"THIS IS NOT
IT'S ONLY

She whirled about and faced him. "That's the problem—it *was* only a few kisses. I shouldn't be feeling this way."

"Just what are you feeling? That a few kisses weren't enough?" David chuckled softly. "I can certainly agree with you on that."

"David, I think you should go."

He frowned. "Do you really think that sending me away is going to resolve your dilemma? I'm not a frightening fellow—you must give me the chance to show you that."

She turned and faced him. "But can I trust you?"

He bent his head and kissed her softly. "Always."

She melted against him, her body warm and inviting in his arms. . . .

Sweet Rewards

by

Melinda McRae

A TOPAZ BOOK

TOPAZ
Published by the Penguin Group
Penguin Books USA Inc., 375 Hudson Street,
New York, New York 10014, U.S.A.
Penguin Books Ltd, 27 Wrights Lane,
London W8 5TZ, England
Penguin Books Australia Ltd, Ringwood,
Victoria, Australia
Penguin Books Canada Ltd, 10 Alcorn Avenue,
Toronto, Ontario, Canada M4V 3B2
Penguin Books (N.Z.) Ltd, 182–190 Wairau Road,
Auckland 10, New Zealand

Penguin Books Ltd, Registered Offices:
Harmondsworth, Middlesex, England

First published by Topaz, an imprint of Dutton Signet,
a division of Penguin Books USA Inc.

First Printing, August, 1996
10 9 8 7 6 5 4 3 2 1

Printed in the United States of America

To my parents,
Forbes and Ruth McRae,
in honor of their
Fiftieth Wedding Anniversary
1946–1996

"Nothing—absolutely and literally nothing—will put an end to the militant suffragist campaign save the removal of its cause . . ."

Christabel Pankhurst
Letter to the London *Times*
Sept. 21, 1909

Prologue

Bixley, Leicester
April, 1909

The short, rotund man at the podium paused for breath and an expectant hush fell over the crowd gathered at the Bixley Meeting Hall. "And now may I present our featured speaker, a man unselfish in his support of the Liberal Party, a man whom I fully expect to see as Prime Minister one day—David Kimbrough!"

Thunderous applause erupted as the tall, handsome politician stepped forward. He looked out over the smoky hall, reveling in the enthusiasm of these party loyalists. Then he held up his hand for silence.

"I thank you, Mr. Hawkins, for that rousing introduction." He grinned. "I also wish to reassure Mr. Asquith that I have no *immediate* designs on his job." The crowd laughed, then David sobered. "I am here to demand your support for the new budget proposals"—he paused to allow more cheers—"a budget that will allow this government to continue their reforms and improve the lot of every person living in England, aristocrat or commoner, miner or clerk, Scot or Irish—"

"What will it do for women?" a shrill female voice demanded from the side of the hall.

David ignored the taunt and continued with his speech. "There are those who claim that our reforms are too radical, too dangerous, but how can they be? Economic prosperity and stability will benefit every member of society."

"Not if you deny women the vote!" another voice at the rear charged.

David took a deep breath to mask his growing frustration. The local party leaders had assured him that women wouldn't be admitted to the hall, in order to prevent just this kind of disruption. It was becoming far too common wherever he spoke and he was tired of it.

"I am not here to discuss voting reform. I am here to speak in favor of the government's budget—"

"A government which refuses to grant the franchise to women!"

The male crowd stirred angrily.

"Remove that woman."

"Get those bitches out of here!"

David turned and glared darkly at the local party man, who blanched and jumped to his feet.

"I'll take care of it."

"See that you do." Turning back to the audience, David raised his hand for silence. "I have no intention of getting into a shouting match with our *uninvited* guests. Once they are gone, I will continue." His pronouncement was met with cheers.

Across the dim hall, he saw one of the protesting women jump onto a chair. "You cannot silence us," she shouted. "We will be heard."

Hands reached up and pulled her down, abruptly cutting off her complaint. Her voice rose with invective as a man slung her over his shoulder and carried her toward the door.

"That's the way! Show 'em who's boss!"

The woman's indignation—and the crowd's approval—brought a grin to David's face.

He jumped backward as something exploded against the podium, splattering his suit with dripping goo.

An egg. Some blasted woman had thrown an egg. His eyes scanned the crowd, looking for the culprit. There, on the left. She was reaching into her bag for another—

Something hit him in the head and he whirled about. Another egg-tossing female climbed onto the stage and began pelting the party leaders with eggs.

The crowd surged forward and two men leaped for the platform, their faces twisted with anger. There'd be a full-scale riot in a minute if someone didn't intervene. David lunged toward the woman and grabbed her upraised arm just as she prepared to toss an egg at the shouting audience. He dragged her toward the side of the stage.

Amid the din, he heard the shrill blast of a policeman's whistle. Thank God.

The woman struggled against his hold. "Let go of me, you brute."

David laughed wryly. "That's a pretty case of the pot calling the kettle black. I'm not the one hurling eggs." Before she could protest further, he pushed her into the arms of one of the local functionaries.

"Here—deliver this woman to the police—she attacked a Member of Parliament." David went back to the podium to see if there was any way to recover the situation.

The women were gone, but the crowd still milled about, talking loudly and angrily. David feared there would be no regaining their attention now.

Damn these provincials! Security was a joke in the country. In a properly run organization, nothing like this would have happened. He would have some sharp words with the local party leader before he caught the train back to London.

Still, he owed it to the party to make the best of things and try to call this meeting back to order. He would be playing into those infernal women's hands if he didn't. He stepped toward the podium and shouted above the noise.

"There's nothing more shattering to a politician's ego than to be upstaged by the crowd," he joked. The nearest man laughed and the hall began to quiet. David waited another moment, then resumed speaking, "But I am not here to talk about myself but about the party and our plans to run this country the way it should be run."

A few cheers rang out and David smiled to himself. He had them again.

From her position across the street from the meeting hall, Julia Sydney watched the police officers escort the women from the building and down the street. She grinned with self-satisfaction. The first phase of tonight's action had obviously succeeded. Now, it was up to her to make certain that the rest of the night went as well.

Not that she had any doubts that it would; she'd planned things too well. As soon as the party leaders left the building, their steps would be dogged all the way to the train station, and she had an equally boisterous welcome planned for them at the London end. If Julia had her way, no Liberal Party member would be able to utter a word in public without being reminded that women wanted the vote—now.

After checking the watch on her wrist, Julia slowly strolled down the sidewalk, making certain that all her soldiers were still in place. She nodded to the sign-wavers who stood outside the hall, ready to shout their slogans and distract the police when the meeting disbanded. The dignitaries' motorcars still stood parked outside the entrance; a sign that they didn't expect further trouble. Julia smiled to herself. Wouldn't *they* be surprised.

At the corner she turned and circled the block to make sure that the cars out front were not a subterfuge. More than one politician had evaded her wrath by sneaking out the back door of a meeting hall. That in itself was a victory of sorts, but Julia preferred to confront her oppressors face-on. All seemed in order and she resumed her post, impatient for her part in the action to begin.

The doors to the hall swung open and she heard the loud roar of cheering voices. The time was here!

The ladies across the street sprang into action, waving their placards and shouting slogans. The first men leaving the building ignored them, pushing past without comment, but as more men flocked out the door and thronged onto the sidewalk, they began returning the taunts and jeers. The few police officers stationed outside turned their attention to the growing confrontation.

Julia stepped into the street, and at her signal two women darted toward the cars. They bent over the outside tires for a moment, then slipped away as quickly as they appeared.

The police had their hands full keeping the angry men away from the protesters when a tightly bunched group stepped through the door. Julia's pulse quickened as the local Liberal party leader appeared, followed by the Under-Secretary for Home Affairs, the Honorable David Kimbrough. Tall and blond, in an expensively tailored suit, he would have stood out in any crowd.

Grace Atkinson appeared at her elbow. "Ready?"

Julia nodded. Ready to move into action, she felt the familiar sense of awareness; everything looked clearer, sharper, and the surrounding world receded into the background. All her attention focused on her target.

The two women ran across the street and darted between the parked cars just as the dignitaries approached. As if conspiring to help her, Kimbrough stood to one side, hat in hand, a disgruntled expression on his face.

"Votes for women!" Grace cried and threw the contents of a wide-mouth jar at Kimbrough.

"Votes for women!" Julia echoed and flung the contents of her bag at him.

A man grabbed her arm and pulled her to the ground, but not before she had the satisfaction of seeing the Honorable MP standing there, sputtering with fury, as molasses dripped down his front. A piece of white down clung to his nose.

The local police station was already in an uproar when the young constable pushed Julia through the door. The small station house smelled of sausage and sweat. Police milled about the room, casting dark looks her way. Julia smiled smugly. No doubt she had disrupted more than one dinner tonight.

She was pushed none too gently before a desk.

"Name?" the irritated sergeant asked.

"Julia Sydney," she replied. "And I demand the status of political prisoner."

"Don't you all," sighed the harassed sergeant, writing her name in his ledger. "Take her away."

The same constable who'd arrested her took her arm and led her across the hall, into a small room.

"Where are the other women who've been arrested?"

Julia asked, scanning the empty chamber. "I demand to join them."

"No doubt you'll have company soon enough," the man answered and shut the door.

Julia sat on the bench and rubbed her bruised wrist. She'd only sat there for a few minutes when the door opened and Grace walked in. Julia jumped up and gave her a hug.

"What a smashing success! Did you see the look on his face?"

Grace laughed. "Mr. High and Mighty didn't look so dignified with feathers clinging to his fancy suit. I only wish we could be in London to see what goes on there!"

Pacing the tiny room, Julia found herself too filled with elation to be still. "Oh, it will be an adventure not to be sent to Holloway this once. And who knows? Perhaps the local magistrate will accept our demand to be treated as political prisoners. Wouldn't that be a coup for us?"

Grace sighed and sat down, unlacing her shoes. "I just hope we get bailed out soon. Standing about all this evening's tired my feet. I'm looking forward to a nice warm bath and a cup of hot tea."

Julia glanced at her watch. "We shouldn't be here much more than an hour—the group at the train station will arrive soon with our bail. Then we can all get a good night's sleep before we have to appear in court tomorrow."

"What do you think they will do for a sentence this time?"

"Not above a month, I would guess."

Grace eyed her curiously. "Are you still determined to stage a hunger strike?"

Julia nodded emphatically. "If they insist on treating us like ordinary criminals, we have to. The government must be made to acknowledge that this is a political matter."

"Maybe I should have dinner along with my tea," Grace said glumly.

"I plan to. Even if you decided not to strike, you

know what prison fare is like. I always have a decent meal before I go in."

Grace wiggled her sore toes. "How many times is this now?"

"Oh, five or six at least," Julia said without bothering to count. "It's become rather a bore, actually. That's why I'm curious to try the hunger strike. With any luck I'll be out again in no time and can get back to work."

"I can't see why you don't let others take your place in jail. You could do a lot more good on the outside."

"But I can't ask others to be arrested if I'm not willing to be arrested myself, can I?" Julia tossed her head. "Besides, someday I'll write a guide to the prisons of England and this is a marvelous way to get firsthand information."

Grace laughed and the door opened. Three other women were pushed inside.

"It was a joy," the youngest one gushed as Julia greeted her. "They finally arrived in a hansom at the last minute and tried to make a dash for the train. We held them up long enough that they missed it and now they'll have to wait three hours for the next!"

"Good job," Julia said. "Someone is telegraphing to London?"

One of the other women nodded

Julia consulted her watch again. "Georgy should be by shortly with our bail so we can enjoy our dinner."

The third girl gave her a nervous look. "Is it really going to be so bad—prison, I mean?"

"No, of course not," Julia reassured her. "The time passes so quickly you hardly notice it. And we'll all be there, together, of course. Think of it as a grand vacation!"

Grace snorted. "I can think of more pleasant places to spend my holidays."

Julia ignored her. "This will be your badge of honor, Marjory. Your first jailing! You are truly one of us now."

The girl managed a weak smile. "Someday, I hope to be arrested as many times as you."

"A worthy goal." Julia grinned, then stifled a yawn. "Come, let's sing, and let them know why we're here."

Their voices joined together:

> "Oh! Women dear, and did ye hear
> the news that's going round,
> They think that prison bars will daunt
> Those born on English ground. . ."

Chapter 1

Sussex
July, 1909

David took a deep breath of the sweet country air as he steered his motorcar along the road toward Cranwood. It felt good to escape from London, away from the ever-increasing pressures of the budget debates in Parliament. Three days in the country came as a welcome break.

As would visiting his aunt. Lady Caroline Marchmont was characterized as a terror by some, but David dearly loved the old lady. She claimed he was the only one of the family who was a credit to his noble heritage, thoroughly irritating the rest of the relatives and making David laugh. But coming from a woman who'd been born in the waning days of George IV's reign, the observation was flattering just the same.

The years had been kind to her, but David couldn't help but notice that she was always a bit weaker, a shade frailer, each time he saw her. He would miss the irascible old lady when she was gone.

As he pulled into the drive, David slowed and came to a halt in front of the Georgian country house. The unpretentious red brick structure was a far cry from the palatial ducal residence where David had been born, and he loved it all the more for its modesty. Here, he felt comfortable.

Before David even shut off the engine, the young stableboy raced around the corner of the house. Motorcars were his obsession, and David's was one of the few he ever saw up close.

David stepped out. "Hullo, Robbie."

"Yer aunt's gone out with the carriage," Robbie replied without taking his eyes off the Rolls.

"She has, has she?" David chuckled. His aunt could well afford to purchase a car, but insisted she was perfectly content with old-fashioned horsepower. Of course, she didn't mind when David took her for a drive at speeds that had only been dreamed of in her youth.

"I'll leave the car here for now," David told the boy. "We'll put the tarp over it later."

The boy nodded, running an admiring hand over the curved bumper.

David smothered a laugh and grabbed his bag out of the rear. What must it be like, growing up in the sleepy Sussex countryside, knowing about all the wondrous marvels of the age and yet seeing them only rarely?

After changing out of his dusty driving clothes, David slipped out of the house and ambled across the back lawn. There was no point in waiting around the house until his aunt returned. He'd come to the country to enjoy the change of pace, and the best way to do that was on foot.

He loved his visits to the country and sometimes wished he'd be content to remain here, away from the noise and bustle of the city, the interminable governmental wrangling. But David knew he needed the challenge of London's rough and tumble political life.

Like last week, when those infernal women had stood outside his window all night, chanting their slogans. Thank God he'd been able to slip out the rear door; they'd wasted their energy infuriating his neighbors. But he'd been tempted to walk around to the front and lecture the suffragettes on their irritating behavior.

He needed a break from work and the Cabinet and the city and everything connected to politics. It was a pity he couldn't spend a month or two here, but right now it would take a miracle for Parliament to adjourn before the end of the year. A good many men were going to have to forgo their autumn shooting. Particularly if the government had to call for elections next year. This year's by-elections had already been a disaster and that didn't bode well for the Liberals in the future.

It was those damned women. They diverted attention from what the government had accomplished, frightened the conservatives, inflamed the liberals and socialists, and hardened opposition in the Lords. One couldn't have a rational discussion of the issues in public without being interrupted, as if voting rights for women were the most pressing problem the government faced.

Ah well, even a few days here with his aunt were bound to relax him. No screaming suffragettes, intransigent Lords, or obstinate party members to bother him here. Just a bunch of little old ladies who were more concerned with local gossip and the deplorable state of today's servants.

He walked along without any particular destination in mind, merely wanting to enjoy the beautiful July sunshine. Already, this summer had been unseasonably warm and the smell of ripening hay mingled with that of baked earth. He traversed fields and stepped over narrow streams, strode down dusty country lanes and overgrown footpaths. In the entire time he walked, he did not see another soul. It was sad, seeing the countryside deserted like this. If things kept on as they were, soon everyone would live in a city and only animals would scamper through the brush.

His rambling walk took him in a wide circle, bringing him back at last to the far edge of his aunt's property, marked by the pond where he'd swum as a boy. It had been a long time since he'd come down here.

A sudden noise brought him up short and he moved forward slowly. It sounded like water . . . splashing? Someone was swimming in the pond. David grinned. He was glad the local lads were still putting it to good use.

He almost called out a greeting, but some sixth sense silenced him, and he was glad. For as he peered around a tree, it was very obvious that it wasn't any village boy swimming in the cool water. A naiad, or a dryad—he couldn't remember which was which—but the swimmer was definitely female.

An encounter like this had been the last thing on his mind when he left London this morning. As a gentleman, David knew he should turn away. But as a man, he wanted to get a closer glimpse of a real-life water nymph.

There wasn't much to see after all, just a white form moving through the water, a flash of skin now and then, and her short, dark hair plastered against her head as she moved with determined strokes across the water. She was a skilled swimmer.

David scanned the shore for some sight of a companion, but the woman was alone. Skirting the edge of the trees, he moved closer to the pile of clothing on the grass. Should he tell the lady she was trespassing?

Leaning against a tree, arms folded across his chest, David watched her swim toward him. She still hadn't spotted him and he smothered a laugh in anticipation of her surprise.

She reached the shallows and rose up like a goddess emerging from the depths. He sucked in his breath at the sight of her naked form. By God, she was magnificent! Droplets of water streamed down her pale skin, tracing every curve of her shapely body. Her full breasts were taut and erect in the sudden chill of the air, and David's groin tightened instinctively.

He must have made some noise, for she looked up and spotted him.

She surprised him by not diving back into the water, or indulging in hysterics. Instead, she stood there, looking at him with a calm, almost defiant expression.

"You're trespassing, you know," he said at last.

She lifted her chin with cool hauteur. "Am I?"

"This pond is on private property."

Ignoring him, the woman walked toward the pile of clothes and grabbed a white garment. David felt a flash of disappointment.

But if she'd thought that putting on her underclothing would make matters better, she was wrong. The thin cotton material clung to her wet skin, accentuating the swell of her hips, the fullness of her breasts. David was consumed with a sudden flash of lust, unfamiliar in its intensity.

Who was this delectable water sprite?

Julia bent down to retrieve her blouse, deliberately ignoring the leering look in the man's eyes. She didn't want him to know that this was her worst nightmare come to life.

She'd been swimming here daily ever since she came down to Cranwood. She found the physical exercise invigorating, and each trip through the water washed away another layer of prison memories. The worst thing she'd anticipated was being spied upon by some prepubescent village boys.

The Honorable David Kimbrough was the last person she'd expected to see, ogling her like a satyr. He couldn't have caught her at a worse disadvantage if he'd planned it.

Even dressed casually, in white shirt and flannels, his sleeves rolled up, he looked every bit as arrogant as he did in formal parliamentary garb. Julia ached to do something to wipe that smirking grin off his face.

"Do you make a habit of this?" Julia began to button her blouse, determined to ignore his avid stare.

"A habit of what?"

"Spying on ladies while they are dressing." She gave him a scathing look. "I believe they have a name for that sort of behavior."

"I wasn't spying," he retorted indignantly. "I wanted to make sure nothing was amiss."

"And what have you decided? Am I so dangerous that you must watch my every move? Unless, of course, that was your intention all along."

"Belive me, I don't get a thrill from spying on strange women in various stages of undress."

"Then why are you still here?" Julia stepped into her skirt and quickly pulled it over her hips. Once she was dressed, he wouldn't have any reason to stare.

A look of pure frustration crossed his face. He glared at her for a long moment, then turned and walked off.

Julia watched him go with a mixture of regret and relief. Regret, that he left too soon. Kimbrough obviously didn't like to have his ego deflated, either in Parliament or at the side of a country pond. His towering rages were famous and she'd have liked to have provoked him further.

Relief, that he hadn't recognized her. She wondered if he would have looked at her in such a lecherous way if he'd known who she was.

An interesting thought.

At least she'd hidden her discomfort well. He'd never know how mortified she'd been.

Returning to her cottage, Julia put a pot of water on for tea.

Sitting on the front step, waiting for the water to boil, Julia gave thanks for the hundredth time to Lady Marchmont for providing the Women's Social and Political Union with this refuge. Julia wouldn't admit it to anyone, but after the hectic spring actions and her last stay in prison, she needed some time alone.

The country offered a golden opportunity to recover from her last hunger strike, to write, and to plan further actions for the fall. Overt political activity had been the last thing on her mind. But if Kimbrough was staying in the neighborhood . . . the opportunity for harassment was too good to resist. He wouldn't be on his guard in the country, the way he was in London. And since he hadn't recognized her earlier, she could get close without him even being aware, and force him to listen to her at last.

First, she had to find out where he was staying. Lady Marchmont would certainly know.

A slow smile crossed Julia's face. Perhaps her stay in the country wouldn't be as peaceful as she'd first intended. She might have an adventure to relate when it was all over after all. Already, after two weeks here, she felt a new rush of energy—energy that had been missing for so long.

The energy to challenge David Kimbrough face-to-face. And wipe that smug expression of male arrogance off his face once and for all.

* * *

Lady Marchmont had returned while David was walking and now awaited him in the small parlor. He walked to her chair and took both her hands in his, kissing her cheek.

"You arrived early," she chided him. "I would not have been away had I known."

"I didn't mind," he said. "I enjoyed taking a walk by myself. It seems I cannot go unmolested in London these days. Those blasted suffragettes are everywhere."

"Perhaps if you gave them what they wanted, they would not be so determined in their pursuit of you." She gave him a pointed look while she poured his tea.

David scowled as he accepted the cup from her. "Unfortunately, there are more pressing issues in the country right now. We're facing the worst constitutional crisis since the days of Cromwell with this budget. If the House of Lords rejects it, the government will fall."

"I would think you would want to increase the size of the electorate, then."

"And create more voters who can by swayed by the bilious propaganda of the vested interests?" David shook his head vigorously. "No thank you."

Lady Marchmont eyed him shrewdly. "You look tired. I am glad you came down for the weekend."

David stretched out his legs and sank lower into the comfortable chair. "So am I."

"I fear I am going to impose on you tomorrow, however. A number of ladies are coming to tea and they are most desirous of meeting with you."

"As long as they don't hurl eggs at me," he said with an easy grin.

"I know some of them hold suffragette sympathies, but I assure you they will not attack you in my house, at least."

"For that, I'm grateful."

Lady Marchmont poured herself another cup of tea and David took the opportunity to study her carefully. Her high-necked, beaded black gown looked too stark against her pale, wrinkled face and white hair, and he thought that she had shrunken in size since he last saw her. Another sign of inevitable decline.

For a moment he wondered what he would do once she was gone. She represented his strongest tie with the rest of the family. His mother, with her new husband, was too busy enjoying the watering holes of Europe to bother to set foot in England more than once or twice a year. And he'd never been close to his uncle, the duke. Particularly now that they were at odds over the budget.

Families could be a damned nuisance at times.

Should he tell his aunt about the young lady he'd encountered this afternoon? Somehow, David didn't want to talk about the vision he'd beheld, fearing the act of putting words to the images in his mind might erase them. He didn't want to forget those impossibly long legs, slim hips, and enticing breasts.

But he had to know who she was. Her cool reaction to his avid perusal intrigued him. That kind of self-assurance in a woman was rare, and he wanted to find out more about her. Perhaps one of the ladies at the tea tomorrow could help him.

With a woman like that in the neighborhood, there might be more advantages to visiting his aunt than he'd first thought.

"I need to check with Mrs. Grayson about dinner." Lady Marchmont reached for her cane but David jumped up, helping her to her feet. She accepted his arm, but waved him off when he tried to escort her to the door.

"I'm not an invalid, yet," she said with a wry grin.

David sat down in the chair again, absently tapping his fingers against the arm until he realized what he was doing. He was here to relax after all.

Having tea tomorrow with a bunch of sweet, white-haired old ladies was exactly what he needed.

But he could not forget his water nymph.

Chapter 2

Julia stood on the front doorstep of Lady Marchmont's house, fanning herself with her straw boater. The early morning breeze had died and the afternoon grew increasingly muggy. She should have taken more effort to keep in the shade while she walked over from the cottage.

She wondered what the other guests would be like. Certainly, not all of them would be so sympathetic to the cause as Lady Marchmont. Julia feared she would be on display, like a zoo exhibit of some rare South American animal, but she owed it to Lady Marchmont to attend and talk with her neighbors. She had, after all, given a great deal of money to the WSPU, and offered the use of the cottage for those women who needed rest "after their harrowing ordeal in prison," as her letter had so aptly put it.

Lady Marchmont's offer had intrigued Julia. When several women returned from their sojourn in the country with glowing reports of their benefactress, Julia had decided to take advantage of the opportunity herself.

They had shared tea several times and Lady Marchmont had shown herself to be an astute follower of the political scene, even if she rarely ventured up to London anymore. On the whole, her views were more conservative than Julia's, but on most issues relating to women, they saw eye-to-eye, despite the differences in age and upbringing. Lady Marchmont took a keen interest in the suffrage campaign—hence her donation—and Julia spent several delightful afternoons regaling her with the various humiliations that had been heaped upon opposition politicians.

The butler finally responded to her summons. He took Julia's plain straw hat and led her to the drawing room.

If she hadn't been here before, Julia would have been intimidated by the sheer volume of furnishings in the blue and gold room. Lady Marchmont might be modern in her politics, but she was firmly Victorian in her tastes. Every surface was covered with objects—vases of flowers and ornamental bric-a-brac on the tables and shelves, layers of carpets on the floor, gilt-framed pictures obscuring the patterned wallpaper.

Lady Marchmont beckoned from her thronelike chair at the end of the room and Julia hastened to her side. The elderly lady clasped her hand and a smile brightened her face.

"So glad you are here, my dear. So many of the ladies are eager to hear what you have to say. I promised you would speak a few words." She leaned closer. "I think you may be able to make a few converts."

Julia gave her a conspiratorial grin.

"I believe we have two or three more guests due to arrive and then we shall begin." She turned to the plump woman at her side. "Margaret, be a dear and introduce Miss Sydney to the ladies."

Margaret, whose surname Julia never quite learned, took her by the arm and circled the room, introducing her to Lady this and Mrs. that. Julia wondered if the entire county had been invited. She realized with sudden awareness that this was no simple tea—Lady Marchmont had neatly arranged a campaign meeting for her. Perhaps they would form a Cranwood branch of the WSPU this very afternoon.

Lady Marchmont banged her cane against the side of her chair and the room fell silent.

"As you know, we have a special guest with us today. A lady whose courage and determination in fighting for the rights of women have made her the thorn in the side of stubborn politicians everywhere. I am pleased to introduce Miss Julia Sydney, who will say a few words about the work she does—and how we all can help."

The applause following this introduction was more

than polite. Julia flashed Lady Marchmont a grateful smile and stepped in front of the fireplace.

"I'm pleased to be invited to speak here with you today. And I must give thanks to Lady Marchmont, who has been so generous in her support of the WSPU." Julia nodded at her benefactress. "It proves that the cause we fight for cuts across the lines of class and occupation—the work we do is designed to help *all* women, rich and poor, aristocrat and commoner, city dweller or country resident. The denial of the vote to women is only a symptom of the larger problem—the systematic repression of women in every area of life, from work to the home, in education, politics, and the law."

She examined her audience, silver-haired ladies in dresses dripping with lace, jewels at their throats and fingers. Women raised in homes of wealth and privilege. Would they really understand what she had to say?

Or where they, too, tired of the restrictions under which they had been raised? Were they willing to break the chains of bondage and forge a new freedom, if not for themselves, for their daughters and granddaughters? Julia vowed to speak to those hopes.

"Winning the vote is only one step in the direction of righting this wrong—but it is a very big step. When women have the vote, politicians will at last be answerable to their female constituents. With the power of the ballot, we can force change, until we have a society where men and women are treated fairly and equally."

Julia paused to take a breath and fought back a gasp as she caught sight of the man who strode into the room.

David Kimbrough.

Anger filled her. He must have heard that she was to be here today and intended to interfere, imposing on Lady Marchmont's hospitality in the process.

Kimbrough gave a brief glance in her direction, then halted in midstride and stared. Julia's heart sank as recognition flared in his eyes, and she watched helplessly as he went to Lady Marchmont's side and engaged in a whispered exchange. He looked at Julia again, a startled expression on his face.

Julia met his gaze with a challenging look, realizing he now knew who she was. David Kimbrough was not going to turn her from her purpose.

Taking a deep breath, Julia turned back to her audience. "Despite the popularity of our cause, the government still refuses to take us seriously. The Prime Minister refuses to meet with us and we are arrested when we attempt to assert our legal rights of petition. There are men in the government who are determined to prevent us from obtaining the vote." She tossed Kimbrough a scornful look. "Men like the illustrious Under Secretary for the Home Office—David Kimbrough."

Julia pointed at him. "I'd like to know why you're spending so much time and effort fighting women's suffrage, Mr. Kimbrough. Perhaps you'd care to tell these ladies why you think we are so wrong?"

As she hoped, everyone turned to stare at him, and Julia smiled with deep satisfaction at his uneasy expression.

Kimbrough smiled weakly. "I hardly think this is the time or place—"

"Where is the proper time and place?" Julia demanded. "Within the confines of a Parliament composed entirely of men? In a Cabinet led by a man whose strong opposition to the cause is well known? Where is the proper forum for women's concerns and questions to be heard and discussed, if not in drawing rooms like this?"

Sympathetic murmurs passed among the women. Several leaned forward, as if urging her to continue.

Kimbrough tossed up his hands in a gesture of defeat. "All right, let's discuss it. What do you want to know?"

Julia gave him a stern look. "When will the government grant us the vote?"

"Women will have the vote when the House of Lords is willing to approve the legislation. Any action in the Commons is futile until that time."

"How are we to know what the Lords will do if the bill is never forwarded to them?" Julia demanded.

"Don't be ridiculous," Kimbrough snapped. "Of course they will toss it out."

"Not if the government stood firmly behind it," Julia countered. "It's doomed to fail until it does. When is the government going to support the bill?"

"We have more important things than women's suffrage to worry about," David said heatedly. "The Irish question, land taxes, armaments."

"And so we women are to stand aside politely and wait?"

"Yes."

Julia turned to her audience, who were following the exchange with rapt attention. "Is that what we want? To wait patiently on the sidelines until the *men* decide what we can have—and when we can have it?"

"No!" the women chorused.

"Or are we going to demand our rights now?"

"Now!"

She directed a triumphant look at Kimbrough. "The women have spoken."

"None of you has any idea how government operates," he said. "It's a process of give-and-take, and compromise. Issuing demands won't help you achieve your goals."

"We've been patient long enough." Julia gave an angry toss of her head. "We saw what happened when we agreed to wait the last time—nothing. The government must learn that it can't ignore us."

"Perhaps if you acted more like *ladies* than hoodlums you would—"

"It's the government that forces us to take drastic measures to draw attention to our demands," Julia replied. "If the Prime Minister would listen to us, if we were allowed to speak at party rallies instead of being locked out of meeting halls like criminals, we wouldn't have to take such steps."

His face clouded with anger. "If we didn't lock you out, you'd disrupt every meeting we have."

"Because that's the only way we can be heard." She waved an accusing finger at him. "You refuse to listen to us when we approach you with our *legal* petitions."

"Do you think I'm going to be more willing to listen after you've smeared me with molasses and feathers?"

"When you've ordered women to be physically removed from your meetings, what do you expect? Tea and biscuits served on a silver platter?"

"No one is going to listen to you as long as you act like wild-eyed harridans." He gestured at the ladies seated around the room. "Look at the women here. Ladies, every one. You won't find them throwing rocks and scuffling with policemen."

"Now that they realize how intransigent you are, perhaps they'll be willing to." Julia appealed to her audience. "You can see why we need your help. The government has to know that *all* women care about this issue. Let your voices be heard, either through your own efforts or from your support of others. Send letters and petitions to Parliament, talk with your MPs. Let them know what you think. Money is always needed to fund our work.

"Thanks to the generosity of women like you, our newspaper, *Votes for Women,* is now published weekly. We have a full-time, paid staff working in our office."

Julia smiled. "I know not all of you may agree with everything I say. But if you have doubts, listen to the stories of your neighbors, your mothers, sisters, and daughters. And ask yourself whether you and they should continually be denied the same privileges that have been held so long by men."

The women erupted in applause. Julia shot a triumphant glance at Kimbrough, pleased by the dark look in his eyes.

He quickly strode to the front of the room.

"Before you get carried away with Miss Sydney's skilled oratory, remember one thing. This women has been arrested and imprisoned numerous times. She is not merely a member, but a strategist for the most virulent group of militants. Are they really the type of women you want to support? These radicals are doing more damage than good."

"David, we didn't come here to listen to *you.*" Lady Marchmont's imperious voice rang out.

A hushed silence filled the room. Several ladies darted

anxious glances between Lady Marchmont and Kimbrough, as if waiting for the next explosion.

"I didn't intend this afternoon to be a debate," Lady Marchmont continued. "Let Miss Sydney finish her talk."

To Julia's amazement, he sat down.

Several women crowded around her with eager questions, and she soon lost sight of Kimbrough. Julia patiently explained how the London office operated, what it was like to speak to crowds in the thousands, and why she was willing to go to prison for her convictions. Women pressed money into her hands. Julia wished she had an assistant here to take names, but she could get those later from Lady Marchmont.

At last, the crush subsided. Someone thrust a welcome cup of tea into her hand and Julia sipped it, looking around to see if Kimbrough was still here. She spotted him on the far side of the room, talking with Lady Marchmont.

The elderly lady caught her eye and motioned for Julia to join them.

"A stirring speech, my dear," Lady Marchmont said when Julia reached her. She darted Kimbrough an amused glance. "I apologize for my nephew's interruption. He is so accustomed to public speaking that he sometimes does not know when to be quiet."

It was Julia's turn to stare at him. "You're Lady Marchmont's nephew?"

"Oh, don't sound so surprised." Kimbrough's voice dripped sarcasm. "You had this all planned, didn't you? Thinking you could use my aunt to get at me."

"You certainly have a high opinion of yourself if you think that I'd go to such efforts to seek you out. Particularly when I know exactly where you live in London." Julia took in an angry breath. "Furthermore, until five minutes ago I had no idea you were her nephew."

"And pigs fly." His eyes grew hard. "You have accomplished your goal, Miss Sydney. I suggest that you leave, now."

Julia laughed. "And insult your aunt? I hardly think so. After all, I'm here at her express invitation."

His eyes narrowed threateningly. "Don't give me a cock-and-bull story like that."

Lady Marchmont cleared her throat. "Oh, dear, I must have neglected to tell you yesterday. Miss Sydney is staying at the Apple Cottage for a time."

David glared at his aunt. "You rented the cottage to her?" He shook his head. "This woman is the bane of my existence. Why in God's name have you invited *her* here? She's dangerous."

His aunt laughed. "I hardly think 'dangerous' is the right word. Determined, perhaps. I thought that was a quality you admired, David."

He scowled. "I admire determination, not intransigence."

"I am sure you will manage to survive the encounter. After all, what can one woman do to a seasoned politician like yourself?" Lady Marchmont patted his hand, then crossed the room to the knot of women gathered about the tea table.

Julia turned to Kimbrough, trying to hide her amusement at his anger. "We're so grateful that your aunt offered the cottage to the WSPU. It's been such a restful retreat."

"She did what?"

Julia's smile widened. "So you see, I'm merely here to spend a few quiet weeks in the country. It's sheer coincidence that you chose to visit at the same time."

He glanced around the room. "I wouldn't call this little fund-raising venture 'quiet.' "

"That was your aunt's idea. I thought I was having tea with the ladies from the neighborhood, but she wanted me to talk about my work." Julia grinned. "Not everyone considers me an ogress, you know."

His expression soured. "Only those who've been on the receiving end of your political 'actions.' "

"I do what I feel I must in order to get the attention of the government. If you would listen to us, it wouldn't be necessary."

Kimbrough crossed his arms over his chest. "I'm listening now, Miss Sydney. What do you want me to know?"

Her heart pounded in anticipation. Had she actually gotten through to David Kimbrough? Then she looked at his face and saw the mocking expression in those icy blue eyes. He slowly scanned her from head to toe and back again, with a knowing look that left her feeling as naked as she had at their encounter yesterday. Which no doubt was his plan.

She wasn't going to give him the satisfaction of knowing that he'd succeeded.

"You obviously have no intention of seriously listening to anything I say." Julia turned on her heel and crossed the room.

There was no reasoning with a man like that. It shouldn't surprise her. He was David Kimbrough, after all. A loud and vocal opponent of the suffragettes and everything they stood for. He would take great delight in doing whatever he could to humiliate her.

Why, of all men, had he been the one to catch her swimming yesterday? She knew he'd be mentally stripping her of her clothes every time they spoke. Julia hated the idea of such an arrogant man having an advantage over her. Somehow, she had to find a way to even the score.

And find a way to do it without antagonizing his aunt. It couldn't be a public confrontation, but something just between the two of them. There had to be some way to convince David Kimbrough that she couldn't be intimidated.

David frowned as she walked away. He wouldn't have minded continuing the debate. All in all, he thought he'd come off pretty well in the duel of words with Julia Sydney.

Thank God she hadn't been able to read his thoughts. Even while arguing politics with her in the drawing room, he couldn't forget how she'd looked when she stepped out of the pond, droplets of water glistening on her skin, her breasts firm and crying for a man's touch.

Suffragettes weren't supposed to look that good. He'd thought Julia Sydney would be a tall, thin woman with a face like a horse and a voice as shrill as her tactics. Instead, she was the most damnably attractive woman he'd set eyes on in a long time.

Julia Sydney. She had the shape of an angel and the political acumen of an anarchist.

David slipped out of the room and headed for the library. Pouring himself a generous glass of whiskey, he eased himself into one of the comfortable leather chairs and contemplated today's turn of events.

He'd come down to the country for some peace and quiet, and who did he find—Julie Sydney, staying at the estate cottage, at his aunt's invitation. Was this a sign that Lady Marchmont's sharp-as-a-tack mind was finally going?

Instantly David chastised himself for the uncharitable thought. Auntie had always had a strange affection for odd characters. That she should have latched on to a radical suffragette was no surprise. A few years ago it had been Fabian socialism that caught her attention. Next year it would be something else.

But Julia Sydney? Aunt had to have known that this suffragette had a vendetta against him. Lady Marchmont might have given some thought for his feelings before staging this tea—or at least warned him that Julia Sydney would be here.

Or had she planned this all along? He wouldn't put it past her; Aunt loved controversy. Today's confrontation would be the talk of the neighborhood for weeks, and she'd bask in her triumph.

The library door opened and David glanced over his shoulder.

"The ladies have all gone home," Lady Marchmont announced with a wry grin. "You can come out of hiding."

"I'm not hiding," David said stubbornly.

Lady Marchmont took the opposite chair. "I own, I am a bit disappointed in you, David. I do not like the idea of you being rude to a guest in my home."

"Rude? To that woman?" He snorted derisively. "She doesn't know the meaning of the word."

A faint smile crossed her face. "I thought you had greater political tact than to allow an opponent to rile you so."

"That woman isn't a political opponent—she's an annoying pest."

"Goodness, I haven't seen you get so worked up over a political difference since you and Churchill disagreed on the Russian situation."

"I would rather enter a den of wolves than entertain Julia Sydney for tea." David gave a mock shudder.

"Aren't you being a bit too harsh, dear?" Lady Marchmont looked bemused. "I know you don't approve of her tactics, but she is working for a good cause."

"If she wanted to accomplish some good, she'd stop disrupting my speeches and my life and let me go about my work to get this budget passed." He leaned forward. "Doesn't she realize that if the government falls, we'll have a general election? Who knows what will happen then."

"Which, since she is not permitted to vote, means little to her, I'm sure. It is rather tiring to be told to take a back seat to *more important* matters year after year."

He gave her a quizzical look. "Don't tell me she has infected you with her blathering propaganda. I thought you had more sense than that."

"I have more sense than to think only *men* are capable of governing. They've been in charge all this time and see what good it has done us! Perhaps it is time for a change."

"Not the kind of change she wants. She'll have men at home taking care of babies and cleaning house while the women run the show."

"Would that be so bad?" His aunt smiled.

"It isn't natural!"

"I believe that's been said about a lot of things over the years. Gas lighting. Trains. A great many people believe the motorcar is the invention of the devil." An impish smile creased her face. "What if they are right? You could face an eternity of damnation."

"I'm not talking about science and progress, I'm talking about human nature. It goes against all logic for women to be involved in the government. They simply are not suited."

"Oh?" She snickered. "Then how do you explain Victoria's success?"

"Look who advised her—the Prince, Melbourne, Palmerston, Disraeli. They held the real power, with Parliament doing all the work."

Lady Marchmont looked surprised. "However did poor Queen Bess manage?"

"All her administrators were male."

Laughing, his aunt patted his cheek. "You are not going to listen to reason on this point are you? Just like your grandfather, with that stubborn Kimbrough streak in you. Now, be a dear and pour me a glass of whiskey."

David raised a brow. "Are you sure?"

"The doctor said I shouldn't, so of course I will."

David poured the amber liquid from the crystal decanter on the table. "Perhaps you should listen to the man."

Lady Marchmont dismissed the doctor's opinion with a wave of her hand. "And if a daily glass of whiskey shortens my life by a month or two, what difference will it make? I've lived far too long as it is."

"*That* is totally wrong and you know it." David handed her the glass. "You're younger in spirit than any of those ladies who came for tea."

"Excepting Miss Sydney?" She laughed. "Did she really cover you with molasses and feathers?"

"Ruined one of my best suits."

Lady Marchmont took a long sip of her drink. "Nevertheless, I should like you to make amends to her."

He arched a brow. "I thought I was the injured party."

"I'm talking about your disruption of my tea today."

"She was the one who insisted on a debate," David stubbornly insisted. "I would've been content to remain silent."

"Perhaps you should have followed your instincts," she replied dryly. "In any event, you did say some things that upset me—accusing her of manipulating me to get after you. Really, David, do you think I am such a fool?"

He winced. "No."

Lady Marchmont smiled. "Good. Now run along to the cottage and apologize. I should like to take a nap before dinner."

David knew when he was beaten. She was the only woman who could order him around like this. He escorted her to her room, then, with marked reluctance, struck out across the lawn toward the Apple Cottage.

Chapter 3

Relaxing in the garden behind the cottage, Julia slowly sipped her tea and leaned back in the chair. Overgrown roses tumbled over the fence, perfuming the yard with their heady fragrance. It was so peaceful here, quite unlike the heated debate in Lady Marchmont's drawing room earlier today.

Julia fondly remembered summer afternoons like this, when she and her sisters played fanciful games amid the flowers and trees of their grandfather's garden. They had chased fairies, scaled mountains, wrestled tigers, and slain dragons in those far-off days.

Julia laughed. Things hadn't changed much. She and her sisters were still searching for dragons to slay. Sara, fighting the ignorance and poverty of the slums; Catherine, exploring the strange land of America; and Julia, challenging the government.

Challenging men like David Kimbrough.

He was certainly a dragon that deserved slaying. Not only for his political views, but for the way he'd looked at her today. He hadn't said a word, but his eyes told her he recalled every minute of that humiliating encounter yesterday.

Sara would insist Julia receive partial blame for the incident—if you swam naked in a pond, you had to accept the consequences. But how could she have known that David Kimbrough, of all people, would come strolling by? It wasn't fair.

And it would only make her work more difficult. No doubt when he returned to London he would regale his cronies with the tale and they would be even less likely to take her seriously.

She shrugged. That didn't matter. Other women could approach the politicians face-to-face. Her major job was tactical operations, after all. Organizing and planning, coordinating and implementation. She could do that no matter what any man thought of her.

But Julia admitted she would like the chance to debate David Kimbrough again—preferably in a more public place, with a huge audience. She would show everyone that all his excuses and explanations were really a pretense for his refusal to accept the idea of women's suffrage.

"You look so peaceful I almost hate to disturb you."

Julia didn't have to turn around to know who'd invaded her privacy—again. Kimbrough.

"Then why did you?" she asked with sweet sarcasm.

Laughing, he plopped down on the grass facing her. "I'm here on a mission of peace. My aunt thinks I offended you today and insists that I make amends."

"That's hardly necessary."

He went on as if Julia hadn't spoken. "I think she was more offended that I thought you were trying to take advantage of her. She's very sensitive about the slightest hint that she isn't as sharp as she once was."

Julia eyed him closely. "Shouldn't you be apologizing to her, then?"

"That would only be adding insult to injury," he explained. "By pretending the offense was against you, her honor is preserved, I'm taken down a peg, and you have the satisfaction of seeing me thoroughly cowed by a member of the fairer sex."

"That's certainly one of the most *sincere* apologies I've received in some time."

"Do you want me to pretend that I'd bruised your tender, womanly feelings?" He grinned. "I think you'd find that far more offensive."

Julia was forced to laugh. There was a perverse logic to his words.

Kimbrough leaned back, propping himself up on one elbow. Julia studied him more carefully. He looked as if he could be relaxing on the edge of a cricket green, in his white shirt and flannels. The perfect picture of the dashing young aristocrat at leisure. A shock of his sandy hair fell over his brow and he brushed it back. In that moment, she thought he looked too young to be the Under Secretary for the Home Office.

But even stretched out casually on the grass, he exuded an aura of masculine confidence and strength. If it had been any other man, Julia might have found the image attractive. But this was Kimbrough, after all. A man she dared not admire.

As if sensing her thoughts, he looked at her and smiled.

"She really is a dear, you know."

"What?"

"My aunt. Great-aunt, actually." He uttered a melodramatic sigh. "Although she still treats me like a twelve-year-old schoolboy."

"Perhaps she's found that's the best way to deal with most men," Julia observed.

He laughed loudly. "You never give up, do you, Miss Sydney? Tell me, just what would you women do in a world without men? I suspect you'd find it tiresome before long."

"I never said I wished for a world without males. I only ask that women be treated equally."

"Then how can you support legislation reducing the number of hours women can work in the mills? Shouldn't they work equal hours?"

"For less pay?" Julia gave a scornful laugh. "I'd like to see how many men would stand at the weaving machines all day for women's wages."

"How many women are willing to shoulder a gun and attack a bunch of bloodthirsty Boers?"

"Perhaps if women were running the country, we wouldn't need an army."

His laugh was harsh. "This from a member of the rock-throwing brigade? You set a fine example of pacifism."

Julia clenched her fists. He was twisting everything she said, trying to make her look foolish. "That is damaging property—the only thing that seems to gain the attention of the men in the government."

He laughed again. "Oh, there are other ways to gain our attention." He raked her with a heated gaze. "I imagine if you marched down Piccadilly without your clothes, you'd garner all sorts of male attention."

She glared at him. "That is a perfect example of your refusal to take women seriously."

"We can only take you seriously when you behave in a serious manner. Property destruction or civil disobedience doesn't fit that mold. Nor does swimming in the nude."

Julia eyed him haughtily. "A gentleman wouldn't refer to that incident."

Kimbrough guffawed. "That is rich, coming from you. You can break windows, toss eggs, flatten tires, and attack Members of Parliament, but *I'm* in the wrong for admiring an attractive woman?"

"Admiration has nothing to do with it," she said heatedly. "You only bring it up to humiliate me."

His eyes lit with the same delighted look with which he'd appraised her at the pond. "Oh, admiration has everything to do with it. I may despise your politics, Miss Sydney, but I'm forced to admit you have the shape of an angel. I can still picture those long, lithesome legs and those exquisitely shaped bre—"

"Oh, for God's sake." Julia had no desire to hear his exaggerated description of her. "Can't you men think of anything else?"

"What?" He arched a brow. "Does talk of the naked human form make you uncomfortable, Miss Sydney? I thought you were one of those progressive females, not a hypocritical Victorian."

"I have nothing against the human form, male or female," Julia said with more vehemence than she intended. Kimbrough had an unfortunate knack for destroying her equanimity. "I resent the male inability to look beyond the mere physical when it comes to their admiration for women. We aren't just a collection of legs and breasts and hips and thighs. We have minds and opinions and rights that should be ours. *That* is what I want you to see."

"But it is hard to remember when it comes wrapped in such an alluring package . . ."

"I thought you came here to offer me an apology."

He looked at her with a lazy grin. "Most women would be pleased at my compliments."

"That only shows you don't understand women very well." Julia jumped to her feet. She'd had enough of his infuriating behavior. "Good day, Mr. Kimbrough. I trust we will manage to avoid each other for the rest of your visit." Grabbing her teacup, Julia walked toward the cottage, head held high. She walked regally through the doorway and shut it firmly behind her.

Safely inside, Julia leaned against the door, shocked at the violence of her feelings.

Why had she reacted so strongly to his taunts? He was baiting her deliberately and she responded like an outraged old maid. The greenest campaigners in the WSPU showed more control than she had. She'd been called far worse things by others; why couldn't she brush off his remarks?

Because they were too personal. He wasn't talking about the vote, or women's rights, but about *her*.

The whole problem wasn't made any easier by the fact that Kimbrough was a damnably attractive man. In the halls of Parliament, dressed in his striped trousers, frock coat, and top hat, he appeared the very symbol of an oppressive male government. But in the country, with his casual dress setting off his trim, athletic form, he presented a much different image. He seemed more approachable, more human. And male—far too male. He enjoyed looking at her far too much. He'd never take her seriously if he was mentally undressing her every time they met.

Worst of all, deep inside, it pleased her that he found her attractive. That was the most frightening thing of all. She'd struggled against that side of her nature, the one that appreciated male attention and admiration, submerging it in her work. She'd learned too well the disaster that could occur if passions were left unchecked.

She would have to learn to firmly ignore him.

Unless she found some way to even the score between them.

A slow smile stole across her face. She knew all about Kimbrough's political life, but little of his personal one. Maybe there she would find the weapon she needed to deflate his enormous ego and make him look at her as a political opponent again, and not just a woman. Suffragette sympathizers moved in even Kimbrough's elite circles; someone would know something about him.

Then Julia would be able to challenge him with her own taunts. And that unfortunate meeting at the pond could fade into insignificance.

David slowly got to his feet, unable to hide his grin. Lord, she was a feisty one. Those wide brown eyes glowed with righteous indignation whenever she argued her cause. What a challenge it would be to tame her!

Then he grimaced at the thought. That would take a lifetime of effort, with little chance for success. Women like that didn't want a real man—only emasculated ones they could ride roughshod over.

It was a pity. Suffragettes should be unattractive, embittered spinsters, not enticing nymphs. Somebody needed to tell Julia Sydney she was working with the wrong group.

He wondered what she had done before becoming a suffragette leader. Had she dabbled with Fabian socialism? The labor movement? It would be interesting to find out.

He was curious, too, about her personal life. Somehow, he didn't think any woman who swam in the nude was a straight-laced, prudish Victorian. He'd be willing to bet her background was far more bohemian. There might even be a lover or two hidden in the past. *That* would be a valuable bit of information to possess. He didn't like the idea of staging personal attacks against anyone, male or female, but it was always best to be prepared. No telling what the WSPU might resort to it they felt desperate enough. He wanted to be ready for anything.

When he got back to London, he'd start asking a few questions. He'd suddenly wanted to know everything he could about Miss Julia Sydney.

Thursday evening, David sat in his room at the Home Office, staring at the print of eighteenth-century Venice on the far wall. The House had been in session for hours now, but he doubted they would be dividing for any votes this evening. He wasn't needed to steer the debate and he relished the chance to retreat from that noisy chaos for a few hours.

He fingered the papers before him, surprised at what he'd been able to find out about Julia Sydney in such a short time. Nearly everyone he'd spoken with had some tidbit of gossip to impart. Most of it was exaggerated, or repetitive, but after sifting through the dross, he had a much better understanding of his opponent.

Her family history had been interesting. What a bizarre childhood she'd had! Raised in a freethinking household, the three sisters educated at home by an exponent of whatever cause had caught their parents' fancy at the time. A household where they'd read Mill instead of Shakespeare, Rousseau over Browning, the Webbs instead of Kipling.

And despite such an unconventional education, she'd gone on and taken honors in law at university—knowing full well that she wouldn't be allowed to practice. Had that restriction fueled her support of feminist causes, or had she studied law for that very reason?

She'd been politically involved since an early age, attending meetings with her parents. They'd been active in labor causes and she'd been an organizer for several years before and during her university stay.

There was less information about her personal life. He unearthed a few hazy rumors about a male companion during her days as a labor organizer, but discovered nothing concrete. Suffragettes, as far as he could tell, led boring lives. There wasn't any sign that she had a man in her life.

Had her work for women's rights soured her so much on men that they didn't interest her?

David laughed aloud. No. She'd looked at him all right, though she'd tried hard to pretend she wasn't. He knew when a woman was examining him, and Julia Sydney had been doing just that when he sat in her garden last Sunday.

He wondered what conclusions she'd reached.

Now, he must decide how he was going to deal with her.

Attacking her for her suffragette activities was unnecessary—she harmed herself more every day with her radical activities. No, he needed to get to her in a more personal way, so she'd avoid him in the future.

He remembered her consternation whenever he teased her about his observations at the pond. Was she merely reacting to his mention of her nakedness, or was it the male attention that disturbed her? Either way, he sensed it was the key.

What if she thought he was interested in a sexual liaison? If she was a man-hating suffragette, she'd run screaming if he came after her, and he'd be rid of her once and for all.

And if his hunch about her interest in him was right, he might find out if there was any truth to those vague stories about a lover. He wanted to see those brown eyes burn with passion, instead of political zeal.

Either way, he won. He'd frighten her away, or lure her to his bed. Attempting to seduce Julia Sydney would be an interesting challenge—and a hell of a lot more entertaining than butting heads with the Unionists in Parliament.

By midmorning Saturday David pulled his motorcar in front of his aunt's house. There was no time to waste; if he intended to launch his campaign against Julia Sydney, he needed to get to work right away. He wanted to make sure that by the time she returned to London, she would run at the very sight of him.

Or be content to stay in his bed.

Lady Marchmont expressed mild surprise at seeing him again so soon, but David explained it away with a morose description of the continuing struggle over the budget. He told her he needed to escape to the country as often as he could manage it—which was not a complete lie.

She did arch a questioning brow when he suggested that Julia dine with them that evening, but agreed to his plan. David mentally rubbed his hands with satisfaction. Dinner was an excellent place to start. Miss Sydney wouldn't be suspicious—not with Aunt there—and he'd have the opportunity to observe her closely while he decided the exact form of his attack.

Whistling cheerfully, he ambled off toward the cottage after luncheon. In the city, a few hours notice before dinner would be a gross insult, but here in the country, life wasn't as formal. And if by chance she had other plans, there was always tomorrow. But he couldn't imagine that she had anything else to do.

He rapped loudly on the cottage door but she didn't answer. Frowning, he walked around to the back to see if she was in the garden, but it was empty. Frustrated, he walked back to the front and knocked again. Then he reached for the door handle and pushed it open.

"Miss Sydney? Are you here?"

He stepped into the room, which was blessedly cool behind the thick stone walls. "Miss Sydney?" he called again.

She obviously wasn't here. Now what should he do? Leave her a note, at least.

He looked around the front parlor for pen and paper. The room was a picture of disorder—a skirt lay draped over a chair and books sat in towering piles. A vase of wilting flowers stood on the small table by the window.

As long as she wasn't here, it wouldn't hurt to take a closer look. Curious to learn more about this woman, David crossed the room. A book lay facedown on the upholstered chair by the window. He craned his neck to read the spine. *Howard's End*?

He laughed. Julia Sydney wasted her time on novels? He found it hard to imagine.

A table had been pushed into the corner and was obviously doing duty as her desk. Books balanced in precarious stacks and papers cluttered the surface. He grabbed one of the books. *Women and Economics. That* sounded more like her style. David glanced at another title, and another. An eclectic mix of economics, philosophy, and political theory.

Grabbing a sheaf of papers, David darted a guilty glance at the open door as he did so. He'd be furious if he found someone riffling through his papers. But what did they say—all was fair in love and war? This was certainly war.

The pages he held were obviously notes on her reading. He riffled through another pile. Scraps of ideas were scrawled across the paper in a bold hand, many followed by question marks, as if she were considering some aspect of them. "Role of women in the proletariat—did Marx consider? Where does Bentham's utilitarianism fit in? Would Aphra Behn be a literary success today?" Her questions were as eclectic as her reading.

But they still told him little about *her*. He knew her political views; he wanted to discover something about her personally. Shamelessly, he sifted through the rest of the papers, looking for anything useful.

He found a letter with a London postmark. It was probably from one of her suffragette chums, but it might tell him more. Folding back the flap, he started to remove the letter.

"Do you make it a habit of snooping through other people's papers, Mr. Kimbrough?"

David dropped the envelope with a guilty start and whirled to face her. She looked as if she knew exactly what he was up to.

"I'm glad you're back—I was looking for a pencil to leave you a note." David willed himself to relax. "My aunt and I would like you to join us for dinner tonight."

Anger clouded her features. "And that gives you a

reason to go through my papers? Did you find anything interesting?"

"Only that organization isn't your strong suit."

Julia crossed the floor and stood in front of him, hands on hips, a scowl darkening her face.

Her stance only accentuated the curve of her full breasts beneath the lacy fabric of her blouse. An appreciative grin spread over his face when he realized that Julia Sydney was not wearing a corset.

"Really, Mr. Kimbrough!"

Her furious tone snapped him back to attention.

"It may be acceptable in London to apply your bullying tactics to intransigent party members, but we're not in London and I'm not some junior MP."

"I'm not trying to bully you," he protested. "I came to ask you to dine with my aunt this evening."

"Why?" she asked with open skepticism.

David knew he had to disarm her suspicions. "Oh, you've caught me out! It's actually a nefarious government plot. I knew I couldn't pull the wool over your eyes." He gave her a sardonic look. "It's dinner. With my aunt, and myself. Just the three of us."

"I'd love to dine with your aunt," she said at last. "I'm not so sure about you."

"I'll be on my best behavior." He grinned ruefully. "After all the wrangling in the House last week, the last thing I want to do is discuss politics over my meals."

She looked doubtful. "Whatever will we talk about, then?"

"Oh, I am sure we can find some safe topic. The weather is always a possibility. Should we wish to grow daring, we might tackle sporting events—or the musical stage."

"All topics of *your* expertise?"

He sensed her weakening resolve. "I'll motor over to pick you up." David moved toward the door. "Around seven—Aunt likes to dine early."

"Wait—I haven't said I'd come."

"You will." He grinned widely. "Curiosity will get the better of you."

Her brow furrowed. "You don't need to come for me; I can walk."

David hid his triumph at winning this first battle. "No, as your host for the evening, I insist." He arched a quizzical brow. "You don't have an aversion to motorcars, do you? I could bring my aunt's carriage if you prefer."

She gave an exasperated sigh. "The motorcar would be fine."

"Good." He smiled cheerfully. "Forgive my intrusion, Miss Sydney. Next time I drop by with an invitation, I'll be sure to bring a written one—just in case you are out." He bowed quickly and slipped out the door.

David pursed his lips thoughtfully. That had been an awkward situation; he *had* been snooping and she'd caught him red-handed. He thought he'd covered his discomfort well.

Worse, he hadn't learned a single new thing about her. Other than that she was an indifferent housekeeper and didn't mind wrinkles in her clothes. It was hardly unexpected. He couldn't picture a woman like her concerning herself with something as traditional as housework. No, she was much more interested in doing battle in the streets than dusting a mantel.

At least she'd be coming for dinner tonight. By then, he'd be at his flirtatious best—a little light banter, some flattering remarks, and an admiring glance or two should be enough to get things started. He'd toss in a bit of sexual innuendo to keep things spicy. Nothing too threatening—he didn't want her frightened; just confused. And intrigued.

Julia stood in the parlor, still stunned by the audacity of the man. She'd caught him standing in her front room, blatantly snooping through her papers. What had he hoped to find—strategy notes for the next WSPU action? Didn't he remember she was on holiday?

He hadn't even had the sensibility to look embarrassed.

Kimbrough probably hadn't even seen anything wrong with his actions. That was the type of man he was—

confident to the point of being aggressive, so convinced that he could do nothing wrong that the concerns of others were brushed aside.

Julia glanced at the letter Kimbrough had been holding and her breath caught. Had he read it? She hoped not, for the letter contained detailed information about the Honorable Member from Colton. Julia didn't want him to know that she'd been inquiring about him. With his male arrogance, he'd put the wrong interpretation on that. She only sought to gain a political advantage over him.

His childhood was what she would have expected—schooling at Eton and Oxford, as befitted the grandson of a duke. Julia vaguely recalled stories of his father, Lord Frederick Kimbrough, who'd been a darling of the Tories until he resigned in a fit of pique over some minor issue—then died suddenly in a sailing accident. Kimbrough's mother was an American heiress, one of the many who'd flocked to England in search of a titled lord.

The marriage, by all accounts, had been a disaster. People predicted it would have ended in a scandalous divorce if not for Lord Frederick's death. Kimbrough's mother ultimately married one of her lovers, and now lived abroad.

Julia wondered if his parents' rocky marriage had affected Kimbrough, and his attitude toward women.

After university, Kimbrough spent a few years working as a secretary to various government officials, then stood for election to a safe Liberal seat. That had been the one surprise—one would expect a man of his background to be a Conservative. But he was generally considered a reformer on several issues—women's suffrage the notable exception—and his meteoric rise within the party was legendary.

That rise was generally credited to his ability, but Julia suspected family connections had helped there as well. He was admired in the House, although some who had felt the rough side of his tongue said he could afford to learn to be a bit more conciliatory. Kimbrough apparently did not suffer fools gladly. The picture was that of a driven, arrogant politician intent on making a name for himself in the halls of Parliament.

Julia concurred with that assessment.

But it was the information about his private life that interested her the most. There had been discreet rumors about the unattached and very eligible bachelor, who seemed to match his pursuit of fine living with a fondness for other men's wives. Yet it was only gossip; there was no definite proof.

Still, it was an interesting piece of information. Could it be the weak point she'd been looking for? A man with a fondness for married women could be vulnerable, and a juicy scandal would certainly reduce his effectiveness. David Kimbrough was a formidable political opponent, and Julia wanted to face him from a position of equal strength—or, even better, superiority.

She'd try to learn more about him tonight.

Promptly at three past seven, she heard the motorcar pull up in front of the cottage. Julia was at the door before he knocked.

"I see you're ready. Promptness is an unexpected virtue in a woman." His piercing blue eyes skimmed over her in critical appraisal, then widened with admiration.

Did he look at every woman with such intensity? Julia shrugged off her discomfort and forced herself to examine him with equal intensity. "When so many women's lives are filled with inconsequential activities, what motivation do they have to be on time?" Julia asked dryly. "You'll find that few working women can afford the luxury of tardiness."

"And even though you are a working woman on holiday, you aren't going to slip out of the habit." He gave a mock salute. "Commendable discipline on your part."

"I've known a great many men who couldn't keep track of time," she observed. "But since they were *men,* and obviously engaged in *important* pursuits, it was acceptable."

"I don't want to get in a debate on the subject," David

said, handing her a motor coat. "Remember, we promised to confine our conversation to safe topics."

"Ah yes, the weather." She pointedly ignored his proffered hand and climbed into the passenger seat, and squinted at the setting sun. "I don't think it will rain soon."

David jumped up beside her. "We could use a bit of rain to keep the dust down." Carefully, he turned the car around, then gunned the powerful engine and pulled away with a spray of gravel.

Julia grabbed for her hat and the door handle. Kimbrough obviously drove with the same arrogant attitude that he applied to every other activity. She couldn't wait to deliver him his comeuppance.

Upon arriving at the house, Julia jumped down before he had a chance to assist her and walked toward the front steps without waiting for him. Let him have a taste of his own imperious attitude.

He caught up with her at the top of the front steps and pulled open the door. "I can't tell you how much Aunt is looking forward to this evening."

Julia darted him a sideways glance. "She must be glad to have you visit again."

"On the contrary, she's highly suspicious of why I'm here." He took her coat. "You'll have to reassure her on that account."

Julia regarded him with confusion. "Whatever for?"

"She thinks I've come down to see you."

He couldn't possibly be serious. She stared at him. "What on earth are you talking about?"

He shook his head as if he, too, were surprised. "Yes, she thinks I've developed a partiality toward you." Kimbrough took her elbow and steered her toward the drawing room. "I tried to tell her that I was merely eager for any excuse to get out of the city, but she doesn't believe me."

"I hope you'll do your best to disabuse her of *that* notion," Julia said stonily as they paused outside the drawing room door.

He laughed again. "Are you so sure it isn't the truth?"

The arrogance of the man! Julia suspected all those rumors must be true if he thought every woman was eager for his attentions. Before she could give him the set-down he well deserved, he pushed open the door. Placing his hand on the small of her back, he guided her forward.

Julia wanted to slap him silly. Instead, she walked into the room, escaping his touch.

Lady Marchmont greeted them warmly. "I'm so glad you could come, my dear."

Julia leaned down to kiss her cheek. "Thank you for the invitation."

"I promised her I would stay away from political topics." David winked broadly.

"That will be a relief," his aunt said dryly. "I suppose it is too much to hope that you know any good gossip." She turned to Julia. "He spends so much time at work that he is neglecting the *important* things."

David laughed. "Believe me, there's nothing worth gossiping about in London these days. I think the entire city is on holiday except for Parliament."

Lady Marchmont waved a chastising finger at him. "I will expect more from you this fall. Now, be a dear and pour us all a drink."

He glanced inquiringly at Julia.

"Whiskey and soda," she replied.

Lady Marchmont turned back to Julia. "Now I hope you're taking time to rest and not working all day long. That was one of the stipulations I made about your stay at the cottage—it is for *rest*."

"I've done woefully little work, I'm afraid." Julia gave a rueful shake of her head. "I hope that pleases you."

Lady Marchmont nodded. "You needed a good rest. Why, you already look much better than you did when you first arrived."

Kimbrough regarded Julia with blatant admiration as he handed her the drink. "It's hard to believe she could ever look anything less than lovely."

His gaze made her feel naked again and Julia felt her skin warm beneath his heated gaze. Why was this man able to unnerve her so? Julia turned away, determined to ignore him.

"You should have seen her when she first came down," Lady Marchmont said. "Pale as a ghost and thin as a rail." She gave Julia a critical examination. "She's still far too thin, but at least her color is returning. A few more weeks at the cottage will do wonders."

"That's the lady of the manor talking," said David. "Country air and fresh food will cure anything that ails you. She's convinced we'd all be much happier if we abandoned the cities and returned to the land."

"I think there's a good deal of sense in what she says," Julia said, eager to seize on a new subject. "The cities are breeding grounds for disease and crime."

"Well, tear down the factories, rip up the rail lines, and destroy every invention of the last hundred years and you can have your pastoral Eden." David raised his glass in mock salute. "It would be an unmitigated disaster. The 'good old days' were never as good as they seem. I'll take the modern city any day."

"Yet in the same breath you admit how much you enjoy escaping the city for the country." Lady Marchmont glanced slyly at David. "Or, at least, that's what you say."

"I don't mind *visiting* in the country. I find it extraordinarily relaxing after a long week in the city. And there's so much to do." He darted Julia an amused look. "I understand you swim, Miss Sydney. There's a lovely pond on the edge of the property that is well suited to that endeavor."

Julia nearly choked on her drink, wishing she could fling it in his face.

Chapter 4

The butler stood in the doorway. "Dinner is ready, madam."

David helped Lady Marchmont to her feet, then offered his other arm to Julia. He felt a smug sense of satisfaction that she only hesitated a moment before taking it. His plan was working already.

In the dining room, David sat at the head of the table, with the ladies on either side. It gave him the perfect opportunity to study Julia.

Her appearance tonight surprised and delighted him. The high-collared blue gown she wore was tastefully elegant, not quite formal enough for dinner in the city, but just right for the country. The lace trimming around the neck and cuffs gave her a delightfully feminine look.

Flirting with her was not going to be a painful experience at all.

"Looks like we're having good country food tonight," David said, reluctantly turning his attention to his plate. Thin slices of rare roast beef were surrounded by carrots à la orange and creamed peas.

Lady Marchmont nodded. "Just what you need, David. If I can't keep you in the country, I can at least send you back to the city healthier."

David gave Julia a rueful look. "See how she bullies me? I'm really quite helpless to fight her."

"Perhaps you should listen to what women tell you more often," Julia responded tartly.

He smiled warmly, caressing her with his eyes. "I might be willing to do that—if I had the right woman to give me advice."

She looked nonplussed for a moment, then rallied. "I can name any number of women who would love to advise you—Mrs. Pankhurst, or Christabel, or Annie Kenney."

"I already have someone in mind for the position," he said, giving her a sly wink.

Julia frowned. "Someone to echo your own opinions, no doubt."

David tossed back his head and laughed. "That's the last thing I'd expect from *this* particular woman. No, the lady I have in mind has most unusual views."

"It's a good thing, too," said Lady Marchmont. "You'd be bored to tears, otherwise."

"But what about you?" David glanced at Julia. "Do you want a man who always agrees with you?"

Her lips tightened. "On important matters, yes."

"What do you consider important? Politics? Social issues?" He couldn't resist teasing her. "Economic philosophy?"

"All of those," Julia replied.

"Do you really think you'd be content with a mirror image of yourself?" David regarded her with feigned astonishment. "I suspect you'd grow bored. There needs to be some occasional sparks to fan the fire. Arguing has its advantages—you can always kiss and make up later."

"Arguments require that there be a winner and a loser," she retorted heatedly. "Unlike most men, I don't have a need to dominate my partner. When a couple think alike, they can work together for the same things."

"Yes, you want a relationship based on full equality, one for all, all for one, and all that rot." He raised a brow, determined to rile her further. Her cheeks turned such a delightful shade of pink when she was angry. "There is one aspect of that idea that puzzles me—how, exactly, do you propose to share the childbearing task? I don't recall that they've perfected a male pregnancy."

Julia dropped her fork and it clanked against the plate. "You're being absurd. No one has ever suggested that we find a way to make men pregnant—although I suspect if we did, they would suddenly become far more sympathetic to women's lot."

"But if you are going to be equal, shouldn't you be equal in all things? Why should women be the only ones to bear the young?"

"Perhaps because we are the *stronger* sex. Men would wilt under the strain."

He waved a warning finger at her, smothering a smile. "Now be careful, Miss Sydney. You're veering dangerously close to political matters."

"I am?" She glared at him. "You're the one who brought the matter up."

He tossed a pleading glance at his aunt. "See? Miss Sydney contradicts herself again. Earlier, she said she didn't want to dominate anyone, but she's trying to win this argument."

Julia shot him an angry glare and opened her mouth with a retort, but Lady Marchmont spoke first.

"Now, David, you promised . . ."

He attempted to appear chagrined. "That I did, and I am sorry." He darted Julia a smoldering look. "I suggest we resume this discussion later—when we're alone. I'd like to hear more of your views on childbearing."

Her eyes widened, then she quickly looked away.

Score a point for him.

"I received a letter from your mother this week," Lady Marchmont announced, firmly changing the subject. "She spoke of visiting England in the fall. Should I suggest to your uncle that we have a grand family reunion?"

"And count the dead bodies afterward?" David shook his head. "You know those two can't stand each other."

His aunt regarded him innocently. "But that is what would make it fun." She glanced at Julia. "The family has never forgiven his mother for being an American."

"They've never forgiven her for making my father's life a living hell," David said. "It's a crime topped only by his treatment of her. She'll be happier if she stays in France."

"I hope your family gets along better?" Lady Marchmont turned to Julia.

"Oh, we argue constantly, but it's all in great fun."

"Your parents are still alive, then?"

Julia nodded. "They're in the north—Manchester. I also have two sisters—one in London and the other in America."

Lady Marchmont's eyes brightened. "America—how exciting. What is she doing there?"

"Causing trouble, no doubt," David mumbled under his breath.

Julia gave him a reproachful look. "Traveling, mostly. She's a journalist."

"I should like to have visited America," Lady Marchmont said with a sigh.

"Let's go, then," David suggested. "Parliament's bound to adjourn someday. I'll take you to New York. First class all the way. We'll sip champagne and eat caviar as we sit in our deck chairs."

"These old bones can barely endure the trip to London, let alone New York." Lady Marchmont regarded Julia. "Have you been to the States, my dear?"

Julia shook her head. "There is some talk of arranging a speaking tour next year. If Sarah is still there, I might go."

David snickered. "Planning on lecturing those upstart colonists on the proper role for women?"

Julia glowered at him. "In case you didn't know it, women already have the vote in several states. We would do well to follow their example."

He wasn't going to let this opportunity slip by. "Why don't you emigrate, then? I'd think you'd want to live in a land where they honor your claim to equality. Why, you could even be elected Lord Mayor or some such thing."

"I won't leave England while my sisters here are still shackled by male prejudice."

He cast an amused glance at his aunt. "I must not be very observant. I've missed seeing these women in chains—where do you suggest I find them?"

Silently, Julia held out her arm and pulled back her sleeve, exposing her wrist. A livid red scar marked her skin. "Two months ago," she said evenly. "In the transport on the way to Holloway. The jailer fastened the manacles too tightly . . ."

David winced at the image of those delicate wrists encased in hard steel. Lace suited them so much better.

"How dreadful," Lady Marchmont said. She turned to her nephew. "I really think you should do something about this, David. Miss Sydney and her friends are not dangerous criminals. Is it really necessary to transport them in chains?"

"I will make some inquiries when I return to London," he said, his voice subdued. In the abstract, he approved of harsh measures against the suffragettes. But when they applied to Julia . . .

Lady Marchmont kept up a running chatter through the rest of the meal, for which David was glad. Somehow, the conversation had gotten away from him. He was supposed to be flirting with Julia Sydney, not feeling sympathetic toward her.

That is, unless he intended to seriously pursue this flirtation with her. And in that case, tenderness was not the tack to take; he suspected she'd despise that. No, if he intended to conquer her, it must be from a position of strength. She had to submit to him—willingly.

Julia laughed at something his aunt said and spooned a bit of strawberry trifle into her mouth. Her tongue darted out and licked a drop of red juice from her lip. David's groin tightened at the sight. He found that simple act more erotic than any number of posed French postcards.

He really did want her, in the most physical sense. There was something indefinably sexy in her refusal to wilt before his taunts, her ability to return his jabs with equal strength. If she sparred with him in bed like she sparred with him at the table, they would both be exhausted before the night was out.

Exhausted, and satisfied. Sex with Julia Sydney might be one of the memorable experiences of his life.

There were some areas where this notion of equality between the sexes was not such a bad idea.

* * *

To Julia's relief, they ate dessert quickly, and returned to the drawing room. Soon, she'd be able to go home. Kimbrough's puzzling behavior this evening disturbed her. One minute, she'd swear he was flirting with her; in the next, he was administering a set-down. What did the man hope to accomplish?

"A pity you never sat still long enough to learn to play the piano, David." Lady Marchmont's voice jolted Julia back to her surroundings. "I don't suppose you play, Miss Sydney?"

Julia shook her head.

Lady Marchmont reached for her cane. "Then I'm afraid I will have to leave you two alone. Without music, I'll fall asleep in my chair and I refuse to subject myself to that sort of indignity. Thank you for coming tonight, Miss Sydney." She waved off Kimbrough's hand and walked out of the room.

Julia rose, uneasy at the thought of being here alone with Kimbrough after he'd been acting so strangely all evening. "I should go also."

David held out a restraining hand. "And leave me by myself? I think not." He walked over to the sideboard. "Another whiskey?"

Reluctantly, Julia nodded and sat down again. Perhaps, by staying, she could discover the reason for his erratic behavior. She almost thought he was flirting with her—but for what point?

And Julia had to admit that sharing a drink with a good-looking man wasn't the worst thing in the world, even if he was a member of the government.

He poured their drinks, then lounged in the chair across from her. "I envy your opportunity to stay in the country, Miss Sydney. Monday morning will come far too soon for me."

"Why doesn't Parliament recess?"

He shook his head. "Now, no, you're talking politics. We had an agreement . . ."

"Don't tell me that you are so wrapped up in your budget work to take a break. Commons would probably get more done if you went home for two weeks."

"Confidentially, I agree. But I'm not the one in charge." He grinned ruefully. "I don't want to talk about Parliament. When I'm alone with a pretty girl, I'd much rather she talked about herself."

"I suggest you confine your outrageous flattery to your political speeches," she said, determined to dismiss his phony flattery. "I have no need of it."

"Oh, I never flatter outrageously," he said with an easy smile. "Only truthfully. You note I didn't call you 'beautiful'—that's going too far. But you certainly qualify as pretty."

She gave him a withering look but he blithely went on, scrutinizing her with a critical eye.

"Your mouth is a trifle too large, and your nose too narrow for a true beauty," he said with a grin. "But those big brown eyes make up for a lot." He reached over and tousled her hair. "It's only a pity you cut your hair so short. I can almost imagine it cascading over your shoulders in long, soft waves—"

"Stop it." Julia jumped to her feet and started for the door. She wasn't going to listen to this nonsense any longer. "I'm leaving."

David was on his feet in an instant. "Not alone, at this hour. I'll have the car brought round."

"I prefer to walk."

"That's even better." He glanced out the window. "There's nothing like a moonlit summer night for a walk in the country with a pretty lady."

"I don't need an escort."

He took her arm and firmly led her into the hall. "I never said you *needed* an escort. I merely want to go with you."

Stopping in the front hall, he handed her the duster. "I don't want you to take a chill on the way home."

Julia bit her lip to keep from uttering an angry retort. The sooner they left, the sooner she could be home and rid of the man.

Stepping out onto the moon-drenched drive, they walked along quietly for several minutes. Julia maintained a brisk pace to show Kimbrough that she had no desire to dawdle with him. If he thought she'd be impressed with his silly flirtation, he'd learn the truth soon enough.

He finally put a hand on her arm. "Is this a race? Must we run the entire distance?"

Julia smiled with smug satisfaction. "I don't want to keep you out past your bedtime."

She saw him grin, his teeth gleaming white in the light of the moon.

"Oh, it's not even close to my bedtime, yet." He took her arm. "Or at least my sleeping time."

Julia sighed with exasperation. Must the man put a sexual twist on every remark she made? Pulling her arm free, she continued on, pointedly ignoring him.

He walked beside her silently until they came in sight of the cottage.

"I hope you're planning to ask me in for a nightcap."

Julia smothered a derisive snort and gave him a disdainful look. "On the contrary. Good night, Mr. Kimbrough."

Surprisingly, she thought he looked disappointed.

"What? The night is still young." A smile tugged at his lips. "We might even take a midnight swim."

"Don't be ridiculous."

He grinned apologetically. "Well, you do like to swim, don't you? You can't be ready to go home yet; the night's barely begun."

Julia eyed him warily. "I see no reason to stay out anywhere—with you."

Taking her hand, he drew her to him. "Oh, but I do."

The bright gleam of desire in his eyes sent a reluctant thrill of anticipation up Julia's spine. She might despise his politics, but something drew her to this man.

"Admit it, we've both been fighting this from the moment we laid eyes on each other." He leaned closer. "Don't you think we should do something about it?"

"About what?" Julia cringed at the shaky quaver in her voice. She didn't want him to hear the thumping of her heart, feel her racing pulse.

"Us. This attraction. It's the most damnable thing, but you can't deny it's there."

Julia took a deep breath. "Oh, can't I?"

He gently walked her backward until she was pressed against the tall oak that stood beside the drive. Pinning her hips with his, he trapped her against him and a sharp jolt shot through her at the intimate contact. She smelled the subtle scent of his cologne, the sweet odor of whiskey on his breath.

Kimbrough ran his fingers down her cheek, then cupped her chin in his hand.

"I spent the last week wondering what this would be like," he said, his voice a low whisper. Slowly he lowered his mouth until their lips touched.

Julia wanted to turn her head, wanted to avoid his kiss, but she couldn't move, could barely breathe in that excruciatingly long instant before his mouth came down on hers.

The contact was electric and she clenched her fists to keep from making a sound. Despite her denial, Julia had been as aware as he of this strange—powerful—attraction between them. She wanted to bury her hands in his thick blond hair, pulling him closer. Her breasts tightened in anticipation of being crushed against his chest. It took every ounce of her strength to keep her body rigid, to keep from responding to him.

He stepped away so suddenly that she was thrown off balance, grabbing his arm to keep from tumbling to the ground.

Kimbrough was staring at her, wide-eyed, as if he, too, didn't believe what had just passed between them. Then a smirk spread across his face.

"I commend you on your self-restraint, Miss Sydney. But don't grow too overconfident." He started off down the lane. "I don't give up easily."

Julia watched him until he was out of sight, then touched her fingers to her lips, as if to capture the feel, the taste of him again. Her skin tingled at the memory of his touch.

Her mouth was a "trifle too large" indeed! The man was an outrageous flirt.

But it was the truth. Her mouth was too large. And

he hadn't lied later either, about the attraction between them. The unspoken invitation was tempting—too tempting. She had to stop and try to think clearly. Kimbrough was her political opponent, after all, a symbol of all the men in government who refused to listen to women's demands.

There was no question he was flirting with her, but to what end? There was more going on here than the simple attraction between a man and a woman. What exactly did he want?

Power. Of course. It was a typical male move, thinking he could use the spark of sexual attraction to gain mastery over her, to soften her opposition to him.

But what if she played along with his little game? Let him think she was interested, let him think she was responding to his lures. Once he thought he was succeeding, she'd be able to show him just how wrong he was.

Entering the cottage, she kicked off her shoes and curled up in the chair by the window. The moonlight cast mysterious shadows across the garden.

It wouldn't be hard to pretend she enjoyed his attentions—Julia had to admit she liked it. And for an instant, a frisson of apprehension chilled her. What if she couldn't resist his entreaties?

She shrugged off her worries. David Kimbrough might be a powerful force in the government, but he was no different from any other man. Once they were in hot pursuit of a woman, all their sense vanished. She'd learn his weaknesses, his failings, then turn them against him. He'd rue the day that he'd thought he could intimidate her.

And that incident at the pond would be forgotten.

Julia awoke in the morning with half-formed plans swirling in her head. She must decide how to respond with Kimbrough. She couldn't appear too eager; he might grow suspicious.

But he'd be going back to London tomorrow, so she had to work quickly; there was no guarantee he'd be back next weekend—unless he thought he was making progress with her. She had to make sure he thought he was.

Inviting him for tea this afternoon would be a start.

Julia tossed on her dressing gown and hastened into the parlor. She quickly penned a note to Kimbrough, requesting his presence for tea. Lord knew what she would feed him, but she'd worry about that later. Now she had to deliver this blasted note.

Some things were certainly easier in the city, when dispatching a message meant handing it to a willing helper, instead of struggling into her clothes and tromping across the dew-covered grass herself.

Back at the cottage, the note delivered, Julia fixed herself a cup of tea and sat by the window again. Just how was she going to let David Kimbrough think she was interested?

After last night, she didn't think it would take too much effort on her part. A few subtle hints to imply her attraction should be enough. He was so full of himself, it would only confirm his belief in his irresistibility to women.

And then she'd have him under *her* power.

Once again, she reminded herself that there was nothing wrong with being attracted to Kimbrough—if she wasn't, she wouldn't consider playing along with his plan. But as long as she was, she might as well make use of the situation.

She knew that some members of the WSPU would be appalled by her willingness to play up to him, but Julia had never paid much heed to their antimale views. Wasn't a woman's sexual equality as important as her political and social rights? Women had been sexual slaves to men for centuries; now it was time to turn the tables and enslave the men. And because they were such fools, it was an easy task.

Julia couldn't wait to bring David Kimbrough to his knees. Preferably begging.

Chapter 5

David grinned when he read the note from Julia. Tea at four. Such a ladylike thing to do.

The invitation bolstered his spirits. He'd worried when she hadn't lingered with him last night, but this showed she was still willing to see him after that kiss. It was a good sign—he was making progress, albeit slowly. A pity he couldn't take the week off and remain here; things would surely move quickly then.

He'd have to lay the groundwork well today for his return next weekend. Taking pen in hand, he scribbled a hasty acceptance and dispatched it to the cottage. Then, with a resigned sigh, he returned to his work. Slaving over government papers on a Sunday was the price he had to pay for a weekend in the country.

But his attention kept veering back to last night, and the kiss he'd shared with Julia. She'd trembled in his arms and he knew it wasn't from fear or revulsion—she'd been struggling against reacting to his kiss. It only bolstered his belief that there was an intense attraction between them, and that she was as aware of it as he. Now he must convince her that there was no point in fighting it.

Or had she already come to that conclusion, and the invitation to tea was the admission? David grinned to himself. Maybe he'd be able to take some inspiring memories back with him to London.

Promptly at four, he rapped on the cottage door.

There was no response and he knocked again, louder. He heard footsteps and Julia opened the door.

She was dressed plainly today, in a simple skirt and

blouse, but the wide belt set off her tiny waist, and the severe tailoring of her blouse only accented those full, uncorseted breasts. His fingers ached to touch them.

"Here already?" She smiled a warm welcome. "I just put the water on to boil. I thought we'd sit outside, in the garden. It's such a pleasant day."

David nodded silently and followed her to the back, curious as to what would develop.

In the garden, two wrought-iron chairs flanked a lace-covered table. An array of biscuits and tiny sandwiches filled two plates and a vase of flowers stood in the center.

"This looks . . . amazing," David said.

Julia laughed. "Make yourself comfortable while I check on the tea."

David sat down and grabbed a biscuit. He hadn't expected Julia to fling herself into his arms, but she hadn't appeared nervous or flustered by his presence, either. Had he been too optimistic, thinking she meant something by inviting him here?

When he heard Julia's step, David jumped to his feet, taking the tea tray from her. He set it on the table and they both sat down.

"I hadn't realized this was to be such an elegant affair, or I would have dressed," he said, examining his rolled-up sleeves with mock chagrin.

Julia waved his protest away. "This is the country, remember? It was your aunt who insisted on all the finery—and the sandwiches. Watercress and cucumber." She made a moue of distaste. "Tell me, can anyone really survive on watercress and cucumber sandwiches?"

David laughed and grabbed one off the plate. It disappeared in one bite.

"No," he announced. "But it is the expected thing."

Julia filled their cups. "My mother had people in for tea all the time, but they'd usually get so wrapped up in their discussions that they barely ate anything. My sisters and I particularly appreciated that. Lots of biscuits and cakes for us."

"Don't you hold teas in London for your political supporters?"

Julia handed him his cup. "I usually don't attend those."

"Too tame for you, eh?"

Her lips quirked in amusement. "Indeed."

David sat back, sipping his tea and openly admiring her.

He still admitted he liked what he saw. Her short, dark hair might give her face a boyish appearance, but from the neck down it was obvious she was a woman. A woman he wanted to possess, in the strongest sense of the word. He wanted her naked beneath him, those long legs wrapped around his back, giving and taking pleasure.

David suddenly realized that he was going to be bitterly disappointed if his attentions frightened her away.

Julia gave him a hesitant look. "I fear I was rude last evening."

Her words wiped the erotic images from his brain. David arched a brow. "Oh?"

"I should have invited you in for a drink." She spread her hands in an apologetic gesture. "I know tea is not quite the same, but I hope this makes up for my lapse in hospitality."

"I assure you that I find every moment in your presence pleasurable." David took another sandwich and downed it in two bites.

She cleared her throat. "Then I can hope to see you again?"

David gave her a long, languid look. "I have every intention of seeing you again, Julia."

Averting her gaze, Julia took a sip of tea, then peered at him over the rim of her cup. "Next weekend, perhaps?"

His pulse quickened at her words. She *was* interested. "I'd like that very much." He reached out and took her hand. "Is it too much to hope that you might be persuaded to come to London during the week?"

She darted him a nervous smile. "Unfortunately, I cannot—at least this week. But perhaps later . . ."

His thumb moved in sensual spirals across the back of her hand. He heard the quickening of her breath, felt the rising heat in her skin.

Oh, yes, she was eager. Nervous, but interested. It looked as if she wasn't going to run after all. He just might be able to lure her into his bed.

But he didn't want that—yet. No, he wanted to wait, wanted to tease and tantalize her to a fever pitch, then leave her aching and unfulfilled. She would have five long days to think about him, to imagine what was to come, so that when he returned, she'd be putty in his hands.

Still, there was no harm in taking *some* advantage of the situation.

Glancing at her, he saw that her gaze was focused on their two hands, her delicate, feminine one held firmly between his strong male fingers. Possession. That was what this was about. He would possess her; she would submit. And in submitting, she would acknowledge his victory, the power of his sexual dominance.

She wouldn't be thoroughly tamed, but she'd be forced to acknowledge who was the stronger in this battle between the sexes.

And she certainly wouldn't be flinging any more pots of molasses at him.

Her own gaze lifted and met his. Her dark brown eyes were warm, inviting.

There was nothing wrong with a little taste.

David leaned over and pressed a gentle kiss on her lips. Her fingers convulsed in his and he squeezed them.

"David," she whispered against his mouth.

"Ssh."

He clasped the back of her neck, pulling her closer as his tongue flicked along her lips, caressing them, demanding entrance. She gave a startled gasp and he took advantage of it, plunging his tongue into her mouth, feeling her, tasting her.

Her hand brushed tentatively across his shirtfront and he grabbed it, pressing it against his chest. His mouth worked against hers, coaxing her, urging her to surrender to passion and desire.

Julia moaned softly, swaying toward him. She wasn't resisting him now. Her mouth and tongue moved with his, proving he'd been right about her passionate nature. David wondering if he needed—or wanted—to wait until next weekend.

Abruptly she pulled away. He caught a glimpse of the startled expression in her eyes, before she hastily looked down.

He grasped her chin and turned her head to face him. "There's nothing wrong with what you're feeling," he said softly.

The thick lashes that framed her brown eyes fluttered. "I . . . I shouldn't."

"Are you afraid of consorting with the enemy—or any man?"

Julia jumped to her feet and strode about the garden in long, agitated steps.

"I don't know what you want. I don't know what *I* want. It's all very confusing."

David regarded her with an amused expression, pleased that she was reacting as he hoped. "Does it really matter right now? This is not life or death—it's only a few kisses."

She whirled about and faced him. "That's the problem—it *was* only a few kisses. I shouldn't be feeling this way."

He stood and walked toward her. "Just what are you feeling? That a few kisses weren't enough?" David chuckled softly. "I can certainly agree with you on that."

As he neared her, she stepped away.

"David, I think you should go."

He frowned. "Do you really think that sending me away is going to resolve your dilemma?"

Julia shook her head. "But it will give me time to think."

David came up behind her and placed his hands on her shoulders. He felt her tense beneath his fingers.

"I'm not a frightening fellow—you must give me the chance to show you that."

She turned and faced him. "But can I trust you?"

He bent his head and kissed her softly. "Always."

She melted against him, her body warm and inviting in his arms.

God, he wanted her.

But not on a Sunday afternoon, when he had to leave in the morning. Not as skittish as she was. He needed more time to do this properly. He'd have to wait.

With a sigh, he touched his lips to the tip of her nose.

"I thank you for inviting me to tea," he said, slowly relaxing his hold on her. "And I look forward to seeing you next weekend."

Her eyes widened. "You're leaving?"

He nodded. "I think it would be best." He tapped his finger lightly on her nose. "But I fully intend to continue this *discussion* when I return."

She smiled shyly. "I'd like that."

David bowed and strode out the gate.

Julia sank into the chair, smothering her laughter behind her hand.

Her touching display of budding passion mixed with agonized reluctance had reduced him to jelly. He was firmly convinced she was succumbing to his male charms.

Yet it wasn't far from the truth, and she had to keep remembering that she was only playacting. Those kisses today had shaken her more than she cared to admit. She couldn't recall being drawn this strongly to any other man. By rights, he was a man she should detest. But the more she spoke with him, the more she was forced to admit she liked him.

David might be infuriatingly arrogant and stubbornly antisuffrage, but he didn't threat her with the condescension of most men. He talked to her as an equal—even when they disagreed.

And he spoke to the deeply buried part of her, that secret, feminine core that she tried to ignore while she did her work. But David made her feel defenseless before him.

She must be very careful to make sure she didn't succumb to his whispered endearments and thrilling touches. Always, that must be foremost in her mind. Because if she did succumb, it meant he was the winner—and she wanted it to be her.

Saturday couldn't come soon enough.

During the week, Julia threw herself into her work, spending most of the day reading and taking notes. In the evenings she organized her work, and began outlining story ideas for *Votes For Women,* the WSPU newspaper.

She felt alive and energized again, and it wasn't from the country air. Julia usually preferred action instead of writing, but this week it suited her mood. Anticipation fueled all her activities, giving her an enthusiasm for her work that she hadn't felt in a long time.

Anticipation of David's return, and the challenge of dueling with him again. What new compliments would he devise to flatter her? How many more kisses would he dare?

She could hardly wait for Saturday to arrive.

The interminable wrangling in Parliament irritated David even more than usual that week. He could barely stand to sit in the chamber and listen to all the idiotic comments, when all he wanted to think about was Julia—and the unspoken promise of the upcoming weekend.

His office provided little escape, for it seemed someone was always darting in with a new paper to read or a new proposal to evaluate. He agreed with Julia's remark that they'd all get a lot more work done if they took a vacation. Everyone's tempers were short and the summer heat did nothing to cool them.

As a result, he found himself spending far too much time imagining what *she* was doing. Probably reading in the garden while he was shut up in his stuffy office, or having tea with his aunt while he had to listen to boring speeches.

His favorite thought envisioned her swimming naked in the pond, a vision conjured up from the image seared on his brain. Soon, he hoped to find out how well reality matched his memory.

This weekend needed a delicate hand. She was fighting against her impulses and he had to move carefully to make sure he didn't frighten her away.

That was the very last thing he wanted. He no longer cared a whit for his original plan. He wanted Julia now for herself, for the fascinating, enticing, alluring woman that she was.

From the moment she awoke on Saturday morning, Julia tried to pretend that it was just like any other day. She drank her customary cup of tea in the parlor, then dressed and reviewed her work from yesterday. She'd nearly finished her article on the hidden costs of women's low wages; she would finish it today and start taking notes for her next project.

She certainly wasn't going to sit here waiting, wondering when—or if—David would arrive. He would be here when he chose to, and if he didn't come at all, it merely meant she would have to work all the harder to encourage him the next time they met.

That's what she told herself, but it did little to dampen the mixture of apprehension and anticipation that had her jumping to her feet every other minute. She tried to tell herself she wasn't eager to see *him;* she only wanted to know if she'd done a thorough job of convincing him she was flattered by his attentions. His return today would merely be a mark of her success.

Yet Julia knew she was lying to herself. She wanted to see him again, pure and simple.

With a frustrated sigh, she put her work away and slammed out of the cottage.

If he did come, she didn't want him to find her here, looking as if she were waiting for him. He was already far too arrogant about his masculine appeal; he'd be insufferable if he thought she was eagerly waiting to see him. If need be, she'd spend the entire day walking, so she wouldn't be home when he came to call.

But what if he came, found her gone, and went back

to London? She could leave a note, saying she would be returning. But that would tell him that she'd expected him to come, when she didn't want him to think that at all.

Lady Marchmont. David would never leave without visiting with his aunt. Julia could stop by for a cup of tea, casually mention she was going walking, and know that David would find out.

Except that Lady Marchmont was perceptive enough to realize exactly what Julia was doing.

Julia threw up her hands in disgust. There was no easy answer. She could walk and risk David coming and going, leave him a note and let him know that she expected him, or tell her plans to Lady Marchmont and have her know as well.

Finally, Julia decided that if David was so easily discouraged that he left because she wasn't in when he called, she needed to know. It meant that she had more work to do.

With that decided, Julia took off down the lane and crossed the field, determined to let fate decide the course of events.

Whistling a jaunty music-hall tune, David steered the car down the lane toward the cottage on Saturday morning.

It had been a hellacious week in the city and all he wanted to do was feast his eyes on Julia and steal a few more kisses. Ironically, despite their political differences, it was easy to forget politics when he was with her.

Maybe because he was so consumed with lust that he couldn't think about anything else.

His pulse quickened with the thought that he'd see her again in only a few minutes. Last Sunday seemed ages ago. He couldn't wait to touch her, hold her, possess her. She hadn't rebuffed him on Sunday; he could take this a few steps further this weekend.

Halting the car in front of the cottage, David set the brake and turned off the engine. Jumping out, he barely stopped himself from running as he hastened toward the door and rapped briskly.

David knocked again, louder, but there was still no response. She must be in back, in the garden.

He walked around the corner of the house, stopping to peer through the parlor window, but there was no sign of Julia inside.

The garden was deserted and he felt a sharp stab of disappointment. She knew he was coming today; why wasn't she here?

He shook his head. He shouldn't expect Julia, of all women, to be sitting here patiently waiting for him to arrive. She wasn't that type of female—and he wouldn't be so eager to see her if she was. Wasn't it that independence of spirit, her unconventionality, that drew him to her?

Although she could have at least left him a note saying when she would return.

Slowly he walked back to the car. He'd visit with his aunt and come back later. He bent to pull the starting crank on the car, then halted. If he left the car here, it would be a pointed reminder to Julia that he'd arrived, and she hadn't been here to greet him.

David started walking toward his aunt's house.

He took the shortcut across the field and as he climbed the stile, he caught a glimpse of a woman emerging from the copse at the far end. Shading his eyes with his hand, he squinted at the distant figure. Was it Julia?

Just the thought that it might be made his heart pound at a ridiculous rate. Why did she have such an unnerving effect on him? He was acting like a randy schoolboy, not a sophisticated man-about-town. But from that first encounter at the pond, Julia had a knack for destroying his composure.

As the woman drew closer, David recognized the lithe female figure and he jumped off the stile, striving to appear casual. He shouldn't appear *too* eager. He didn't need Julia, of all women, feeling too sure of herself.

He raised his arm in greeting and she gave him an

answering wave. Watching her approach, with her long-legged, masculine stride, David once again appreciated her uniqueness. She was, surprisingly, one of the sexiest women he'd met, even while she ignored society's conventional standards of feminine appeal. And she seemed remarkably unaware of the fact—which probably was part of the attraction. Julia's actions held no artifice; if he found her sexy as hell it was because she was, not because she was trying to be.

"Where have you been?" he demanded when she was within hailing distance.

"Out walking."

He opened his mouth to berate her for not being at home when he'd arrived, then stopped himself. He didn't want her to know just how badly he wanted her. Julia, shouldn't think she had a hold over him.

Stopping a few paces from her, David tried to hide the delight in his eyes.

"Since you weren't home, I was going to visit my aunt."

Julia gave him an impish look. "Don't let me stop you."

He grabbed her hand and pulled her closer. "Do you really think I want to see my aunt, now?"

She looked at him, her brown eyes wide with innocence. "I don't know what you want to do," she said simply.

Leaning over, David planted a gentle kiss on those full, lush lips. "That, for one." Then he pulled her into his arms and kissed her again, slowly, deliberately, tasting her lips, her mouth, her tongue. She tasted like sweet summer grass.

"That, for another," David said as he drew back for a moment. "I hope that meets with your approval."

For an answer Julia put her hands to his head and pulled his mouth down to hers again for a brief kiss.

David barely hid his surprise. Things were moving faster than he could have hoped!

He took her hand and they strolled back to the cottage.

"How was your week?" he asked.

She laughed. "I should be the one asking that question. I don't need to tell you how uneventful my life is. What did you do?"

"Let's just say I was very glad to leave London behind this morning." He squeezed her fingers. "Particularly knowing what was waiting for me here."

She arched a brow. "Oh? And what is that?"

He stopped and placed his hands on her shoulders, gazing down into those chocolate eyes. "You."

A wide smile crossed her face. "Have you been practicing your flattery all week?"

David laughed lightly and took her hand again. "Daily. I spent all my time in committee meetings thinking of outrageous things to say to you."

"No wonder so little gets done in Parliament," she said dryly.

He grinned.

When they reached the car, he dropped her hand and rummaged in the boot for the package he'd brought, then followed her into the cottage.

"Did you get much work done this week?" he asked her, noting the unchanged chaos in the parlor and on her worktable.

"Not as much as I wished, but the delights of the country offer too much temptation," she said with a laugh.

He eyed her teasingly. "Swimming in the pond again, eh?"

Her eyes brightened mischievously. "I'm not going to say."

Laughing, David handed her the package. "Here, this is for you."

She took it from him, an eager expression on her face. "For me? How exciting. I don't often get presents."

"I thought you could use a little more light reading," he said, basking in the glow of her pleasure—and she hadn't even opened it yet.

Julia tore the paper off and held the slim volume in her hand. "*The Wind in the Willows.* Isn't this a children's book?"

He grinned. "It's all about life in the country. The perfect thing to read in the garden after working all day."

Laughing, Julia glanced at the inscription: *For Julia, in hopes that she finds I drive better than Mr. Toad.*

"I take it Mr. Toad is an abominable driver?"

"The worst," he replied.

She gave him an assessing look. "I'm not sure I'm familiar enough with your driving to make a comparison."

"Then by all means, let me show you." David jumped at the opportunity to spend more time with her. "I'll take you to lunch in the village."

"How delightful."

"Don't expect too much," he said as he steered her out the door. "It's only the local pub."

"Lunch with you would be a pleasure wherever we ate," Julia said.

David grinned to himself. She *was* glad to see him.

Now, he just had to take advantage of the situation.

They had a leisurely lunch in the village, then David took a circuitous route back to the cottage, ostensibly to show off his driving skills, but really to give him an excuse to spend more time with her.

The longer he talked with Julia, the more he liked her. She wasn't the strident militant he'd expected. Her aura of calm self-assurance attracted him—as did the way she rose to the bait whenever he teased her. He couldn't remember enjoying himself this much with a woman in a long, long time.

It was a struggle to keep his hands off her. But he was determined to seduce her, and he didn't want to do anything to scare her now, with victory looming on the horizon. Julia Sydney was too grand a prize to let slip through his fingers. He'd court her diligently, flatter her outrageously, and hope by the end of the weekend that they'd be sharing more than a few kisses.

Unfortunately, his aunt was not going to cooperate with his plan. The minute he walked in the door, she announced he was escorting her to dinner at the vicar's, and no amount of protestations on his part could free him from the obligation.

Julia would have to wait until tomorrow.

Chapter 6

On Sunday morning Julia restlessly prowled the parlor, her uneasiness increasing with every stride. She hoped David would come by today—and at the same time berated herself for her desire to see him again.

She was supposed to be teasing him with her attentions, letting him believe she was flattered and enticed by his words. But Julia found it increasingly difficult to remember that this was merely a game. If she wasn't careful, she'd find herself responding in earnest.

And that was not good. David Kimbrough was her political enemy, and she couldn't believe there wasn't a deeper reason for his increasingly attentive behavior. Men like him had their pick of women—why would he choose her?

Unless he had some ulterior political motive in mind.

A light knock sounded on the door and Julia's heart leaped at the sound, knowing it was David. All her resolution vanished.

He greeted her with an easy smile, his blue eyes alight. "I'm here to invite you up to lunch at the house. Aunt wishes to see you."

"Goodness, you make it sound like a summons."

David laughed. "Let's just say she is plotting to foster the relationship between us."

Julia wasn't sure that they needed any help. She grabbed her hat and followed him out the door.

"Between the two of you, I shall be so thoroughly spoiled by all this fine food that my life in London will seem plain after this."

"I want to spoil you," he said, his blue eyes lit with barely restrained desire.

Julia looked away, disturbed by the intensity of his gaze.

At the house, the butler escorted them to the terrace, which overlooked the rear garden and a broad swath of green lawn.

"The weather is so nice I thought we could eat on the terrace," Lady Marchmont said when she greeted them. "Everything is ready."

David pulled out Julia's chair and she sat down, amazed at the elegant table before them. The crisp white linens, heavy silver, and patterned china all looked as if they belonged in the dining room.

"I've had less casual luncheons at the club," David said as he sat down. "Who are you trying to impress?"

"Just because we're dining on the terrace doesn't mean we have to let standards slip," his aunt said with a sniff.

The unobtrusive butler served the cold cucumber soup and tiny sandwiches of salmon and watercress. A large platter of fruits and cheese completed the meal.

"I can't eat another bite," David said, pushing away his second plate of dessert.

Lady Marchmont smiled. "That's why lunch on the terrace is so pleasant—it increases the appetite."

"All I need now is a good cigar and a glass of whiskey."

"Nonsense." Lady Marchmont shook her head. "Some good physical activity is what you need. Where's that old croquet set we used to have?"

David groaned. "You don't expect Julia and me to play croquet? It's been years."

Lady Marchmont gave Julia a sly wink. "Afraid she might beat you?"

David's eyes gleamed a challenge. "Can you wield a croquet mallet, Julia?"

"I've played a time or two," she replied airily, hiding her delight. She was acknowledged the family champion at croquet, and couldn't wait to take on David.

"My money's on Julia," Lady Marchmont said with a grin.

Julia gave David a superior look. "I think I'm up to the task—you're out of practice, after all."

He jumped to his feet. "That does it. I'm not going to let *that* remark go unchallenged. I'll see if I can find the set."

After he left, Lady Marchmont gave Julia a shrewd glance. "Croquet is your game, is it?"

Julia stifled a giggle. "My sisters and I played it endlessly when we were growing up."

"David always wanted to be the best at everything." Lady Marchmont shook her head in warning. "He spoke the truth when he said he doesn't like to lose—ever."

"Neither do I," Julia replied.

"That's why you two make such an interesting pair," Lady Marchmont said. "I wonder who will be the ultimate winner?"

Julia knew Lady Marchmont wasn't referring to the upcoming croquet match. Julia, too, wanted to know who would come out the victor in this duel. It wasn't a political battle anymore, and she didn't feel as confident of her superiority in matters of the heart.

"Goodness, you make this sound like an electoral campaign." Julia tried to keep her voice casual. "It's only a simple game."

"Is it?" Lady Marchmont looked thoughtful. "You two are seeing a lot of each other."

Julia avoided her knowing gaze. "Believe me, your nephew and I won't be crossing paths in town. I'm not exactly popular in government circles, and I don't expect David to attend many WSPU meetings."

"If David wants something bad enough, he'll find a way to get it. You should be prepared. He wants you, you know."

Julia laughed uneasily. "He'll have to change his views on the suffrage bill, for a start."

Lady Marchmont gave her a conspiratorial look. "We'll both put pressure on him—he can't fight the two of us."

"I think you're the only one he'd listen to."

"Nonsense. He's impressed with your political acumen."

"That doesn't mean he's going to agree with me."

"Perhaps I will go up to the city this fall," Lady Marchmont said, half to herself. "We can confront the boy together."

"I'm not allowed within a block of Parliament."

Lady Marchmont patted her knee. "Well, if you can't go there, I will. They won't dare ask me to leave."

"Who would be foolhardy enough to try?" David stood at the foot of the terrace, a croquet ball in his hand.

"We wondered what would happen if we tried to join you in the members' dining room," Julia said with a grin. "I know I wouldn't get past the front door, but I think your aunt would be more successful."

David laughed. "You two are plotting to get me in trouble, aren't you?" He tossed the ball into the air. "Are you ready to wield your mallet, Miss Sydney?"

Julia jumped to her feet and went down the steps. "Let's see how good you are."

"I thought you already knew that," he said in a low whisper that sent a chill of remembrance up her spine. She wanted to feel his lips on her again, feel the gentle touch of his hands. "I'll set out the far wickets—you do the rest."

They set up the six-wicket course in short time.

"Those last two wickets are out of line," Julia called to him as he trotted back to the start.

Shading his eyes with his hand, David glanced down the course. "They look all right to me."

Julia rolled her eyes. "It's a good thing you didn't choose engineering for a career."

Pulling off his jacket, David rolled up his sleeves. With a flourishing bow, he gestured toward the start line. "Ladies first."

Julia glared at him. "You're saying that just so I will insist that you go first."

"It was worth a try." He grinned sheepishly and

reached into his pocket and pulled out a coin. "Heads or tails?"

"Heads."

David flipped the coin and caught it. "Tails. I'll take blue and black."

He positioned himself behind the blue ball and with a tap of the mallet sent it spinning toward the first wicket. Julia followed his path with her red ball.

To her amazement, instead of heading for the wicket on his next shot, David deliberately knocked his ball against hers, then sent it shooting toward the far sideline.

"What are you doing?" Julia demanded.

"Keeping you out of play," he replied with a wicked grin. "You didn't think this was going to be a *civilized* game, did you?"

"I should have known there'd be foul play from a member of the government," she said in a loud undertone.

He shrugged off her concern. "It's in the rules, you know. I've just as much right to keep you away from the wickets as I have to knock my ball through."

"If that's the way you want to play, so be it." Julia took her mallet and aimed for David's ball.

His game strategy didn't change—keep her balls away from the wickets at all costs, even if it meant he didn't score many points himself.

Julia battled back with determination, but she knew she was fighting a losing battle. She and her sisters might have knocked a ball out of the way if a wicket was blocked, but they hadn't made a practice of deliberately sabotaging each other. She'd have to learn quickly. Julia didn't like to lose any more than he did.

Worse, he didn't play fair. Oh, he didn't violate any of the rules of croquet—it was the rules of human decency he ignored. Yelling "Miss!" as she struck her ball, causing her shot to go awry. Deliberately sending her balls to the same far corner of the court turn after turn, without making any attempt to advance his own.

His very presence was an unfair distraction. He stood there, hands on his hips, the accustomary arrogant expression on his handsome face, his hair glinting gold in the sun. With his sleeves rolled up, exposing his tanned, muscled forearms, David looked delectable—and he knew it.

Attempting to ignore him, Julia eyed the angle between her ball and the wicket. This was the first time she'd had this good a shot and she wanted to get the ball through. Grasping her mallet with both hands, she bent over, taking careful aim.

David suddenly encircled her with his arms.

"Here, let me help you." His hands closed over hers where they grasped the mallet.

Icy chills danced up her arms and Julia sucked in her breath. She was trapped, captured in his arms. And she didn't want to get away. The solid strength of his body, pressed against her in a far too intimate manner, felt too good.

He's doing this on purpose. The conscious part of her brain reminded her of that, but the thought did nothing to temper her reaction to him. She wanted to melt against him, to dare him to kiss her again.

His lips brushed against her neck and she started, suddenly aware of her surroundings. A quick glance at the terrace told Julia that Lady Marchmont was thankfully dozing.

"Croquet," he whispered, his breath warm against her ear. "We're playing croquet, Julia. Hit the ball."

As if it hadn't been his goal to distract her all along. She let him guide her swing and tapped the ball through the wicket.

"Good girl." He planted a kiss on the side of her neck, just below her ear, and stepped away.

Julia bit down on her lip to stifle her protest—until she caught a glimpse of the smug expression in his eyes. He *was* trying to distract her from the game.

With her free stroke, she took aim at his nearby ball, sending it spinning toward the left side of the course.

"What are you doing?" Dismay crossed his face.

"Playing croquet," she replied with a triumphant smile.

The game deteriorated into a parody of the genteel garden pastime. Amid laughter and cries of despair, they both concentrated on preventing the other from gaining an advantage.

"You don't play fair," he grumbled after she'd knocked his ball away from the wicket three times in a row.

"I don't believe there is anything in the rules that specifically forbids that situation." Julia grinned. "It was a perfectly legal move."

"I'll get you for that later."

Julia calmly aimed for his other ball and shot it into the hinterlands of the court.

A bell clanged loudly and Julia glanced around.

"My aunt," David explained. "It's her discreet way of telling us we've been out here long enough." He aimlessly brushed his mallet over the grass. "Care to declare my victory?"

"Your victory?" Julia scoffed. "I'll concede no such thing."

"I believe I am ahead on points."

"The game isn't over."

He took the mallet from her hands, squeezing her fingers as those deep blue eyes probed hers. "Isn't it? I think we've been playing games long enough, Julia."

His expression sent shivers down her spine. She knew exactly what he meant.

But it was too soon to say who was ahead in *that* game.

She started toward the house. "We shouldn't keep your aunt waiting."

A pitcher of iced lemonade sat on the table next to Lady Marchmont. She looked up eagerly when Julia and David appeared.

"Well, my dear, did you defeat this overarrogant nephew of mine?"

David coughed and Julia shot him a dark glance.

"We didn't finish the game," she explained. "He *claims* he was winning, but I think we have to call it a draw."

Lady Marchmont shook her head. "I hoped you would soundly trounce him."

"Oh, there's always the opportunity of a rematch." David gave Julia a sharp look. "I don't think either of us will be satisfied until there is a clear winner."

Lady Marchmont pointed to the pitcher. "Pour us some lemonade, dear."

"Lemonade?" David raised a brow. "Surely I deserve something a little more—robust—after my athletic endeavors."

Lady Marchmont rang the silver bell that sat at her elbow and the butler appeared instantly. "Bring the whiskey, Heevers."

Julia sipped her icy lemonade and watched and listened while David continued to fondly tease his aunt.

Here, in the country, he was so different from the arrogant politician she'd first thought him. It was easy to forget the political differences between them. And harder and harder to resist the man.

Intoxicating was the only word Julia could use that came close to describing the effect David had on her. When she was with him, all other things faded into insignificance. And she didn't care. Julia wanted to be with him.

Somehow, David had brought back enjoyment and enthusiasm to her life; a thing that had been sadly lacking after her last term in prison. He'd reenergized her with his attentions, and despite the fact that he'd distracted her abominably from her work, Julia felt happier than she had been in a long time.

She only wished she knew where this would all lead.

A sudden breeze danced across the terrace.

"You'll catch a chill if you stay out here longer." David helped his aunt to her feet, then looked at Julia. "Do you wish to come inside also?"

She shook her head. "I'll wait here."

"You'll have to resume your match another day," Lady Marchmont said. "I am counting on you to beat him, my dear."

Julia smiled. "I look forward to doing that myself."

While she waited for David to return, Julia walked to the end of the terrace. Leaning her elbows on the railing, she gazed out over the park. The garden blooms were at their height as bright splashes of crimson and sun-bright yellow stood out against the more subdued blue and white hues. In the afternoon heat, the scent of roses drifted across the terrace. Julia could have stood here forever, soaking it all in.

David came up beside her, casually wrapping an arm around her waist. "You look deep in thought. Contemplating your strategy for the next match?"

Julia leaned against him, enjoying the solid strength of him. "Just wishing that summer would last."

"You make it sound as if the grim snows of December are going to be upon us next week." He turned her toward him and kissed her gently. "It's barely August, my dear. Plenty of time left for frolicking under the golden orb."

"Plenty of time for me to defeat you at croquet—if you choose to play fair."

"I play as fairly as you, sweetling." He squeezed her tightly. "You stood so innocently on the grass, knowing how enticing you are . . . I never knew a woman who could look so ravishing in a plain skirt and blouse."

Julia fingered one strap of his braces. "And I suppose you know nothing of how you appear, with your sleeves oh-so-casually rolled up . . ."

He laughed heartily. "I never considered croquet to be such an erotic sport before." He leaned over and kissed her slowly, lingeringly. "But then again, you make the very act of breathing an erotic experience."

Julia wrapped her arms around his neck, pulling his lips down onto hers again, touching him, tasting him.

Like the game they'd just played, she wasn't sure exactly who was ahead right now.

In the morning he rejoined her at the cottage and they sat at the little table in the garden, feasting on the jam and scones he'd purloined from the main house for their breakfast.

"I am not sure if I am going to be able to come down next weekend," David said, stretching out his legs. "I may have some speaking engagements."

Julia tried to hide her disappointment. "Where are you going?"

"Planning to send your cronies there to greet me?"

She gave him a withering look. "I thought we'd banned political remarks."

He held up his hands defensively. "I know how organized you ladies are—and how creative."

"I am on holiday, remember? I am officially forbidden to do any WSPU organizing until I go back to London. So you can venture out, unafraid."

"That doesn't mean someone else won't undertake the task."

"True." She grinned. "But you can't blame me for *that*."

He gave her a speculative look. "I wonder what will happen when you do take up your work again."

Julia willed herself not to shudder at the thought. She wondered about that, too, but she didn't want to think about it. Now now. That was a problem for the future. She gave him an enigmatic smile. "Who knows what my duties will be when I go back? I may be stuck in the office writing articles all winter."

"I doubt it." David stood. "I'll let you know by the end of the week what my plans are. If we make progress, I may be able to get away after all."

"I'll hope to see you, then."

"Eagerly?"

Walking over to him, Julia placed her palm against his chest, feeling the heat of him through the fine white lawn of his shirt. "That depends. Should I be anticipating something special?"

He laughed. "I promise to find some way to surprise you."

"Then I will be *eagerly* awaiting your arrival."

David hugged her close. "I can't wait," he whispered into her ear before he kissed her good-bye.

* * *

An hour later Julia forced herself to take a brisk walk to combat the emptiness she felt at his departure. She knew she shouldn't enjoy his company so much, knew she shouldn't be so eager to see him again.

But she did and knowing that didn't make it any easier. Someday she was going to have to come to terms with her feelings for him.

Feelings. She was supposed to be flirting with David, not developing "feelings" for him. But feelings she had, and they were rapidly moving into an area that she didn't want to examine too closely.

Julia knew she was playing with fire, but like a moth drawn to a candle flame, she couldn't stop herself. Where it would all lead, she didn't know, and didn't want to guess. She wanted to pretend that there were no worries, that no problems loomed on the horizon, that she and David could tease and laugh like this forever.

That was childish reasoning. Nothing lasted forever, especially a relationship as tenuous as this. It would come to a screeching halt someday, when the reality of their political lives intruded. But until it did, Julia wasn't going to spend her time worrying about it. She'd enjoy the time she spent with David, and not worry about what was to come.

Chapter 7

David spent the week in London in a frenzy of anticipation. He sensed Julia weakening. His feeble hold on his desires was nearly gone and he ached to pursue her without the need for caution. Surely, she wouldn't grow skittish after all this time?

Her eagerness grew every time he kissed her. Surely, it was time to move on to the next step. He could go about this in the traditional way—wooing her as any man would woo a lady. Flowers. Candy. Gifts. Except he didn't think those things would make much of an impression on her.

He could go for the practical—a bottle of fine wine, or whiskey, since she seemed to like that. There were probably any number of fine delicacies that she couldn't get in the country; a trip to the food counter at Harrods would offer up a number of choices.

Food. His mind raced. That was it. A time-tested method. And in the country, what could be more appropriate than a picnic? A lazy afternoon spent on a blanket spread out beside a stream, their stomachs filled with tasty food and warmed by some potent wine. The perfect setting for the final step in a seduction.

His body ached at the very thought of it.

He wore a cheery smile for the remainder of the day.

On Saturday morning David arrived at his aunt's in record time. He barely popped in long enough to greet her before he took himself off to clean up from the dusty trip. Then he was out to the stables, with his picnic basket, and instructions to Robbie where to take it so all would be ready.

Whistling cheerfully, David struck out across the lawn toward the cottage.

Julia promptly opened the door when he knocked, but he could see from the surprised look on her face that she hadn't been expecting him this early.

David gave her a long, searching, head-to-toe look, thinking she looked good enough to eat. He wanted to wrap his hands around her slim waist, and crush those soft breasts against his chest.

Instead, he took a deep breath. "I'm glad to see you're properly dressed for the occasion."

Her eyes danced expectantly. "Oh? What are we doing?"

Grabbing her hand, David pulled her out the door. "I've a surprise planned. Down by the stream."

She gave him a doubtful look. "Not swimming, I hope."

He laughed. "No, a picnic."

Shading her eyes, Julia glanced at the sky. "Those clouds look ominous."

"It's August and it hasn't rained in ages." David grinned. "Or is it that you don't want to picnic with me?"

Julia smiled winsomely. "I am very willing to picnic with you, David Kimbrough."

"Good."

She looked at his empty hands. "What do you propose to eat on this picnic?"

He took her arm and started down the drive. "Oh, it's waiting for us there. I wanted to have my hands free for other things—like holding a lovely lady's arm."

The route he followed was more from memory than any path, but soon they reached the stream. In the spring it was probably an impressive torrent, but now only a bare trickle of water coursed between the banks.

There, as he'd planned, stood the hamper. Now, if only the rest of his plans worked out as well. He firmly intended to make Julia his today.

She helped him unfold the blanket and set it out, then plopped down indecorously and removed her shoes and socks. David admired her ankles, thinking her feet looked as good as the rest of her.

He held out the hamper to her. "I packed it myself," he said with pride, hoping she liked his choices.

Lifting the lid, Julia inspected the contents. She pulled out a jar of pickled mushrooms, a tin of pâté de foie gras, and toast crackers. Cold meat pastries, red, ripe strawberries, a jug of cream followed.

She grinned with delight. "This looks wonderful."

Beaming from her praise, David pulled a bottle of wine from the stream and uncorked it, then groaned in chagrin. "I forgot the glasses."

Julia laughed and took the bottle from him. "We'll have to be savages, then." She lifted the bottle to her lips and took a swallow, then handed it back to David.

Without taking his eyes off her, he brought the bottle to his own lips, in an action as intimate as a kiss. He saw her watching with rapt attention, turning away she caught him looking at her.

Good. David sat down beside her and spread pâté on a cracker, then handed it to her.

"How was your week?" she asked.

"Dreadfully dull. All I could think about was seeing you today." His gazed at her with undisguised longing. "Dare I hope you thought of me?"

She popped a strawberry in her mouth and chewed. "Perhaps."

Laughing, he munched a cracker. "That's hardly a balm for my male ego. I expected a bit more enthusiasm."

Laughing, Julia took the pâté knife from him. "It's a woman's prerogative to keep a man guessing."

David took another sip of wine and handed her the bottle. "Then my goal for the weekend is set—I mean to discover what thoughts lurk behind those inscrutable brown eyes."

She gave him an amused glance. "I wish you luck."

They devoured most of the food in a short time. His

stomach full, David reclined on the blanket, content to watch Julia.

Suddenly she scrambled to her feet and danced toward the stream, hiking up her skirts before stepping into the cool water. David watched her with an appreciative gleam in his eye as she revealed a great deal of curvaceous leg.

"Are you sure you don't want to go swimming?" he asked with an exaggerated leer.

"I prefer to swim where I can get my entire body wet," she replied in a teasing tone. Stepping out of the water, she walked back to the blanket where David lay stretched out, propped up on one elbow, and sat down beside him.

"We'll have to go to the shore, then," he said. "There's plenty of water there for swimming."

"Is that a formal invitation?"

"I could use a long holiday." David reached out and took her hand, twining her fingers in his, and searched her face, desperate to know where he stood with her. "Will you come with me?"

Her expression turned thoughtful, as if she was weighing the ramifications of his suggestion. He watched her eagerly, barely daring to breathe, waiting for his answer.

"Yes," she whispered.

Bringing his hand to the nape of her neck, David pulled her head down, until their lips were only a breath apart. "I promise we'll have a wonderful time."

He didn't wait for a response, but pressed his lips against hers, pulling her down atop him. She responded to his kisses with an enthusiastic ardor that only fanned his own desire. His tongue invaded her mouth, seeking hers. Julia's breasts, pressed against his chest, grew taut.

He wrapped his arms around her and rolled over, pinning her beneath him. His weight pressed her into the blanket as he kissed her fiercely, his tongue exploring her mouth. She tasted like wine and strawberries, a mix that grew more intoxicating with each kiss.

A clap of thunder exploded overhead. David reared up and glanced at the roiling black clouds.

"Oh, no," he groaned as the first drop of rain hit his nose. He sat up.

Julia scrambled upright, and they frantically stuffed the remains of their lunch into the hamper. Ignoring her socks, she shoved her feet into her shoes.

"Here, wrap the blanket around you." David handed it to her. "It'll keep you drier."

She shook her head. "It's too much trouble. I can run faster without it."

With her help, he struggled to fold the blanket as clouds opened and the rain pelted down. After shoving it into her hands, he grabbed the hamper and they raced for the safety of the cottage.

Breathless and drenched, they finally arrived on the front step. Julia pushed open the door and David followed her inside. They stood in the flagged entry, water dripping onto the stones.

David intended to make some joking remark about their interrupted tryst, but as he turned to look at her, he sucked in his breath at the sight. Soaked by the rain, Julia's blouse clung to her breasts, creating an even more erotic picture than her naked form at the pond. He grabbed her and pulled her into his arms, planting a heated kiss on her mouth.

She responded eagerly, her hands clutching his shoulders. His lips pressed against hers, insistent, demanding. Despite his soaked clothes, a fire burned inside him. He couldn't believe how much he wanted this woman.

Wrenching his mouth away, David gulped in air, his body aching with desire. "You should get out of those wet clothes before you take a chill," he said, his voice gruff with passion. His hands reached for the buttons on her blouse.

David felt her tremble as his fingers fumbled with the tiny fastenings. Peeling off the wet garment, he flung it on a chair. Her camisole hugged her skin, the rosy hue of her nipples dark against the sheer fabric. He undid the waist of her skirt, letting it fall to the floor in a sodden pile. Julia's knickers molded to those enticing hips and slim, long legs.

He wanted those legs wrapped around him, wanted to hear her moans of pleasure as he eased himself into her body.

Stepping back, David gave her a long, steady look, unable to tear his eyes away from her delectable body.

"I want you, Julia," he said, his voice cracking with desire. "And if you don't want me, I suggest you flee to your bedroom and lock the door."

Julia saw the need in his eyes, knew that this was no feigned emotion, no silly flirtation between them. *He wanted her.*

Just as much as she wanted him. Julia felt powerless to resist her own longings.

Taking a deep breath, Julia stepped closer and reached for his shirt. "I don't want you to catch a chill, either."

He shivered as she unbuttoned his shirt. Despite the drenching, his skin was hot to the touch when she brushed her fingers across his chest. She felt the rapid pounding of his heart, echoing the rhythm of her own racing pulse.

Grabbing her hand, David brought it to his lips, kissing each finger with aching slowness. His blue eyes seared hers with a white-hot heat and Julia's knees weakened as her own desire coursed through her.

David led her into the bedroom. Running his hands up her sides, he pushed the camisole over her head and arms, then pulled her down onto the mattress. A rush of anticipation flowed through her as he took her in his arms.

"You're so damn beautiful," he whispered against her skin, kissing the valley between her breasts. Then his mouth came down on a nipple and Julia arched at the exquisite sensation, her breast growing taut and aching under his caresses. His lips moved to her other breast and a soft groan escaped her. It felt so good, so right . . .

"David," she moaned, her body thrumming with excitement.

His tongue traced a path down her abdomen as he pushed her knickers down, his mouth following the descending waistband. With a muttered oath, he rolled to one side and pulled the sodden garment off her ankles, then settled himself between her legs, his heated skin scorching hers. His hand teased the dark curls between her thighs while his mouth ran kisses along the line of hair, sending her quivering with need.

Slipping his hands beneath her bottom, David raised her to his lips.

Julia gasped when he touched his tongue to her. She'd never . . . he shouldn't . . . But the sensation captured her as he expertly teased her, leaving her panting for breath, convinced it was possible to die from too much pleasure. She buried her fingers in his hair, moving instinctively beneath his mouth, barely able to breath, to think, to do anything but succumb to the pleasure he gave her.

A bolt of heat shot through her and Julia couldn't stifle her cry as she exploded, arching and twisting beneath his tormenting mouth. He didn't pull away, staying with her until the aching stabs of pleasure faded.

Sated, overwhelmed by the intensity of the passion he'd aroused, Julia lay silently, coherent thought gone. Her previous experiences with sex had been hesitant, fumbling, and generally unsatisfying. But this . . . She'd never expected this kind of passion. He knew everything she wanted—before she did.

Julia ran a caressing hand down his chest, struggling for words.

"That was . . . astounding."

He grinned. "We've barely begun, Julia."

His words sent a shiver down her spine.

Rolling to one side, he pulled off his shirt and pants, and knelt naked before her. Julia couldn't tear her eyes away from him. David was gorgeous—every part of him.

He stretched out beside her and pulled her into his arms, his hardness pressing against her. His mouth dipped again to her breast, his hand kneading the flesh. Julia ran her fingers down his back, hearing him groan, pleased she could bring him pleasure.

"That feels so good," he said, his voice taut with passion. He put his hand atop hers, pressing it against his heated skin. "Touch me, please."

With growing boldness, Julia ran her hand across the tautness of his back. Her fingers explored his body, the hard muscles of his arms, the wiry blond hairs of his chest. Touching a finger to a nipple, she was surprised to see it harden beneath her touch. He groaned again and she suddenly realized her power as a woman. The power to give and take pleasure.

She hadn't known it could be like this, that loving was equal parts of giving and taking. She wanted to give David everything.

Growing braver, she skimmed her hand lower, brushing across his abdomen, feeling his muscles harden as he drew in his breath. Julia reveled in his reaction, finding herself eager to bring him pleasure. Slowly she curled her fingers around him and he shuddered at her touch.

"Am I hurting you?" she asked teasingly.

He laughed, a low throaty sound that caused her skin to tingle. "Oh, yes, I'm in agony."

In a lightning-fast movement, he was on top of her, kneeling between her legs, pressing himself against her. "There's only one way to ease this pain," he whispered.

Julia wrapped her hands behind his neck, pulling him down against her as he eased himself into her body. She opened herself to him, drawing him inside her until he filled her.

It had never felt like this before. With David, there was a sense of completeness, of fulfillment as their bodies joined. It was exhilarating—and frightening. It felt too good, too right, to be here with him, holding him inside her, moving against him as her desire throbbed again. She could lose herself in the pleasure.

He pulled away, then pushed into her again, moving with ever increasing urgency. Julia caught the rhythm and moved with him.

"That's it," he rasped. "Faster. Harder. I want you to come again, with me inside you." He slipped his hand between them and touched her with his fingers.

Julia gave a long cry as a thousand nerves exploded and she shuddered against him.

David continued thrusting, rhythmically, prolonging her pleasure until he cried aloud at his own release. He collapsed atop her heaving chest, struggling for breath.

Cradling his head against her breasts, Julia smiled with dreamy satisfaction. She never imagined it could be like this. He'd uncovered a depth of passion in her that she never would have suspected, until now.

All that smug, male arrogance hadn't been misplaced. He was a master at arousing a woman. But had this been like any other time for him? Or had their loving been special for him, too?

Julia feared to ask.

Finally, he stirred and pulled the covers over them, gathering her into his arms.

It felt so nice.

Bundled beneath the blankets, Julia snuggled against him. The rain still pounded against the roof and windows, but here, inside, she felt warm and secure in his arms.

"Sleepy?" David murmured.

"Comfortable," Julia replied, snuggling closer. "And exhausted."

"Better rest, then, because I'm not done with you."

"Oh? What else did you have in mind?"

"I'll think of something."

Julia laughed.

When she awoke later, the room was nearly dark. David lay asleep beside her, his breathing slow and even. Rain still tapped against the roof, but the storm's intensity had waned.

Julia slipped from the bed and threw on her kimono. The floor was cold against her bare feet, but she walked to the kitchen. Lighting the paraffin stove, she set a pot of water on to boil, then moved into the parlor to light a lamp.

She gathered the damp clothes she and David had

flung to the floor and hung them over the backs of chairs to dry. As she grabbed for her crumpled blouse, a broad smile creased her face as she remembered the intensity of their lovemaking, the primitive need that had consumed them both. No matter what came later, it was something she wouldn't forget.

David Kimbrough was the lover of a lifetime.

How long would she be able to enjoy him?

Returning to the kitchen, she checked on the water and prepared the tea.

"Ah, tea. Just the thing."

She whirled about. David stood in the doorway, a towel wrapped around his waist, his eyes still droopy with sleep. He ran a hand through his rumpled hair. Julia thought he looked adorable.

"Are you hungry?" Julia asked. "I've some eggs. And I think there's a few things left from the picnic."

"Starving." He glanced ruefully at the towel. "I don't suppose you have any dry clothing that would fit me?"

Julia laughed. "As a matter of fact, I do. My father's old robe is hanging behind the door in the bedroom. I like to bundle up in it on cool nights."

He disappeared and returned a few minutes later, clad in worn, plaid flannel. "Elegant," he muttered.

After pouring the hot water into the teapot, Julia took it into the parlor. David followed, pausing at the door to retrieve the picnic basket. He pulled out the remnants of their picnic and set the food out on the table.

"A veritable repast," he said.

"We'd be better off with those cucumber and watercress sandwiches you were complaining about last weekend," Julia said with a laugh. "Pickled mushrooms and strawberries. Delightful."

"What do you usually eat?" he asked.

She shrugged lightly. "Soup, or eggs, mostly. Your aunt often sends food over since she knows I don't do much cooking."

"I imagine your mother didn't consider that a necessary part of your education."

Shaking her head, Julia laughed. "Political theory was

far more important. I can't sew a stitch either—although my youngest sister does fine embroidery."

David grabbed her hand and traced along the lines of her palm. "I don't think any man would mind hiring a cook for you."

"Why not cook themselves? Men are certainly capable of that task."

"Our mothers didn't teach us, either."

"Then you must have a cook."

"No, actually. I generally dine out."

"Well, then, our situation is the same—except no one thinks oddly of you for it." Julia grabbed a strawberry and bit into it, then looked at him curiously. "Does your aunt know you're here this weekend?"

David nodded. "I stopped at the house this morning before I came over."

"Won't she wonder where you are now?"

"I think she knows where I am."

Julia fought a blush. She shouldn't care what Lady Marchmont knew—or thought—about her dealings with David. Julia only wished she had a better idea what they were.

Pushing back his chair, David stood and stretched. "Show me where those eggs are. The one thing I can cook is an omelet."

Julia perched atop the kitchen table and watched while he prepared the food. Despite his protestations of ineptitude, he moved with confident competence, whisking the eggs with a skilled hand, checking the temperature of the pan like a gourmet cook. Julia delighted in watching him, thrilled to have a man doing something for her.

He inspected her bare cupboards with a look of growing dismay. "Don't you have anything here? No spices or greens?"

Julia shook her head, laughing. "I guess I grew too accustomed to plain fare in prison."

David tossed her a challenging look. "Well, I'll work to change that. If I can't teach you how to cook, I can at least teach you how to eat."

They were nearly finished with the meal when a knock sounded on the door.

"Who can that be?" Julia pulled her robe closer and went to answer it.

One of Lady Marchmont's servants stood on the doorstep, a valise clutched in his hand.

"Mr. Kimbrough still here?" he asked.

Julia nodded.

The man gave her a knowing grin. "Here's the bag he told me to bring."

Julia stood in the doorway, clutching the valise, staring bemusedly at the man as he walked down the drive. Then she slammed the door shut and stomped back into the parlor, flinging the bag at David.

"Of all the arrogant, insufferable—"

"What did I do?"

"You had the audacity to have this sent over, so confident that you'd be here—"

"Was I wrong?"

Julia longed to wipe that arrogant smirk off his face.

"Oh, come on, Julia, don't act like an outraged virgin. You can't tell me that you didn't expect this to happen. As I recall, you were as eager as I."

"I didn't expect you to tell the entire neighborhood of your intentions—ahead of time!"

"You certainly don't know much about country life—everyone knows everything—usually long before it happens." He put his arms around her. "I've been in agony for the last week—wanting you, dreaming of you. Can you blame me for being so eager?"

Julia sighed. He was right. Hadn't he told her that Lady Marchmont was voicing her own suspicions last week? No doubt the entire neighborhood was speculating about the nature of her relationship with David.

Let them speculate. She wasn't sure she understood what was going on any more than they did.

She nodded at the valise. "What's in the bag?"

He grinned. "My shaving kit. A nightshirt. And a bottle of brandy."

"What, no change of clothes?"

"See, I didn't consider every possibility. I hadn't planned on getting soaked, or I would have packed some." He fingered the worn robe he wore. "I think I still cut a dashing figure in this, though."

Julie laughed. "I'll make more tea. It's a perfect day for tea and brandy."

David admired the gentle sway of her hips as she crossed the room. He'd made love to her twice now and he couldn't wait to do it again.

She was everything he'd wanted her to be—fierce, passionate in her responses. And although she was no virgin, he didn't think she'd had many lovers. She'd been too overwhelmed by the fire that consumed them both.

He felt a smug sense of satisfaction in the thought that *he'd* been the one to unleash her passions.

And it made him feel better about his own reaction to her. He couldn't recall any woman who'd so enthralled him sexually. It had nothing to do with their political conflict—and everything to do with who she was and how she lived her life. She approached lovemaking the way she approached life—with enthusiasm. And her eagerness only fueled his own pleasure. He could give her what she wanted—and take the same back from her.

God, he was going to enjoy this.

She came back with the new pot of tea. David poured a generous dollop of brandy into their cups while they waited for the brew to steep.

He chucked her under the chin. "Am I forgiven for my presumption?"

She gave him a teasing look. "That depends. You'll have to work to put yourself back into my good graces."

"What did you have in mind?"

He saw the gleam of anticipation in her eyes and knew exactly what she wanted. David reached for the belt of her robe.

Chapter 8

He awoke the next morning with a start, staring in confusion at the unfamiliar room. Then the soft shape next to him stirred and he knew exactly where he was. David wrapped an arm around her waist and pulled Julia tightly against him. She mumbled something and kept on sleeping.

Sometimes he thought that watching another person sleep was a far more intimate act than possessing their body. In sleep, you were unaware, vulnerable, defenseless. And although vulnerable was not a word he would normally apply to Julia, in this moment she was, as she nestled in his arms like a sleeping child. He felt oddly protective of her.

Carefully he stretched his cramped muscles. He ached everywhere and his only consolation was that she was probably as sore as he. Restraint hadn't been on either of their minds last night. David wished he were back in London, where he could have a soothing soak in a hot tub.

Of course, it would be ungentlemanly of him to bathe alone, and Julia's presence wouldn't be conducive to a relaxing soak.

But it would be a hell of an enjoyable bath.

He realized with a sudden shock that it was only Sunday morning. It was hard to believe that he'd only come down from the city yesterday, and that he wouldn't have to go back for another full day. He could spent the rest of the weekend in bed, if he wanted to.

His stomach rumbled and he realized one thing would drive them out—hunger. If he slipped out now, he might be able to get to the main house and raid the kitchen before Julia woke up.

Carefully, he withdrew his arm and sidled off the bed. His clothes were still damp, but he'd grab some dry ones at the house. He scribbled a hasty note to Julia, which he propped up against the half-empty bottle of brandy still sitting on the table, and let himself out of the cottage.

The sky was gray with low-hanging clouds, but it wasn't raining. Not that it mattered. The grass was so wet that he was soaked to the knees by the time he reached the house.

Lady Marchmont's cook was in the kitchen, stoking the range and getting ready for her day's work. David pleaded for her sympathies and she promised to pack up some food for him, while he raced upstairs to get some dry clothes.

After changing, he stopped long enough to leave a note for his aunt. Old gossip that she was, she deserved to have her suspicions eased—at least to a certain extent. He promised to bring Julia by for tea later that afternoon. That would put a damper on his aunt's nosy questions.

Back in the kitchen, he grabbed the basket and returned to the cottage.

Stretching lazily in bed, Julia felt like a cat who'd fallen asleep in the sun. Perhaps she would just roll over and go back to—

Her eyes snapped open. The other side of the bed was empty. David was gone.

The sharp stab of disappointment surprised her. How could she miss him this much already?

Because she feared he might not come back.

Julia heard the cottage door open and shut, and quick steps crossed the flagged hall.

David's face appeared around the door frame, smiling broadly as he caught sight of her. "Oh, good, you're awake. I've brought us breakfast."

"From the fairies in the forest?" Julia hoped her answering smile wasn't as fatuous as she felt. He'd come back.

"From the kitchen at the estate. I told the cook we were in severe danger of starvation." He gave her a teasing look. "If you get dressed, I *might* share some of it with you." He disappeared into the hall.

Julia scrambled from bed and pulled on her kimono. She was starving, in fact. How resourceful of him to come to their rescue.

Padding into the kitchen, Julia stared in amazement at the food spread out on the table. He must have told the cook a pitiful story, for he'd brought back more food than they could possibly eat in two days.

David was already seated, buttering a thick slab of bread. "Help yourself," he said, pointing at the food.

"Are you sure there's enough?" She sat down, setting a napkin on her lap.

His eyes twinkled. "Barely. I'm counting on you to eat your share."

"I could eat a horse," Julia admitted, forking a thick slab of ham onto her plate and slicing off a piece.

"I left my aunt a note, telling her we'd come by to visit later this afternoon."

Julia's fork halted halfway to her mouth. "Do you really think that is wise?"

He arched a mocking brow. "Afraid to be seen in public with me?"

"Won't she wonder where you spent the night?"

"I hardly think she'll be surprised."

"David, I am staying here out of her generosity. I don't care to anger her."

"Do you think she'll throw you out because you're sleeping with her favorite great-nephew?" He laughed. "On the contrary, she'll be delighted. The news will be the highlight of her week."

Julia gave him an indignant look. "What do you intend to do, regale her with every intimate detail?"

"She won't need that—one look at you will tell her everything."

"What is that supposed to mean?" Julia feared his

answer—were her own feelings so transparent? Could he see how contented—and confused—she felt?

He leaned back in his chair, a self-satisfied smile on his face. "Just that you look like a woman who's been thoroughly tumbled."

Julia rolled her eyes, relieved that he hadn't seen more. "You certainly aren't lacking in self-confidence."

Reaching across the table, he clasped her chin in his hand. "Am I wrong? Or was that someone else I heard moaning with pleasure during the night?"

"Perhaps it was all an act, calculated to soothe your enormous male ego."

He burst out laughing. "Sorry, Jules, but that won't wash. I've enough experience in these matters to know when a woman's pleasure is faked or genuine. The greatest actress in the world couldn't have duplicated your performance."

"You've slept with enough actresses to know?"

"If you've any complaints over my performance, I'd be more than willing to make another attempt." His eyes lit with expectancy.

Laughing, Julia threw up her hands. "All right, I concede defeat. You are a very talented lover."

"Thank you." He bowed his head with false modesty. "And I confess that I have no complaints either."

She gave him what she hoped was an enticing, sensual perusal. "I have no intention of letting you grow bored, David Kimbrough."

His smile widened. "I'll willingly sacrifice myself for the cause—in the interest of research, of course."

"I look forward to the experiment." Julia popped a piece of cheese into her mouth.

His fork landed on the table with a clatter. "What shall we do once we've finished breakfast?"

The hopeful expression on his face made him look like a little boy begging for sweets. "I would like to have a bath," Julia said tartly.

"That sounds like great fun," David replied. "Can I wash your back?"

"Only if you help haul the hot water," Julia said.

Surveying the Victorian-era kitchen, his gaze settled on the pump at the sink. "Good God, I forget you live in such primitive surroundings. Come back to the house with me. There's hot *running* water in the upstairs bath."

"I really don't think your aunt would appreciate—"

He shook his head. "You do have a hidden streak of propriety behind that militant facade, don't you? Would you feel better if I told you that you won't be the first lady I've entertained at her house?"

"Does she approve or merely tolerate your misbehavior?"

David laughed. "If you'd seen all the things she has over the years, you'd know that she has a very open mind. I don't think there's anything left that could shock her."

"Well, I don't want to be the one to find out," Julia replied. "I'll bathe here, thank you."

"Suit yourself." His expression turned apologetic. "I had to bring some work down with me. I could bring it back here—that is, if you aren't thoroughly sick of my company."

Julia slowly licked a drop of butter off her finger, amused by his rapt attention. "Oh, I think I could stand to have you around for a bit longer."

He grinned. "Good. I'll help you with the water, then dash back to the house while you're in the tub." He sighed loudly. "I guess that means I won't be able to scrub your back."

"I'm sure you'll have other opportunities."

"I certainly hope so." His face wore a smug expression.

Once the water was heated and the old tin bathtub filled, David left. Julia stripped off her clothes and sank into the soothing water, uttering a deep sigh of contentment as the heat soaked into her limbs.

She had finished her bath, dressed, and was rinsing the dishes when David walked back in, a bulging portfolio under his arm. His hair was damp and curly.

"I see you took advantage of the *hot running* water," Julia said, briskly drying a teacup.

"I didn't think you'd mind." He set down his satchel, grimacing. "I'm going to be damn happy when this session is finally over."

"Find yourself a comfortable spot in the parlor and you can work away to your heart's content. I have plenty of work myself."

"What exactly are you working on?" he asked.

"Oh, this and that," she said airily as they walked into the other room. "Mostly newspaper articles."

"I didn't know you were a writer."

"I don't get the chance to do it very often; I'm usually too busy with other things. That's why I'm working so hard now. I want to have a batch of articles when I go back to London."

"Who are you writing for?"

"Why, *Votes for Women,* of course."

He grimaced. "That propaganda sheet?"

"On the contrary, we're one of the few papers that prints the truth," she retorted. "We're certainly more accurate than *The Times.*"

"That depends on your point of view."

Julia smiled between gritted teeth. "I promise not to bother you about your work if you don't bother me about mine."

David nodded. "That's a good idea."

Taking her book and tablet, Julia sat in the chair by the window, prepared to take notes on her reading. David settled himself on the sofa and pulled out a sheaf of papers from his portfolio.

Only the turning of a page or the scratching of a pencil broke the silence, but Julia found it difficult to concentrate on her reading. David's presence proved too great a distraction. She couldn't forget the pleasure he'd brought her, his lovemaking skills, her own urge to touch and caress him.

It was an unnerving experience, to be so consumed with thoughts of another that her work suffered. Always, before, her work came first. But with David in the room, Julia could almost forget her own name.

Peeking over the top of her book, she watched him

work. His brow creased in concentration as he thumbed through the report he held, making occasional notes in the margin. A lock of still-damp hair fell over his forehead and her fingers itched to brush it back.

But Julia knew if she touched him, she wouldn't be able to stop. She wanted him too much.

As she watched him, Julia realized what a complex man he was, a study in contrasts. An urbanite who enjoyed country picnics. An arrogant politician, yet a considerate lover. What other contradictions would she discover about him as she came to know him better? And she admitted she wanted to know more—about his childhood, his entry into politics, his life in London.

And any other women in his life.

The flash of jealousy gave her a momentary uneasiness. Had she stepped too blithely into this affair without considering the consequences? It was her very attraction to him that had made this flirtation sound so attractive, and when flirtation had led to something more, she'd been willing, eager. Now, she wondered if danger lurked as well.

Danger to her peace of mind.

She couldn't lose sight of her work, her purpose. David must remain a diversion, not an all-consuming passion.

He looked up, catching her watching him. Julia responded with a guilty smile and he set down his work.

"This isn't fair," he declared, standing and stretching. "If I'm working, you must, too." He came up behind her and kneaded her shoulders. "You're not living up to your part of the bargain."

"Perhaps there are other things I'd rather be doing," she said in a low voice.

"Oh?" He bent over so his mouth was next to her ear. "And what do you suggest?"

"We are in the country, after all. A nice walk would be in order."

Glancing over her shoulder, Julia saw the twinge of disappointment cross his face. Good. He needed to learn that she wasn't going to succumb to his raging desire at the drop of a hat.

And it would be best if she didn't give in so readily to her own longings, either. It would make it easier to remember the place he must play in her life.

Lady Marchmont greeted them warmly when they arrived for tea later that afternoon.

"How nice of you to come," she said as David ushered Julia into the drawing room. "Tea by oneself is such a bore."

The butler arrived promptly with the tea tray and Lady Marchmont poured. She handed Julia her cup. "I hope you two have been enjoying yourselves."

Julia's teacup rattled in the saucer as her hand shook, and she exchanged a guilty look with David.

"Caught you out, haven't I?" The elderly lady cackled loudly. "Ah yes, I remember what it was to be young, and in love. The rest of the world ceases to exist."

David laughed. "Considering the current state of Parliament, I find that a great relief."

Lady Marchmont turned to Julia. "Tell me, my dear, is he treating you well?"

Julia darted David a mischievous glance. "Well enough."

"You're a nosy old lady," David said, but with fondness in his voice.

"Humor this 'old lady,' then," she said. "I need a little excitement in my dull, dreary life."

David shook his head. "We should all lead such dull lives. Sit through a finance committee meeting and you'll see what dull truly is."

"Oh, you love politics and you know it." His aunt chided him. "You have to take the good with the bad."

"Like being covered with molasses and feathers?" he asked with a wry look at Julia.

"You can't complain that was a boring experience," she replied with mock innocence.

"I'd willingly sit through any number of committee meetings before I went through that again. That was one of my favorite suits!" His expression grew tender. "At least I won't have to worry about that happening again."

Julia calmly sipped her tea but her insides roiled at his words. Did he think she would stop her campaign against the government—and him—just because they were lovers?

If so, he certainly had a surprise coming.

"I hope this doesn't mean you will go dashing back to the city now, Miss Sydney." Lady Marchmont gave Julia a searching look. "I enjoy having you here."

"Oh, I have no plans to leave soon," Julia assured her. "I still have a great deal of work to do."

"Good. You are still far too thin, but your color is coming back. The country air is doing you good."

"Don't forget the exercise." David grinned. "Plenty of opportunity for that in the country."

Julia shot him a dampening look. "I do love to walk."

Lady Marchmont looked wistful. "A good idea for the city. Oh, to be young again! These old bones are now at the mercy of carriages, trains, and those infernal motorcars."

"And they get you where you're going faster than you could ever have dreamed as a girl," David said.

"Speed, speed, speed. That's all you young people think about. There's something to be said for a nice, leisurely progression across the country. Why, I remember when a trip to Scotland was an enormous undertaking. Now, you're whisked there by train in no time at all."

"Which, if you don't enjoy travel, is a marvelous improvement." He glanced at his watch. "If we're going to have anything to eat for dinner, I need to speak with cook." He gave his aunt a chastising look. "You should have warned me Julia didn't know how to cook before you introduced us."

Lady Marchmont dismissed his complaint with a wave of her hand. "You can always hire a cook, David. Other qualities are less easy to come by. You both are welcome to eat here anytime."

David glanced at Julia. "Shall we? Otherwise it's probably cold sandwiches for us."

Julia laughed. "I am starting to realize the importance food plays in your life. If Lady Marchmont is so generous as to offer, I wouldn't dare think of dragging you away for *cold sandwiches.*"

"It's that ducal blood," Lady Marchmont said in a stage whisper. "The Kimbroughs have always had a reputation for being gourmands."

"You'd make a poor suffragette." Julia tossed David a pitying look. "No hunger strikes for you."

"An abominable practice," Lady Marchmont said with a shake of her head. "Ruining your health to make a point."

"It is the only way we *can* make our point," Julia said. "We only ask that the government treat us as political prisoners, not common criminals."

"If you didn't get arrested in the first place, you wouldn't have to worry about it," David said.

"If *your* government would give women the vote, we wouldn't need to go to extremes to demand your attention. Protests would stop."

"Oh, I doubt that. You wouldn't be happy unless you were agitating for some cause."

"Is that so different from what you do, David?" Lady Marchmont asked with a shrewd smile. "I seem to recall you belong to the Liberal Party, not the Conservatives."

"I don't throw things to get my point across."

"That's because you don't have to," Julia said, leaning forward eagerly. "How would you like it if women ran the government and men couldn't vote? I imagine you'd be throwing things then."

Lady Marchmont laughed gleefully. "She has you there, David. You'd be at the front of the crowd, yelling 'Off with their heads.' "

David held up his hands in defeat. "I know when I am outnumbered. I will bow to the ladies' opinions—today."

Julia looked at Lady Marchmont. "Have you ever considered coming to London for one of our meetings? You would be an impressive speaker."

Lady Marchmont shook her head. "I'm too old to get involved—I bow to the younger generation. I'm content to confine my help to the financial arena."

David rolled his eyes. "Couldn't you have found a more innocuous cause to support—like finding homes for lost puppies? That's much more appropriate."

"But not nearly as much fun." Lady Marchmont gave Julia a broad wink.

Chapter 9

They lingered for dinner, and longer, and it was nearly dusk when Julia and David strolled back to the cottage, arm in arm.

"Your aunt is a wonderful lady," Julia said. "I hope you appreciate her."

"Oh, I do. She was a godsend when I was a child."

"Oh?"

"My father's idea of parenting was sending me expensive presents when he was in funds, while my mother only wanted to hide me from her lovers. Aunt saved me from having to spend every summer and holiday at that mausoleum of my grandfather's."

"She has no children?"

David shook his head. "There was a son—killed in India before I was born. I became the grandson she never had."

"Do you ever see your mother?"

"Rarely."

Julia took his hand, feeling a twinge of sadness for the young boy who'd been so ignored.

"Don't feel sorry for me," he said, as if reading her thoughts. "My parents were miserable together and it was a good thing they did ignore me—I rarely saw the confrontations."

He wrapped an arm about her waist. "Besides, if I wasn't close to my aunt, I wouldn't have met you. I'd still think you were a man-hating militant, with a beaked nose and skinny body . . ."

"Suffragettes come in all shapes and appearances," Julia said. "Just like all other women."

"I don't think there's another one as lovely as you."

Julia's heart thrilled at his words, even as she dismissed them as outrageous flattery.

As Lady Marchmont said, it was far too easy to ignore reality when one was . . . infatuated.

Julia awoke first in the morning, and slipped out to the kitchen to heat water for tea. Fixing herself a cup, she took it into the parlor and sat in her favorite chair by the window.

The time had flown by; Monday had arrived with surprising suddenness. David would be leaving shortly.

With a pang, Julia realized she didn't want him to go. She'd miss his teasing words and that slow seductive smile that curdled her insides.

Julia smiled wryly. This was a new and exciting experience.

She needed to be careful. Physical pleasure couldn't distract her from her work. Like her summer in the country, David was a holiday. All too soon, reality would come crashing in on them.

If only she could enjoy herself for a little while longer.

She sipped her tea in contentment.

"You look like you're thinking far too hard for this time of morning."

Julia set her cup down and looked up at David. He stood there with a crooked grin on his face, his shirttail hanging out and his hair still tousled from sleep.

He had a surprisingly winsome little-boy look to him and for an instant she wanted to grab his hand and haul him back to the bedroom, keeping him there for the rest of the day—and tomorrow as well.

Instead, Julia rose and walked toward the kitchen. "I'll get your tea."

He grabbed her wrist as she walked by. "You're not going to get away that easily. You could at least say good morning." David planted a smacking kiss on her lips.

With a sigh, Julia melted against him. He would be leaving soon, after all. She might as well take advantage of the time they had left.

* * *

Julia lay in the crook of his arm, her head resting against his shoulder as they lolled in bed after a languorous lovemaking. David sighed with reluctance. "I really should be leaving if I have any hope of making today's sitting."

She ran a teasing finger across his chest.

"Must you? Surely the government can function without you for one day."

He grabbed her hand and brought her fingers to his lips. "It's flattering to think that you hold me in such high esteem."

Julia laughed. "I think you're the one overestimating your value. No one is indispensable—not even the PM."

David grimaced. "I hope you don't tell him that to his face. You'd set the suffrage movement back fifty years."

"Asquith has already managed to do that on his own," she said dryly.

Rolling over, David eased his weight atop her. He clasped both her wrists with his hand while his tongue traced lazy circles around her nipple. There was nothing more that he wanted to do than to spend the rest of the day, the week, the month, here with her, in bed, exploring each and every part of her enticing body and intriguing personality.

He prayed that the Commons would take a break soon, so he could spend more than the weekend with her. Or that she would return to London, so he could see her there as well. But that wasn't going to happen today, and if he didn't leave now, he would never make it back to London before dark.

Reluctantly, he gave her breasts a final kiss and climbed out of bed.

David was acutely aware of her scrutiny as he pulled on his clothes. She lay there, watching him with those dark, smoldering eyes, as if she ached to undo each and every button he'd just fastened. Almost as badly as he wanted her to.

"I'm hoping to be down next weekend," he said, fastening the cuffs of his shirt.

"Oh?"

"I thought I *might* stop in."

"Hmm." She adopted an air of indifference. "I'll have to check my schedule and see if I can fit you in. I'm a busy woman, you know."

He leaned over and kissed her. "Just make damn sure you're here on Saturday."

She grinned wickedly. "I'll see if I can arrange that."

David lingered, still unwilling to leave. Saturday seemed a very long time away. "I thank you for a most enjoyable weekend."

"The pleasure was *all* mine," she replied.

Laughing, David bent over and gave her another kiss. "That's highly debatable, but we can argue about that next weekend. Good-bye, Julia."

"Good-bye."

He turned and walked into the hall, knowing if he didn't leave now, he'd never get out of here. He grabbed his jacket off the chair and let himself out the door.

The car started easily and David climbed in. After carefully backing around, he cast one last look at the cottage as he started down the drive.

Julia was standing at the window, waving her farewell. Stark naked.

Please let Saturday arrive soon, he prayed.

After David left, Julia took a leisurely bath, then took her books out to the garden. She'd accomplished nothing during David's entire visit and would be woefully behind if she didn't apply herself. Her days in the country were limited and she needed to finish her work before she returned to London, and the fall campaign to force the government to grant the vote to women.

She didn't want to think how that was going to impact her relationship with David. Not yet. Selfishly, she wanted more time with him first. More time to indulge in all the sensual fantasies he inspired.

Julia didn't realize how many there were until she went to bed that night. The sheets smelled of sex, sweet, glorious, exhilarating sex, and she felt a sharp pang at the thought that it would be five more days until she could see him again. Hugging his pillow to her, she breathed in the male scent that permeated it.

Setting the pillow aside, she sighed.

During the week, Julia attempted to work on her articles, but she found herself being distracted at the oddest times, by the smallest things. A light rain shower on Tuesday reminded her of their abortive picnic—and the exhilarating pleasure that followed. As she swam in the pond on Wednesday, she recalled their first, embarrassing encounter—and his veiled promise that they should go swimming in the nude together.

Even the dry economics tome that she tackled on Thursday could not free her thoughts of him. In fact, it made things worse—the book was so boring that her mind drifted away constantly.

It was no help that the cottage was so small—every room held a reminder of David. The garden in back was no escape, either. His presence lingered everywhere.

Late in the afternoon she threw down her book in disgust and put on her walking shoes. If she couldn't work, at least she could walk, and try to think about something other than David Kimbrough. She couldn't afford to lose sight of her goal—gaining the vote. She had to remember David was an opponent.

Perhaps, now that they were close, she'd be able to persuade him to change his views. While she captured his body, she might also capture his mind.

But why did she have the uneasy feeling that he was the one doing the ensnaring?

By the time David reached London on Monday evening, Parliament had already been sitting for several hours. He hastily changed at his office and took his seat on the bench, irritated and out of sorts. His mood didn't improve when debate on the finance bill lasted until five a.m. When David finally went back to his house, he collapsed on his bed and fell asleep in an instant.

The rest of the week wasn't any better. Commons'

energy was taken up with the budget debate, a difficult enough process at any time, without the opposition of the Lords hanging over their heads. More than once David thought the government should just pass the damn bill and let the Lords veto it, even if it meant new elections. True change wasn't going to take place until the power of the Lords was broken, and this budget was as good a cause as any. But too many people thought it would be possible to work out a compromise and struggled to create provisions that the Lords would accept.

He knew Julia would understand his attitude. She had no fondness for the Lords, since they were the biggest bar to enacting any changes in the voting laws. In fact, by setting up a showdown over the budget bill, he might ultimately be helping her cause.

That was an amusing thought.

David had to admit that as much as he would like to discuss his work with her, he also wanted her here for far more personal reasons. He couldn't forget the satiny feel of her skin beneath his fingertips, her soft moans of pleasure as he made love to her, her womanly smell. No matter how many times he'd made love to her over the weekend, it hadn't been enough. He wanted her worse than ever.

He'd never met a woman as uninhibited, as comfortable with her body and her desires as Julia. She let him know what she wanted in no uncertain terms, and was equally enthusiastic in meeting his own needs. He'd learned more about women in that one weekend with her than he'd learned from all his previous lovers.

And he was stuck here in London until Saturday, slowly going mad with frustrated desire.

David eagerly anticipated her return to the city, when he could see her for more than a few fleeting days every week. When he could have her in his bed whenever he wanted, falling asleep beside her after sating their desires, waking in the morning to make slow, languorous love to her.

He could not wait.

* * *

Eagerly pulling his car in front of the cottage on Saturday morning, David set the brake, turned off the engine, and jumped down. Julia raced out of the cottage and flung herself into his arms.

"Miss me?" he asked, surprised and delighted at her welcome.

In answer, she touched her lips to his.

"A lot?"

She laughed. "Enough."

"Good." He caught her up in his arms and carried her into the cottage, down the hall, and into the bedroom.

She felt the mattress move as he stood up and she rolled over. He was looking down at her with a arrogant, possessive look in his eyes as he hastily unbuttoned his shirt. A look that both frightened and thrilled her.

His fingers clumsy with desire, David hastily stripped off her clothes, pressing her down on the mattress while he tore at his own. Her dark eyes smoldered with anticipation and David knew he'd have to struggle mightily to keep himself under control.

Lying beside her, David kissed her deeply, thrusting his tongue into her mouth, tasting her, teasing her, showing her his need. His fingers skimmed along her satiny skin, tracing her collarbone, the curve of her breast, the swell of her hip before he touched the spot between her legs.

She was ready for him. David spread her legs with his knee and settled between them, easing himself into her welcoming warmth.

Oh, God, she felt so good.

Trying to restrain himself, David moved with deliberate slowness, but she urged him on, wrapping her legs around him, forcing him deeper, higher inside her. It was an exquisite mixture of pleasure and pain as he fought to restrain himself. His mouth found her breasts, licking them, biting them as she moaned beneath him.

Julia arched against him, crying out his name in a long,

drawn-out moan, and he unleashed himself, thrusting into her with deep, drawn-out strokes until he exploded inside her.

Reluctantly, David pulled away and rolled onto his back, cradling Julia against his chest. He couldn't believe that any woman could feel this good, bring him such pleasure.

"That was even better than I remembered," he said.

"Why, thank you."

He ruffled her hair. "It's a good thing there aren't any mind readers in Parliament—they'd be shocked to know what I was really thinking about during debates this week."

"You really should apply yourself to your job," Julia said. "How is the country to be governed if the MPs are spending all their time thinking about sex?"

David laughed. "No one else could possibly have anything this good to think about." He gave her a squeeze. "I'm the lucky one."

"That's a pretty smug remark. Didn't your mother ever tell you not to be so sure of yourself?"

"And I suppose you're going to tell me that you aren't enjoying yourself."

"Well . . ." Her lips curved in a smile. "Perhaps a *little* bit."

David ran his hand down her back and cupped the curve of her buttock. "I'm more than willing to give it another try. I'd hate to think that you weren't thoroughly pleased."

Julia snuggled closer. "I have no complaints."

He planted a kiss on her forehead. "And did you spend your week thinking about the same thing I did?"

She laughed. "Don't you think I have more important things to do?"

"No."

Julia pinched his chin. "Do you ever grow tired of being so arrogant?"

"Oh, admit it, you know you thought about me once or twice."

"You, or the sex?"

"Is there a difference?" he asked, his voice deliberately casual, yet wondering how she would respond, hoping she would say yes.

"They're certainly intertwined," she replied.

Frustrated by her noncommittal answer, David rolled her over and sat straddling her legs. She gazed up at him, a self-satisfied smile on her face.

Did she want *him*—or merely the physical pleasure he gave her? He needed to know.

Stroking her breasts, his fingers teased over her nipples, watching them harden beneath his touch. She was so responsive, so sensitive. And she had the same effect on him. Only moments before, he'd felt exhausted, yet now he was hard and wanting her again.

And he found that frightening, because he wanted her *too* much. He hadn't anticipated that when he'd first planned her seduction. Then, he'd only wanted the satisfaction of conquest. But now he found himself more concerned with what she wanted, what she felt, rather than his own pleasure. And that, surprisingly, brought him greater pleasure.

And because he wasn't at all sure what she thought about him, the whole idea made him uneasy. Did she really want him as badly as he wanted her?

The only hold he had over her right now was sex, a tenuous one at best. But he intended to use it until he'd welded her to him. A woman as sensual as Julia needed a lover, and he intended to be the one she wanted, the one she had to have. He planned to make damn sure she realized that.

He slid his hand slowly down over her abdomen until his fingers reached the curls between her legs. Slowly, deliberately, he stoked the fire within her.

Much later, he reluctantly opened his eyes, content but hungry. Julia lay curled up beside him. He stroked her arm until she stirred.

"Planning to sleep the rest of the day away?"

"Sounds lovely," she murmured drowsily.

Snapping the covers back, he slapped her lightly on

the rump. "Out of bed, you lazy wench. It's time to eat and I'm starving."

Julia rubbed her backside. "You expect me to feed you after that rude awakening?"

"No, I'm going to feed you." He raked her naked form with an exaggerated leer. "But I don't think they'll allow you through the door unless you put on some clothes."

He swung his legs over the side of the bed and sat up. Their clothes were strewn about the room where they'd been tossed during the mad frenzy of their first coupling. David wondered if they'd ever succumb to restraint.

He hoped not.

Julia pulled on her chemise. "I take it we're not dining with your aunt."

"No, I'm taking you out to dinner. It's not the Savoy, but the food is nearly as good. Cheaper, anyway."

"And where is this grand dining parlor?"

"Oh, that's a surprise. So be a good girl and get dressed. We'll take the car."

The place he had in mind was the inn at the neighboring village—once a major coaching stop that had nearly ceased to exist with the advent of the railroad. But now, with the increased popularity of motoring, they'd found a new source of customers. It was small, unpretentious, and cozy, and he preferred it to any of the fancy restaurants in London.

He thought Julia would feel the same way.

"I can't believe you haven't been here yet," he said as he ushered her into the timbered dining room, the last remnant of the original eighteenth-century building. "For someone who can't cook, this place would be a godsend."

"Unlike you, food doesn't play that great a part in my life. As long as I have something to eat, I'm happy."

"I'll have to do something to change that. I'll turn you into a gourmand despite yourself."

She smiled brightly. "Do you enjoy taking on impossible challenges?"

He grinned back. "I took you on, didn't I?"

Arching a brow, she gave him a quizzical look. "And why is that?"

"Lust, pure and simple," he said with feigned lightness. "Naked women have that effect on me. I've wanted you since I saw you rise like a mythical nymph from the water."

She actually blushed.

"As a gentleman, you shouldn't have been watching."

"As a lady, you shouldn't have been swimming naked."

"I'm not a lady."

He grinned. "And I'm no gentleman."

"That's patently obvious."

"And you wouldn't want it any other way." David laughed. "Ah, Julia, you're such a delight. I wish I'd met you sooner."

She gave him a startled glance before consulting her menu.

David hid a grin. He was getting to her, he knew it. She wasn't sure how to react, what to say, but give her time. He fully intended to have her firmly in his grasp before long.

He realized this was more than great sex and the challenge of subduing the radical suffragette who'd assaulted him with molasses and feathers. He liked her. She was bright, politically aware, and fiercely determined. All the things that most women were not, either by choice or by society's dictates. Julia didn't care about any of that.

And even though he'd followed the rules and played the game, he didn't either. He recognized in her a kindred spirit—except she wasn't afraid to say what she thought or act on her views.

A much braver soul than he was.

But then again, she didn't have anything to lose. If he wanted a political career, he had to do what was expected of him.

Perhaps that was why he enjoyed spending time with Julia so much. With her, he could be himself. He loved to provoke her with outrageous remarks, just to watch her reaction.

When their food arrived, David watched with amusement as Julia devoured hers. No ladylike picking at her food.

"Worked up an appetite this afternoon, did we?"

"I have to keep up my strength," she said tartly, but with a smile.

"Good idea." He gave her a lascivious look. "I've plans for you later tonight."

"And here I thought we were going to sit up and discuss politics."

David laughed. "You know what a dangerous idea that is. No, I had something safer in mind—and much more fun."

"Cards? Charades?"

"Something better suited for two people."

Julia smothered a grin. "Billiards? Chess?"

He gave her a mock-stern look. "My dear woman, have you no imagination? Saturday night, a man and a woman, alone, in a cottage? A cottage with a very *comfortable* bed, I may add."

Julia didn't suppress her giggle. "Sleep?"

David shook his head. "If that's the only thing you want to do there, I'm hurt."

She leaned across the table, a mischievous look in her eyes. "Sex in bed is so bourgeois, David. I thought you had more imagination than that."

Sex in the public dining room of an inn crossed his mind, but he dismissed it, albeit with reluctance. "Well, if it's variety that you want . . . I think I can accommodate you."

Her dark eyes widened with interest. "Oh, do tell."

He shook his head. "If it's surprise you want, it's a surprise you will get."

"Not even a hint?"

David's groin ached to even think about what he wanted to do to her. "Finish your dinner," he growled. "It takes us thirty minutes to get back, remember."

Julia pushed her plate away. "I'm ready."

David hastily paid the bill and hustled her out to the car. He resisted the urge to take her in his arms, knowing that he wouldn't be able to stop if he did.

Thirty minutes. He'd have her back to the cottage in thirty minutes.

David wondered if she'd ever been loved in the front seat of a motorcar.

Chapter 10

They spent a lazy Sunday morning in bed, drinking tea and scattering biscuit crumbs over the sheets.

And making love. Even if it was a bourgeois location, Julia herself admitted it was more comfortable than the kitchen table where he'd taken her, fully clothed, the moment they reached the cottage last night.

Intoxicating was the only word that came close to describing the effect he had on her. Like a drug she couldn't get enough of, a growing addiction that would spell her ultimate doom, but brought sinful pleasure in the process. Julia didn't care.

She'd only felt such an all-consuming passion for one other thing in her life—the cause, and her work for the Union.

Yet this was totally different, an obsession that drew her in body and soul, a physical yearning that didn't slacken no matter how many times they made love.

Lying next to him, in a drowsy, contented haze, Julia realized that she was rapidly losing control of herself. She'd never anticipated she would feel like this, would need David so badly, and it was scary to realize that she wanted him as much as he wanted her. So far, she'd managed to keep him off balance enough not to notice, but Julia didn't know how much longer she could keep up the illusion.

She didn't want him to know just how much she thought about him, longed for him, his touch, his body joining with hers.

Julia pushed the thought away. Nothing could ever be *too* good. She'd worked hard over the last year; she deserved to have some fun. Hadn't she come to the country for that very reason? It wasn't her fault that David happened along when he did—or that they'd been so instantly attracted to one another.

David mumbled something sleepily and tightened the arm that lay across her chest.

Turning on her side, Julia pulled the sheet up over them and snuggled closer to David. There was no point in ruining a marvelous day with too much thinking.

After he left on Monday, time dragged at an interminable pace. Five entire days lay ahead until she could see him again.

The thought of taking the train up to London and surprising him was tempting, but ultimately, she did not have the nerve. Not because she thought he'd be displeased, but because she wasn't ready to think about the city, and how she and David would fare once she returned. It was safer in the country, when they only had to think about each other.

A stab of shock shot through Julia when the messenger boy handed her the telegram Friday morning. Fearing bad news, her hands trembled as she opened it until she read the message.

> ARRIVING TOMORROW. HAVE BAG PACKED AND BE READY TO GO BY TEN. DESTINATION??? D.K.

Julia tipped the boy and refolded the paper, trying to quell the excitement inside her. Not only was he coming, he'd planned the surprise he'd promised. He was taking her somewhere for the weekend.

And just as quickly as elation filled her, so did fear. She shouldn't be feeling this pleased. But all she could think about was the delightful things she could do to the body of David Kimbrough—and the equally delightful things he could do to hers.

Saturday morning David was in the car and heading across the river as soon as there was light enough to drive. He couldn't wait to see Julia again, hoping she would be pleased with the plans he'd made for them.

Memories of her had been an even worse distraction this week than the last. If he'd been full of anticipation before, he was flaming with desire now.

It still seemed unbelievable that he was involved with Julia Sydney. It was the ultimate of ironies, yet he didn't mind a bit.

Sitting in interminable committee hearings in hot, stuffy rooms, David had been tempted to stand up and announce to all and sundry that he was involved in a heated affair with the notorious suffragette. It would certainly wake everyone up. But he discovered he was reluctant to speak to anyone about Julia, even when he had to alter his plans in order to take her to the shore. What they had was too important to be shared with anyone—especially those who wouldn't understand.

He knew he was falling in love with Julia, but the thought was more frightening than reassuring. Frightening, because he wasn't at all sure what she felt about him—or if she would be willing to admit it.

He couldn't have picked a worse woman to fall in love with. It had nothing to do with unequal backgrounds or the social disparities between them; David gladly ignored the fact that he was the grandson of a duke. And despite his regular attendance, he didn't much care for the glittering London social scene. He went for political reasons, not personal enjoyment. He thought an evening reading by the fire with Julia would outshine any number of fancy dinner parties and dress balls.

As he left the edges of the city behind and started out into open country, David increased his speed. It shouldn't take more than a hour to reach Cranwood. If Julia was ready, they could be to Middleton by midafternoon. He thought longingly of the tiny seaside inn that was their destination, where they could spend a peaceful weekend within sight and sound of the ocean.

An entire weekend at the beach, alone with Julia. Where he could further explore Julia's penchant for creativity in bed, and further tie her inexorably to him.

During the last, bumpy quarter mile to the cottage, he was almost tempted to toss his carefully planned schedule out the window and delay their departure. He couldn't wait to sink himself into her warm body. But David tried to convince himself that the pleasure would be all the better for the anticipation. By the time they reached Middleton, he would toss her onto the bed and remain there the entire weekend if he wanted. They could eat, sleep, walk naked, and make love all without setting a foot outside the door.

And if they did decide to venture out, he knew the perfect stretch of deserted beach that was suitable for a number of highly improper activities.

In order to stiffen his resolve, he left the car running and rapped on the door. It opened in an instant and the warm smile that lit Julia's face made him want to rethink his entire plan. It would be so easy to spend the entire weekend here.

David swept her into his arms and kissed her with an abandon that left them both breathless.

"I think," he said when he finally tore his mouth away to gulp in air, "that I missed you."

"Oh, really? I hadn't noticed."

He swatted her rear. "Scamp. Are you ready to go?"

"Are you going to tell me where we are going?"

"Well, if you were the type of lady who wore a bathing suit, I would have told you to pack it," he said as he took her bag and stowed it in the boot of the car. "But since you prefer to swim naked, you've probably brought everything you need."

"Hmm," she said as she pulled on the duster he held out. "That certainly eliminates a few possibilities. Are you talking about freshwater or salt?"

David helped her into the seat, handed her a pair of goggles and a veiled hat, then climbed in beside her. "If I told you, it wouldn't be a surprise."

"Are we taking the waters at Tunbridge Wells?"

He laughed. "I *know* they won't allow you to bathe naked there."

"Ah, you've found a more private location. It must be

a lake or the sea then—but are there any lakes in Surrey?"

"A few." David calmly turned the car around in the drive.

"You aren't going to tell me, are you? How infuriating." Julia gave him a withering look. "How was your week?"

"Abominable," he replied. "Which is the most I am going to say on the matter. I don't want to think about a single bit of government business for the next two days."

"Well, I had a most productive week," she announced smugly. "I wrote two articles for the newspaper, and took notes for three more. I finally threw aside Worthing's book on economics—it was the most boring thing I have ever seen in print."

"Economics seems to have that effect on most people."

"What I can't understand is why an author would write something so boring when it is just as easy to make it entertaining—or at least understandable."

David shook his head. "You don't understand the proper principle. The less understandable the work, the more profound it must be."

"That certainly sounds like male logic," she said with a wry grin. "Women have a great deal more sense than that."

"See? That is why you are always fighting for respect. If your writings were more obscure, they would impress more people and hence earn more respect for the cause."

She laughed. "That's utter rot and you know it. But what can I expect from a government representative whose very job is devoted to obfuscation and excess verbiage?"

"I said I wasn't going to talk about work on this trip and I meant it," he said with a laugh. "You'll have to find some other way to pick an argument."

"I'm not trying to pick an argument," Julia protested. "See, that is another male tendency. Men are free to express their opinions, but when a woman does, it is considered arguing."

"Only when her opinions are confrontational."

"You think anyone who doesn't parrot your own views is being confrontational," she retorted. "I would call that spoiled and arrogant."

"And it's just like a woman to turn the attack to a personal level. Men never do that."

Julia let out a loud peal of laughter. "That's the most ridiculous thing you've said yet. I've never seen anything more vicious than a political campaign."

"But we don't resort to eggs and molasses."

"Oh, I've seen any number of speakers pelted with everything from rotten garbage to horse dung in the provinces," she said. "I can't take credit for developing that tactic."

"It's a pity you have to wear those blasted goggles," he said. "I love to look at your eyes when you're steamed up like this."

She gave him an exasperated look. "And you know perfectly well that I'm teasing you as much as you're teasing me. Which serves you right since you won't tell me where we are going."

"A quaint little inn," he said, reaching over to squeeze her thigh. "The ideal place to take a certain lady . . ."

"It sounds like you have something in mind."

"I'm not driving all day just to take you walking on the downs. The activity I envisioned involved a room and a bed"—he grinned—"unless you have a preference for the floor."

"I'll have to give the matter some thought," she said with a look of deep concentration.

They stopped for lunch in Horsham, where they ate quickly and David refilled his petrol tanks. This wasn't a leisurely drive in the country; he wanted to reach their destination as quickly as possible—and without mishap. Running out of petrol was one thing he wanted to avoid.

He was only one-half hour off his estimated schedule when he pulled in front of the rambling country house that was his goal.

"This is your cozy inn?" Julia asked with surprise. It looked more like a private house.

"Like it? It may not look like much, but the food is good and the privacy unparalleled."

"You don't think you'll run into any of your fellow MPs here?" she asked with a teasing smile.

"I try to avoid them as much as possible on the weekend," he said, ushering her into the entry parlor.

The landlady greeted David like an old friend and a twinge of jealousy shot through Julia. How many other women had he brought here?

She firmly told herself it didn't matter. She was here to enjoy herself with David and jealousy did not fit in. Jealousy only mattered if she wanted a future with him, and that wasn't possible.

They followed the landlady down a long, narrow hall, up and down two half flights of stairs, until she threw open a door at the end of the corridor. Private was an understatement—they could shoot off a gun back here and it wouldn't be heard in the main hall.

"I'll be serving tea at four," the landlady said as David dropped their bags. "Will you be joining us?"

David shot Julia a scorching look, then turned back to the landlady. "We had a late lunch. I think we will wait until dinner."

"Very well, then. Enjoy your stay with us, Mr. Geary." She shut the door behind her.

Julia arched a brow. "Mr. Geary? How sly of you, David. Am I Mrs. Geary?"

He grinned. "I didn't go quite *that* far. But over the years, I've found it easier to travel under another name when I'm on holiday. It's simpler than denying I'm *that* David Kimbrough."

Julia walked to the open window and pushed the curtain aside. The room overlooked the Channel and she took a deep breath of the sharp, tangy air. Sun sparkled on the water and several sailboats dashed across the waves.

David came up behind her and placed his hands on her shoulders. "Well, what do you think?"

"Very nice."

"I wanted to get away—just the two of us."

His hands dropped to her waist and she leaned back against him. "Sometimes, you have some very good ideas."

"Only sometimes?"

David nuzzled at her neck, giving her gooseflesh. "Well, most of the time."

He began undoing the buttons of her blouse. "I think I am having another one of my wonderful ideas. As soon as I get your clothes off, I'll show you."

"Stop wasting time."

Sometime later they pulled back the covers and lay down properly, with only the sheet over them. Julia watched drowsily as the sea breeze fluttered the lacy curtains. David slept, his breathing deep and even.

She didn't care if he'd brought a hundred women to this place. He was here with her now, and that was all that mattered. For them, it would always be the here and now. This wasn't a grand passion; it was an expedient soothing of lust among two very different and ultimately incompatible people. She had to remember that.

But lying here, feeling lazy and smugly satisfied, she dared to wonder what it would be like to keep seeing him. For a while, at least, after she went back to London. It would be a welcome break from the endless rounds of rallies, meetings, and demonstrations that would start again only too soon. The sheer physical release of sex would be a needed respite from all that.

Yet even that was too far into the future to think. This weekend was dedicated to the moment, and as she drifted into sleep, Julia thought only of how pleasant a change that would be.

David awoke with a start, unsure of his surroundings. Then he realized his arm was wrapped around the curvaceous female form curled up against him and he let out a deep sigh of contentment. Julia. His groin instinctively tightened.

His desire for her never seemed to flag. It was a miracle they were so evenly matched, that he hadn't already frightened her away with his insistent demands. But she was equally demanding—which in turn made him want her all the more.

He wished they could have more than these two brief days together. A week, even two, would be indescribably pleasant. They could lay abed until noon, swim in the ocean in the hot afternoon sun, then make love again and again as the sun went down. He didn't think he would ever tire of making love to her.

Which could pose a problem in the future. It was one thing to be together in the privacy of his aunt's estate. It was quite another to maintain a discreet affair in London.

Unless, of course, they continued to meet in the country on the weekends. As much as he would regret not being able to be with her more often, that offered the safest solution, and one he thought she would also appreciate. He guessed she would have a difficult time explaining him to some of her suffragette cronies—especially those who advocated celibacy as the natural way of life for women.

For Julia, he thought that would be as unnatural as stopping breathing. She was a woman of unbridled passion.

She'd obviously been diverting that passion into her political work. But he'd provide a more natural outlet for that energy—and if she had less need for her political work as a result, so much the better.

That was what this was all about, after all—reducing her effectiveness as a political opponent. And if keeping her satisfied in bed was the best way to do that, David was willing to make the sacrifice.

They ate in their room that night; a simple but hearty country repast. They made love again and fell asleep in each other's arms, listening to the roar of the sea.

Waking early, they feasted on a massive breakfast.

"What shall we do today?" David asked her.

"You are the one with the plans," she said. "I am here to be entertained."

He cast a whimsical glance at the bed. "You mean I haven't succeeded?"

She uttered a low, throaty laugh. "You've done well—so far."

"Then I offer you several choices. We can take the car and explore the countryside—Arundel Castle isn't far. Or we could even take the train into Brighton and pretend to be real tourists."

"Or?"

"Or I could take you to that secluded spot I mentioned. The beach here is nice, but rather exposed. The landlady can pack a lunch for us."

"That sounds fun."

He pushed back his chair and stood. "I'll tell her now."

When David returned, they gathered up their things and by the time they'd gone down to the car, the landlady had their luncheon ready. David stowed everything in the boot and started the engine.

He followed the narrow road that ran along the coast, through Bogner, and then turned onto a rutted country lane. The road grew more and more torturous.

"Are you sure you know where you're going?" Julia looked doubtfully at the track they followed. "This looks more like a cow path than a road."

"I told you the place was secluded." David gave her knee a quick squeeze. "If it was easy to get to, everyone else would be there."

When the dubious lane vanished altogether, he stopped the car. "We have to walk the last bit." He took the lunch basket from the boot and motioned for her to come with him.

Julia followed behind him as they traipsed across the field and struggled up a tiny hill. David stopped at the crest and looked at her. "Now, wasn't this worth it?"

Spread out below was a circular bay with a wide, sandy beach. A tall church spire off to the west was the only sign of human habitation anywhere.

"This is marvelous!" Julia exclaimed.

David beamed at her approval. They started down the other side of the hill as the vegetation turned to beach grass and sand.

"I've run into a rare fisherman and a local or two, but this place is usually deserted. People on holiday go to the resort towns."

He spread out the blanket and Julia sat down, yanking off her shoes. She stuck her feet into the warm sand and wiggled her toes.

"It's been an age since I've done this," she said.

David stripped off his shirt and pants. "Come on, let's test the water. You're the one who claims to have such a mad passion for swimming."

"It'll be cold," she warned.

"I'll find a way to warm us up later." He gave her such an outrageous leer that Julia laughed.

She stepped out of her skirt and unbuttoned her blouse. When she was down to her knickers and short chemise, David lunged at her and picked her up, then strode toward the water.

"Put me down!"

"Are you sure?" he asked as he splashed through the surf.

Realization dawned on her. "No!"

"Typical female—always changing her mind." David grinned wickedly.

"Our minds are no more changeable than any man's," she retorted.

"Oh?" David lifted his arms and held her out over the water. "Then you *do* want me to put you down?"

Julia gritted her teeth. "Yes."

He dropped her and she hit the icy water with a splash.

Julia scrambled to her feet and lunged at David, knocking his legs out so he fell into the knee-deep water. "Turnabout is fair play," she said, standing over him with a haughty look on her face.

"You're right," he said, grabbing her arm and pulling her back into the water. Laughing and splashing, they struggled playfully to further drench each other.

"Uncle, uncle," David finally called, holding up his hands defensively. Julia flung another handful of water at him.

"You acknowledge the superiority of women?" she taunted.

"In the water, yes."

She considered him carefully. "Well, I guess I could accept that answer." Julia struggled toward shallower water.

David watched her progress, enamored of the sight of her dripping wet frame. Her lacy chemise was plastered to her skin, her nipples hard and erect with cold as they thrust against the water-soaked fabric. Knickers molded to the curve of her rump.

Splashing toward her, David knew exactly what he wanted.

He chased her up on the beach, falling atop her as they collapsed laughing onto the blanket. He mouthed her breasts through the thin cloth, nipping at the puckered tips.

"God, I want you," he whispered against her neck before his mouth came down on hers, his tongue thrusting into her hot warmth. His fingers fumbled with the ties to her knickers.

"Damn." The wet strings wouldn't come untied. He sat back on his haunches and grabbed for the slit in the fabric, exposing the triangle of dark curling hair and the opening that he sought.

He looked up and saw her eyes close, her breath already coming in short gasps. She was ready, and wanting. He thrust into her, enveloping himself in her moist heat.

She felt so damn good.

Pure, raw animal lust coursed through his veins as he pushed into her again and again. Her hips rose in welcome, as she clasped him inside her, releasing him with reluctance only to welcome him again.

His fingers found her sensitive spot and she moaned when he touched her. "Do you like me to touch you there?"

"Oh, yes," she breathed.

He gave an exaggerated thrust. "And do you like me to touch you *there*?"

She answered with a low moan that fanned the heat of his desire. He moved against her, with her, in her, working to bring them to a mutual pleasure. As she shuddered beneath him, he let his own release flow.

"You're going to be the death of me," he said, finally, when he had enough breath to speak.

"It's another sign of male weakness." Julia smiled smugly. "You haven't heard me complaining, have you?"

He squeezed her breast. "You are a shameless hussy," he said. "It's the scourge of modern times—proper Victorian women didn't make these kinds of demands on their men."

She laughed. "You are a complete hypocrite, David Kimbrough."

"Then we're two of a kind."

Julia sat up and looked at him. "What is that supposed to mean?"

He pulled her back down beside him. "Simply that we were made for each other, Jules." His mouth sought hers. "Nothing is going to keep us apart."

Chapter 11

Back at the inn, after a delicious dinner of fresh sole, they took a walk on the beach in the gathering dusk.

"On nights like this, it's easy to forget that we have motorcars, telephones, and electric lights," David said, looking out over the darkening water.

"You need to spend more time in the country." Julia laughed. "It's easier to imagine after a few weeks without all that."

"I'll wager you miss the excitement of the city, though."

"A bit." Julia took his arm. "Right now, I enjoy the peace of the country more."

David scuffed at the sand beneath his feet. "What would you be doing with your life, if you weren't involved in the suffrage campaign?"

She thought for a moment. "I planned to be a teacher once, and inculcate the right thoughts into those little minds. But I decided I needed to do something more active, where I had a chance to really change things."

"Few people are ever able to do that."

"Well, I want to be one of them. That's why I studied law."

"Why set yourself up for the disappointment? You could have studied something you knew you could use."

"But why should I have to? Why should someone say that I can't be a barrister or a solicitor simply because I'm female? What possible difference can my sex make?"

It was, David admitted, damned unfair. He could just see her in front of a jury, filled with righteous indignation in her client's defense.

Of course, her clients were likely to be stone-throwing suffragettes, so perhaps it was for the best.

As if reading his thoughts, Julia spoke. "I conducted the defense at four of our trials."

"Your suffragette friends?"

She nodded.

"Did you get them off?"

"Of course not. The government isn't going to listen to logical argument."

"Then I'd say you're not that great a lawyer." David laughed at her outraged expression. "I'm teasing you, Jules. I'm sure you strike terror in the heart of every prosecutor who faces you."

She wrapped her arm around his waist. "I'm doing what I want. Are you?"

"Yes," he said emphatically.

"And how high do you want to go? A cabinet post, surely. Will you be prime minister one day?"

David laughed ruefully. "If I said yes, you'd accuse me of being too full of myself." He sobered. "I'm not sure I would like to be PM. But a Cabinet post . . . that's a different thing."

"So you could order your staff around, instead of being ordered yourself."

"Exactly."

"I fear we're a lot alike in that regard," Julia said with a laugh. "I think that's one reason I decided not to teach—there's always someone to tell you what you can and cannot say, even in the most progressive schools."

"You were a born rebel." David shook his head. "You must have caused your parents endless torment."

"On the contrary, they delighted in my rebellions." Julia smiled ruefully. "Except the time I organized a nursery strike over the condition of the oatmeal."

"Your first hunger strike."

"I guess it was, wasn't it?" She walked beside him silently for a moment. "Do you ever imagine what you would have been like if you'd been born into a different family?"

"No. Do you?"

"Of course. What if *I'd* been the grandchild of a duke? Would I be more concerned with fashion, balls, and social niceties than the plight of the poor or the status of women?"

"You'd find some other cause to espouse. I can't picture you being anything else than what you are."

"Think how different things might have been if I'd been born a male."

David gave her waist a squeeze. "I'm certainly glad you weren't."

"I could be an MP." She darted him a teasing glance. "You'd have to face me in Commons, then."

"You'd only be a backbencher," he scoffed. "Inflicting annoying pinpricks, but having no real power."

"Then I'd start a radical paper and attack government policies from that forum."

"You're already doing that."

"True." Julia giggled. "You mean that I'm more politically effective as a disobedient woman than a backbencher in Parliament?"

"That's not what I said . . ."

"I am glad to be female," Julia continued. "Since we are the superior sex."

"Oh, no, I'm not going to respond to *that* remark."

She punched him lightly on the arm. "Coward."

"That's right. I know better than to pick an argument with a barrister."

"What would you like to be, if you weren't a politician?"

He shivered in mock horror. "You say that word with such distaste. It's an honorable profession."

"So you say." Julia smiled.

"When I was very young, I wanted to be a sailor, and sail exotic seas, explore strange countries, and bring back wondrous treasures like the ones in my grandfather's display cases."

"Why didn't you?"

"I get seasick."

Julia whooped with laughter. "You poor thing."

"Oh, well, all the exotic areas were explored long ago

and I'd only be following in someone else's footsteps. I decided to settle for something a little less exciting." He gave her a sideways glance. "Although the excitement level of my life has a tendency to rise at times."

"I wouldn't want you to get bored."

Boredom would be the last problem in his life with Julia around.

During the night, the fog rolled in, obliterating the channel from view and filling the air with damp.

"Good thing we're leaving today," David observed as they ate breakfast. "We'd probably get lost if we tried to go for a walk on the beach."

"Will the driving be treacherous?" Julia half hoped they would have an excuse to stay.

He shook his head. "This'll clear off after we're a few miles inland. There's probably brilliant sunshine on the other side of the village."

They dawdled over their meal, taken in the common room. Julia wondered if David was as reluctant to leave as she. These two short days had been an idyll, a true escape from the real world. She didn't want it to end. It was far too easy to forget that there was another world beyond the misty blanket that surrounded them.

But David had to go back to London and she needed to finish her work at the cottage.

He made love to her one last time in the little room overlooking the sea, with a strange combination of fierceness and tenderness that exactly suited her mood. Then they stowed their luggage in the car and headed back toward Cranwood.

David had been wrong about the weather, for the fog never lifted, and by the time they reached Horsham on the return trip it was beginning to drizzle. They hastily raised the cover on the car before dashing into the inn for a quick lunch.

His temper grew shorter as the weather worsened and the roads grew muddier, slowing their progress. It was nearly six when they reached the cottage.

Julia's eyes widened with surprise when he brought his bag in with hers.

"Aren't you going back to London tonight?"

He shook his head. "The roads are only going to get worse in this rain, and it'll be dark soon. They can hold one session of Parliament without me."

Julia's heart pulsed with pleasure at the thought that she would have him for one more evening.

"I'll dash up to the house and find us some food," he said, giving her a quick kiss. "I'll be back in a trice. See if you can get a fire going."

The rain continued all through the night, but Julia didn't mind. She and David built up the fire in the parlor and toasted bread, laughed, and talked.

In the morning he lingered as long as he dared, not driving away until after noon. Julia watched him go with an aching sadness. Four long days before she could see him again.

The thought of moving back to London grew more tempting. He'd only be a phone call away and she could see him anytime, not just on the weekend.

But if she was in London, she'd be working also, so busy she'd be hard-pressed to find time for him. And his schedule was equally hectic. Perhaps it was better this way, when they could count on two undisturbed days together.

Yet even that couldn't last much longer.

She shook her head. It was the weather that made her feel so pensive. The rain after all those glorious sunny days would dampen anyone's spirits. David would be down again on Saturday and they would have another wonderful weekend together. Julia refused to think how few weekends were left before she had to return to town, or what would happen when she did.

The first surprise of the week arrived on Wednesday, with the delivery of another telegram. Julia tore it open eagerly, expecting a message from David, but instead it announced that several members of the WSPU were coming to visit on Friday. It was a jarring reminder that she was going to have to take up her life again, soon.

The ladies arrived by carriage, having taken the train down from the city. Julia greeted them at the door: Selena Rood, a former labor organizer from the Midlands; Katherine Ames, who'd been with Julia in prison several times; Lady Mary Cowles, who'd traded her privileged life for a small room in London and was one of their most persuasive speakers; and Beryl Tennant, whom Julia didn't like very well for her rigid opinions, overbearing manner, and lust for power.

"What a lovely place," Lady Mary observed as she examined the parlor. "You must have had a wonderfully relaxing summer."

"I hope you finished all your articles for *Votes for Women*," Beryl said. "You'll be far to busy to write anything this fall."

Julia poured tea and handed the cups around, feeling almost overwhelmed to be surrounded by suffrage friends again.

"We came down to see how you were doing." Selena gave her an uneasy smile. "We hadn't heard from you for so long . . . we wanted to make sure your health was all right."

"As you can see, the country air has done wonders." Julia grinned. "I feel marvelous."

Katherine sipped her tea. "When do you propose to come back to town? Christabel was hoping you would lead the demonstration in Birmingham next month."

"What's the plan?" Julia leaned forward eagerly.

While Katherine explained the plans for Birmingham, and other demonstrations in September, Julia listened carefully, growing more and more excited. She *had* been away from the political fray too long and her eagerness to return grew. And leading a mass demonstration was a great way to start.

"Tell Christabel I think it sounds good." Julia checked the tea water. "Is she planning for many arrests? I'm not sure I'm ready for that yet."

"Oh, we don't want you arrested there," Selena said

hastily. "We want to save our big arrests for London—the publicity is so much better."

"And Holloway is *so* much more comfortable," Julia said wryly. They all laughed.

"Perhaps you and I can go together again," Lady Mary said with a wistful look.

Katherine tossed her a warning glance. "I thought your doctor had forbidden any more jail time for you."

Lady Mary waved her off. "He doesn't think *any* woman should be in prison. It is nothing."

"Do we intend to continue hunger striking as a tactic?" After enduring two of them, Julia's eagerness to participate was waning. She remembered just how long it had taken her to recover from this last one.

Beryl gave her a sharp look. "Do you have any problems with that?"

"No." Julia forced a smile. "It gets all of us out of prison sooner."

The ladies had brought their own lunches, so while they ate, they continued talking and planning through the afternoon.

Sometime after two, during a spirited discussion of proposed targets, Julia heard the front door open. She glanced over her shoulder, then recoiled in shock at the sight of David standing in the parlor doorway.

"Surprise, Jules!" He strode into the room. "You see before you the most irresponsible member of Parliament who just chucked the Friday session and—"

Julia wondered who looked more surprised—her guests or David.

"Oh, excuse me." David came to a sudden halt, staring at Julia's guests. "I didn't realize you had company." His eyes met hers and she sent him a silent plea. "I'm here on behalf of my aunt, who wished you to dine with her this evening—that is, if you are available. Around eight?"

"That would be fine," Julia said.

"Good. I'll tell her then." David backed out of the parlor. "Pardon my intrusion."

Julia heard the door shut behind him.

Four pairs of eyes turned toward Julia.

"Wasn't that David Kimbrough?" Lady Mary asked.

Nodding, Julia struggled to appear unconcerned. "Imagine my own shock when I discovered that Lady Marchmont is his great-aunt!"

"Sounds like you're on friendly terms now." Beryl's eyes narrowed suspiciously.

Julia shrugged. "I can hardly be rude to him when I'm here as a guest of his aunt."

"Think what a marvelous opportunity this is!" Selena exclaimed.

They all looked at her.

"Remember how we've had such trouble arranging a meeting with anyone in the Home Office? Julia will have access to him now."

Julia felt a sinking sensation in the pit of her stomach. They couldn't send her after David. "I hardly think—"

Katherine looked thoughtful. "You might have an idea there, Selena." She looked at Julia. "Do you think you could get an invitation to his office?"

"I doubt it," Julia replied, thinking hastily. "We try to behave in a civil manner because of his aunt, but he knows what I think of him."

"Perhaps we could use the aunt, then," Katherine mused aloud. "Invite her up to London. She'd be able to get in to see him and you could go along."

"What do we hope to accomplish?" Julia asked.

"We have the opportunity to get someone inside the Home Office and you're wondering why?" Beryl stared at her. "Julia, where are your brains?"

"But what good comes from confronting him in private?" Julia still felt confused.

"Once you're inside, there's no end to what you can do. Barricade yourself in his office!" Katherine's voice rose with her enthusiasm. "Can't you picture a suffrage banner hanging from a window of the Home Office? It would be exquisite."

"I don't think it would work," Julia said flatly, hoping they'd forget the whole idea. "I won't take advantage of Lady Marchmont."

"Perhaps you're losing your enthusiasm for direct action." Beryl eyed her with a challenging gaze. "Or your aversion to Kimbrough has faded."

"And what is that supposed to mean?"

"You heard him, calling you 'Jules.' " Beryl grimaced. "That doesn't sound like a bitter enemy."

Julia willed herself to remain calm, to not betray her feelings. "I told you, we've tried to be civil because of his aunt."

Beryl's grimace tightened. "Since when is any person more important than the cause?"

"Lady Marchmont has been a generous supporter," Julia said vehemently. "Both with money and the use of this cottage. It would be sheer folly to antagonize her."

"I think Julia's right," Lady Mary said quickly. "Sometimes a spoonful of honey accomplishes more than a dash of vinegar."

Beryl gave her a sour look, but didn't reply.

"There's no point in discussing Kimbrough—or any other member of the government—until I get back to London," Julia said evenly. "Katherine, tell Christabel I need another week or so to finish up down here, and then I'll be back." She smiled brightly. "Do we have time for another cup of tea before the need to leave for the train?"

Julia kept that same false smile pasted on her face until they were gone and the door shut firmly behind her. Then she staggered across the parlor and collapsed onto the sofa.

She *thought* she'd been able to deflect their suspicions—all except Beryl's, and that woman was suspicious of everyone. Thank God she'd been so stunned when David walked in that her face hadn't registered any other emotion.

But even if they had no idea that she and David were lovers, their other plans were equally disastrous. There was no way she could take on David as a target again, subjecting him to the humiliation and insult that the campaign demanded. The idea was impossible.

Why the voice in her head asked.

Because she couldn't do that to the man she loved.

There. She'd said it, admitted it to herself. She loved him. It was probably the stupidest thing she'd ever done in her life, but it was too late for recriminations now. Instead, Julia needed to find a way out of the coil she'd entangled herself in. Her clever little plan to ensnare him had trapped her as well.

Why did this have to happen on a Friday, with the whole weekend still in front of them? They could have spent two more carefree days together, ignoring the world outside. But now, the world had intruded and she couldn't ignore it any longer. She had to face the future, and the wide gulf that yawned between them because of their political differences.

She knew, once they were back in London, that the forces attempting to pull them apart would be enormous. No one at the Union must know of their relationship—their attitude toward David this afternoon made that clear. Their meetings would have to be arranged as carefully as for an adulterous affair under the watchful eyes of a suspicious spouse. Not at all what she wanted.

But the alternative of not seeing him at all was worse.

Julia sighed. She would try to push aside her doubts and her worries for the weekend. Try to recapture the magic of their weekend at the shore, when everyone and everything seemed so very far away. There was so little time left; she wanted every minute of it to be perfect.

Julia gathered up the dirty cups and plates and carried them into the kitchen. She'd change her clothes before she went up to the house; the invitation to dinner was probably legitimate.

It would be a welcome relief to face David in front of Lady Marchmont. They wouldn't be able to talk privately, to kiss, to make love until much later this evening. By then, she'd have her emotions under control.

She uttered a grateful prayer for Lady Marchmont's invitation.

A mixture of confusion and anticipation hung over Julia as she mounted the steps to the house. Would she be able to convince David that nothing had changed? That this weekend was the same as all the others?

The door opened and she was suddenly face-to-face with him. A wide grin crossed his face.

"It's about time! I was just getting ready to come after you."

Throwing herself into his arms, Julia realized she didn't have to feign delight at seeing him. Crushed against his chest, it was easy to forget all their problems for a moment.

"Sorry to have interrupted your little social gathering," he said, when he finally finished kissing her.

"That's all right," Julia said with a frozen smile. His reminder was like a dash of cold water in her face. "You merely added another topic to the discussion."

"Gossiping about me with your girlfriends?" David grinned. "I trust you told them how wonderful I am."

Julia laughed wryly. "Not exactly."

"I'm wounded. If you won't say good things about me, who will?"

"I think you do well enough on your own. Is your aunt in the drawing room?" Julia suddenly wanted the safety of Lady Marchmont's presence, fearing David would see through her mask of false serenity. "I don't think we should keep her waiting too long."

"You're right." David sighed deeply. "But you must appreciate the sacrifice I'm making in not dragging you back to the cottage this minute."

"We have all weekend."

He shook his head. "Not exactly. That's why I came down today—I have to leave tomorrow afternoon—I'm giving a speech in Manchester on Sunday."

Regret and relief ripped through her. They would only have one day together—but she wouldn't have to keep up the pretense that nothing was wrong as long, either. Julia didn't know if she was more relieved or disappointed.

Lady Marchmont greeted her with a warm hug.

"I hear the poor boy wandered into a tea party this afternoon," Lady Marchmont said, casting David a teasing smile. "You should have seen his stunned expression when he returned to the house. I think it came as a shock to him to realize that you do have a life."

"Of course I know Julia has a life," he grumbled. "I just didn't expect her to be entertaining the ladies' sewing circle when I arrived."

Julia couldn't smother her laugh. Sewing circle, indeed.

Lady Marchmont gave her a knowing look. "I hate to disparage your domestic talents, my dear, but I suspect you don't know which end of a needle is which. I imagine those were some suffragettes from London."

Julia nodded.

"I do so wish you had invited them to the house. If they come down to visit again, please bring them to tea. I would so like to chat with them."

"So, the troops are checking up on you." David looked annoyed. "Are they trying to drag you back to town?"

"I do need to go before long." Julia patted Lady Marchmont's hand. "And I cannot say how enjoyable my stay has been. I hope everyone who stays at the cottage will find the situation as pleasing—and as healing."

"You certainly look healthier than you did when you arrived," Lady Marchmont observed. "I only wish you would promise to stop that horrid hunger striking. It cannot be good for your health."

Julia shot a pointed glance at David. "We will do what we must to get the government to hear our grievances."

"Perhaps we should have the prison food catered by the Savoy," David suggested. "I suspect the women would be less tempted to refuse food then."

"I know, it isn't a great hardship to avoid eating at Holloway." Julia grimaced at the memory of the gluey porridge. "But enough *political* talk. I meant to tell you how lovely the asters at the cottage look, Lady Marchmont. They seem to all have come into bloom during the last week."

"Not more dead flowers in vases." David gave Julia a

disparaging look. "Can't you leave the poor things alone to die in peace in the garden?"

"I'll have you know that every flower in the cottage is fresh," Julia said archly.

"That's a first."

Lady Marchmont laughed. "Trust David to be concerned over something as trivial as a few wilted flowers." She gave Julia a sly wink. "I don't think it's your floral arrangements that draw him back here week after week."

"No, it's her cooking ability." David's grin was triumphant.

"At least I'm honest about my failings," Julia said. "I don't have to cheat at croquet to win."

"Did you hear that, Aunt?" David adopted a wounded expression. "She accuses me of cheating. I should call her out for that."

"Dueling has gone out of style, David." Lady Marchmont laughed. "Why, I remember what a fuss there was over the Earl of Cardigan's duel in 1840. Somehow, pistols at dawn seemed less romantic after that trial in the Lords."

"Then I suggest a rematch." David's eyes brightened as he looked at Julia. "We should have enough time if we start first thing in the morning."

"It would be a pleasure to take you on again—if you agree to play fairly."

"Don't they say that 'all is fair in love and war.'" David grinned. "I'm sure croquet fits in there somehow."

Julia winked at Lady Marchmont. "Who said that trial by combat went out of style? Men just moved their combats to the more accepted arena of sport."

"I do play a mean game of cricket," David offered with a glib smile.

"Is there anything that you don't do well?" Julia regarded him with amusement.

"Not that I'm aware of."

Lady Marchmont rang for the butler. "All this talk of war and combat is making my hungry. I'll have the tea tray sent up." She glanced anxiously at her guests. "You two are staying for dinner, aren't you?"

"Of course," Julia said. It was a good excuse not to be alone with David, yet.

Chapter 12

David couldn't quite put his finger on it, but there was something bothering Julia tonight. Oh, she looked the same and talked the same, but an uneasiness lurked at the back of his mind as he watched her chat with his aunt. She wasn't her usual self.

Was she angry because he couldn't stay the full weekend? Or was it that blasted croquet match that had set her back up? He didn't give a damn who won or lost; if it would make her happy, he'd let her win.

But either possibility seemed silly. More likely, the explanation involved those gaggle of suffragettes who'd gathered in her parlor earlier today. Had his interruption offended her? Granted, he shouldn't have just walked in like that, but how was he to know she had guests? He'd covered his intrusion well; she shouldn't have any complaints on that part.

Was she embarrassed to let them know she actually had an acquaintance with a man? He had read some of the antimale drivel put out by some of suffragettes. He knew Julia didn't subscribe to that mush, thank God, but they might not know that.

Or was he the real problem? That visit could have been a vivid reminder of the very large political gulf that lay between them, and the recognition that their differences weren't easily resolvable. If his political views were too grounded in reality, hers were unrealistic.

Even if he could sympathize with her demands—which he wasn't at all sure that he did—there was no way the government was going to give women the vote at this time. The Lords would veto the bill, the government would fall, and Asquith would have to explain to everyone why he'd driven the Liberal Party to suicide.

But Julia didn't understand that. It was one very good reason for not giving the vote to women—they didn't consider the practical realities of the situation. Why should women vote when half the male population couldn't? And how many women would actually spend a minute of their time studying the issues and the candidates? They'd vote as their fathers, or husbands, or brothers suggested, which meant that their vote would mean nothing. So why cause such a ruckus to get it?

Julia wouldn't see it that way, of course. She would say that once women had the vote, they would take an interest in politics, and would use their newfound power to change things for the better. But David knew just how difficult it was to effect change.

The endless wrangling over the budget bill was a case in point. It was critical to the running of the country, yet they couldn't even get the Liberal members to agree on what it should say, let alone the other parties.

And Julia thought giving the women the vote would change all that. For a woman who had such a sharp sense for disruptive tactics, her grasp of political reality was appalling.

But how could he explain all that to her? She'd accuse him of being patronizing, antiwoman, and reactionary, all in the same breath. Any explanation he gave would be considered self-serving, antifemale, and influenced by his government position.

Perhaps it would be easier to give women the vote and then let them straighten out the chaos that followed.

Whatever the problem today, he and Julia were going to have a talk tonight, after dinner. He wanted this straightened out before he left tomorrow.

David waited until they were safely back inside the cottage, seated on the sofa with a glass of whiskey, before he broached the subject.

"Something is wrong," he said bluntly. "What is it?"

She regarded him hesitantly. "I'm not sure what you mean."

"You've been acting strangely all evening. Are you angry with me for some reason?"

"No."

"Then what is it?" He set his glass down. "Did I offend your London friends when I walked in? Was the sight of a virile male too shocking for their delicate constitutions?"

"You're being absurd."

David arched a brow. "Am I? Then tell me what's bothering you."

"Nothing is bothering me, David."

Her nervous fidgeting belied her words. "Do you wish I could stay longer this weekend?"

"Of course I do, but I know that you have responsibilities." She laughed lightly. "Goodness, is that what you think? That I'm having a fit of pique because you can't stay for the entire weekend?"

"No, I don't think that."

"Well, that's what you're implying."

David raked a hand through his hair in frustration. "Something is bothering you and I'm trying to discover what it is. Talk to me, Julia."

Abruptly jumping up, she strode to the window, then came back to stand in front of him. "And in your vast male arrogance, you're convinced it has everything to do with you?"

"Doesn't it?" He watched her with growing suspicion. She was trying to hide something from him.

"No, it doesn't." She sighed. "If you must know, I've been preoccupied because my visitors today reminded me that I need to get back to work."

"You didn't mind that I interrupted your meeting?"

She grinned. "Well, you might have knocked first."

"And the ladies weren't shocked to discover that you were on speaking terms with a member of the opposite sex?"

Julia gave him an odd look. "Why would they think anything abut that?"

"I've read some of their antimale diatribes." He shook

his head. "According to their arguments, we men are responsible for every ill on the face of the earth."

Julia giggled. "I don't think they're far wrong."

David grabbed her around the waist and pulled her down onto his lap. "Do you care to elaborate on that point?"

"No."

He examined her closely, seeking the truth lurking behind those dark, mysterious eyes. "Did you tell them you're sleeping with a Member of Parliament?"

"Of course not. That's none of their business."

Cradling her in his arms, he hugged her against his chest. "It might be, Jules. Once we're back in London, and seen together, people are going to talk."

Julia twisted on his lap so she faced him. "Then they are just going to have to talk." She pressed her mouth to his and David quickly forgot about anything except the alluring softness of her body.

Long after David fell asleep, Julia lay beside him in the bed, staring at the ceiling. She hoped she'd deflected his concerns. She didn't want to waste what little time they had with more questions.

He'd been right about one thing—if they were ever seen together, people would talk. The attitudes of her WSPU colleagues would range from suspicion to outrage and Julia would find herself in an uncomfortable position. Some would be offended by her involvement in a sexual affair. Others would wonder how she could bring herself to even speak to a man like David Kimbrough.

And a few would question her sincerity and devotion to the cause, seeing any involvement with a member of the government as a defection from their side. That was what Julia feared most, and after listening to Beryl today, she knew it would be the hardest charge to fight. Her refusal to act against David would be seen as proof.

The only way to allay everyone's suspicions would be to make sure she was never seen with David. That was easy enough in the country—today's unexpected exposure hadn't been that damaging—but the city was different. Their lives would revolve around secret meetings, in out-of-the-way places. The very thought made her uncomfortable.

It would be far easier if she broke off with David—now, before she went back to London.

But it was one thing to contemplate it, and quite another to carry it out. She'd fallen in love with the man, after all. For a moment she railed against the strange quirk of fate that had brought them together, and the forces that were now threatening to tear them apart. If David were anyone other than a member of the government, there wouldn't be a problem. It wasn't fair.

But very little in life was. And some things were more important than the feelings of two people—women's voting rights, for example. If being David's lover affected her ability to work for that cause, Julia knew she would have to give him up. It was as simple as that.

She only hoped she'd find a way to manage both.

Embarking on this foolish course had been pure folly. She was tied to David more tightly than she could ever have imagined.

Thank God he was leaving tomorrow. It would give her more time to think and plan for the complications of life in London.

One thing was clear: she had to go back to the city. It was too easy to stay here, to go on as they had been. The time had come to face life again, to find out if there was any way this would work.

Sleep didn't come easily to her. Julia woke once, hearing the sound of rain tapping against the roof before she resumed her tossing and turning.

The pungent aroma of freshly brewed coffee finally shook her from sleep in the morning. She heard David puttering about the kitchen, whistling while he no doubt fixed their breakfasts.

Julia lay back against the pillows, savoring the calm for a few extra moments. It was comforting to know he was out there, taking care of her needs. With a shock, Julia realized she'd grown accustomed to him taking charge on the weekends. She liked the fact that he fixed her breakfast, brewed her tea. It was a further sign of how much she'd let him into her life.

Jumping from bed, Julia donned her robe and walked into the kitchen.

David turned around and his blue eyes warmed with a welcoming smile that tore at her heart. Why did he have to be so handsome?

"You were sleeping so soundly I didn't want to wake you."

Julia glanced at the cup he held. "Coffee?"

He nodded. "One of my recent vices. Would you like to try some?"

"I love coffee."

"Really? Why didn't you tell me sooner?"

Julia accepted the cup he offered and sat down. "I guess I never thought about it. I fell back into the habit of making tea here; it was easier. But I always drink coffee in London at the office."

"I wonder how many other things there are about you that I don't know?" He sat down across from her, his gaze intense.

Julia laughed nervously, looking down at her cup. "I think you're pretty well versed in all my faults and foibles."

He nodded toward the window. "Looks like we won't be able to play croquet after all today—unless you want to bundle up in a mackintosh."

"I think I'll wait—we can resume the challenge at another time."

David sipped his coffee. "I'm determined to win, you know."

"So am I." Julia returned his challenging gaze.

"Not much to do on a rainy morning." David toyed with his cup. "Can't play croquet, or go for a walk, or a drive."

"Have to stay indoors," Julia agreed.

"We could play cards."

"Or read aloud."

"Or go back to bed."

Setting her cup down, Julia stood and held out her hand.

There was a desperation to her loving that she hoped he didn't notice. She wanted to imprint every part of him on her memory, as a reminder of this golden summer together. As if to assist her, he made love to her with excruciating care, bringing her again and again to the edge, without letting her fall over it. Julia thought she would go mad before he relented and gave her release.

She focused her attentions on him then, seeking to torment him in a similar manner, while she reveled in the feel, the smell, the taste of him. She would remember this, all of it, for ever.

And when they finally collapsed with exhaustion, she cradled his head against her chest and held him in her arms, struggling to fight back tears as she did. She didn't want to let him go, and feared that she would have to. London loomed in their future, a constant threat to their life together.

Because of the weather, David left shortly after noon. They visited Lady Marchmont again, so Julia stood beside the elderly woman on the front steps as they waved good-bye.

Lady Marchmont turned to Julia. "Do come back in. We can have some more tea and a decent chat, now that David's gone."

Julia didn't have to be asked twice. She didn't want to go back to the cottage yet, not without him.

"I suppose it is too much to hope that you will be staying much longer?" Lady Marchmont asked.

"I am afraid I have to return to town—this week, in fact." Julia shook her head ruefully. "As my friends reminded me yesterday, I've been away long enough."

"Well, I hate to see you go, but at least I can send you back knowing that your health is restored."

Julia smiled. "And I am grateful for that."

"Although, if you plan to destroy it again, I'm not sure I will be so generous next time." Lady Marchmont waved a warning finger. "Let others do the hunger striking—you've proved your courage. No one will think less of you."

"I'll do what I have to do," Julia said, although she was touched by her hostess's words.

Lady Marchmont sighed. "I knew you would say that. And you know that you are welcome to come back here at any time—as is anyone else who needs the rest."

"Thank you."

"Now, I do expect you and David to visit me from time to time. I can't keep abreast of all the news here in the country. I'm counting on you two to keep me informed."

Julia smiled weakly. Maybe it would work. Maybe they could still flee to the country on weekends, leaving the city, and all the difficulties it posed, behind.

"What day are you planning to leave? I shall have the coachman take you to the station."

"Wednesday," Julia replied. "It'll take me at least that long to pack."

"Well, if you need any help, let me know. I can send one of the maids over."

"I think I can manage," Julia said. "It's more a matter of sorting all my papers and books before I box them up so I can find everything again."

"Are you returning to your room at Clement's Inn?"

"I hope so—unless they've given it away! It is so convenient living 'above the shop.' "

"Oh, if I were still young . . ." Lady Marchmont's eyes twinkled wistfully. "I'd show you girls a thing or two about female determination!"

"I'm sure you would." Julia smiled at her enthusiasm.

Reluctant to be alone, Julia spent the entire afternoon with Lady Marchmont, talking some, but more often listening as the older woman recounted tales of her long life, filled with anecdotes about nearly every famous politician or personage of the last fifty years. Julia hoped someday others would find her memories as interesting.

Finally, noting her hostess tiring, Julia took her leave. She had to go back to the cottage eventually; she may as well get this over with.

Stepping over the threshold, Julia felt as if she were entering it for the first time again. Just knowing that she and David might never be together here again made everything look different.

She wandered from room to room, looking for reminders of his presence, then seeking to exorcise them from her mind when she found them. But it was a futile effort. There were memories aplenty; she just couldn't get rid of them.

Her task wasn't helped by the discovery of a number of things he'd managed to leave behind during all his visits. A sock, hiding under the bed. A handkerchief, crumpled on her writing table. Even the dregs of their morning coffee, still in the cups, was a vivid reminder of his presence, as was the tin of coffee and the percolator he'd left just this morning.

All signs of how deeply he'd twined himself into her life.

Julia took a deep breath. She'd never shrunk from a battle before. Somehow, she would find a way to keep David and continue with her work.

Bright and early Wednesday morning, Julia settled herself into Lady Marchmont's elegant traveling carriage, surrounded by her trunks and boxes. In a few hours she'd be back in London.

Arriving at Victoria Station, Julia arranged for her luggage to be sent on, then descended the stairs to catch the tube. Soon she'd be home. But instead of the excitement she should feel at returning to the city and her work, all she felt was regret. Regret that she had fallen in love with David, and regret that worry over it was going to taint both her work and her relationship with him.

She would have to get control of her tumbled emotions, and soon. If she moped about the WSPU headquarters for very long, everyone would be curious—just like David had been last Friday.

Julia sat up a bit straighter. If she had to make personal sacrifices for the cause, she meant to work all the harder to make sure that their goals were realized.

Her arrival at Clement's Inn was greeted with cheerful

surprise and delight by the women in the office. Julia quickly saw that there were many new faces, the old hands having been sent into the provinces to advance their work. London was the training ground for many new recruits.

Her cozy room at the top of the stairs waited for her. Enthusiastic girls—she could hardly call these young ladies anything else—forced her to stand aside while they willingly hauled her luggage up the two flights of stairs. They thought it an honor to give a hand to Julia Sydney.

In the isolation of the country, Julia had forgotten that her name and face brought such an enthusiastic response from the "troops." It was a pointed reminder of the importance of her work. They looked to her for leadership, and she had to provide it.

After stripping off her traveling cloak and gloves, Julia joined the office staff in the front room for afternoon tea. They were full of questions about her time in the country, the articles she'd written, the plans she had for new actions. Laughing, Julia waved away most of their questions. She didn't want to make any pronouncements until she'd spoken to Christabel, who was speaking in Coventry with her mother and the Pethick-Lawrences.

By the time Julia went to bed, she felt better about returning. This was her home, after all. Living in a house full of suffragettes was a comforting experience—the closest thing she'd felt to family life since she'd left home. Already, her mind whirled with ideas for new tactics, bold and decisive ones that would capture the attention of the newspapers, and hence the public.

In the morning Julia eagerly jumped into the thick of things. Christabel wanted her to go to Bristol, for a planned demonstration a few days hence. Julia hastily packed her bag, then dashed off a note to David, telling him she was back in London, but out of town for the weekend. She posted it on the way to the station.

She hated the thought of not seeing him until next week, but reasoned it was for the best. Establishing her schedule at Clement's Inn was important; it would be easier to fit meetings with David into her schedule then.

* * *

Sitting in Parliament, listening to a fellow MP drone on about the Irish Land Bill, David could hardly wait until Saturday morning. He'd be off at dawn to see Julia. Every day they spent apart seemed like a week to him.

He wondered how long it would be before she came back to London. It couldn't be soon enough for him; it would make it a hell of a lot easier to see her. Granted, they'd have to be careful when and where they met, but Julia, with her vast experience in the guerrilla tactics of the suffragettes, would find a solution to their problem. The kind of woman who could sneak into a Liberal Party meeting would not have any difficulty finding a place to meet her lover.

His house would be the perfect location. No one would notice her coming and going—the only ones who ever bothered him were the suffragettes, and Julia could make certain the shouting figures were reassigned elsewhere on the nights she visited.

The very thought of having Julia in his bed whenever he wanted made him regret even more that he couldn't see her for two more days.

His only concern was as the fight for the budget heated up, his time would become less and less his own. The late-night sessions would only increase, and the PM wanted to blanket the country with speakers to gain support for their position. And where there were government political rallies, there were suffragettes trying to disrupt them. He and Julia could easily find themselves at opposite ends of the country.

But the budget would pass eventually and then Commons could finally adjourn. They could travel—to Paris, Italy, even farther. They wouldn't have to return until spring.

If he could persuade Julia to take a break from her WSPU activities.

He hoped he could.

Chapter 13

On Saturday David reluctantly conceded to the threatening weather and took the train to Cranwood instead of driving. He didn't want to waste endless hours stuck in a mud hole when he could be with Julia instead.

Hailing the old carter at the station, David jumped onto the seat and told him to drive to the cottage. At the top of the lane, David jumped down, grabbed his bag, and started down the lane.

As he caught sight of the building, his steps quickened and he took the last few paces at a near run. Halting on the doorstep, David knocked loudly. Receiving no response, he pounded harder.

"Julia?" he called.

He tried the door but to his surprise, it was locked.

Confused, David walked around the side of the cottage and peered into the window, then stared in disbelief at what he saw. The furniture was under holland covers, the tabletops bare. No stacks of books, no piles of papers.

Julia had gone.

Stunned, he took a few faltering steps toward the front door, then stopped.

Something must have happened, some emergency that caused her to leave suddenly, without time to let him know.

Picking up his bag, David started out for the main house at a trot. His aunt would know what was going on.

He almost forgot his worries about Julia when he walked into the drawing room and saw his aunt. Her face was pale and drawn, her nose red, her eyes weeping, and she looked as if she hadn't slept for several nights.

"You're looking a fine picture of health," he said, trying to mask his worry.

"It's this dreadful cold." She waved her handkerchief at him. "I'll be better soon enough."

He knelt by her side. "Have you seen the doctor?"

"That old fool doesn't know anything." Lady Marchmont coughed hoarsely. "Gave me some vile-tasting stuff and told me to stay in bed."

"Which is probably a good idea."

"Nonsense. I do just as well in the drawing room and I won't die of boredom." She bent over with another fit of coughing, gratefully accepting the cup of tea David handed her.

Lifting the lid, David inspected the pot. "The water's cold—shall I ring for more?"

Lady Marchmont nodded.

"Julia's left the cottage."

He saw the surprised look in his aunt's eyes.

"Haven't you seen her? She went back to London on Wednesday."

David took a deep breath. "Obviously, she didn't choose to tell me."

Lady Marchmont looked at him closely. "Have we had a falling out?"

Jumping up, David paced across the floor. "None that *I* was aware of. Everything was fine when I left last Saturday. What happened?"

His aunt's face didn't betray anything. "I think you'll have to ask Julia. I can't presume to speak for her."

"But you know?"

Shaking her head, Lady Marchmont took another sip of the tepid tea. "She merely told me it was time she went back to work. We didn't discuss you."

The fresh tea arrived as David poured it for her.

"Put a dollop of brandy in mine," his aunt commanded.

"Are you sure that's good for you?"

She laughed. "At my age, nothing is good for me."

David complied with her request, adding more than a dash to his own cup, and sat down beside her.

So Julia had gone back to London, without telling him; she'd been there for two days and hadn't made any effort to contact him. If he was a pessimistic person, he might think she didn't want to see him.

But that was absurd. She didn't have any reason to run from him like that.

It was those damn suffragettes. They were probably keeping her so busy that she hadn't had a chance to do anything. For all he knew, they'd shipped her off to Manchester or Glasgow to rally the troops. As soon as she came back to town, he'd hear from her.

Still, she might have told him what was going on.

Glancing up, David felt relieved to see his aunt dozing in her chair. She might downplay this cold, but he'd never seen her looking so poorly. David prayed it wouldn't turn into anything worse. She refused to make concessions to her age, and no doubt would continue to insist she wasn't that sick. He would have a word with the doctor before he left, to make sure she was closely watched.

David could catch the late train back to town, but he decided to stay the night. He'd feel better if his aunt looked better in the morning, and there was no reason to rush back to town if Julia wasn't there.

Still, as soon as he did get back, he was going to find out where the hell she was, even if he had to go to the WSPU offices to do so.

In the morning he was pleased to discover that his aunt still lingered in bed. The weather was cool, but not raining, so David decided to take a walk. He'd join his aunt for lunch, and then catch the afternoon train.

He wasn't surprised to find that his steps took him to the pond. A few yellow leaves drifted across the surface, a firm reminder that fall was near, but David knew he would always remember it in the blazing summer sun, when he'd seen Julia naked for the first time. The image was imprinted on his mind.

As was the image of her in his bed, beneath him, atop him, beside him as he loved her. Inside, he felt a deep, aching emptiness without her here. They'd been apart for far too long.

David wondered if the WSPU offices were staffed on a Sunday evening. If he called, he might be able to find out where she was.

With renewed enthusiasm, he continued his tramp across the park. Even if he had to follow her to Scotland or the north of England, he would track her down. Soon. Finding her was rapidly becoming an obsession.

After lunch, David took his leave of Lady Marchmont. He was still deeply concerned about her health and if it hadn't been for his eagerness to find Julia, he might have stayed another day. To soothe his conscience, David penned a note to the doctor before he reboarded the train.

He regretted that he couldn't have a phone installed at the house, but David resolved to telegraph daily to check on her condition.

When he arrived in London, a message from the Home Secretary awaited him. He wanted David to join him at a rally in Bristol on Monday.

David jumped at the opportunity to do something. He called the WSPU to verify Julia was out of town, then repacked his bag and caught the train to Bristol.

He wasn't at all surprised to see suffrage picketers outside the hotel. David deliberately walked through their ranks with a confident expression. There was something about knowing he was the lover of one of the leading suffragettes that reduced his irritation at their protests.

The local Liberals greeted him effusively and immediately took him to the Secretary's suite. Gladstone and the local leaders were planning their route to the meeting hall with the skill of a military campaign.

"Ah, Kimbrough. Glad you could join us." Gladstone motioned for him to join them. "Tell me, have you developed any good techniques for avoiding the ladies outside? Should we try decoys?"

David shook his head. "Just make sure the police have barriers installed, and that they keep everyone behind them. And be damn sure that no one sneaks into the hall."

"We've had a guard on it for the last two days—no unwanted guests are going to get inside." The local Liberal leader exuded confidence.

For David, tired from traveling, dinner, and particularly the cigars and whiskey afterward, lasted far too long. But he was here as a government representative, and it was his duty to be politely attentive to his hosts. He carefully hid his sigh of relief when the gathering broke up shortly after midnight.

In the morning he ate a leisurely breakfast in his room, then joined the others at the rear entrance of the hotel, where the cars had pulled up. David climbed into the first car, the Home Secretary followed in the second, with the rest of the locals in the third.

The drive to the hall was uneventful, which only made David uneasy. If it had been only himself speaking, he wouldn't worry, but the suffragettes would hardly give up the opportunity to annoy the Home Secretary. But only a small group of women stood outside the barriers at the end of the street, holding their VOTES FOR WOMEN signs high.

David glanced quickly at the protesters, then looked away, momentarily confused.

My God, had that been Julia?

He twisted around but the car was now too far down the block for him to see any of the women clearly. David sank back into the seat. That was all he needed—an unplanned confrontation with her at a political rally.

At least he knew she hadn't come here deliberately to confront him, since his presence was unannounced. He only hoped she wasn't intending to get herself arrested—he didn't relish having to visit with her in a jail cell.

The men climbed out of the cars, the street eerily quiet. The women at the far end of the block stood silently, waving their placards but not shouting their usual slogans. Their silence bothered David. They were up to something, he knew. But what?

Taking the local party leader aside when they entered the building, David offered a warning. "Those women have some sort of plan; they're far too well behaved. You're sure the hall is secure?"

The man nodded.

Taking his place on the stage with the others, David listened patiently to the local speakers. At his turn, David rose and gave a short speech, then introduced the Home Secretary. He'd only uttered a few words of his speech when a loud male voice interrupted, crying out, "When is the government going to grant women the right to vote?"

David couldn't suppress a grin. Banned from the hall, held a block away by barricades, these women had figured out a way around things after all—utilizing the men in the organization to cause trouble for them!

The crowd reaction was immediate and violent. The men who dared to speak out for suffrage were dragged from their seats and hauled from the auditorium. The men continued to harangue the speakers from the hallway, until the sound of loud scuffling told David that someone was taking care of the problem.

David's nervousness grew. The suffragettes outside certainly had an equally boisterous reception planned for the speakers.

Order restored, the Secretary finished his speech to thunderous applause, then David followed him through the throng to the waiting cars.

As they stepped onto the street, several women broke through the police barricades and ran toward them. Gladstone and the others ran for the cars but David stood his ground, squinting at the approaching women. Was Julia among them?

"For God's sake, Kimbrough, get in the car." The Home Secretary pulled at his sleeve and David reluctantly climbed in. The driver gunned the engine and sped down the street. David stuck his head out the window, trying to catch a glimpse of the attacking suffragettes, but the car moved too fast.

Another angry, sign-waving group of women met them at the station. David eagerly scanned the crowd, but didn't see Julia. If she was in Bristol, she was back at the meeting hall.

Jumping from the cars, David and the others scrambled aboard the train and made their way to the first-class compartment reserved for them. The train pulled away, and everyone gave a sigh of relief.

Until it came to a halt with a sudden lurch.

"What the—?"

Fearing more trouble, David jumped from his seat. He hastened down the corridor toward the front of the train, meeting a police officer partway.

"What's wrong?" David asked.

"Those blasted women put a log across the tracks," the policeman explained. "We'll have it gone in no time."

"Are you guarding the train? They might try to board."

The man shook his head. "There's no sign of any protesters here. They're corraled back at the station."

Nervously, David returned to his seat. They were prime targets, stuck here like this, and he couldn't believe those women wouldn't take advantage of the situation. But the train began to move again and the return trip to London passed without incident.

Reaching home at last, David intended to spend the evening catching up on his work. He glanced through the pile of mail that had accumulated during his absence.

He paused at the sight of a plain envelope, addressed in an unfamiliar hand. But as soon as he saw the WSPU's trumpeting angel imprinted on the flap, he knew who'd sent it. Eagerly he tore it open.

It was from Julia, telling him not to come to Cranwood on the weekend, as she wouldn't be there. He glanced at the postmark. Thursday. The damn thing had probably arrived on Friday but he hadn't bothered to look through the mail before he'd left.

Relief flooded him. She wasn't hiding from him after all.

But where was she now?

In the morning he called the WSPU office again, but to his frustration; they would not tell him where she was, and said they didn't know when she would return.

The lack of information was for her protection, he knew, but it infuriated him that he'd have to wait for her to contact him. He didn't like the fact that she held all the cards.

Was she doing it on purpose—trying to keep him off balance and unsure of her feelings? That seemed too coquettish a game for Julia—she was too honest for that.

But she damn well better get back to town—soon.

After trudging off to that night's Parliamentary session, he spent most of the evening with a bored look on his face, listening to uninspiring oratory on the Irish Land Bill. Finally, he left before the end of the session; the vote on this was not going to be close. Returning home, he poured himself a glass of whiskey and relaxed in the comfortable armchair in his office.

He missed Julia. Wished she were here at his side, sharing a drink, enchanting him with her expressive eyes and sharp wit. With a shock, he realized that he wanted to talk with her even more than he wanted to take her to bed.

If she didn't contact him soon, he would go mad.

In the morning he scanned the papers for articles about the Bristol demonstrations. A few women had been arrested, but to his relief, Julia wasn't among them.

She must be back in London. If he didn't hear from her by tomorrow, he was going to stage his own protest march on Clement's Inn.

He'd just left a boring committee meeting at the Home Office when one of the secretaries handed him a note. David unfolded the paper and, seeing Julia's signature, eagerly scanned the note.

David—I want to see you. Can we meet for dinner? The Bridge House Hotel, at 6. Ring me at Clement's Inn if you cannot come.

David folded the note and put it in his pocket, not caring who saw the fatuous smile on his face.

Where in the hell was the Bridge House Hotel? He darted after the secretary to see if he could find a city directory.

Leaving the House before the dinner break, David arrived at the hotel at a quarter of six. Even if Julia had extended the invitation, he didn't want her to experience the awkwardness of being a lone woman in the dining room, waiting for him.

She'd chosen this obscure hostelry well, he thought, inspecting the small lobby. It was convenient, but being on the south side of the river was unlikely to be visited by anyone either of them knew. It was small and unpretentious, but probably served decent food.

And they charged a reasonable price for their rooms. He didn't know if Julia had chosen to dine at a hotel for that reason, but David certainly hoped she had more in mind than dinner. He might be longing for her company, but he was longing for her body as well. As a precaution, he'd reserved a room for them.

He'd rather take her back to his house, but he feared it might be under siege by suffragette protesters. They seemed to choose their targets at random, and he never knew when they would come around to disrupt his life. He didn't have anything against hotels, but he preferred the comfort of his own home. In those comfortable surroundings, it would be easier to pretend that things weren't going to change now that they were both back in London.

It was a ridiculous idea. Of course things would be different. For one thing, he couldn't drop in on Julia whenever he wanted. Perhaps he could convince her to find a flat somewhere else, one that would provide a safe retreat for both of them. One where they could forget their political lives and concentrate on each other.

David sighed. Somehow, he didn't think she'd agree.

He jumped to his feet when she walked in the door. His heart lurched at the sight of her, thinking she looked more beautiful than ever. A broad smile crossed her face when she spotted him and he had to clench his fists to keep from embarrassing them both in public.

She was wearing a tailored suit that made her look enticingly slim, and a wide-brimmed hat that was surprisingly stylish. He wanted to rip everything off her and just gaze at her naked body.

"You're early," she said.

David took her hand, unable to tear his eyes off her. "I didn't want you to think that I wasn't coming."

"Shall we be seated, then? I'm famished."

The waiter took them to a corner table, made all the more intimate by the low lighting. David ordered the first thing on the menu, not really caring what he ate. Julia was the only thing that mattered.

"I had a rather severe scare last weekend," he said with a wry grin. "I went down to see you at the cottage and it was a bit shocking to find you'd gone."

"Didn't you get my note?"

"My fault entirely—I didn't bother to check the mail before I left." He shook his head. "But the trip wasn't a complete waste—my aunt had a miserable cold and I'm glad I checked on her."

"I hope she's better."

"I'm sure she is—she isn't one to let a thing like that get her down for long. And since I couldn't find you, I joined the Home Secretary in Bristol on Monday." He looked at her closely. "Was I mistaken, or did I see you there as well?"

She stared at him. "I had no idea you were there."

"As I said, it was a last-minute thing." He paused while the waiter brought the soup. "I was surprised at how well behaved your troops were—and at your new tactics for infiltrating meetings."

Julia grinned. "As long as you lock us out of the meetings, we'll find a way to be heard, one way or another."

"The train blockage frightened me. At first, I envisioned suffragettes throwing themselves across the tracks. Thank goodness you had more sense than that."

"Don't be surprised if it comes to that one day," she

said soberly. "The government can't continue to ignore our demands."

"There's no need for anyone to get hurt in the process," he said.

"We're not afraid to suffer for the cause."

David glanced up in relief when their food arrived. He hadn't come here to discuss politics with her. "Let's see how good the food is here."

He deliberately turned the conversation to a lighter note while they ate.

They ordered dessert, but David only picked at his crème caramel. Sitting across from Julia for an entire meal had only whetted his appetite for something else.

"That was delicious," Julia said, pushing her custard dish aside. "And I'm stuffed. I couldn't eat another bite."

"I engaged a room for us," David said quietly.

Her dark eyes widened and a smile flitted across her face. "Awfully sure of yourself, aren't you?"

David signaled the waiter to bring the bill. "I thought you might be persuadable." He leaned closer. "It's been a monumental struggle to keep my hands off you all evening, and my self-control is wearing thin. I'm not sure how much longer I can restrain myself."

"I hate to see you suffer." Julia's eyes twinkled with anticipation. "And I'd hate for you to pay for a room you didn't use."

After paying the dinner bill, David took Julia's arm and led her upstairs. By the time they reached the room, he could barely draw a breath, so eagerly did he want to hold her. Unlocking the door, he led her inside and pulled her into his arms.

"God, I've missed you."

His mouth came down on hers.

Chapter 14

Julia melted against him, returning his kisses with eagerness. She wanted him, needed him so much that it frightened her. From the moment she'd spotted him in the hotel lobby, she'd been unable to tear her eyes away, longing to touch him, and feel his touch herself. They'd been apart far too long.

"I can't believe how much I want you," David murmured, nuzzling against her neck.

"It's merely the thrill of a clandestine meeting in a hotel."

"Do you mind?" He gave her a long look. "I would have taken you home but sometimes your fellow—"

"David, this is perfect," Julia said. "I know we need to be careful; that's why I chose this place."

David kissed the tip of her nose. "Do we really need to be so careful? Would the country fall apart if they discovered we were lovers?"

"The country might not, but there'd be a lot of questions asked at Clement's Inn."

"Are they running some type of convent? Good God, this is the twentieth century. They can't dictate every aspect of your life."

"I'm a paid employee of the Union," Julia reminded him. "I need to set an example. They can always fire me, you know."

"They wouldn't dare. Besides, it's not as if you're working against them." He smiled ruefully. "I can testify to your insistent support of the cause."

"Ah, but you are a member of the government, after

all." Julia pinched his chin. "An *antisuffrage* government. I should hold you in contempt."

His arm tightened around her. "But you don't detest me, do you?"

"No," she said softly. "I don't *detest* you."

He laughed and kissed her gently. "That's one of the things I like about you—your honesty."

"What else do you like?" she asked with a teasing smile.

David began walking her backward toward the bed. "That you don't wear corsets."

Julia gave a mock shiver. "Horrible things. My mother was vehemently against them."

Quickly undoing the buttons on her blouse, David parted the fabric and kissed the skin above her chemise. "Your mother was a wise woman." With skillful fingers he unfastened her skirt and pushed it down her hips.

As Julia reached for the buttons of his shirt, he grabbed her hands and pulled them away.

"This is my plan, remember? I'm going to undress you." He wanted to take his time, but his desire warred with his plans.

Julia dropped her hands to her sides and he quickly removed her blouse. Then he bent and pulled off her shoes. Tugging her chemise over her head, David left her only in her knickers and stockings. He tenderly cupped a breast in each hand, squeezing them gently before bending and planting a kiss on the erect tip of each. Then he untied the ribbon of her knickers and let them fall to the floor. Julia stood naked before him and his desire flamed.

"Lay on the bed," he said, his voice hoarsening. "On your stomach."

Julia complied, fighting against the erotic thrill of his words. She'd longed for his touch, dreamed of this, from the moment he'd left her all those days ago. He ran his hands down her back, sweeping over the curve of her buttocks. Planting a kiss along the top of her stocking, he slowly rolled it down her leg, his mouth following the descending path. Julia clenched the bedcover between her fingers, trying not to cry out.

With her stockings gone, he ran his fingers up her legs, tickling lightly, bringing up gooseflesh. David squeezed her bottom, his fingers inching lower and lower toward the junction of her legs. Julia felt his hand sliding beneath her, seeking the part of her that wanted him so desperately.

She cried out when his fingers found her, already wet and wanting. He pushed her legs apart, probing inside her with first one finger, then another. With his other hand, he stroked her leg, her rear, her back. And always were those fingers, stroking, probing, urging her toward her release with a speed that stunned her. Julia spasmed against his hand, crying out in pleasure, satiated yet frustrated at not taking him with her.

She felt the mattress move as he stood up and she rolled over. He was looking down at her with an arrogant, possessive look in his eyes as he hastily unbuttoned his shirt. A look that both frightened and thrilled her.

Lying back against the pillows, Julia watched him undress, admiring his broad chest, dusted with golden hair. She couldn't wait to run her hands, her mouth, over it, licking his nipples into hardened buds.

Julia drew in her breath as he removed his drawers, exposing his thrusting erection.

He must have seen the invitation in her eyes, for he was atop her in an instant, knowing she was wet and ready. His movements were hard and furious, demanding the same response from her. She responded, eagerly, not holding back any part of her desire, her need, from him. This was what she wanted—David deep inside her as she rose again and again to meet him.

She felt the tingling race up her body as she arched against him, crying out his name in a long, drawn-out moan as he pushed her down on the bed in rhythmic motions. He sucked in his breath and froze for a split second, then flooded her with his release. Shuddering, David collapsed atop her.

Julia wrapped her arms around him, reveling in the weight of him, lying between her legs, still inside her body. She had him—all of him—as much as any woman could ever have a man.

Was that what she really wanted?

Leaning over, he kissed her. "I love you, Jules."

Her heart beat faster with his words, but dismay dampened her elation. She saw the unspoken question in his eyes, knew what he wanted her to say. That she loved him. But she feared to put it into words, as if saying it aloud would put them in danger.

Sighing deeply, David rolled away from her.

Julia reached out a hand and stroked his arm, trying to ease his disappointment. "David, I don't know what to say. There are times when I don't think I can live without you, but there is my work, the cause . . ."

"Ah, yes, the cause," he said, his voice heavy with bitterness. "We can't let anything come before that, can we?"

"Don't do this now. Not tonight." Julia pressed herself against his back, running her hands over his chest. "Make love to me again."

This time, when they finished, he got out of bed instead of lingering beside her.

"I have to go," he said. "The dinner break is long over."

Julia sat up. "I understand. I should get back, too."

He laughed. "Bed check at midnight?"

Julia laughed in return. "Not exactly. But I have a meeting early in the morning."

David groaned as he pulled on his shirt. "So do I, now that I think of it." He grinned at her. "What do you think they would do if we both failed to show?"

"I'd be roundly scolded." Reluctantly, Julia climbed from the bed and gathered her clothing.

"What are your plans for the weekend?" he asked. "We could drive down to Cranwood. Aunt would love a visit."

His suggestion filled her with regret. Cranwood sounded like such a safe haven. "I have to go out of town for a few days."

David's face darkened. "Another demonstration?"

Julia shook her head. "Just a visit to some of the other Union chapters."

"I could go with you." His expression brightened. "Surely we could have some time together."

She chuckled. "I can tell you've never been on a WSPU jaunt. Firstly, there are four of us going, and secondly, we always stay in supporters' homes. I'm not sure where I'd manage to put you."

"Under the bed?" he asked wistfully. "Well, I tried. You'll ring me when you get back?"

Julia leaned over and kissed him. "Of course."

"What am I going to do with myself for the entire weekend? It's been so long since I've spent one in town that I don't remember what to do."

"I'm sure you'll find something to do."

He darted her a longing look. "Unlikely—when I can't do the one thing I really want to."

She ran a finger down the front of his shirt. "This will give you something to look forward to next week."

Grabbing her hand, David brought the palm to his mouth, pressing a kiss against it. "Remember, I'm an impatient man. If you leave me alone too long, I'll come by Clement's Inn looking for you."

Julia laughed. "I'd like to see you amid the enemy camp."

"I'd be quaking with terror, no doubt." He flashed her an encouraging smile. "Spare me the frightening experience and ring me the moment you get back to town."

"I will."

Once they were dressed, he escorted her downstairs, insisting that she take a hansom back to Clement's Inn, instead of riding the tube.

Julia didn't mind the rare luxury. The privacy of the cab offered a better atmosphere for reflection than the noisy bustle of the Underground.

She knew David still didn't understand the importance of her work to her—or the danger that their relationship put her in. And despite his protestations she didn't think it would do his own career much good if his superiors found out about her.

She had to make certain that they maintained their secret.

The sensible thing would be to break it off now, before anyone knew. Then they'd both be safe. But tonight had revealed an appalling weakness in herself—a weakness she never thought to find.

But from that first meeting at the pond, David Kimbrough had turned her life upside down. Her emotions were in a turmoil, her thoughts confused, and the only thing she knew for certain was that she couldn't stop seeing him.

As foolish and selfish as that attitude was, it was how she felt. David might be her political opponent, but she loved him despite his politics and his government position. She willingly ignored that, for the joy of being with him.

Julia had never thought she'd be willing to overlook such a major difference. It was compromising her beliefs—sleeping with the enemy, if you liked—but she didn't care. She wanted to stay with David as long as she could.

The offices at Clement's Inn were still brightly lit when the cab deposited Julia in front. Inside, several women laughed and chatted gaily as they folded notices and stuffed them into envelopes.

"Miss Sydney!" one of them called and they all stopped to look at her, several with worshipful expressions on their faces.

Julia hated it when they looked at her like that. She wasn't doing anything special; just the work she was suited for. But these young women—goodness, many of them were in their late teens—considered her and the other old hands their idols.

Would they think so highly of her if they knew she'd just come from David Kimbrough's bed?

One of the girls stepped forward and handed Julia a paper. "These are the flyers we're preparing for the demonstration in Birmingham. What do you think?"

Julia quickly scanned the notice and smiled her approval. "They look good. We should attract a large crowd."

"I wish I were going, but they said I needed more experience in the office. Will you be there?"

"I'm going up to talk with the organizers, but I'm not participating in the demonstration."

"I read your article on women's anger in the last issue of *Votes for Women,*" another girl said shyly. "I like the way you blamed the government for our increasing militancy."

"If they would give us the vote, we wouldn't need to act," Julia agreed.

Looking at their eager faces, she remembered the zeal she'd once applied to the cause, a zeal now worn thin through the many imprisonments, hunger strikes, and the continuing frustration at their lack of progress. She'd gained back some of the old enthusiasm after her relaxing stay in the country, but the dilemma surrounding her and David was rapidly sapping it again.

Taking off her hat, Julia unbuttoned her coat. "I'll help you stuff those envelopes."

They stared at her, aghast.

"You don't need to do that."

Julia laughed and grabbed a pile of envelopes. "I'm not afraid of a few paper cuts, I assure you. Stuffing envelopes was one of my first jobs here."

All too soon, she realized that her presence put a damper on their high spirits, as if they feared to act naturally around her. Julia realized she was doing more harm than good by remaining here. She quickly finished the pile in front of her, then rose.

"I'm sorry for not doing more, but I need to get to bed." She smiled in apology. "I've an early meeting in the morning."

"Oh, thank you so much for your help," the tall, thin girl said. "Good night."

"Good night."

Julia headed down the corridor toward the back stairs that led up to her two small rooms.

Once in her room, she switched on the light in the parlor and tossed her hat on the sofa. Going to the small paraffin stove, she put water on to boil for tea.

It was uncomfortable being a suffragette icon, even if a rather insignificant one. For a moment Julia marveled at the calm with which Christabel and her mother handled the adulation. Did it make them as uncomfortable as it did her?

She shook her head as she waited impatiently for the water to heat. If she'd wanted to stay in the background, she should have kept on typing and stuffing envelopes those three years ago, instead of accompanying Christabel and the others on a march. Once she'd experienced the thrill of confrontation, the mundane tasks of the office no longer held any appeal for her.

Action was what she wanted and action was what she sought. And now it was that which threatened to crash back on her, threatening her relationship with David.

A light tap sounded on her door.

"Come in."

To her surprise, it was Beryl. Julia immediately grew alert. It was unusual for her to visit.

Beryl surveyed Julia's room with cool hauteur. "You're making a late night of it."

"So are you," Julia replied dryly. "Would you like a cup of tea?"

Beryl nodded and perched on the edge of the well-worn sofa. "I understand you're going to Birmingham to help the organizing committee."

"I am." Julia prepared the tea.

"I wanted to go, but Christabel insisted I stay here."

Julia ignored Beryl's jab. Sometimes, being away from Christabel's eagle-eyed scrutiny was a relief. But Beryl delighted in thinking that she was the WSPU leader's favorite.

"Have you given any more thought to tackling Kimbrough?"

Julia sat down, hoping her cup didn't rattle in the saucer. She refused to allow Beryl to maneuver her into a corner.

"I told you, I don't want to offend Lady Marchmont. I won't take advantage of the connection."

"I heard he rang here earlier in the week, asking after you."

"He did?" Julia tried to appear surprised. "Did he leave a message?"

Beryl shook her head and Julia almost laughed at her look of disappointment.

"Where were you tonight?" Beryl asked. "You were certainly gone for a long time."

Julia was growing tired of this clumsy interrogation. Beryl wasn't her boss. "I'm not answerable to you for my whereabouts, Beryl."

A flush crept over her face. "We were just wondering . . ."

" 'We' or *you*?" Julia countered.

"Something might have happened to you. You're a well enough known figure; someone might try to do you harm."

Julia drew the hat pin from her hat. "I was well enough armed."

"Still, I don't think it's safe for you to go out alone."

"Why, Beryl, how nice of you to be concerned for my safety," Julia drawled sarcastically. "But I assure you, I'm able to take care of myself."

"Christabel agrees with me," she retorted. "None of the leaders should go out without an escort. It's too dangerous."

"If I need a bodyguard, I'll hire one." Julia didn't try to hide her irritation. "I'm not going to allow anyone or any group to restrict my movements—be it you or the antisuffrage leaguers."

"Think of it as a friendly word of warning." Beryl hastily finished her tea and rose. "I'll see you at the meeting in the morning."

Julia shut the door behind her with a feeling of loathing. How that woman irritated her! Beryl wouldn't be happy until she'd taken over control of the entire organization, and with it, the minute details of everyone's lives.

Thank God Birmingham offered Julia an escape for a few days. She almost wished she could stay there, and be a part of the demonstration, away from Beryl's prying questions.

But if she did, she'd surely be arrested, and then heaven only knew how long it would be before she would see David again.

Leaning back in the chair, she sipped her tea.

David. That was what this entire conversation had been about. Beryl was obviously suspicious and Julia realized she'd have to be extra careful around her in the future. If Beryl ever discovered the truth, there was no telling what she would do—except that it would be calculated to improve Beryl's standing in the Union. Discrediting Julia would certainly help that.

She never should have allowed a man to complicate her life.

After seeing Julia into the cab, David took the tube from the London Bridge Station to Whitehall, and looked in on the debate in the House. He was relieved to find he hadn't been needed, and no one noticed he'd returned so late.

He retreated to the Liberal caucus room, where they would come for him if he was needed. Pouring himself a drink, he sprawled in a chair.

God, he'd hated every part of tonight. Every part except being with Julia. But the secrecy, the tiny hotel room, the separate journeys back to town, ground at him like a sore tooth. He wanted better than that for her. He loved her, and didn't care who knew it.

Yet he knew that his attitude was unfair to her. He could weather the storm if their affair became known, but for Julia, it was more doubtful. Because she was a woman, and a suffragette. She'd be roundly condemned by both society and her political allies. He didn't think Julia cared a rap for society, but guessed that the pressures from the suffragettes would be harder on her.

Hard enough that she would stop seeing him?

He prayed not. He had to convince her that they could continue to see each other, both in London and the country. And if that meant more furtive meetings in out-of-the-way hotels, so be it. Seeing Julia was the important thing.

The next four days dragged on endlessly. David remained in London—the first weekend he'd spent in the city since June, and he soon remembered why he didn't like it. He allowed himself to be talked into going to the theater on Saturday, but he found it boring, and the desultory conversation over supper that followed only depressed him.

He realized just how dull most of his companions were. Not that he'd chosen them for their brilliant conversation—most of them were political compatriots, not necessarily close friends. Other undersecretaries like himself, men without the cachet of Cabinet positions, but men who were more than mere MPs.

In the past, David had found them more entertaining than his other social circle—the aristocratic one that he was a part of, even if he was on the fringe. At least he could get a reasonable thought from his political cronies. There weren't many people as perceptive as his aunt among the upper crust. Their lives usually revolved around their entertainments, from intimate dinner parties to gigantic balls. All staged without much thought, because it was what they did. David had always attended for the same reasons, because it was what he'd always done, been raised to do. Now, he couldn't believe he'd endured all that nonsense for so long, especially when he didn't enjoy it.

Of course, it was much easier to go along with the crowd than to set his own course. And, admittedly, he didn't have anything against being entertained. It was only after spending so much time with Julia that he'd developed a taste for much simpler pleasures, and the company of more than four or five people felt stifling.

That was a problem he'd have to overcome, because with a political career, he was doomed to attend social functions; they were part of his job.

But how much more enjoyable they would be with Julia at his side. He could imagine her scathing comments on the behavior of the theatergoers, who were more concerned with their own conversations than the play onstage. She'd have a biting remark for the women who came dressed in all their finery—knowing the minimal wages that were paid to the women who produced that finery.

And supper afterward . . . There she would no doubt complain about the excessive quantity of the meals, the food wasted, the money spent.

Just knowing how she would disapprove made David feel disapproving also.

It was an odd sensation, to know exactly what another person would think in a situation. He didn't think he'd known anyone—man or woman—well enough before to have made such accurate predictions.

But with Julia, he felt as if he'd known her for years rather than only several weeks. He laughed to himself. Probably because she *was* so opinionated, and not at all hesitant to express herself, so he knew what she thought on nearly everything.

Except their relationship. She'd been remarkably closemouthed about that. The only thing he could say with certainty was that she enjoyed sporting in bed. Was her enthusiasm due to him, or would she behave the same with any other man?

A sharp pang of jealousy flashed through him at the thought of Julia with another man. She belonged with him.

He merely faced the monumental task of convincing her of that.

A task that would be made much easier if she wasn't so caught up in the suffrage campaign. David admired her determination, but he wished it wasn't so strong at times. He had the uneasy feeling that if it came down to a choice between himself and the WSPU, the WSPU would win easily.

Somehow, he had to make Julia realize that it was possible for them to be together, despite their political differences. That those differences would only add spice, not discord, to their relationship. That she could love a member of the same government that resisted her call for women's suffrage.

It would be the toughest campaign of his life, but David was determined to win it. He needed Julia.

Chapter 15

"David? It's Julia."

He leaned closer to the phone. Just the sound of her voice made his heart leap. These last few days without her had seemed like weeks.

"You're back," he said inanely.

"I could be calling you from Birmingham."

Her tone was teasing, assuring him she wasn't. "When can I see you?"

"Tonight?"

"Perfect." He glanced out the window to the deserted street outside his house. "I don't see any of your ladies out front. Why don't you come here?"

There was a pause at her end. "Don't you think that's a bit risky?"

He laughed. "You're the one who knows if it's safe or not. Find out if anyone plans to picket here tonight."

"And raise even more eyebrows? No, thank you, I'll take my chances."

"Come in a hansom," he suggested, "and have him go up the alley. I'll meet you in the back and no one will be the wiser."

"Oh, so that is how you escape! I should report that to someone."

David chuckled. "You'd only be harming yourself if you did, my dear. How soon can you be here?"

"About half an hour."

"I'll be waiting. Anxiously." David took a deep breath, hoping she wouldn't refuse his next request. "And don't plan on leaving until the morning."

"I'll see you soon."

After she rang off, David leaned back in his chair, a fatuous smile on his face.

She must be missing him to have called so soon after her return. Tonight, he wanted to make her acknowledge that, make her realize that she needed him, too.

Meanwhile, he didn't have much time to prepare for her arrival, and he wanted everything to be perfect. He dashed down to the kitchen to see if there was enough to eat, sent his man out to pick up some last-minute items, then gave him the evening off.

Long before the appointed time, David waited impatiently outside the back gate. His blood hummed with the thought of seeing Julia again, knowing they would be together for the entire night.

Soon his ears caught the steady clip-clop of a horse's hooves and he picked out the dark outline of a cab coming toward him. Grinning, David stepped out into the alley.

The hansom stopped and David paid the driver, then opened the door to help Julia out. His grin widened as he took her hand and led her through the narrow garden to the rear entrance of the house.

He pulled her into his arms the minute they stepped inside, kissing her lips, her cheeks, her forehead.

"God, it's so good to see you again," he whispered. "I've missed you."

"I missed you, too."

"Here, let me take your coat and bag. I've given my man the night off so we'll have to take care of ourselves, I'm afraid."

"I think we can manage." Julia examined her surroundings with frank curiosity. "Come along and give me a tour."

"There isn't much to see," he said apologetically, leading her through to the front hall. He pointed to the first door. "That's the parlor and the dining room's over here."

"I want to see them," Julia said.

"I haven't seen where you live," David teased, but followed her into the parlor, a place to entertain before and after dinner. The wife of a fellow MP had handled the furnishings for it and the dining room—a farewell present when their affair had ended. David hoped Julia liked it.

She gave each room a thorough examination, while David waited on tenterhooks for her opinion. Did she think the striped wallpaper too formal, or the dark mahogany furniture too old-fashioned? He'd make any changes she wanted.

"Very nice," she pronounced at last, halting in front of the dining-room fireplace. She picked up a small Chinese vase from the mantel and turned it over in her hand. "But not at all what I thought it would be."

David laughed with relief. "You've a good eye—I didn't choose any of this."

"Who did?"

Did he see a flash of jealousy in her eyes? "An old friend who knew I had the usual male indifference to these things."

"It's very grand for a bachelor—even if he is an Under Secretary."

"It's actually my mother's house," he explained. "But since she prefers to live abroad, I've acquired it by default."

"You must entertain a lot."

"Not often." He grinned. "It's a hard life being a bachelor—we're always invited out but few people come to us."

"I can tell how disappointed you are."

Julia continued to prowl the room, inspecting the crystal, examining the silver.

Finally, she turned to him.

"There's really nothing of you here, is there?"

"My private rooms are upstairs," he said, holding out his hand. "Would you like to see them?"

She arched a brow. "Is that an invitation to your bedroom?"

"Most certainly."

Julia took his hand.

* * *

He didn't give her time to inspect the bedroom, but pulled her down onto the bed, making love to her with desperate need. They made love twice, then dressed in robes and went down to the kitchen, where David fixed a midnight supper of omelettes and champagne.

"How was your trip to Birmingham?" he asked as they ate. "What new demonstration strategy have you developed?"

"You'll find out soon enough," she said evasively.

"That sounds ominous. Should I warn the police?"

"I'm sure they'll be quite prepared."

He looked at her curiously. "Why didn't you stay?"

"I have things to do in London."

"And here I thought it was because you couldn't bear to be away from me for that long."

Julia laughed. "We had more than enough women to carry out our work in Birmingham. I've other things to plan."

Reaching across the table, David covered her hand with his. "Julia, whatever you're planning, please take care. Both the government and the police forces are losing their patience—I'm afraid someone is going to get hurt soon."

"That will be the government's fault." A flash of anger crossed her eyes. "If they deny us the right of legal protest, they force us to stage illegal ones."

"I just don't want anything to happen to you—in or out of prison."

"Take your concerns to Asquith. He has the power to stop everything with a few words."

"Julia, when are you going to realize it's not that simple? The entire Liberal Party could come out for women's suffrage, but that doesn't mean it will become the law of the land. There are political realities to consider."

" 'The House of Lords will veto it,' " she retorted in a mocking voice. "What if they do? It only shows what a reactionary, obstructionist group they are. Perhaps it will bring about some needed changes."

"That's what Asquith is trying to accomplish," David

said. "But suffrage isn't the issue to make the fight over."

"Why not? Because it's so unimportant?" Her voice dripped sarcasm. "After all, it only affects women."

David took a deep breath, determined to rein in his anger. He didn't want to fight with her tonight, but make love to her.

"Your eggs are getting cold," he said sternly.

"Afraid of the truth?" Julia asked before turning back to her food.

Back in his bedroom, he made love to her one more time and they slept.

In the morning David slept so soundly Julia didn't have the heart to wake him. Silently she slipped on a robe and padded down the hall, bent on exploring the rest of his house. Somewhere, she hoped to find more clues to the puzzle that was David Kimbrough.

There was another, spare bedroom at the far end of the hall, but it was the room at the front, overlooking the street, that interested her. His office. Here, at last, was his personal lair.

The room was a picture of order and neatness. Julia giggled. No wonder David had been so horrified at her vases of dead flowers and scattered piles of work. Here, his things were arranged with military precision; the photos on the mantel were all in identical frames. The top of his desk was bare except for an inkstand and even the books in the tall shelves were arranged by topic.

Standing in front of the fireplace, Julia closely examined the photos. She recognized the one of his parents instantly, finding it surprising that David even had a picture of them. There was another print of his mother and another woman, with a small child standing between them. Julia peered closer and realized that it was David, short pants, knobby knees, and all.

He looked adorable.

He'd been in her thoughts constantly over the last few days, even while she was involved in the demonstration planning in Birmingham. She'd barely set down her suitcase when she'd rushed to the phone to call him last night. After hearing his voice, she couldn't have stayed away for any reason.

It felt odd to be in his house. There were so many reminders of who he was—grandson of a duke, MP, government official. All the things that threw up walls between them.

Yet the only way to deal with these conflicts was to confront them, as she was doing now. To learn as much as she could about the man on his home turf, when he'd be open and relaxed. Julia felt a desperate need to gain some sort of sense of who he was, to understand him, so she could better understand her feelings for him, and the hold he had over her.

Even at the cottage, ostensibly her territory, she'd felt matters slipping out of control. Julia feared it would be worse here, where David held all the cards.

She didn't want to lose herself.

"Snooping, are we?"

Julia jumped at the sound of David's voice. Slowly she turned around, then grinned at the sight of him leaning against the door frame, stark naked.

"You were rather charming as a child," she said at last, pointing to the picture.

"Are you hinting that I'm not now?"

She gave him an amused head-to-toe perusal. "I'm not sure . . ."

He closed the distance between them, and fingered the collar of his robe. "I think you're wearing something of mine."

Julia heard the desire in his voice and her knees suddenly felt like jelly. He wanted her again, and his need fanned her own. "Would you like it back?" she asked, her voice low.

"Eventually." Untying the sash at her waist, he pushed the robe off her shoulders, bending his head to suckle at her breast. Together, they sank to the floor.

After making love, they lay there, arms and legs entwined, too lazy to move. A sharp noise jolted them apart.

"How long did you tell your man to stay away?" Julia asked.

"Longer than this," David said. He got to his feet and strode toward the window. After peering carefully around the curtain, he broke into laughter.

"What is it?"

He beckoned to her. "Come see."

Peering warily over his shoulder, Julia gasped and jumped back in shock at recognizing the picketers below. "David, how could you! Those are Union women! They might have seen me!"

"If they did, I'll make them forget." David flung the window open. "Hey! You down there! What do you think you're doing?"

Covering her eyes, Julia couldn't suppress her giggles. There would be stories bandied about the office for days about a naked David Kimbrough standing in front of his window, lambasting the demonstrators.

David shut the window with a slam and turned back to her, a wide grin on his face. "That scared them off. Should have thought of it long ago."

"Oh, David, you're impossible," Julia gasped between laughs. "I hope they send the constable after you."

"They won't." He grabbed the discarded robe and held it out to her. "Let's have some breakfast. I'm famished."

Julie glanced at the clock. "I should be going soon."

"Not without breakfast. I don't want it to be said that I'm starving you." He eyed her critically. "You could still use a little more flesh on those bones."

"Oh, thank you," she said, sticking her arms into the robe.

In the kitchen, David forced her to sit while he toasted bread, then slathered it with butter and jam. "When am I going to see you again? Is this a busy week?"

Julia took a bite of toast. "David, we have to be very cautious about seeing each other in the city."

"Then let's go to the country this weekend," he suggested. "Auntie would love to see you."

"I'd like that," Julia said. "I think I can go this time."

"But I still want to see you this week. We could have lunch on Wednesday or Thursday."

"Only if you invite me to the members' dining room," Julia said with a laugh.

"Of course. And you can show me off afterward at Clement's Inn. No, I was thinking of a more *discreet* setting."

"Where?"

"I'll keep that a surprise." He smiled mysteriously. "I'll ring you tomorrow morning." He uttered a deep sigh. "I think I can wait that long to see you again."

Julia popped the final bite of toast into her mouth. "You're going to have to."

"Do you miss me when we're apart?"

Julia gave him a surprised glance. "Of course."

"Good." He clasped her hand. "I thought those weeks in August were bad, when I was here and you were in the country, but it's even worse being in the same city with you, knowing how close you are, and not being able to see you."

Julia realized she felt the same way. It was impossible not to think of him when she knew he was only a few minutes away.

"You're looking far too serious," he said.

Julia forced a smile. "You reminded me of how much easier things were last month. Why don't you get Parliament to adjourn, so you can go into the country and I'll visit you on the weekends."

"You won't get an argument from me about that," he said. "I'm thoroughly tired of these endless debates."

Julia stood. "I really have to go."

"I'll call you a cab."

"You don't need to, I can take the tube or the omnibus."

He shook his head. "I wouldn't feel very gentlemanly if I allowed you to do that."

She raised a brow. "Are all my actions subject to your approval?"

"You're free to do whatever you wish," he said hastily. "But since I invited you here, it's my responsibility to get you home."

"Better," she said. "But it would set tongues wagging if I turn up in the middle of the day in a cab."

"Have him let you off at the end of the block."

"Or merely take me to the nearest tube station."

"You're being ridiculously stubborn, you know."

Julia smiled. "That's a silly charge, coming from a member of Asquith's government."

David threw up his hands. "All right, take the tube. I'll let you—I mean you are free to walk to the station if you want."

Laughing, Julia patted his cheek. "You're learning, David. Now call me that hansom you are so enamored of and I'll cross the city in comfort."

David shook his head and reached for the phone.

As she headed homeward, Julia felt a vague sense of relief.

It would be so easy to keep seeing David like this; his house offered them the perfect privacy. She pictured herself spending more and more time there. And she shouldn't. She needed to concentrate on her work.

Julia berated this weakness in her, this weakness that made the thought of giving up David so intolerable. Why, when she could be so strong in prison, was she so weak where he was concerned?

She knew he was distracting her from her work, blunting the enthusiasm that she usually applied to planning new, dramatic methods of harassing the government. It had been others, after all, who'd suggested the tactics they'd decided to use in Birmingham, not her. And she was ashamed to admit that at first she'd wondered if escalating the violence was the right thing to do. But she kept her doubts to herself and helped with the planning as if she wholeheartedly approved.

Could the sentimental emotion of love be the cause of her weakness? Was it true that women lost something of their selves when they cared for a man—a loss that only accelerated when they became tangled in the net of marriage and family?

Of course, there were married women in the WSPU, some even acting against their husbands' wishes. But Christabel and Beryl weren't married, and Julia had always considered the three of them to be the ultimate examples of the dedicated suffragette. Champions of the cause, loudly proclaiming their beliefs, willing to go to prison, and suffer any indignity for the betterment of all women.

But now, Julia began to have doubts. Not about the work of the WSPU, but about herself. Was she really as dedicated as she once had been, or had she lost her edge when she fell in love with David Kimbrough?

The upcoming events in Birmingham nagged at her. Even though Christabel hadn't wanted Julia to participate, there was a part of her that wanted to, that wanted to be involved in this next, escalating step. She had a right to be at the forefront. Yet at the same time, she was glad she wouldn't be facing arrest, for it meant she would be free to see David. And that realization made her feel even worse.

Action was what she needed, Julia realized. By taking an active part in a demonstration, the following arrest and imprisonment would force her mind back onto her task. Now she only had to convince Christabel to plan a new demonstration—one that Julia could lead.

By the time she reached the Strand, Julia was already planning in her head. It was time the suffragettes took their voices to the streets of London again. And she had an idea.

Jumping down from the cab, Julia walked the last two blocks to Clement's Inn with increasing urgency. Birmingham must be followed by an equally strong action in the capital.

And Julia vowed to be at the forefront.

For the rest of the week, Julia poured herself into her work. Christabel liked the idea of a London action, depending on what happened in Birmingham, and told Julia to make plans.

She realized that there was no way she could get away

to the country with David for the weekend. Friday's demonstrations in Birmingham would be only the beginning, and Julia suspected they would be working through the weekend to deal with the aftermath, whatever it was.

She rang David Thursday morning to tell him.

"Let's have lunch tomorrow, then," he suggested. "A *long* lunch."

Julia fought to restrain a blush. She knew exactly what he had in mind and her knees went weak at the thought. Then she willed herself to remain in control.

"Where shall I meet you?"

"I'll pick you up with the car," he said. "I know an inn in Surrey that serves delicious food."

Julia hesitated, then shrugged off her concerns. As long as David didn't dash up the front stairs, no one was going to know she was with him. "I'll meet you at the corner of the Strand," she said.

"At half past eleven?"

"That will be fine."

"Don't plan any meetings for the afternoon," David said, and rang off.

Julia set the phone down slowly.

She should have said no, easily pleading too much work—she'd already begged off from the weekend. He might be disappointed, but what else could he say? But instead, she'd melted at the first sound of his voice and found herself unable to say no—again.

Why couldn't David be something other than he was? A schoolteacher, a university instructor, or even a tradesman. He could even be a MP. Just not such a high-ranking one in the party that had promised women so much at the last election, then reneged on their promises.

And if only he wasn't so insistent on taking the government line, that this was not the time for women's suffrage, that they must be patient and wait for other, "more important" causes to take precedence. But David heartily endorsed the Liberal Party stand. He was totally unalterably opposed to the WSPU's position and, hence, opposed to everything Julia believed.

How could she be so deeply in love with him?

It was a puzzle she didn't understand. And because Julia didn't understand it, the only way she knew how to escape it was to stop seeing him. Over time, she could fall out of love with him.

Except it wouldn't be as easy as falling in love with him.

Julia reminded herself she'd made sacrifices before. Emotional ones, when she'd decided to leave the safe nest of her home for adventure in the world. Financial ones, when she'd decided to work as a union organizer instead of a teacher. Or when she'd given up that job and returned to school to get a law degree she knew she wouldn't be allowed to use.

Personal ones, when she'd suffered the taunts and humiliations of the male law students, who resented her because she was a woman, and even more because she'd been smarter than they.

And there'd been the physical sacrifices. The long days of enforced silence in the government's prisons. The days and nights in solitary confinement, for rebelling against the rules. The days of gnawing, gut-wrenching hunger, when she'd been reduced to the weakness of an invalid.

Julia knew she was strong. Strong enough to endure all those things. She must be strong enough to endure all this as well.

She could go to America with Christabel's mother in October. That would take her far away from David, making it impossible for her to succumb to temptation. Surely, speaking about the suffrage cause to the appreciative American audiences would infuse her with new enthusiasm. Perhaps while she was there, she could visit her sister.

And maybe even stay. American women wanted the vote; they might welcome a British suffragette with open arms. She could give them advice on waging their own struggle.

Julia shook her head. Fleeing to America was the coward's way out. She had to confront her feelings for David and determine what she was going to do. Otherwise, she wouldn't be able to live with herself. Julia had never backed down from anything before, and she wasn't going to back down now.

She was seeing him tomorrow; it was the perfect opportunity to tell him that she didn't want to see him again. But Julia knew she couldn't do it, not yet. A few more weeks wouldn't make any difference. She could enjoy his company for a while longer.

That explained her disappointment when he called and said his schedule had been changed and he only had time for tea. Instead of a leisurely lunch and a long afternoon in bed, she had to settle for a quick, public meeting.

"Sorry about lunch," David said, when he'd seated her at the small tearoom off the Strand. "I'll make it up to you with dinner tomorrow night."

"I'm holding you to that," Julia said, teasing him. At least the place was nearly empty and they could have the illusion of privacy.

"I don't think there's going to be any normalcy in my life until this session is done," he said with a shake of his head.

"You could always resign your seat," Julia said.

"And you could quit the Union," he countered. "And we both know neither of us is going to do any such thing."

"If we had the vote, I could retire."

"Believe me, if I had any say in the matter, I'd give it to you."

Julia's eyes widened. "You're going to support suffrage?"

"It has nothing to do with the issue—I just don't want you putting your life in danger. No political cause is worth your life, Julia."

"Tell that to the Irish—or the Boers—or the Americans. They all fought against political tyranny."

"And not too successfully, except for the Americans. This isn't a war, Julia, it's a political issue." He regarded her sternly. "You have to wait until the time is right, when popular opinion will support it."

Julia carefully sliced her cake. "I intend to make sure that popular opinion turns our way faster."

"Breaking windows and throwing rocks isn't winning you any friends in the government."

"We don't have any friends in the government," Julia said. "As long as they ignore our demands, we'll do what we must to get our message across."

"One thing's clear," he said with a frown. "We don't dare discuss politics. Not while you insist that you are the only one who is right."

"Isn't the government doing the very same thing, by stifling debate and refusing to produce a suffrage bill? They pat us on the head and say 'someday.' Well, someday isn't good enough."

David grabbed a cake from the tray in front of him. "Lovely food, isn't it?"

Julia laughed. "Alright, I will be quiet. I'm sorry you had to work so hard this week. I didn't get a chance to read the paper this morning—how is the budget debate faring?"

"Slowly."

Julia took a sip of tea. Hearing the tinkle of the doorbell, she glanced over David's shoulder at the two women who walked in—and nearly dropped her cup.

Selena and Grace. Dear God, they'd spotted her and were coming over.

"Julia! What a surprise! I see that you're—" Selena came to an abrupt halt when she spotted David.

"Hello, Selena, Grace." Julia struggled to hide her dismay.

"Christabel was looking for you," Selena said. "No one knew where you were." She looked at David as if he were some sort of distasteful insect who'd wandered onto her plate.

Julia pushed back her chair and stood, causing David to scramble to his feet. "I should get back." She gave him a pleading look, praying he would play along. "Thank you for the tea, Mr. Kimbrough. It was nice of your aunt to ask you to treat me."

"You know Auntie; I daren't go against her wishes. She insisted that I personally make sure you were well."

"Stop by my office when you get a chance, Grace. I'd like to hear about the action in Manchester. Selena." Julia nodded and headed for the door.

She didn't know if David was behind her or not, she only wanted to get out of that tea shop, away from him, away from the Union women.

Caught having tea with the enemy.

That was no exaggeration. Anyone in the Home Office, with jurisdiction over the police and prisons, would be considered an enemy right now. If Beryl found out about this, Julia would never hear the end of it.

Blindly, Julia walked down the street until someone grabbed her elbow. David.

"Not a good meeting?" he asked gently, his eyes filled with concern.

Julia shook her head. "This is going to be difficult to explain."

"I did my best."

"You did, and I appreciate it." Julia took his arm. "Oh, well, it was bound to happen eventually. I'm just glad we were seen together at a tea shop instead of leaving a hotel."

"Brazen your way out of it," he advised. "Tell them you were using your feminine wiles to pump me for information."

She gave him a withering look.

"Not a good idea? Then you better stick to the story of my aunt."

"It doesn't really matter." Julia shrugged with an indifference she didn't feel. "They'll think what they want, and nothing I say will make a difference. I plan to ignore the whole thing."

"Good idea." David stopped outside the tube entrance. "I need to get back to Whitehall, but I want you to ring me tonight. And if you have any difficulties, I'll bring a signed affidavit perjuring myself and my aunt if it will help."

Julia forced a smile. "Everything will be all right." She stood on tiptoe and planted a farewell kiss on his cheek.

She only hoped that she was right.

Julia was closeted with Christabel for the rest of the afternoon, so she never knew whether Grace and Selena entertained the office with tales of her tearoom escapade. Julia felt as if she were walking around the office holding her breath all the next day, but no one said anything and she gradually relaxed.

Still, it was a pointed reminder that she was in a dangerous position as long as she continued to see David. She had to make a decision, soon.

Chapter 16

On Saturday morning David sat down to breakfast with his copy of *The Times* and scanned the headlines. His breath caught when he read about the demonstrations in Birmingham. According to the article, women had climbed roofs to throw stones at policemen, then broke their cell windows after being arrested. Julia had helped plan this? What in God's name had she been thinking?

When he finished reading, he was shaken. Was this the sort of thing Julia had been planning all summer, when he wasn't there making love to her? He prayed that she hadn't, that she wasn't responsible for this dangerous escalation of violence. It would only infuriate the public and the government. By upping the ante, the WSPU was daring the government to retaliate, and David didn't want to guess what would come next. Someone was going to get seriously hurt if they weren't careful.

Other articles in the paper were equally disturbing. Four women had been released from jail in Scotland, after fasting for four days. No doubt the women arrested in Birmingham would start a hunger strike as well, endangering their health and subverting the system of justice at the same time.

He couldn't understand their eagerness to bring such harm on themselves. How much longer would they continue this foolish course—until someone died? They'd have the perfect martyr for the cause, and David doubted it would change the mind of a single Member of Parliament. A few might rejoice that there was one less suffragette to contend with.

And it was only a matter of time before Julia waded into the fray again. He wished he could kidnap her, imprison her at the cottage until matters quieted down. He didn't want her risking her life climbing over slippery roofs, or chasing after motorcars, or starving herself in prison.

He wanted her here, with him, in this house.

David threw the paper down. Something had to be done to save these women from themselves, Julia included. But getting her to listen to reason wasn't going to be easy. Thank God she was meeting him for dinner tonight. He'd try to convince her to take care.

He worked on Home Office business for the rest of the afternoon until he was interrupted by the telephone. It was the Home Secretary, ordering David to an emergency meeting to deal with "the deplorable situation in Birmingham."

David sighed. He'd have to call Julia and tell her their dinner plans might be in jeopardy. If the meeting didn't drag on too long, they might be able to have a late supper, at least.

That would be better, anyway. He could bring her back to the house and convince her to spend the night again.

As he'd feared, the meeting at the Home Office was neither short nor pleasant, and by the time they'd hammered out a plan, everyone was exhausted and short-tempered.

David most of all. For the first time since he'd met Julia, his job put him in an awkward situation. He was sworn not to reveal the discussion tonight to anyone, least of all to one of the suffragettes. Yet he desperately wanted to warn her what was coming, to let her know that the government had had enough and was not going to tolerate any more disruptive behavior.

But he couldn't do that without compromising his word.

He found Julia waiting for him in his office when he arrived home. She looked right at home, curled up in a chair, reading a book.

"I thought it would be easier to wait for you here," she said.

"Good idea," he said, bending over to kiss her cheek. "The meeting ran late."

"I'm surprised they have you working on a Saturday night." She put her book aside and wrapped her arms around his neck. "What sort of important government decisions were you making?"

David shrugged, hoping she didn't feel the tension within him. "Routine Home Office things that we didn't have time to deal with during the week."

Julia gave him a lingering kiss. "Goodness, I'd hoped we missed dinner for something more important than that."

David pulled her close. "Don't worry, I'll make it up to you."

"Good."

Later, despite the fact that Julia was curled up asleep beside him, David was unable to drift off. Tonight's meeting had suddenly brought home in vivid detail the real difficulties involved in being with Julia. If any of the men in that meeting room had known she would be sleeping by his side now, they would have shown David the door.

It gnawed at him that he couldn't tell her what was coming. Not because he disagreed with the government plan; on the contrary, he agreed with Asquith and Gladstone that it was the only possible solution. He feared that Julia would get caught up in it before it became public news. It would be well over a week, at least, before anyone learned what was going on, and a lot could happen before then.

It wasn't going to be easy to persuade her to keep away from demonstrations without giving her a concrete reason. Could he convince her that she'd already earned enough campaign ribbons in prison, that she didn't have anything more to prove? It seemed that every new suffragette recruit was eager to be arrested; let them go instead. Julia should stick to her planning and writing.

Maybe she was already doing that. She hadn't participated in that horrible mess in Birmingham; maybe that was her new role. Ultimately, that might prove a problem as well, if the government decided to take on the WSPU as an organization, but for the time being, it would keep Julia out of jail.

And right now, that was what he wanted. He was no fool; he knew she would continue to participate in those insane hunger strikes if she was jailed. It was only a matter of time before someone died, and the government had to prevent that at all cost. They didn't want to create any martyrs for the cause. Tonight's decision would hopefully solve that problem.

David didn't want to think how the women would react to the new government plan. Or what Julia would say when she discovered David approved of it.

In the morning they sat in the parlor before a cozy fire, sipping tea after breakfast.

"I was rather appalled to read the newspaper accounts of the actions in Birmingham." David was nervous about introducing the subject, but knew he had to talk to her about it. "I hope you didn't know that things were going to go that far."

Julia stared at him. "Are you referring to that 'objective' report in *The Times*? The one that failed to mention the vicious police attacks on our people?"

"What can they expect if they're going to throw stones? Someone might have been hurt."

"The only people hurt were our women. They were careful not to hit anyone, but the police didn't bother to give them the same consideration." Her voice rose in anger. "And after being forced off the roof with fire hoses, they had to spend the night in the cells in their soaking wet clothes."

David understood her anger, but she had to see reason. "Lawbreakers don't have much cause to complain about their treatment."

Her eyes flashed. "A government that has to barricade

city streets and hold their meetings behind locked doors is not in a position to say who is breaking the law."

"Julia, this is a very serious matter." David strove to keep his voice calm. "It is one thing to hold protests; quite another to physically attack the police."

"The police show no reluctance to mistreat us," Julia retorted. "And as I said, we weren't attempting to hurt them, just disrupt the proceedings."

"Those women were hurling rocks at Asquith's car. What if they'd managed to hit him or the driver?"

"Perhaps it would knock some sense into both of them."

David jumped to his feet and angrily paced the room. "Julia, this isn't a laughing matter. People's lives are in danger now, and someone is going to get hurt."

"We've been told we don't have the strength to fling open the franchise door. Now, we're showing that we do."

"Do you have any more violent demonstrations planned?" he asked quickly.

Julia gave him an astonished look. "Are you asking that as a friend or as the Under Secretary?"

"Both."

"How dare you!" She stared at him, outraged. "Did they ask you to quiz me?"

"They don't even know I'm seeing you," he said.

"Don't ever ask me anything like that again, David. You know I cannot tell you."

"Then you are planning something."

He shivered at the cold stare she gave him.

"You'll just have to wait and see, won't you?" She set her cup down on the table and stood. "It's late; I need to be going."

"Julia, wait." He reached out for her.

She reached the door, then whirled on him. "Don't you ever presume on our friendship to spy for your masters, David. I thought better of you than that."

"I'm only asking for your own good," he said grimly. "The government isn't going to stand for this kind of violence."

"Then tell Asquith to give us the vote. We won't give up until we have it."

"Even if someone is hurt—or killed?"

"Many men have died for their political beliefs—women are no less capable."

"I don't want it to be you."

"I have a better sense of self-preservation than that," she said, and walked into the hall.

David didn't see her out—there was no reason. She was furious with him and he wasn't much happier with her. Julia might be very practical about some things, but when it came to the vote and the WSPU, she was too stubborn to listen to reason.

And his hands were tied. He didn't dare tell her enough to frighten her away from action, or he'd betray his position. And he knew nothing short of that would dissuade her.

He only prayed he could keep her out of trouble long enough for her to realize the consequences of what she was doing.

Julia hastened down the front stairs, eager to get as far away from David as possible. How dare he tell her what to do—and try to spy on the WSPU as well.

She'd made a great mistake in thinking that there was a way to live with their differences. Today, Julia had seen just how far apart they really were, and how unbridgeable that gap was.

It was obvious she couldn't see him again. Not unless he dropped his automatic support of each and every government action, and she didn't think he would. He was a *member* of that government, after all, a Cabinet Under Secretary, a man with political ambitions. He was more concerned with his own career than in doing what was right.

Riding home on the tube, she felt a sick sense of betrayal at his words earlier. He didn't care at all what she thought; he only wanted her to do what he considered was right.

The idea of telling her what to do! It was the one

thing she could never tolerate from a man. It meant he didn't trust her judgment, wanted to think for her, force her to submit her mind as well as her body to him.

That she refused to do.

At least one good thing had come out of this—it wasn't going to be difficult to stop seeing David. She didn't care if she ever set eyes on him again.

Julia reacted with outrage when she read a telegram from Birmingham on Monday. The harsh sentences given the protesters stunned the entire office. Three months hard labor for the leaders!

Was this what David had tried to warn her about yesterday?

The thought of calling him was tempting. She wanted to tell him just what she thought of this latest government tactic—for she knew the government had ordered the Birmingham judges to impose such harsh sentences.

The prisoners, of course, would have the last laugh. They were probably at the prison right now, preparing to refuse their first meal. Five women on hunger strike at one time. They wouldn't get much hard labor out of them, she thought mirthlessly.

The only question was how long they would have to wait before their release. Two days? Three? The WSPU in Birmingham was ready and waiting with the nourishing gruel the women needed after fasting for several days. All depended on the prison officials, and the strength of the women in prison.

She still felt a twinge of regret that she hadn't been there, that she was free while Mary Leigh and Charlotte Marsh were bravely enduring their ordeal. But Christabel promised Julia that her time would come—in an action that would make Birmingham look like a garden party.

With a sigh, Julia turned back to the letter she was preparing for the newspapers, protesting the harsh sentences handed down in Birmingham. The WSPU wasn't going to let this go unnoticed. Plans for the next big demonstration in London were coming together, and this would only give them further ammunition.

Julia would show David that she had a mind of her own, and government threats wouldn't deter her.

Yet despite her anger and her resolve not to see him, he was never far from her mind. Knowing he was in London, only a scant twenty minutes away, created an insidious tendril of temptation. In her weak moments, she thought about going to him, confronting him and forcing him to admit that her position was right.

But if she saw him again, she was more likely to fall into his arms than attack his opinions. Until she could control her physical reaction to him, she had to stay away.

Thursday morning Julia sat at her desk, scanning the proof sheet for the next issue of *Votes*. Yawning, she wished she had a cup of tea. Everyone had been putting in long hours all week.

It didn't help that her sleep was disrupted by thoughts of David. She missed him with a deep ache, fought constantly against her desire to see him.

One of the new office girls stuck her head in the office. "This telegram just arrived for you," she said.

Puzzled, Julia took it, wondering who would be sending her a telegram. She read it quickly.

Lady Marchmont was dead.

Her face must have reflected her feelings when she read the words, for the office girl offered to run and get her a cup of tea.

Lady Marchmont was dead.

Tears welled up in her eyes. That wonderful, modern lady was dead.

Julia glanced back at the telegram. It was terse and to the point.

AUNT DIED SUDDENLY. FUNERAL SATURDAY.
PLEASE COME. I NEED YOU. DK

Julia gratefully accepted the tea from the girl and sipped the hot brew while she tried to think. There was nothing pressing on her schedule, no meetings or sessions she couldn't miss.

The question was, did she dare go?

With the funeral on Saturday, it would be easy to travel down on the morning train and come back the same day. It would be the smartest thing to do; she wouldn't have to spend that much time with David.

But the words on the paper tore at her. "I need you." She knew what he meant, because she needed him, too.

Julia made up her mind. If David needed her, she would be there. She couldn't get out of here tomorrow, but she'd leave early Saturday morning. And if he wanted her to stay, she would.

Her packing Friday night was interrupted by a knock on the door. Beryl again.

"I hear you are going out of town for a few days," Beryl said in a snide tone.

"Lady Marchmont died and I'm going down for the funeral." Julia folded a blouse.

"For the funeral, or to soothe the grief of her nearest relative?" Beryl's suspicious eyes watched her closely.

"I hope to offer some comfort to Mr. Kimbrough. He loved his aunt dearly."

"I don't think she's the only one he loves." A scrap of paper dangled from Beryl's fingers. "You can't expect a telegram to remain private in this office."

"Think what you will," Julia said. "Lady Marchmont was very good to me—and to the WSPU—and I want to pay my respects."

"Oh, I see nothing wrong with that." Beryl smiled slyly. "In fact, I think we should send a Union deputation to the funeral. We can all travel down together."

"No."

"Oh? Will it interfere with your plans?" She gave Julia's bag a pointed look. "Surely, you don't need all that for such a short trip."

"I may stay. I'm sure there are things I can do."

"Like warm that man's bed?"

Shaking with anger, Julia whirled on Beryl. "I don't have to listen to your insinuations. This is my room and I suggest you leave. Now."

Shrugging, Beryl turned toward the door. "I'll see you tomorrow. Save a place for us at the church."

Julia fought the urge to slam the door behind her. The worse thing was, Beryl was right. If Lady Marchmont's death was the only reason, Julia wouldn't want to stay.

But it wasn't Lady Marchmont she worried about, it was David. Julia's heart ached for him, knowing how bereft he must feel. Despite his teasing ways, Julia knew he'd adored and deeply admired his aunt. Her death must have come as a great blow. If Julia could bring him some small mote of comfort, she wanted to be there.

Political differences, Home Office policies, and even the worry over discovery paled beside her need to go to him and help him through his grief.

Before leaving London, Julia telegraphed Cranwood to say she was coming. A somber-faced Robbie met her at the station with the cart.

"Thank you for coming," Julia said as she climbed in.

" 'Twon't be the same without her," Robbie said.

Julia agreed.

They drove to the house in silence. When the cart pulled up in front of the house, Julia grabbed her bag and started up the stairs. She raised her hand to knock when the door was pulled open and David stood there. He stopped and looked at her.

His face was drawn and pale, with dark circles under his eyes. Julia ached for his pain.

"Thank you for coming," he said quietly.

Julia flung herself into his arms.

Chapter 17

David held her tightly for several minutes without saying a word. Finally, he released her and held her at arm's length, staring at her as if he couldn't believe she was here. Pain etched his face.

"Oh, David, I am so very sorry. What happened?"

"It was that damned cold. Turned into pneumonia and I didn't even know it." His eyes filled with guilt. "I should have come down and made sure she was all right."

She squeezed his arm, remembering that they'd planned to come down last weekend, until her work interfered. "You can't hold yourself responsible. I'm sure the doctor did all he could."

"But to have her die alone like this . . ." With a sigh, David ran a hand through his hair. "Some of the family is here—in the drawing room, with the other guests. Come meet them."

"Is there anything I can help you with?"

He shook his head. "Everything is taken care of. She wanted things to be simple. There's to be a short service at the church and then people will come back here for refreshments—the church ladies took care of all that." He looked at her closely. "You will stay, won't you?"

Julia nodded.

David took her hand and they walked slowly up the stairs to the drawing room. When they entered the familiar blue and gold chamber, David clasped her elbow and guided her to a group of guests clustered around the far window.

"You may as well get the worst over with first," he

whispered to her. "Everyone, I'd like you to meet Miss Julia Sydney, a particular favorite of Lady Marchmont's. Julia, this is Castledown, my cousin."

Julia held out her hand to the marquess, who looked startled for a moment, then took it. He had David's piercing blue eyes, but was shorter, stouter, and darker than his cousin.

"Lady Hawley, my father's sister." David continued with the introductions. "And here we have the remnants of the Marchmont clan—Sir James and Lady Woodfern, and Gerald Wheatley."

Their greetings were all polite but Julia had the feeling they all knew who she was—and wondered why she was here.

"I'd like a cup of tea," Julia said to David.

"I'll get it."

She put a hand on his arm. "You stay with your guests. I can manage."

Relieved to escape the frank curiosity of David's relatives, Julia poured herself a cup of tea and stood back, watching the other guests.

Her fears about being alone with David today were groundless—he had a house full of mourners to deal with and didn't have time to worry about her. She relaxed a fraction. This wasn't going to be such an ordeal after all.

Julia watched David chatting politely with his relatives, amazed at his composure. His face bore an expression of bewilderment, as if he still couldn't believe what had happened. It was a natural reaction to death and Julia's heart ached for him. A part of her wanted to take him in her arms and cradle him against her breasts like a small hurt child.

But if she reached out to him, she might cause herself pain as well. Knowing that they couldn't go on together, because David would never understand her commitment to the suffrage fight, she vowed to keep him at arm's length, if only to protect herself.

A few more guests arrived, and it was nearing half past one when David announced the carriages had arrived to take them to the church. Julia filed out of the room with the others, but at the last minute, David touched her arm and drew her back.

"Will you ride with me?" he asked.

The imploring look in his eyes made it impossible for her to say no, despite her fear of being alone with him. Relief filled her when she saw that the marquess was riding with them as well. They wouldn't be able to talk privately.

In deference to the solemn occasion, the line of carriages moved in a slow, orderly procession through the village and halted in front of the old stone church with its square Norman tower. The number of carriages already parked outside surprised Julia. For a simple funeral, it was well attended.

Their carriage rolled to a halt and David climbed down, clapped on his top hat, then helped Julia out.

"Would you care to sit with me?" David asked softly as they walked toward the entrance.

It was the last thing Julia wanted to do, but she recognized the lines of strain around his eyes and knew that he was barely under control. If her presence brought him some comfort, she would willingly stay with him.

The church was half filled, the men in somber suits and the ladies in dark colors. Julia hoped it pleased David to see how many had come to pay their final respects to Lady Marchmont.

She followed him up the narrow aisle, then nearly stumbled in shock when she caught a glimpse of the three women in the nearest pew. Beryl, Selena, and Grace. Beryl gave her a smirking look and Julia quickly turned away.

Let them think what they liked. Right now, she didn't care.

The front of the church overflowed with flowers, but Julia had no trouble recognizing the enormous wreath sent by the WSPU, with its distinctive white, green, and purple ribbons. For a minute she smiled. Lady Marchmont would have liked that.

Taking her seat beside David in the family pew, she

gave him an encouraging smile and he squeezed her fingers. The service was mercifully short. Julia darted glances at David, sitting so rigidly beside her, his face deceptively impassive. The marquess read the lesson and then David rose to give a short eulogy. Julia clenched her hands until her fingers hurt as she watched him struggle to retain his composure as he spoke about his beloved great-aunt. When he was finished, she wanted to dash forward and hold him in her arms.

Instead, she slipped her hand in his when he sat down next to her again.

After the minister pronounced the benediction, the family mourners filed out of the church. A light drizzle had started and someone handed Julia an umbrella. David stood in the doorway, bareheaded, shaking hands with the local mourners as they filed out. Most of them would be coming to the house later, but David wanted to express his thanks now.

Beryl and the other Union members were the last to leave the church. Julia gulped in dismay when she saw them approaching.

"Are you returning to London with us?" Beryl asked Julia, pointedly glancing at David. "The train leaves in half an hour."

Julia took in a deep breath. "I'm going back to the house with the family."

David stepped closer and pressed his palm against the small of her back, giving her courage.

"Suit yourself. I'm sure Christabel will be impressed with your devotion." Beryl gave David a disparaging look, then walked away.

"I didn't expect *them* to be here," David whispered to Julia. "Does this mean more trouble for you?"

"Beryl is always causing trouble," Julia replied.

"Would you like to leave now?" he asked.

"No," she replied firmly. "I'm not going to let her, or anyone else, guide my behavior."

He patted her on the shoulder. "That's my Jules."

Lady Marchmont had requested there be no graveside

service, so they walked back to the carriage for the short ride to the house.

While they'd been at the church, servants borrowed from the neighbors had laid out the food in an impressive array in the drawing room. Long tables were heaped with hot dishes, cold meats, fruits, vegetables, and plates upon plates of cakes and biscuits. Lady Marchmont's own staff had been given the day off to attend the service, and were holding their own wake below stairs.

Someone handed her a plate of food. Julia nibbled at it but she didn't have much appetite.

Her feeling of awkwardness was more pronounced now that the funeral was over. The wall that had been erected between her and David after that last argument in London was still there, making conversation with him awkward. And if earlier she'd feared to talk with him, now she wished she could, but with all the guests they wouldn't have the chance.

Seeing him here reminded her of all they'd shared, the deep joy and pleasure he'd brought her. Was there some way they could recapture that?

She should go back to London, before she succumbed to temptation.

Just as she had made up her mind to do so, David caught her eye from across the room and motioned for her to join him. She followed him out into the hall.

"God, I don't think I could endure another minute in there," he said, loosening his tie. "Come, let's hide in the library. I've some things to discuss with you."

Julia followed him down the stairs to the airy, first-floor room. David poured them each a glass of whiskey and they settled into the comfortable leather chairs. A fire burned in the grate and the room was warm and cozy.

"I met with my aunt's solicitor yesterday. I'm executor of the estate," David said.

"Is that going to be a great deal of work?" Julia asked.

David smiled wryly. "Hardly. Oh, she had a number of tiny bequests, to friends, and servants, and the like.

But the bulk of the estate goes to me. Including the house."

"Oh, David, how sweet of her." Julia smiled at him. "She knew how much this place meant to you."

"I only wonder how often I'll be able to come down," he said gloomily. "She left some money for the WSPU, as well. It'll be a few weeks before all the legal details are taken care of, but you'll have the funds when they're available."

She couldn't resist the impulse to tease him. "What? You aren't going to challenge that bequest?"

The ghost of a smile flitted across his face. "No. But that isn't all. She gave you a life tenancy on the cottage."

Julia stared at him. "What?"

"It's yours to use as you wish—for yourself alone, or as a refuge for your suffragette friends."

"I can't believe she would do a thing like that." Tears pricked at Julia's eyes. "What a generous lady."

"Technically, I'll be your landlord; the estate is in charge of any repairs or improvements." He gave her a pointed look. "So if you want to install a cooking stove, I will do it."

Julia laughed. "Not unless you install a cook with it."

Setting down his drink, David took her hand. "I can't tell you how much it means to me that you came, Julia." His look turned apprehensive. "I wasn't sure you would."

"Of course I would come. I liked your aunt very much." Julia paused, then took a deep breath. "And I didn't want you to be alone through all of this."

His eyes filled with longing.

Julia went to him and he pulled her onto his lap, wrapping his arms around her. Nestling her head against his shoulder, Julia felt a jolt of surprise at how comforting it felt to be in his arms again.

"It's funny, but somehow, I always thought of her as indestructible." David's voice trembled. "Even in the last few years, when she was growing frailer, I thought sure she'd outlive us all."

"I don't think she minded going." Julia wanted to

soothe his grief. "It must be sad, to be the last one of your generation left. I admire her for keeping up on things, instead of retreating into her memories."

"She always had a new cause or theory that she was supporting."

"Are you going to make your home here, now?" Julia held her breath, waiting for his answer. It might make all the difference . . .

"I honestly don't know; it's all too sudden." David looked thoughtful. "I can't be here during Parliament, of course, but other times . . . Yet that means the place stands empty for over half the year."

Julia gave him a hesitant look. "Do you mind about the cottage?"

"Mind? I think it's marvelous." His arm tightened around her. "I only wish there was some way to keep you there all the time."

She sighed. "Like you, my work is in London."

"Have you thought about what I said—about not getting arrested again?"

Frowning, Julia tried to choose her words carefully. "David, you know I can't promise you that. I will do what I think is right."

Concern crossed his face. "I don't want you getting hurt."

"It's not as though I haven't been through it all before." She smiled wryly. "A hunger strike isn't very pleasant, but at least you get out of prison quickly."

"But what happens when the day comes that they don't release you?"

"They will," Julia said without hesitation. "You know they won't risk anyone dying; the scandal would be enormous."

"You can't tell me the WSPU wouldn't welcome a martyr."

Willing herself to remain silent, Julia didn't reply. She didn't want to argue politics with David. Not today.

"Do you think you should get back to your guests?"

Shrugging, David picked up his glass. "They don't need me. There's plenty of food and liquor." He ran a hand along her arm. "Did you know those Union ladies were coming?"

"I thought they might. Your telegram made the rounds at the office."

He winced. "It was thoughtful of them to attend, but I wonder if they were here because of my aunt, or you?"

"It really doesn't matter," Julia said.

"Are they giving you a lot of grief about me?"

Closing her eyes, Julia shook her head. "Not openly—but there is an undercurrent of distrust and suspicion that was never there before."

Her words dismayed David. It would be just like Julia to participate in some violent protest just to prove her loyalty to the WSPU. And if she did, it would be his fault.

"You shouldn't have come, then," he said flatly, determined to correct his mistake. "I'll see that you get to the six o'clock train."

Julia ran a finger across his cheek. "I came because I wanted to, David."

He gazed deeply into her eyes, hoping to read her thoughts. "Will you stay?" he asked hoarsely. "For the night?"

She nodded silently.

He tightened his arm around her. "Thank you."

At the discreet tap on the door, Julia slipped off David's lap and he reluctantly went to answer it. The butler needed him to say good-bye to the departing guests.

"People are leaving," David said apologetically to Julia. "Do you want to stay here?"

She nodded.

The mourners couldn't leave soon enough for David. He wanted them all out of the house, so he could be alone with Julia at last.

Within half an hour, everyone was gone, and he hurried back to the library. Julia sat in the chair, staring into the fire.

"They're all gone," he said. "Finally."

He stood in front of her and held out his hand, his need suddenly overpowering. "Come upstairs with me."

Silently he led her out the door, up the stairs to the room that had always been his. David shut and locked the door, then turned to her.

"I need you," he said simply.

Her eyes answered yes.

Undressing her with special tenderness, he laid her across the snowy white sheets while he ripped off his own clothes. He needed to make love to her now, to soothe his grief and ease his anger at failing his aunt. And to try to repair the breach between him and Julia.

Julia must have sensed his need, for the moment he took her in his arms, she took the lead. He sucked in his breath as her fingers danced over his chest, firing his blood. A low moan of pleasure slipped from his lips when her tongue lapped at his nipples, turning them into hard pebbles that she eagerly sucked.

And he nearly jumped off the bed when her mouth and hands moved lower, tickling him, teasing him, until he strained in pleasurable agony. When she took him in her mouth, he cried aloud.

He wanted to touch her, to pleasure her, but he couldn't move, could barely breathe as she skillfully drove him toward climax. Willingly, he surrendered to her touch as rising waves of heat washed over him.

"Julia." Her name was torn from his throat as the end came.

He had to make her understand how much he needed her. Not just now, but always. Somehow, he must convince her that they could reach an agreement about their work, because he couldn't bear the thought of being apart from her. This last week had been agony.

But how could he fight against the power of an organization and an idea? Julia fervently believed in the work she was doing, the cause she fought for. Her way wasn't the only way; there were other avenues of protest that didn't involve deliberately breaking the law, taunting the government in the process. Why couldn't she join one of the less radical organizations?

Because Julia was a woman of action. Anything less

would chaff at her. Yet a reconciliation was impossible if she continued to fight violently against the government.

He wished they could go back to the carefree days of summer, when they'd successfully ignored all those problems. But unless they hid forever in the country, they would have to face reality. And until—or unless—they worked out a compromise, last week's dispute would grow, and fester, until it became permanent.

He'd have to call on all his persuasive powers to get Julia to listen to him. The government wasn't going to tolerate further violence, wasn't going to turn a blind eye toward the hunger strikes any longer. For her own safety, she had to stop.

Even then he couldn't be sure that she would be willing to compromise. Yet he had to try, because the alternative was too unbearable to contemplate. He didn't want to give her up.

But David didn't want to discuss it with her now, either. He wanted to pretend, for a little while longer, that everything was all right.

Even if he avoided the subject, the unspoken words hung between them while they ate a late supper of food left over from the funeral party, while they talked about everything except politics and their future. Julia seemed to be trying as hard as he to make things seem normal.

After an awkward supper, Julia took David's hand and led him back to the bedroom. Here, at least, they were in complete accord. As long as they were making love, they couldn't think about their disagreements. In bed, nothing between them had changed.

In the morning David assumed she would go back to London, and Julia was grateful he didn't try to persuade her to stay. She sensed they both realized the present fragility of their relationship and didn't want to endanger it. Right now, it was safer for them to be apart.

David drove Julia to the train.

"I'm hoping to be back to London tomorrow, or Tuesday at the latest," he said as they stood on the platform. "I'll ring you when I arrive."

"Please do," Julia said.

He stood awkwardly, hands stuffed in his pockets. "We need to talk, Jules."

"I know. But it can wait. You have enough things to worry about now." She smiled brightly, trying to convey an optimism she wasn't sure she felt. "There'll be time for that later."

"Don't let those women give you a hard time about me," he warned her. "Remind them of that nice, fat check they are going to receive as soon as the estate is settled."

She laughed lightly. "Trying to bribe your way into their good graces?"

"If it helps me with you, I'll do anything," he said with bald-faced honesty.

Julia kissed him on the cheek. "I hope I'll talk with you tomorrow. Take care, David." She climbed aboard the train and took her seat.

As the train sped toward London, Julia stared out the window, but she wasn't watching the landscape. She was thinking of David.

How could she reconcile her love for him with their conflicts over suffrage?

Momentarily, she hoped that with Lady Marchmont's estate, David might resign from Parliament and take on the life of a country landowner. But she instantly recognized that as a futile hope. Julia knew David too well; he wasn't going to give up his political ambitions—any more than she'd give up her suffrage work.

No, they had to come to some arrangement over their differences. But with David working in the hated Home Office, the prospects appeared dim. She didn't want to confront him now, not while he was grief-stricken over Lady Marchmont's death. Some time apart would do them both good. There was no guarantee that they would be able to work things out, but after the joy she felt in seeing David again, Julia hoped they could find a way out of this maze.

She entered Clement's Inn with an air of optimism.

The office was full of people, unusual for a Sunday afternoon.

"Julia, Julia, have you heard the horrible news?"

Julia looked up as Katherine waved to her from across the room. "No, what happened?"

"In Birmingham. They're forcing food on the women."

"What?" Julia dropped her satchel. "Where did you hear this?"

"Rumors were flying on Friday, but we didn't receive confirmation until yesterday. Christabel has all the details."

"My God." Julia ran out of the office, searching for Christabel.

"Ah, Julia, I see you've heard the news." Beryl smiled grimly as Julia met her in the hall. "Government terrorism knows no limit, it seems."

Julia sagged against the wall. "This is horrible. How could the prison authorities in Birmingham take it upon themselves to—?"

"Oh, don't be silly. Something as important as this wasn't decided in Birmingham. It had to have come directly from the Home Office."

Julia's stomach clenched at the thought. The Home Office. Where David was Under Secretary. Had he known about this, played a part in it—and not said a word to her?

The veiled warnings he'd uttered last week, and again last night, flashed through her mind and she suddenly felt sick. He must have known. "What do the prison officials say?" she asked wearily.

Beryl shook her head. "They refuse to say anything. Christabel spoke with Keir Hardie a few minutes ago and he plans to raise the issue in Parliament tomorrow."

"Have you talked with any of our people in Birmingham? Do they know anything more?"

"It's all very confused—naturally, they aren't letting anyone see the prisoners. But word leaked out and they contacted us as soon as they heard."

"What are we going to do?"

Beryl's eyes twinkled in anticipation. "Can you imagine what the public will say when they learn that the government is torturing women prisoners? Why, the Tsar's brutalities pale by comparison."

"We must find out how this came about." Julia frantically considered their options. "Has anyone been able to reach Gladstone?"

"Do you think he would talk with us?" Beryl laughed. "We're trying to send some solicitors into the prison to find out what is going on." Beryl paused and eyed Julia smugly. "I think you can help us there."

"Me? How?"

"Why, with your excellent contacts at the Home Office, you are in a good position to find out what is going on."

Of course. David. Beryl wanted her to talk to David. Julia knew something like this would happen before long. A test of her loyalty, a chance to prove she hadn't become a traitor.

But Julia was just as eager to talk to him herself. To find out if he'd known, and not told her; to find out if he'd known, and approved.

"He's not coming back until tomorrow at the earliest," Julia said. "But don't worry, I'll talk to him. I want some answers, too."

"Did he say anything to you about this?"

Julia glared at her. "If he had, don't you think I would have said something?"

"Some women do strange things when there's a man involved."

"I would never let a relationship with a man interfere with my suffrage work." Julia gave her a cold stare. "*Never.*"

"Good." Beryl started down the hall, then halted and turned around. "Just be sure that you remember that in the future."

Her blatant accusation stunned Julia. It was what she'd feared all along—that she would be suspected because of her friendship with David. Which was particularly ironic right now, because if she discovered he'd known about this terrible situation in Birmingham, she wanted his head delivered on a platter.

Only her knowledge of David's fragile mood kept her from dashing back to the station and jumping on the train to Cranwood. She'd allow him to take care of Lady Marchmont's affairs and return to town.

But she wouldn't wait one minute longer. Julia had to know if he had been involved in developing this policy.

If he had, she would never forgive him.

Chapter 18

By Monday morning Julia was so full of rage she could hardly concentrate on the letter she was writing to the papers. As more details filtered in from Birmingham, the more shocked and appalled she grew.

What the government euphemistically called "hospital treatment" was nothing short of torture. What else could you call it when women were held down and had a tube shoved down their throat? It was hard to believe that such barbarism had surfaced here in England, the most civilized of all countries.

For Julia, it only showed the government's blatant disdain for women. Forced feeding was a process reserved for only the sickest of lunatics, who were incapable of feeding themselves.

Today, at least, Keir Hardie, the Labour MP who actively supported women's suffrage, would demand some answers when Commons met. But Julia hoped David would return before then and she could get some answers for herself. She rang both his house and the Home Office, but no one answered.

The wait frustrated her. She wanted to know now who'd approved this brutality—and especially wanted to know if David had been involved.

Finally, by midafternoon, she couldn't wait any longer. Julia took the tube across London to David's Belgravia house. His man pulled open the door.

"Is David here?" she asked anxiously.

"Just back within the hour."

"I need to see him now."

The man gave her an odd look, but started to take her up the stairs.

"I can find him myself, thank you." Julia brushed past him and dashed down the carpeted hall to David's office. She pushed open the door and saw him seated at his desk, thumbing through some papers.

His eyes lit up when he spotted her and he jumped to his feet, holding out his arms to her.

"Julia! What a surprise." He smiled broadly. "I hadn't even had the chance to call you—how did you know I was here?"

"I was hoping you were," she said icily.

He stepped toward her but Julia moved away. She didn't want him to touch her, not until she knew the whole story. Not until she knew the role he played.

"Who ordered the forced feeding of the hunger strikers in Birmingham?" she asked bluntly.

His expression clouded. "Where did you hear that?"

"Don't give me the official Home Office denial, David. We know what's happening; Keir Hardie is bringing it before Parliament this afternoon." She watched him intently. "Did you know about this? Do you know who ordered it?"

A tense silence fell.

"I can't tell you," he said finally.

His words hit her like a blow. He knew—had known earlier and hadn't told her. "You can't, or won't?"

"Both."

Her eyes narrowed. "But you admit that it is happening?"

David's face remained impassive. "I admit nothing, Julia. You'll have to direct your questions to the Minister."

"Damn it, David, those women are being tortured! It's positively medieval. Forced feeding is something that's used on lunatics, not political prisoners. I can't believe the government would order such a thing."

His eyes grew cold. "You have to question the sanity of people who won't voluntarily take food."

She couldn't believe this was David saying these

things. "I refused to eat when I was in prison. Do you think I'm insane?"

David sighed wearily. "No. Misguided, perhaps, but not insane." He studied her intently for a moment. "Would you rather these women died? No, don't bother to answer; of course you do. Then you would have a martyr for the 'glorious cause.' "

"If anyone dies, it will be the fault of the government. We are political prisoners, not common criminals."

Lunging at her, David grabbed her arms, his fingers tightening. "Don't be an ass, Julia. Those women were arrested for committing physical violence. They threw rocks and roof slates, broke windows, resisted arrest. If those aren't criminal acts, I don't know what are."

Julia pulled out of his grip. "What about the police? They turned water hoses on the women. Hardly the act of a humane government."

"If someone had been pitching roof slates at me, I don't think I'd be inclined to be very sympathetic, either."

"The police threw things as well—and didn't care who they hit." Her voice rose in fury. "Several women were hurt and bleeding, while not a single policeman was injured."

"If you're going to resort to violence, you have to expect violence in return."

His calm manner infuriated her even more. "That might make sense in Tsarist Russia, but England is a country of laws—laws the government is violating."

"Julia, I'm not going to argue with you about the righteousness of your cause."

She clenched the back of the chair until her knuckles were white. "Did the Home Office order the forced feedings?"

"I am not at liberty to say."

"But you knew about it, didn't you? Knew and didn't tell me." She laughed harshly. "Funny, how I thought *I* would be the one who chose work over our relationship. You're more coldhearted than I thought."

"The government has an obligation to protect its citizens."

"Protect? Don't make me sick, David." Julia waved an angry finger under his nose. "The government isn't going to get away with this. Public sentiment will be on our side."

"Suicide is a felony," David said evenly. "It's within the government's right to prevent it."

"A government made up of and elected by only one sex cannot purport to speak for *all* the people."

"It's the only government we have," David said. "Change it, if you must, but you have to work within the law."

"We tried that," she said bitterly. "Did it accomplish anything?"

"Then maybe the time isn't right."

"When will the time be right? In the next generation? Or two or three? We will not wait that long."

David slammed his hand on his desk. "Then as long as you insist on breaking the law, you'll be sent to jail. And if you continue this mad policy of hunger striking, you'll be fed to prevent your death. The government isn't going to cower before your violent tactics, Julia."

She regarded him with utter loathing. "I can't believe that I actually thought there was a streak of humanity in you, David. I've never been more wrong about a person in my life."

"I'm doing my job, Julia." His eyes pleaded with her. "Try to understand."

"And I'm doing mine. Be prepared."

With that, she turned on her heel and left the room.

It made her skin crawl to think that she had thought—even for a moment—she was in love with that man. He wasn't a man; he was a government lackey who couldn't think or act for himself.

Julia wondered what his aunt would have said about David's involvement in this heinous crime.

Reaching the street, she gulped in air, cleansing her lungs of the air from David's house, the stench of his betrayal. For that's what it was—betrayal. There was no better word to describe his actions.

During the ride back to Clement's Inn, Julia began

planning for an all-out attack on the Home Office, and the men within it. The people must learn what the government was doing to its citizens. The newspapers must be contacted, picketers organized, protests planned.

Julia smiled grimly to herself. She'd wanted to get involved in some action—this was her chance. It would be her personal answer to David.

David sat at his desk, a dark frown on his face.

How had those damn women found out about Birmingham so fast? Gladstone thought it would take a week or more for the news to get out.

Now the Home Office had to convince the public that the government was doing the right thing. It shouldn't be too hard. Noble sentiments about how the government couldn't allow prisoners to commit suicide, they were doing the humanitarian thing by feeding them, and so on. Public opinion would be with their decision, he knew.

But he couldn't forget the look of horror in Julia's eyes when she'd realized that he knew what was going on. She wouldn't understand that he'd supported the move because of her, that he was only trying to save her from herself. He didn't want Julia to be the first suffragette to starve herself to death in prison.

She resented his attempt to protect her, but he couldn't sit by and watch her destroy herself. If she wouldn't act sensibly, someone had to do it for her. Even if it widened their estrangement. Her life was the most important thing.

Wearily David reached for the phone. He needed to call the Secretary and let him know the WSPU was fully informed. He would want to have an official response ready before the question period in Parliament.

The WSPU offices were buzzing with activity when Julia returned.

Beryl accosted her the moment she stepped through the door. "Did you see Kimbrough? What did you find out?" Beryl asked her eagerly.

"Very little—officially, the government is saying nothing." Julia grimaced at the memory of his evasive replies. "But I am certain they authorized the feedings. They're afraid someone will die and create a 'martyr for the cause.' "

"That's all we need to know," Beryl said brusquely. "We must make plans."

Julia sat down. "I have some ideas . . ."

By the following morning, the entire country read that the Birmingham prisoners were being forcibly fed in a manner that varied from "humane" to "barbaric," depending on the political views of the reporting paper. Julia found the editorial in *The Times* particularly repellent. Arguing that women had been using the hunger strike to defy the law and reduce their prison sentences, it applauded the new measure that would keep them in jail.

WSPU meetings were scheduled in London, Middlesbrough, and Manchester to protest the action. Keir Hardie and other suffragette sympathizers continued to confront the government representatives in the House of Commons, forcing them to admit that the Home Office had ordered the procedure.

Protests flooded the newspapers, including letters from numerous doctors, who warned of the procedure's danger.

The government paid no attention to the arguments and protests. The official line was the forced feeding had to be done in order "to prevent them from committing the felony of suicide." The same words David had used.

Julia longed to be in Birmingham, to see for herself what was going on. But the prison officials refused to allow anyone to see the prisoners—even their solicitors. Pleas from friends and family were ignored, since their concerns were about medical matters, not legal business.

"It's frightening to think that this kind of thing can be happening in our own country," Lady Mary said to Julia as they worked on the text of another editorial letter.

"The government is merely showing their true colors." Julia tinkered with a phrase. "First they treat us as common criminals, instead of political prisoners; now we're classified as insane. I wouldn't be surprised if they start deporting us."

"They wouldn't do a thing like that," Lady Mary protested.

"They'll try to suppress our demonstrations next," Julia said. "They won't be happy until they've stifled every avenue of protest."

Beryl joined them. "They'll have to send every last one of us to jail to achieve that. We have to take stronger action. Attack Gladstone, your friend Kimbrough, and everyone associated with the Home Office."

"The Home Office didn't decide this on their own," Julia said. "The entire government must bear responsibility."

"What if we appeal to the King?" Lady Mary asked. "Surely, he doesn't want his female subjects to suffer like this."

"Our best hope is with the public—we must make sure they know exactly what is going on," Julia insisted. "If the protests are loud enough, the government will have to back down."

"I think the legal avenue is the best way to go," Lady Mary argued. "They've already violated prison rules by refusing to allow the solicitors in."

"We're preparing a lawsuit, but that takes time," Beryl said. "We need something dramatic to arouse public indignation. Massive demonstrations in London and other cities."

"Birmingham must be included," Julia said. "We must have protesters outside the prison night and day."

Beryl nodded. "Do you want to go up and help them organize that, Mary?"

"Yes," she replied eagerly.

"Good." Beryl turned to Julia. "I still think we must go after the main targets—Asquith, Gladstone, and Kimbrough."

"Why not the entire Cabinet? They all must bear responsibility."

"Do we have enough people?" Lady Mary asked.

"New recruits are arriving in droves since the forced feedings were announced. A great many men included."

"Let's send them after the Cabinet," Julia said. "They won't be suspected and could get close enough to have a real effect."

"Good idea." Beryl glanced at her watch. "Christabel is due back in half an hour. Can we have a plan on paper by then?"

Julia nodded. "Mary, find out who can go with you to Birmingham. I imagine they have enough people there to cover the prison, but they'll appreciate a show of support from London. Have one of the secretaries bring me a list of the men we can count on."

Lady Mary left Julia's office, but Beryl remained.

"Have you seen the light about your friend Kimbrough, now?"

Julia had no intention of giving Beryl the satisfaction of knowing what she felt about David.

"I wonder just exactly what went on with you two." Beryl leaned forward, a nasty look in her eyes. "Tell me, Julia, were you lovers? What was it like sleeping with the enemy?"

"You know how Christabel detests gossip." Julia looked at her sternly. "Our goal is to win the vote, you know. I suggest you direct your energy to that effort."

Beryl slammed the door shut behind her.

The woman was a man-hating witch, Julia thought. She would have made an enthusiastic puritan, delighting in preventing everyone from having any fun.

It didn't help a bit that Julia was bitterly disappointed with David. She had expected more from him, a sign that he at least respected her positions, even if he didn't agree with them. But his actions on the forced-feeding issue showed that he didn't care a fig for what she thought.

Why did they have to be on opposite sides about this? She'd hoped, when she'd gone to him today, that he would be as horrified and appalled as she. If he'd shown any sign of abhorrence at the forced feedings, she could forgive him for having known about the policy change.

But instead of shock, he'd admitted he agreed with the atrocious action.

Julia realized that she knew far less about him than she'd thought. They'd made a pact not to discuss politics, and in retrospect, that had been a mistake. She would have discovered much sooner the type of man he was, would have sent him on his way.

And wouldn't have fallen in love with him.

That was why his attitude hurt even worse.

He was a politician, after all, and he wasn't going to do anything that would jeopardize his rise to the top.

Had he given any thought to how this was going to affect her? He knew she'd staged a hunger strike during her last stay in prison—did he think she'd behave differently the next time she was arrested?

Of course not. Which meant he didn't care whether she was tortured by her jailers. Pleasing his superiors, protecting his political career, was more important.

Thank God she'd discovered his true nature before she'd made a complete fool of herself. Julia had been filled with regret ever since they'd argued; had lain awake nights thinking over his words, wondering if they could make amends. After Lady Marchmont's funeral, she thought it might be possible.

But now, she had no desire to. She couldn't love a man who'd approved of torturing prisoners.

Julia was more determined than ever to be arrested—the sooner the better. And she would make certain that David knew about it—and that she was going to be tortured in prison because of him.

Perhaps it would cause him a few restless nights.

David knew better than to try to ring up Julia. After she'd stormed out of his house on Monday, he knew it would take time for her anger to settle. Fortunately, time was all he could give her right now. They were entering the final phase of the finance bill discussions, and he was busier than ever.

Everyone in the government waited anxiously to see what the suffragettes would do. So far, they'd confined their anger to writing letters, and pushing for visits to the prisoners in Birmingham. David thought it had been an error on Gladstone's part to keep family members from visiting the prisoners, but his opinion hadn't been asked.

If only they had a source inside the WSPU, so they could know what they were planning. Would they confine their activities to speeches and mass demonstrations, or would they undertake a more dramatic show of anger? With Julia involved in planning, David knew that was a real possibility. There was the potential for a Birmingham-like incident in London. An action in the city would gain far more press attention than one in the provinces.

Or, they could go after individual members of the government. He would be high on the list. Would he lose another suit to molasses and feathers—or would they behave in a more violent manner? The Home Secretary had taken to going out with a bodyguard, but David wasn't ready for that.

Not that he thought Julia would try to prevent him from becoming a target. It wouldn't surprise him if she came after him personally; she'd been that angry. But apart from checking the door and window locks at home, he wasn't changing his routine. If they wanted to get him, they would.

As one day passed into two, then three, without any dramatic action, David became more nervous. Those women were planning something; he just didn't know what. The only announced activity was at Manchester, on Saturday. He eagerly scanned *Votes for Women* when it came out to see if there was a hint of a plan, but all he saw were articles vociferously attacking the government.

He read the two authored by Julia very carefully, but they offered no clues as to her intentions. He suspected the WSPU was waiting, biding their time until they decided to move. David wished they would get it over with. The suspense was wearing.

Finally, on Friday, he sent a note to Julia, hoping her temper had cooled enough that they could talk. He asked her to meet him for dinner, ostensibly to deal with some paperwork from his aunt's estate. But he wanted to repair the breach with her, to convince her that he still cared.

He waited for her at Sweeney's, a small restaurant tucked in behind the more elegant avenues along the Strand. They didn't need to meet in secret, now, but David didn't want this meeting in too public a place, in case Julia was still furious with him.

Anticipating her imminent arrival, David ordered a table and sipped a glass of whiskey while he waited. She was a few minutes late, but he knew that the streets could be jammed at this time of day.

But after twenty minutes and another drink, his optimism flagged. It looked very much like she wasn't going to come. Shrugging, David ordered dinner. He was hungry, in any case, and if she finally did arrive, it would show her that he was unperturbed by her failure to appear.

But after finishing his dinner, David was forced to admit that she wasn't coming. Deliberately—or had his note somehow failed to be delivered? He remembered she'd said that his telegram about the funeral had been read in the office. Before he let his full fury rage, he should find out.

David drained his glass, paid his bill, and pulled on his overcoat. He was going to go to Clement's Inn and find out exactly where he stood with Julia.

Chapter 19

Even if David hadn't known that Number Four was his destination, it would have been obvious once he arrived. Suffragette banners hung from the first-floor window ledges, proclaiming VOTES FOR WOMEN as the cause and WE WILL NOT BE STILLED as their motto. David stopped and watched as several women went in and out of the building, some carrying bundles when they left. Leaflets—or did they keep an endless supply of eggs and rocks in their headquarters?

David tipped his hat to the surprised woman on the stairs and entered the building. The clatter of typewriters echoed from his left and he stuck his head through the door.

"I'm looking for Julia Sydney," he shouted above the racket.

A bespectacled typist peered at him. "Who?"

"Sydney." David's voice rose. "Julia Sydney."

A tall, dark-haired woman on the far side of the room turned and looked at him. "What is your business with Miss Sydney?"

David recognized her immediately. Beryl Somebody. She'd been at his aunt's funeral—the one who'd tried to coerce Julia to go back to London.

He smiled and doffed his hat. "Good evening. I'm here to see Miss Sydney."

"Is she expecting you?"

David smiled to himself. Now he knew she was here and he wasn't going to leave until he'd seen her. "In a manner of speaking, yes."

She gave him a scrutinizing look, then walked toward the far door. "I will see if she is available."

The openly curious stares of the women in the room only made David's nervousness worse. They seemed to have forgotten all about their typing.

"Someone's here to see me?"

David heard Julia's voice in the hall behind him and turned, eager to surprise her.

"Hi, Jules."

Even in the dim light, he saw her go rigid.

"What do you want?" Julia demanded in a chilly voice.

"Is that any way to greet an old friend?" David took her arm and pulled her back down the hall. "Where can we be private?"

She shook her arm free. "My office."

They continued down the hall, through two small rooms crammed with piles of pamphlets and papers, and into a tiny chamber. A desk and two chairs were the only furniture, while precarious stacks of books and papers covered most of the bare floor. Handbills from WSPU demonstrations decorated the walls.

He would have known this for her office from the chaos.

Trying to adopt a relaxed pose in the uncomfortable hard-backed chair, David waited for her to sit down. Instead, she perched on the corner of her desk, as if she didn't think this would take long, and eyed him warily.

"Afraid of me, Jules?" He arched a brow. "I promise you, I'm not here to do you any harm."

"I'm not particularly pleased to see you," she said. Her voice dripped ice.

"So I gather. I wanted to know if you deliberately skipped my dinner invitation tonight—or didn't you receive it?"

"What do you think?"

David sighed, realizing this was going to be harder than he thought. "I was afraid of that. Look, Julia, this is ridiculous. We need to talk."

"We don't have anything to talk about. You've made your position perfectly clear."

"And since it contradicts yours, you aren't going to

have anything to do with me." Her indifference irritated him. "That's rather high-handed of you."

"I don't care what you think." She shifted uneasily on the desk.

"Then you aren't afraid to dine with me. How about tomorrow night? Or Saturday." He frowned when she did not respond. "Next week? Next month? Or is it 'never,' Julia?"

She stared down at the floor for a moment, then lifted her gaze to a spot on the far wall, just over the top of his head. He almost laughed at her obvious attempt to avoid his eyes.

"David, it is over."

Her words tore through him. This was what he had been dreading, fearing, all week. But that didn't make the shock of hearing it from her own lips any easier. "Why?"

She shook her head. "You know very well why."

"No, I don't. Tell me."

Julia didn't answer.

David stood up, wanting to wring a response from her. "I thought we agreed not to let politics come between us."

"You tossed that aside when you approved of the plans for the forced feedings."

David needed to storm around the room, easing his pent-up emotions, but in the cramped cubicle there was barely room to turn around. "We were happy together, Julia, don't deny it. You're willing to throw all that away because of this damned fight that you can't win?"

"We *will* win and yes, right now, it is far more important than anything else."

He didn't try to hide his disgust. "I thought you were a smarter woman than that, Julia. Smart enough to make your own decisions, instead of letting others make them for you."

She laughed harshly. "What do you think you're doing by imposing your forced feedings? You claim to be doing it 'for our own good.' Making decisions for us."

"That's different. It's a matter of life and death."

"Which women, of course, aren't capable of deciding for themselves." Her lips curled in distaste. "That kind of attitude sickens me."

"It sickens me that you'd rather die than listen to sense."

"Isn't it my right to choose?"

"No!" he said with more vehemence than he intended. "I won't let you—or anyone—do that to themselves."

Slipping off the desk, Julia stood in front of him.

"I want you out of my office and out of my life, David. Now."

Her words left him no room for argument.

"Very well, then." David stalked to the door and jerked it open so hard the glass rattled. "I won't bother you again."

Everyone stared at him with avid curiosity as he left, but David didn't care. He just wanted to get out of here as soon as possible. When he reached the sidewalk, he started walking, ignoring the direction he took.

Had it all been a sham? Had he deluded himself into thinking that she really cared for him?

No. Julia couldn't have faked that passion. What she had shown him was real; what she just told him was real, as well. Her political work was the most important thing to her and anything that got in the way would be cast aside.

Including him.

He supposed he should be grateful. If they were still seeing each other, it would have been awkward watching Julia picket his house, harass his carriage, and storm his office. But it didn't make the hurt any easier. David truly thought he'd found the woman he could spend the rest of his life with. Certainly, they had political differences, but they'd find some way to work those out. With love, anything was possible.

Julia obviously thought otherwise; stubbornly, David was unwilling to give up hope. He loved her too much to give up without a fight. Time, the ebb and flow of politics, was on his side.

In the meantime, he had to make sure that Julia didn't

do anything foolish before he could change her mind. Such as stage another hunger strike if she was arrested—as he had no doubt she would be before long. The suffragettes made a cause célèbre of every woman arrested, and Julia had been out of the limelight for too long.

Of course, maybe that Pankhurst woman recognized that Julia could accomplish a hell of a lot more outside of prison than in, and would keep her out of the fray. He couldn't imagine allowing one of your major speakers and planners to be out of commission for months.

David smiled wryly. Maybe he'd write Christabel Pankhurst a letter and suggest that very thing.

His smile faded, replaced by a sinking feeling as David realized that whatever transpired, he'd be reduced to watching from the sidelines for the time being. There was no appealing to Julia's good sense in this matter—she didn't have any. He'd have to be patient and wait for his opportunity.

Patience was not one of his stellar virtues. But David thought he could muster a great deal of it if it meant that he could get Julia back.

Julia sank into her chair after David left, shaking with the effort she'd expended in appearing indifferent to him, resisting the urge to run into his arms.

Deciding to give up David was one thing; reconciling her heart to that decision was another. She still wanted him far too much.

This surprising weakness shamed her. Julia Sydney, the woman for whom the cause was all. Julia, the dedicated suffragette, eager to do battle where and when she was needed. Not Julia, the lovesick woman who pined for her lost love.

Jumping to her feet, Julia knew what she had to do to free herself from this emotional turmoil. She needed action, a good rousing demonstration to get her thoughts off David and back on her work.

She'd have that all tomorrow, and it couldn't come too soon.

* * *

Julia dressed carefully in the morning, putting on her most comfortable clothing. She'd probably spend the night in them.

Even from her room she sensed the upswelling of excitement surging through the halls of Clement's Inn. This was more than an ordinary demonstration today; it was an outpouring of indignation against the government's brutal torture in Birmingham.

As she laced up her sturdy oxfords, Julia thought about her valiant sisters there, suffering at the hands of the prison medical staff. How could anyone who'd taken the Hippocratic oath participate in such a process? Their names should be in a medical hall of shame.

Lady Mary stuck her head into the room. "Are you ready, Julia? Christabel wants us in the front room before we leave."

Tying the last lace, Julia grabbed her jacket from the chair. She tucked an extra handkerchief into the pocket of her tweed skirt and followed Lady Mary into the hall.

"I think Christabel wants one last chance to persuade us to let her be arrested."

"No." Julia was adamant on this matter. "She needs to stay out. Enough of us are going to jail as it is."

"Are you scared?"

"A little," Julia confessed. "But the sacrifices we make in prison will help us win the vote. Others are strong; I have to be, too."

She didn't voice her growing nervousness about what would happen in prison, the threat of forced feedings. She tried to push her worries away, determined to be strong.

The room was already crowded when they arrived. As Lady Mary predicted, Christabel hinted that it was her duty to be arrested as well, but they roundly voted her down. With her mother off to America, Christabel had to coordinate the Union activities and keep the issue of government torture in the public eye.

After some encouraging words, and a few choruses of the suffrage hymn, the demonstration leaders left Clement's Inn for Trafalgar Square. There, despite the short notice, they expected a gathering of a few thousand supporters. After a rousing program of speeches, designed to inspire and encourage the crowd, they'd lead a march toward Whitehall and the Home Office, and on to Parliament. They hoped to arrive just as the MPs showed up for the daily session.

Julia doubted they would get that far; she expected the police to turn them back long before that. But that was all part of the plan. Once the police tried to stop them, all hell was going to break loose.

She hoped they got as far as the Home Office, however. It would give her the greatest pleasure to heave a rock at David's bailiwick.

The crowds at Trafalgar Square exceeded even Julia's optimistic expectation. It showed her people were not going to tolerate officially sanctioned government torture.

The speakers stood at the base of Nelson's column, facing north, flanked on either side by the massive stone lions. Supporters filled the square, threatening to spill out onto the surrounding streets. Uniformed police watched uneasily from the sides.

As the WSPU leaders stepped forward, a roar went up from the crowd. People pressed forward, eager to hear the exhortations.

Today, the speeches were short and succinct, with two main themes: there was no place for torture in England and it must stop; give the vote to women and remove the need for protest.

Julia spoke last and she felt the old thrill course through her as she stepped forward. People stood atop the fountains' rims, straining to see as well as hear.

"We are here today," she shouted, "to protest the foul and inhumane behavior of our government. A government that does not represent us, does not give us a voice, nor believes that we need one. They are wrong!"

The crowd roared its approval.

"A civilized nation cannot torture its citizens. A civilized nation cannot treat political prisoners as common criminals. A civilized nation cannot deny the vote to women. If England wishes to be seen as a civilized nation, these things must stop! And we know who is responsible for these injustices!"

"Men!"

"The government!"

"The Liberals."

"They are all guilty," Julia agreed. "We have been betrayed by the Liberals, abused by the government. A government composed entirely of *men*!

"Today, we intend to show those men that we will not tolerate their behavior, that we will not allow them to torture us, that we will not allow them to continue to ignore and dismiss us. We want the vote and we shall have it!"

Julia felt an upswelling of power as the spectators hung on to her every word. This was what she missed, this was what she was here for. To inspire them and to lead.

"Today, we will show the government that we are a power to be reckoned with." She pointed south, toward Whitehall. "We will beard the lions in their den and force them to listen to us. To Parliament!"

A great roar erupted from the crowd and it surged south across Charing Cross, flowing around the statue of Charles I. Banners sprouted from all sides as angry women followed the suffragettes. Jumping from the platform, Julia ran to catch up. The few policemen assigned to watch the speeches weren't prepared for the onslaught and hastily moved back.

Julia knew it would be a race to see how far the marchers could get before reinforcements stopped them. The women had a head start, but the Metropolitan Police office at New Scotland Yard was only a block off their route. She hoped they would get as far as the Home Office, at least.

Across Charing Cross and onto Whitehall they marched, voices raised in song.

> "Shout, shout, up with your song!
> Cry with the wind, for the dawn is breaking,

March, march, swing you along,
Wide blows our banner and hope is waking."

The words, sung by over a thousand voices, sent a chill down Julia's spine. How could they fail, with such determination?

Traffic on the road hastily pulled to the side and onto the curbs as the flood of women streamed down Whitehall toward the government buildings. Guards standing outside the War Office gawked at the procession but made no move to stop them.

Chanting their slogans, the demonstrators marched forward, swelling in size as they moved south. Ahead, Julia saw the bend in the road where Whitehall became Parliament Street—at the junction with Downing Street, their first objective.

Julia tapped Katherine on the shoulder. "Move toward the back and ready your group when we reach the PM's. We want to make sure Asquith knows we're here." Julia turned to Lady Mary. "As soon as we see the police, lead your troops toward the Embankment and play hide-and-seek with them. We want to tie them up for as long as possible."

"Police ahead!" someone shouted.

Julia shaded her eyes and looked ahead. Men in dark uniforms were racing toward them.

"Link arms!" Julia commanded and the front ranks joined together. "WSPU—forward!"

Running down the street, the women fought to reach their first target before the police stopped them. The charge ended in a draw. The police barely had time to form up and block the street when they reached the Home Office Building.

"We demand to see the Home Secretary," Julia shouted. "We want to know why he supports the torture of women."

"This is an illegal demonstration," the police commander replied. "Disperse immediately or I'll have you arrested."

An expectant hush fell over the crowd. Julia glanced

up at the building, spotting curious faces staring out the windows.

Was David there, watching?

"We will not be turned back until we have spoken with Mr. Gladstone," Julia said. "Tell him to come out and speak with us."

"Send him a letter next time!" one of the policemen shouted and a few of the men laughed.

Julia turned to face the press of women behind her. "Remember how so many in the House of Commons profess support for suffrage, yet they won't pass the bill out of committee? Remember how this Cabinet and the Prime Minister espoused the suffrage cause, then betrayed us once in office? This is the same government which ordered and approved the torture of our sisters in Birmingham. Do we want to communicate with them by letter?"

"No!" the crowd roared in unison.

Raising her arm as a signal, Julia and the small cadre of women chosen to lead the action reached into their pockets and pulled out their paper-wrapped rocks.

"Here are our *letters* to Mr. Gladstone!" Julia cried. "Women, forward!" A flying wedge of women raced at the police, forcing an opening in their ranks for Julia and the others to follow. They raced toward the Home Office, police in pursuit.

"Stop government torture!" cried one protester and threw her paper-wrapped rock at the nearest window.

"Votes for women!" shouted another and flung her missile.

Julia pulled her arm back, preparing to throw, when an iron hand clamped down on her arm.

"Oh, no you don't," a policeman said.

Julia struggled to get free of his grip, seeing she had only seconds before another police officer reached her. Grabbing the rock with her left hand, she threw it as best she could at a window. Her target didn't break, but she heard the satisfying crack of broken glass as others succeeded.

A burly sergeant grabbed Julia around the waist, lifting her off her feet and hauling her backward. Squirming and struggling, Julia tried to free herself, but he only tightened his grip.

The loud wail of a siren heralded the arrival of a Black Maria. At the sight of the police van inching its way up the street, Julia grinned in triumph. They hadn't made it to the Parliament buildings, but had come close. And with the police entangled with the window breakers, she knew that Katherine and Lady Mary would be wreaking havoc on their routes.

Julia stopped struggling. She'd succeeded in being arrested, and there was no way any government official—and the London papers—were going to be able to ignore this protest. Several sympathetic reporters had been alerted ahead of time, and the bright flash of their camera lightbulbs told her they were here, watching the scene. The whole story would be in the morning papers.

The sergeant who'd grabbed Julia marched her to the waiting Black Maria and shoved her in. Unlike the prison vans, this one did not have separate compartments for the prisoners, but merely benches along either wall. Julia took her seat and grasped hands with the prisoners on either side of her.

"Where will they take us?" the woman on her left asked.

"Probably Rochester Row," Julia replied. "It's the closest one."

"I managed to break a window!" a woman near the front announced proudly.

"Good for you." Julia knew the action had been an enormous success, both in the damage caused and in the number of women arrested. London hadn't seen a demonstration like this in a long time. No one would be able to ignore it.

And unless things changed quickly, this was only the first act of the new campaign.

The charge room at the Rochester Row Police Station was already crowded with protesters when Julia was pushed through the door. A cheer went up when the women caught sight of her and they all began chanting "Votes for women, votes for women."

"Stop that!" cried the harassed station officer in charge of booking the prisoners.

"Stop government torture," a woman retorted.

Julia watched the milling group with wild excitement. Usually, the Union asked their followers to behave docilely when arrested, having proved their point. But this group was too excited, too enthused to pay attention to that rule. They shouted, whistled, and stomped their feet every time someone tried to bring order to the room. Julia had no intention of encouraging them to behave.

Finally the station officer threw down his pen and marched out, to the hoots and cheers of the prisoners.

In a few minutes the man returned with two other officers. Grabbing the nearest woman, they hauled her through the rear door.

"Where are you taking her?" Julia cried, but they didn't answer. Two more police came through the door and took another woman away.

"Are they going to put us in the holding cells without booking first?" the woman on Julia's right asked.

"I think so," said Julia triumphantly. They'd made a total ruin of normal police procedure. Another victory for the WSPU.

As more women were taken out, the room gradually quieted, bowing to the inevitable. Julia went peacefully when they came for her.

The police took her down the stairs at the end of a short corridor, to the holding cells in the basement, where prisoners stayed until they were approved for bail. Julia suspected most of them wouldn't be.

A police officer sat on a stool at the bottom of the stairs, logbook on his lap. "Name?"

"Sydney, Julia."

The man glanced up. "Seems I've heard that one before."

"I've been arrested six times in London alone," Julia replied proudly.

"Address?"

"Four Clement's Inn."

"Put her in number six," the weary man said.

The man hustled her down the hall and pointed to the cell. Julia stepped inside and the door shut behind her with a resounding clang, enclosing her in the ill-lit room.

Wrinkling her nose, Julia sat down on the plank bench against the wall. The cell stank of stale urine and she wondered when it had last been cleaned.

Oh, well, she'd been in worse places. Immediately she turned to the wall behind her and began to tap out a message to the next cell. An answering tap came through the wall and Julia responded. Prison life had begun.

Chapter 20

Staring at the filthy walls of her cell, Julia wondered what lay ahead. Not tonight—she knew nothing would happen to her here. No, it was Holloway she worried about. Would the suffragette prisoners be force-fed if they hunger struck? More importantly, would Julia be strong enough to endure? They'd still only received the sketchiest of reports from Birmingham and no one was quite certain what to expect—other than the worst. She only knew they wouldn't subdue her without a fight. The prison officers would learn, to their regret, that she was a force to be reckoned with.

Anxiously, Julia wondered what had become of the other leaders. Had Katherine reached Asquith's, and had Mary led the police on a wild chase down the Embankment? She hoped she'd find out in the morning; there'd be supporters at court who'd let them know what had happened.

Julia didn't doubt she'd be sent to prison in the morning. The trial before the magistrate was merely a formality; he'd give her the choice between a fine and the promise not to disturb the peace in the future, or a jail term.

There wasn't any question in her mind which option she would choose.

The only light in the cell came from the small gas jet above the door. Julia resisted the temptation to look at her watch. It would be taken from her tomorrow; another luxury of the world that she would soon be without.

She only knew it was dinnertime when a policeman

arrived with a tray of food for her. The Union made sure that the prisoners had an excellent meal the night before their arraignment, knowing that the hunger strikes would start the next day. Julia wondered what London restaurant had provided this feast.

Despite the enticing smells and delicious taste, Julia ate sparingly. She'd learned from experience that the first day of a hunger strike went better if she didn't gorge herself the day before. She eagerly downed the thick broth, and ate a roll, but only nibbled at the lamb cutlets and creamed carrots.

When she felt tired enough, she lay down on the board plank, wishing she'd thought to have someone bring her bedding for the night. Somehow, in all the excitement of planning the demonstration, that had slipped past her mind.

To her surprise, she managed to get some sleep and didn't wake until she heard the noisy clang of cell doors down the hall. She sat up. It must be breakfast.

Sure enough, soon a policeman appeared at her door, unlocked it, and stepped in with another tray.

"They sure send in fine food for you ladies," he said as he handed it to her.

Julia grinned. "We deserve the best."

"Course, I suppose if you're gonna go 'unger strikin' you want to have some fancy meals. Kinda like fattening up cattle before the slaughter, eh?"

"Not really. It's better if we don't eat too much." She took a glass of orange juice and a piece of toast from the tray and handed it back to him, knowing there were other prisoners who were hungry. The police didn't feed the prisoners in the station holding cells. "See if there's someone who would appreciate this."

He left quickly, taking the tray with him.

Julia ate slowly, concentrating on the chewy texture of the bread, savoring the sweet tartness of the orange juice. It would be several days before she tasted anything other than water.

Not until the forced feedings began.

She tried not to think about that.

Shortly after breakfast, she heard the doors clang again and guessed they were taking the women upstairs to the magistrate. Julia was ready when they came for her.

The small courtroom was packed with spectators, most of them suffragettes. Ignoring the entreaties of the magistrate, they broke into loud applause when Julia and the others stepped before the bench.

As per arrangement, none of those arrested offered any defense for her behavior. A policeman read the list of their crimes—disorderly behavior in a public place, assault, malicious injury to property. Julia grinned widely when her charge included "inciting to riot."

"Do any of you ladies wish to offer a plea?" the magistrate asked in a bored tone.

"Oh, we're all guilty," Julia said gaily. The crowd laughed and the magistrate motioned for quiet.

He began reading the list of fines in a hasty manner until he came to Julia. Then he stopped, and peered at her over the rim of his glasses.

"Julia Sydney. Ten pounds, damages. Fifty pounds bond for good behavior."

The crowd gasped at the size of the bond.

"I won't pay anything to a government which denies me my rights," Julia said loudly.

"Fine, then," replied the judge. "Two months imprisonment in the Second Division."

The loud gasps of the crowd told Julia they were as shocked as she at the length of the sentence.

"I demand to be assigned to the First Division," Julia insisted. "I am a political prisoner."

"Request denied."

As she was led out of the courtroom, Julia smiled and waved gaily to the partisan crowd.

At least the uncertainty was over. She was going to Holloway, and to the indignities of the Second Division, where she would be forced to wear prison clothes, forbidden to speak with the other prisoners, and couldn't write or receive any letters.

She'd been through all that before. Only the threat of forced feedings made this a new experience.

Joining the other women in the anteroom, they waited for the prison van to arrive. After a few minutes, the police came and escorted them down the hall to the Black Maria waiting outside.

It was time for the ride to Holloway.

By the time Julia climbed inside, the tiny cells lining the interior were almost full. Sitting where the guard told her, Julia took a deep breath before he shut the grated door, squashing her into the tiny space. The thud of doors told her that the other cells were being filled, then she heard the outer door of the truck slam shut.

Immediately the women started talking, identifying themselves, greeting each other. Someone began singing the chorus of the "Women's Marseillaise" and they all joined in. One perceptive protester still carried a scarf in the Union colors of purple, white, and green, and she shoved it through the ventilator in the back door. As the van drove north toward the prison, the scarf fluttered behind them and people on the street cheered encouragement as they passed.

Having made this journey several times, Julia recognized when the van halted outside the rear gate of the prison, then pulled into the yard.

They were here.

Relieved to be free from the cramped cell, Julia followed in line as several guards escorted the prisoners inside. Before going through the door, Julia paused for a moment, taking a last look at the outside world. It could be two months before she saw it again.

In the reception area, they were met by the wardress.

Julia stepped forward. "We don't intend to cause you trouble, but as long as we are being treated as common criminals and assigned to the Second Division, we will not take food."

The wardress didn't reply, and motioned for the prisoners to go to the changing cubicles. Julia waited quietly until another wardress and two female officers entered.

"I do not accept this imprisonment and I am not going to undress myself," she announced.

The wardress heaved a sigh and began to pull off

Julia's clothes. Julia didn't resist, but she didn't offer any help either. In exchange for her own clothes, she was gowned in the coarse blue serge of the Second Division, with the incriminating white arrows that branded her a prisoner marching across the material. A wardress tied the apron around her waist and placed the white cap on her head before taking her back into the hall and putting her in another cubicle.

Julia leaned against the wall, suddenly weary after all the excitement. When the door opened, the matron handed her a pair of sheets and a blanket.

"I suppose you're planning to refuse food."

Julia nodded. "The government refuses to heed our petitions; we have no other choice. It's a small price to pay to win our rights."

"They're gonna feed you, you know."

"They can try," Julia retorted defiantly.

The prison doctor arrived. Julia refused to answer his questions about her medical health, and he didn't try to examine her.

Finally, after an interminable wait, a guard escorted her to her cell. Dropping her bedding on the pallet, Julia surveyed her cell, closely examining every inch of the wall, looking for slogans left by other suffragettes. There, in the corner, a faint VOTES FOR WOMEN could be found. She made her bed and sat down on it. Now, the dull routine of prison had begun.

The unlocking of her cell door startled her. Julia pulled her knees up to her chest and wrapped her arms around them, instantly wary. This wasn't part of the routine.

It was the matron, and an unfamiliar man.

"Miss Julia Sydney?" the man asked.

Julia nodded, watching him carefully. What was going on? Surely, they weren't going to feed her already.

"Come with me."

Her suspicions aroused, Julia didn't move. "Why?"

He gave her an exasperated look. "Because you're not going to be staying with us after all."

Julia's eyes widened. "What?"

"I just received word from downtown. You're to be released."

"They've dropped the charges?" she asked.

"They didn't tell me why," the man said. "Please come."

Bewildered, Julia followed him. "Are the others being released?"

"Yours was the only name given to me."

Julia couldn't understand what was going on. Had the government relented, recognizing their cause at last? It was almost too much to believe, but why else would she be released?

In the wardrobe room, she eagerly ripped off the hated prison dress and put on her own clothes. Then she impatiently waited for someone to tell her what was going on.

But the officer who led her down the long corridor to the front door didn't know anything. Her mind awhirl, Julia stepped into the courtyard and took a deep breath of fresh air. On the far side stood the open gate and freedom.

She'd made this walk many times, but never under such mysterious circumstances—and without a cluster of supporters to welcome her. Julia suddenly realized she didn't have enough money to pay for her trip back to town.

She stood outside the gate, looking anxiously up and down the street. Surely, someone knew of her release and they'd soon be here to take her away.

As if on cue, a hansom came around the corner. It pulled over to the curb and the door opened.

David stepped out.

"Get in," he said roughly.

David, standing at the rear of the police court that morning, had cringed when he heard Julia refuse to pay her fine, and winced when the magistrate imposed the two-month sentence.

He couldn't let her do this. He knew what was waiting for her at Holloway. They'd let her refuse food for a few days, then start the forced feedings. And knowing Julia, she'd resist and cause herself further harm.

But there was still time to get her out of this fix.

Dashing out of the courtroom, he whistled for a cab. He had to get to the bank.

Forty minutes later, he returned with a bank draft for the amount of sixty pounds, her fine and the bond for Julia's good behavior. He knew *that* was money thrown away, for he had no illusions Julia would refrain from future protests. But he could save her from the forced feedings this time, and he intended to make damn sure that she pledged to give up the hunger strikes before she was arrested again.

More than a few eyebrows were raised at the police court when he paid the fine, but David ignored their curious looks. He realized he should have sent his secretary, but there hadn't been time. He needed to get Julia out of Holloway as quickly as possible.

The cabman he hailed was more than willing to earn the huge fare for taking David to the prison north of the city. Settling himself in the back of the cab, David unfolded *The Times* and tried to read the accounts of yesterday's riot.

But he couldn't concentrate. All he could think about was Julia and her role in the disturbance. When he'd rushed to the window to see the angry mob outside the Home Office, he hadn't spotted her, but guessed she was there. After learning the women had been taken to Rochester Row, he'd sent his secretary over to get the names. Once he learned Julia was among them, David knew he had to do something to help her.

So here he was, on his way to Holloway, to take Julia back to town once she was released.

Until now, he'd refused to worry about her reaction to what he'd done, but as they passed to the west of Islington, he began to wonder what she'd say.

No doubt she'd be unhappy with him. But with the demonstration, her arrest, and sentencing, she'd already made her point. She shouldn't complain about not having to suffer the consequences. What more could she ask for?

David knew the answer to that one. Julia, and the other radicals at the WSPU, wouldn't be happy until they had the vote. And no one was going to tell them that rioting in the middle of Whitehall and breaking windows at government offices would harm, not help, their goal. There was a strange streak of irrationality in suffragette logic.

The cab pulled down the street leading to Holloway and David leaned forward in the seat. He'd been assured that Julia's release would be taken care of quickly and he hoped he wouldn't have to wait too long for her.

To his shock, he saw her standing outside the front gate of the prison.

Julia stared at David in disbelief as he climbed out of the cab. "What are you doing here?"

"Offering you a ride back to town," he said.

"How did you know I was going to be released? Did the Home Office order it?"

"I paid your bloody fine," he said.

"You what?" Julia stared at him, wondering if she'd heard correctly. "You can't be serious."

"I can, and I did." His expression was dark. "Now will you please get in? I'm sure the cabman doesn't want to spend the rest of the afternoon standing here."

Julia boiled with anger. "What on earth possessed you to do such a thing?"

"Because I wanted to talk some sense into you before you hurt yourself in there. Hunger strikes aren't going to be tolerated any longer. They would have fed you."

She glared at him. "Don't you think I know that? We *want* them to feed us. The more it happens, the more we can show that it's a deliberate government policy of torture."

"You're a fool," David snapped.

"So are you, if you think you can keep me out of here."

Julia started to march back toward the prison, but David grabbed her arm and jerked her toward the carriage.

"If you don't get in the damn cab, I swear I'll pick you up and toss you inside myself." His blue eyes bored into her. "You know who is going to win *that* battle."

Giving him a look of pure loathing, Julia held her head high and climbed into the cab. David sat beside her and the driver headed toward town.

Trembling with rage, Julia couldn't even put her feelings into words.

David was showing his true colors at last. Thinking he knew what was best for her. After all, she was a mere female, a helpless woman who needed his superior male guidance.

How could she have misjudged him so completely? She had actually thought, for a while, that although David disagreed with her politics, he respected her on an intellectual level, thinking of her as an equal. His actions today showed that he thought her a child.

"Did they treat you well?" he asked finally.

Julia gazed pointedly out the window, ignoring him.

He leaned back in the seat and continued talking. "I was watching the demonstration out of the window yesterday. It's a miracle no one got hurt."

"If the police hadn't stopped us, no one would have been in any danger," Julia replied tartly.

"Tell that to anyone who was sitting by a window in the Home Office."

"They could have moved out of the way."

"You shouldn't have staged an illegal demonstration."

"When the government refuses to talk with us, we have no recourse but illegal demonstrations," she said, her fury rising. "The fault is Asquith's, not ours."

"You enjoy painting yourselves as the innocents, don't you?" David gave her a disgusted look. "You lure hundreds of misguided women into your ranks with your warped view of the situation and blind them to the reality. That riot yesterday was nothing more than the action of common criminals."

"I hardly expect you to think otherwise—after all, you're one of the oppressors."

"I'm not oppressing anybody. This is a country of laws and they must be obeyed."

"This is a country of *male* law," Julia retorted. "As a woman, they don't have any jurisdiction over me."

"You're being ridiculous. The law applies to everyone."

"How can I accept laws made by men who are elected only by men?" She eyed him coldly. "Men who claim to know what is best for me."

"I wouldn't call your actions yesterday particularly sensible." David glared at her. "I think you *need* someone to look after you."

Julia felt as if he'd just slapped her. He was treating her like a child who wasn't old enough or sensible enough to make her own decisions.

How could she have ever thought she loved him?

"I don't know what's happened to you in the last month. You've turned into an entirely different person."

"*I'm* not the one who changed." Julia spat out the words. "I thought you had some element of respect for me, but I was obviously wrong."

"What has respect got to do with this?" he demanded. "I'm trying to save you from your own folly."

"I don't need to be saved."

"You don't?" David's lips twisted in a sneer. "When you persist with these damn-fool hunger strikes, what else am I supposed to think?"

"That I know exactly what I am doing."

"Do you?"

She stared at him with deliberate coldness. "Yes."

Unwilling to waste more time arguing with a man who wouldn't listen, Julia turned away. They were passing King's Cross Station, and soon she'd be home.

How was she going to face the women at Clement's Inn?

David had dealt her a greater blow than he could ever imagine. While the other women were at Holloway, facing the horror of forced feedings within the next few days, she was free. Freed by a Cabinet undersecretary whose relationship with her was already suspect. No matter what she said about her and David, no one would ever believe it.

Beryl wouldn't be able to control her glee, and Julia didn't think Christabel would be too pleased. If she knew half the truth about Julia and David . . .

Her only chance at redemption was to take advantage of her sudden freedom and strike an even harsher blow against the government. Something so outrageous and so different that it would capture the imagination of the entire country—and make everyone at Clement's Inn forget what had happened today.

A small smile crossed Julia's face. She would show David Kimbrough that she could think for herself.

When the cab pulled up in front of Number Four, David jumped out first. Julia ignored his helping hand and marched up the steps without a backward glance.

It took only a few seconds after she stepped through the door for the office to come to a total standstill, as everyone stared at her in disbelief.

"Julia! What are you doing here?"

"I've come back to lead us in an even bigger protest against the government," she said bravely. "Is Cristabel in?"

"She's gone up to Holloway to lead a support march," the office manager said.

"And Beryl?"

"She's there, too."

Julia realized she must have just missed them. Well, back to Holloway she would go.

In the privacy of her room, Julia sank down onto the bed. The confrontation with Beryl was postponed, but not eliminated. At least she could discuss her plan in front of the others, when restraint would be a watchword. Christabel wouldn't attack one of her chief lieutenants in public.

Julia's plan had better be spectacular.

Hastily stripping off her clothes, Julia dressed and headed out the door. The train would drop her a few blocks from the prison. She'd have plenty of time to devise a plan on the way.

* * *

After dropping Julia at the WSPU offices, David paid the cabdriver and started out for Whitehall on foot. He needed to walk.

He hadn't expected her to be thrilled by what he'd done, but her harsh words of condemnation stung him. He wasn't trying to treat her like a child; he merely wanted to save her from being hurt.

Maybe if they hadn't made that pact not to discuss politics in the country, he would have discovered Julia's views were much more radical than he'd thought. If she wasn't downright crazy—anyone who actually *wanted* to be force-fed needed to have their head examined.

But after this set-down, he wasn't going to come to her aid again. There was no point in wasting his time.

Despite the walk, his mood didn't improve. He'd spent the entire morning and part of the afternoon taking care of Julia's problem, and to what end? She was furious with him.

He placed the blame on the WSPU and those bloody Pankhursts. Julia was an eminently sensible woman, but they'd poisoned her mind so she couldn't think straight. They wanted to turn everyone into martyrs for the cause, with their imprisonments and hunger strikes. And if someone died in the process, all the better, as it would give them an excuse to increase their attacks on the government.

Stacks of reports sat on his desk at the Home Office. David glanced through them quickly, but nothing required his immediate attention. He tucked two of them into his briefcase and headed out again, for the House. They were getting closer and closer to the critical vote on the budget and he didn't dare stay away.

Outside the members' entrance, he was accosted by a reporter from one of the sensationalist papers.

"Mr. Kimbrough!" The reporter pushed in front of him. "Is it true that you paid the fine for one of the suffragettes arrested yesterday?"

David stopped in midstride.

"Wherever did you get that information?"

The reporter held out his hand, which David ignored. "I'm MacKay. I cover the police beat in Westminster. Heard you effected the release of"—he consulted his notes—"Miss Julia Sydney."

"I was undertaking a commission for a friend." David suddenly realized that he had put himself into an awkward position. He hadn't expected the news to be spread all over the papers. "As a law-abiding citizen and member of the House, I cannot approve of the lawbreaking tactics of the suffragettes."

"But you did pay the fine."

"As I said, I performed that task for a friend who was unable to take care of the matter. As abhorrent as I found the idea personally, I felt obligated to help."

"So Miss Sydney wasn't sent to Holloway with the other prisoners?"

"I have no knowledge of Miss Sydney's whereabouts," David said. Which wasn't a total lie. She could be anywhere by now.

"Did you approve of the fines and sentences handed out? Some say they were far too harsh."

"When any group tries to put itself above the law, they must face the consequences." David chose his words carefully, knowing they would be read by both his bosses and Julia. It was futile to think he could please them both, but he wanted to try.

"What about the forced feedings in prison?" the reporter persisted. "Do you approve of that as a measure against the hunger strikes?"

"When prisoners are under the care of the state, we are obligated to make certain that they remain healthy."

"But doesn't the forced feeding endanger their health?" the reporter persisted.

"It is far less dangerous than starvation," David said. "Now, excuse me, I am late for this afternoon's session as it is." David walked away and entered the safety of the halls of Parliament.

He couldn't believe it was already common news that he'd paid Julia's fine. David had the sinking feeling that there'd be hell to pay when word reached the Home

Secretary—or the PM. Should he offer an explanation now, or wait until they asked him?

David took a seat at the rear of the Liberal benches, wondering why everything was going wrong for him today. He hadn't thought about the political ramifications of what he'd done this morning; all his concern had been for Julia. Now, his connection to her was bound to come under scrutiny and people were bound to ask questions.

Let them. He could honestly say that he had no relationship with Julia. She was furious with him and this wasn't a mild disagreement that would blow over soon. He'd be lucky if she ever spoke to him again.

David wondered what the hell he could have been thinking of, too.

He didn't arrive home until half past two, following another lengthy session. Wearily, David stripped off his coat and threw it over the banister and climbed the stairs. He'd grab a glass of whiskey in his office, then head to bed.

He flicked on the light, poured his whiskey, and thumbed through the mail.

One envelope puzzled him. It merely had his name written across the front, with no stamp or return address, so it obviously hadn't come through the post. Curious, he grabbed the letter opener and slit the flap. He reached in and pulled out a check for sixty pounds.

Drawn on the account of the WSPU.

Without hesitation, David tore it in shreds and tossed the pieces into the wastebasket.

He wasn't going to give Julia the satisfaction of paying off that debt.

To emphasize his point, David fished out the pieces of check from the wastebasket, stuffed them into a fresh envelope, and addressed it to her at Clement's Inn.

He'd like to see the look on her face when she opened *that*.

Chapter 21

No one, not even Beryl, had confronted Julia when she joined the demonstrators outside Holloway, but she knew there would be a reaction eventually. The only question was when and where. She had not had the chance to talk with Christabel, which only made Julia more nervous. She'd stayed in her room last night, anticipating a barrage of curious questions, but no one sought her out.

Obviously, the story behind her release had sped through the office, for when Julia came down, she sensed that everyone was watching her carefully this morning—while pretending not to. She wanted to shout at them to simply ask her what had happened, instead of whispering in corners, but she resisted the urge. They could speculate all they wanted; she knew the truth.

The only thing that mattered was the reaction of Christabel. So far, she hadn't said a word to her. Julia poured herself a cup of tea and retreated to her office.

Edgy and restless, Julia felt confined in the small, cramped space, but she didn't dare leave Clement's Inn. Not until she'd talked to Christabel, and tried to redeem herself with the new plan.

Julia's agitation increased after learning that Beryl had been closeted with Christabel all morning. Knowing how bitterly Beryl resented her, Julia wasn't encouraged by that news. She could only imagine what Beryl was saying, the sly innuendos and outright exaggerations she would be feeding Christabel in order to discredit Julia.

David couldn't have devised a more effective way to eliminate her political effectiveness than if he'd exposed her as a secret member of the Conservative Party. He must have known how his action would harm her. After harping about her safety for weeks, he'd done this on purpose in a final effort to keep her out of prison.

If that was his goal, he'd made a big mistake. On her desk, in a manila folder, was the action plan she'd prepared for Christabel. A plan that would capture the attention of every member of the government—and land Julia in prison again. An action so militant that there would be no question about where her loyalties lay.

This time, David wouldn't be able to rescue her. Julia intended to make sure of that. Timing was critical—an early morning arrest would put her before the magistrate that same day and she could be safely behind the gates of Holloway before David learned what had happened. And this time, she knew better than to come out if they offered her freedom.

As the minutes ticked by without a summons from Christabel, Julia's nervousness grew. The delay was ominous.

She couldn't believe that Christabel would listen to Beryl without talking to Julia as well. They had been through too many things together. They'd shared cells in police stations, linked arms at the front of a demonstration, spent late nights laying out the paper, discussing political strategy and idealistic philosophies into the wee hours of the morning. How could she turn on Julia for something that hadn't even been her fault?

Julia had just made up her mind to go out for lunch when Beryl appeared at her office door.

"Christabel wants to see you now."

Julia swallowed hard, and followed her down the hall.

To her great relief, Beryl wasn't included in the discussion. It was just Julia and Christabel, together, for over two hours. When they were finished, they'd mapped out a strategy for dealing with the issue of Julia's release from prison, and agreed to carry out Julia's plan.

Julia insisted they go on the attack against David, using the publicity about her release to attack the government, claiming that paying her fine had been a deliberate attempt by the Home Office to discredit her. Christabel agreed, saying she'd issue a statement declaring that Julia was, and always had been, a devoted and loyal member of the Union. In fact, it was her very effectiveness as a leader that had led to this underhanded government plan, and if they tried anything like this again, the public should be aware of the reasons behind it.

It gave Julia a smug sense of satisfaction to imagine what David would think when he read *that*.

For the office, they developed the story that Julia had been using her connection with David to gain information about Home Office activities.

Smiling to herself, Julia guessed what Beryl would say about that tale, but she had no way to prove otherwise. Christabel was willing to ignore the truth of Julia's relationship with David, and Julia was grateful for her understanding. She could have thrown Julia to the wolves, as Beryl no doubt wished her to do.

However, Julia knew that her plan had been her ultimate salvation. "Brilliant," Christabel had called it, and Julia felt relieved when she heard the words. She knew everything was going to be all right, now. No one would dare question her loyalty after this.

Christabel gave her a free hand to set the plan into action and Julia couldn't wait to get started. The first step was to recruit her team, then plan and rehearse until everything was perfect.

She thought they'd be ready in two days.

Back in her office, Julia hastily went over her notes, making a list of the supplies they needed, the people she wanted to use.

The door flew open and slammed into the wall with a resounding crash. Beryl stormed in, eyes blazing.

"She should have thrown you out of the Union. That's what I told her to do."

Julia didn't bother to hide her smugness. "How fortunate that you don't have the final say around here."

"Oh, you survived this, but you're a fallen idol, now."

Beryl sneered. "Your loyalties are always going to be suspected, Julia."

"Oh?" Julia raised a skeptical brow. "And why is that?"

"You and I both know what you were doing with that man." She spat out the last two words as if they were an oath.

"What makes you so sure that you know?" Julia gave her a pitying look. "Imagination is no substitute for facts."

Beryl glared at her and Julia smiled at her frustration.

"I'm going to keep my eye on you," Beryl declared, finally. "You'll be caught the next time, and then Christabel won't be able to ignore it."

"Well, Beryl, you're going to have a long wait. I'm planning to be out of the office for the next few months."

"She's not sending you to America!" Beryl's voice screeched with jealousy.

Julia laughed. "Hardly. No, I'm looking forward to another restful stay at Holloway."

"She's going to let you stage some foolish action again?"

"Foolish? I think the term she used was 'brilliant.' "

Beryl flushed scarlet. "You still think you're the favorite, don't you? Well, if you're going out on this action, I am, too. You can't have all the glory."

"Why, Beryl, how generous of you to offer your assistance." Julia didn't try to hide her contempt. "But we can't possibly have both of us in jail at the same time. You'll just have to wait your turn."

"We'll see about that," Beryl snapped and stomped out of the office.

Julia didn't know whether to laugh or hire a bodyguard. That woman grew more odious each day. It would be a real pleasure to get away from her, even if she had to go to Holloway to do it.

If only there was a way to make sure Beryl was going to prison the same time Julia got out. That would make life at Clement's Inn far more pleasant.

As she'd intended, two days later the participants had been chosen, the preparations made, and the intricate plan rehearsed. Only Julia and Diana Morgan would officially participate in the action, with two other women as backup. The four made several secret forays to a deserted warehouse at the docks to practice with their tools until they felt confident they could accomplish their task.

To make certain that the target would be at home, the attack was planned for early morning—at seven. With Parliament sitting until after midnight in these last frantic days of the session, all the members would still be in bed at that early hour.

Particularly a Cabinet minister.

Long after midnight, Julia lay in her bed, unable to sleep, listening to the slow ticking of the clock on the table. She was always nervous before an action, and this one was more important than most. Important, because it would prove to everyone in the Union that she was still one of them. Important, because it would show the Home Secretary that the Union held him personally responsible for the torturing of their sisters in prison.

And it would show David just how bitterly she resented his interference in her life. She hoped this incident proved highly embarrassing for him. He deserved it after what he'd done to her. She'd been walking on eggshells for days, trying to live down his insult. Now, the tables were going to turn and he could see how it felt to be manipulated from afar.

She refused to consider what this might do to his career. He hadn't given her work any consideration when he'd paid her fine; she didn't owe him anything.

Julia was glad Lady Marchmont couldn't see how bad things had become.

Jumping out of bed before the alarm sounded, Julia dressed quickly and slipped down the stairs to put the water on for tea. The office was deserted at this hour; her comrades wouldn't be here for at least another twenty minutes.

She looked around with a sharp pang of longing, knowing she wouldn't be back here for some time. The typewriters were all silent now, but in a few hours they would be clacking away with the work of the Union, cheery voices bubbling over with excitement.

The tea was ready when Diana arrived.

"I've brought the flowers," she said eagerly, laying the massive bouquets across a table.

"Good." Julia pulled out the two axes from the closet and they hid them within the blooms.

Julia examined their work and laughed. "We shall look so innocent, with our armload of flowers. No one will suspect a thing."

Two other women arrived; if anything happened to Julia and Diana before they could carry out the action, they would step in and replace them.

Their fifth confederate waited out front with the car. The four conspirators piled in and drove off toward the house of the Home Secretary.

Julia quizzed the driver, who'd been in charge of preparation. "Now, you're certain there isn't a police guard at the house?"

The driver shook her head. "We've had the place under surveillance for the last three days. There's nothing out of the ordinary."

Two blocks from the residence, the car pulled over and they climbed out. They clasped hands for a moment in a silent salute.

"Votes for women," Julia whispered, and they broke up to take their positions.

They hurriedly marched down the nearly deserted streets. Only a few delivery wagons traveled through this part of town and they saw two or three servants scurrying about on errands. This quarter of town did not come alive until later in the day.

Diana, dressed in the plain clothes of just such a servant, walked boldly down the street in front of Gladstone's house to the corner, then came around the block.

"Everything looks fine," she said.

"Good." Julia checked their flowers, making sure the

ax handles would come free easily. "I'll pay you a shilling for every pane of glass you break!"

Julia marched boldly up to Gladstone's door, with its elegant gold knocker. Pulling her axe free from the flowers, she smashed the head into the door.

The sound of glass breaking echoed in her ears, telling her that Diana was at her task. Julia battered at the door, pulling her weapon free from the splintering wood, then striking deep again. Over the sounds of her blows she heard frantic noises coming from inside: the shriek of a woman, the loud voices of two men. She hoped one of them was Gladstone.

"I've run out of rocks," Diana exclaimed in dismay.

"Here, take over for me." Julia stepped back and let her take the axe to the door. Splinters of bright wood stood out against the dark paint.

"This is harder work than I thought," Diana said between breaths. "I'd rather toss rocks at windows any day!"

Julia swung the other axe against the stair railings, chipping away paint. "Opening the door for suffrage *is* hard work," Julia replied.

"What happens if the door caves in?" Diana asked with a grin.

Julia heard the first faint strains of a police whistle. "Why, perhaps Mr. Gladstone will invite us in for breakfast."

In seconds she saw policemen converging on them from all sides. Julia nodded to Diana and they lay down the axes, sitting patiently on the front steps while they waited for the police to arrive.

Julia thought she saw Gladstone peering from an upstairs window as they were dragged away.

They were taken directly to Bow Street.

"You ladies are out bright and early this morning," the charge officer greeted them as they were brought in. He glanced at the paper the arresting officer handed him. "Disturbing the peace, destroying property, assault—"

"There was no assault," Julia corrected him. "We only attacked the door, the windows, and the stair railing."

"Someone could have been injured by the glass," the policeman growled. "Assault."

Julia shrugged. The more charges, the worse the sentence. And that was what she wanted.

The charge officer waggled his finger at them. "Naughty, naughty girls. You're going to be in for a long time with this. Let's get your names and start the process."

Diana and Julia were placed in the same holding cell while they awaited the arrival of the magistrate. Julia crossed her fingers that they would be taken in first thing when court commenced at ten.

She was right, for promptly at a quarter of, they were called from their cells and marched up the stairs to the courtroom.

Christabel, Beryl, and Katherine sat in the front row. Julia gave them a triumphant smile and shouted, "Votes for women."

The magistrate was not impressed with her outburst and frowned as he scanned the charge sheet. "Ah, the notorious Miss Sydney. What have we been up to today?" He consulted the list. "Hmmm. This is very serious. Very serious indeed."

He sat silently for a moment, thinking. "Damages alone will be substantial, I'm afraid. You will need to pay those. And since this is not your first, or second, or even third appearance in this court, I'm not even going to give you the option of a fine." He banged his gavel. "Three months in the Third Division—at hard labor."

A gasp erupted from the onlookers.

"The Third Division!" Julia's voice rose in protest. "That's for hardened criminals. I'm a political prisoner and I demand to be treated as such."

"Third Division," the judge said firmly.

Julia abruptly sat down on the floor. "You'll have to carry me out, then," she said. "I'm not going to accept such an outrageous sentence."

"Carry her out," the judge said wearily, and looked at Diana.

Julia didn't fight back, but allowed the police officers

to lift her by the arms and drag her stumbling from the courtroom. She was put back in the holding cell, to wait for Diana and the inevitable trip to Holloway.

She'd done it this time. David wouldn't come to her rescue now. And she'd be able to experience firsthand the barbarous torture imposed by the government.

They had probably started to force-feed the women arrested in the last demonstration.

A quick shiver shook her body but she willed herself to calm. This was her purpose, to show that the Union would not bend no matter how abusive the government became. Two more women were going to jail; two more women would undertake a hunger strike, and two more women would have to be force-fed.

Public outrage would build.

The ringing of the phone jolted David from bed. He stumbled down the hall to his office and lifted the receiver. It was the Home Secretary.

When the conversation was over, David hung up the phone with a sick feeling in his stomach. He couldn't believe what Julia had done.

She may have attacked Gladstone's house, but it might as well have been David's front door she destroyed. He knew very well the action had been aimed at him.

He'd only been trying to save her from hurt, when he'd paid the fine to get her out of prison. Now, because he was the one responsible for her freedom, he had to share the blame for her attack. David had the sick feeling that Julia knew that; that it had been a part of her plan.

For a moment he had to admire the cleverness of it all. She could have attacked his house, taking her anger out on him directly. But that was too obvious. Instead, she'd gone after the Home Secretary; an even bigger target. Yet she'd also managed to strike out at David without coming near him.

Very, very clever.

If he was very lucky, he wouldn't lose his job over this, although he wouldn't blame Gladstone for firing him. It would be hard to ignore David's connection to Julia after this and questions were bound to be asked. Many would wonder just where his sympathies lay.

They wouldn't care that Julia was furious with him. He suddenly understood her anger the day he'd rescued her from Holloway, when she accused him of interfering in her life, making decisions for her. She'd effectively done the same thing to him now, and he didn't like it one bit.

Sighing, David walked to the window and peered out, almost hoping to see some axe-wielding suffragettes in the street below. It would soothe his conscience—and improve his standing with the Secretary—if they attacked his house. But he only saw a coal wagon and a vegetable cart lumber past.

Turning away from the window, David went back to his room, jerked open a drawer, and pulled out a shirt. It was going to be a very long day.

Chapter 22

Julia discovered that life as a Third Division prisoner at Holloway was different from what she'd experienced before.

First, the prison clothing was a coarse brown serge dress, not the blue of the Second Division. And her cell was smaller, with a tiny window high up in the wall. Since there was no way to open it, Julia grabbed her crockery mug and hurled it at the glass, shattering it.

Now she could have fresh air.

Over the door, a gas jet sat behind a thick pane of glass, providing the only source of artificial light. Besides the mug and a bowl, her furnishings consisted of a chair, her wooden sleeping pallet, a tin washbasin, and a chamber pot.

As she surveyed the room that was going to be her home for an indefinite period of time, Julia discovered one more dismaying difference about the Third Division. There were no encouraging words scratched on these cell walls by earlier imprisoned suffragettes. She was the first one to be sent to this cell.

From her pocket, Julia pulled the slate pencil she'd hidden in her stocking and made an ink of sorts from the dirt on the floor and spit, then wrote VOTES FOR WOMEN on the wall in large letters. Smiling, she sat back on her heels and admired her efforts. Now, she'd made the cell her own.

She tried tapping on the walls of the adjoining cells, but there wasn't an answer from either one. Were they empty, or occupied by regular prisoners who didn't know to tap back?

The midday meal had already been served before she arrived, so it wasn't until half past six that a wardress entered Julia's cell with the evening porridge and saw the broken window.

"What have you done?" she cried. "The governor is going to be very angry about this."

Julia shrugged. "Tell him to transfer me to the First Division, then."

"You'll have to clean this up," the wardress insisted. "We can't risk anyone getting cut on the glass." She left and returned a few minutes later with a broom and dust-pan. Julia swept up the shards of glass and let the officer take them away—along with the porridge she refused to eat.

They wouldn't tempt her with food again until morning.

The cell grew so dark it was difficult to see before the gas jet came on with a soft hiss. It was the prison clock; now, it marked the coming of evening, and when it went out in the morning, dawn was arriving.

Julia scratched a line on the wall to mark her first day.

This wing of the prison was eerily quiet and Julia feared that she was the only prisoner here. Where had they put Diana? She'd been assigned to the Third Division as well—shouldn't she be nearby? Julia held her breath, listening carefully, but only silence reached her ears.

Julia didn't think she'd ever felt more alone.

During the night she found the dark, brooding silence of the prison more disturbing than any noise. Sharp pangs of hunger gnawed at Julia's stomach; she'd already fasted for more than a day. Tomorrow would be the worst, then the pains would go away, to be replaced by the creeping weakness brought about by slow starvation.

How long would they wait before they tried to feed her?

When she awoke from her fitful sleep, Julia saw that the gas jet no longer flamed. It was morning, her second day in prison.

She left the morning porridge untouched by the door

of her cell. The wardress gave her a disgusted look when she came in later, with a bundle of sewing. Julia's sentence included "hard labor," which in a women's prison consisted of needlework. Julia found the idea amusing, knowing her ineptitude with the needle. It would serve them right if she ruined a good piece of material. But on principle, she refused to do the work. She was already in trouble for breaking her window. They could add this to her growing list of crimes.

"I won't work," Julia told the wardress. "Political prisoners do not perform labor."

The wardress sighed, taking away the sewing and the porridge.

Julia sat on her bed, struggling to focus her mind on the mental article she was composing for the newspaper. It was the only way to cope with the boredom and the isolation. As long as she kept her mind busy, she wouldn't have time to dwell on what was to come.

She refused to think about David.

Dinner, the usual meat and potatoes at twelve, smelled unusually delicious and Julia struggled to ignore the temptation. The second day of a hunger strike was always the worst, when even the unappealing aroma of porridge sent the saliva flowing. In the past, when Julia had declined food, they took it away immediately, but now they left it, a deliberate provocation.

Late that afternoon, two prison officers appeared and escorted her to the governor's office.

Julia couldn't restrain a shiver of apprehension. More than likely, this was about the window and the sewing, but she carried the nagging fear that David would interfere again, would arrange another release and humiliate her further. Julia vowed that they would have to bodily carry her if he had; she wouldn't leave willingly.

The governor, a short, stout man with a bristling mustache and florid face, gave her a stern look as she stood before him. "I understand you refuse to do the labor assigned to you."

Julia stared at him, a defiant look on her face. "I claim the rights of a political prisoner."

"You were sentenced to the Third Division." He consulted the papers in front of him. "That'll be three days on bread and water for not doing your work."

Julia smothered a smile. A fearsome punishment for a woman on a hunger strike.

One of the officers approached the governor and whispered in his ear. He regarded Julia with a fierce look.

"So, you're refusing to eat, are you? Your appetite might improve after some time in a special cell."

Julia couldn't smother her grin this time. A punishment cell on her first full day. And he hadn't even brought up the matter of the window.

The guards led her down two long flights of stairs, and through a passage to a level that she thought was below ground. Her new "punishment" cell was larger than the one upstairs, with a window looking out at ground level. The wide bed was nailed to the floor.

Inspecting the window, Julia saw it was barred from the inside. She wouldn't be able to break this one. But the air seemed fresher here than upstairs. Julia sat down on the mattress and shut her eyes. She knew she wouldn't sleep, but she would rest. Already, she felt a slight dizziness, as her body rebelled against the lack of food.

How long would they let her go before the doctor ordered the forced feeding?

As it grew dark, she scratched a mark in this new cell to mark the passing of another day.

Late in the night, Julia struggled awake, feeling smothered by the lack of air. She climbed out of bed to smash the glass before she remembered that she couldn't. When she was let out in the morning to draw her water, Julia gulped in the fresh air of the corridor with relief.

From time to time, she heard muffled noises from the hall, but Julia couldn't tell if there were other prisoners in the punishment wing. Several times, she called out, listening intently for a reply, but no one answered.

Another night came, another mark scratched on the wall.

Late in the afternoon—she could tell from the fading

sunlight—of her second day in the punishment cell, the senior medical officer came in, introduced himself, and asked how long she'd been without food. Julia refused to answer. He checked her pulse and listened to her heart, then went away.

Julia's heart didn't stop pounding for several minutes. It wouldn't be long, now.

Curling up on the mattress, she determined to save every ounce of her waning strength for the fight to come. She would not be a willing partner to her torture.

She awoke later, the cell dark. It was night outside. The small of her back ached and she felt faint from hunger, but those were torments she could endure. They were familiar.

It was the fear of the unknown—the forced feedings—that made this prison stay such a torture. Not knowing when they would come, how long she could keep them at bay, and what would happen once they overcame her resistance. Julia wished they would get it over with and end the suspense.

Another mark on the wall. The third day.

She barely slept that night. Every tiny sound jolted her from sleep, for she feared they'd come in the middle of the night to catch her unawares. To ease the tension, she went over every detail of her planned resistance. There was little hope of turning them from their task; the women in Birmingham had fought them to no avail. But Julia vowed that she'd give the doctors a memorable fight.

When she heard the heavy tromp of many footsteps in the hall, shortly after dawn, she knew it was time. Quickly Julia retreated to the far corner of her cell, her back against the wall, arms crossed over her chest with her fingers in her nostrils and mouth. They'd practiced this position at the Union office.

The steps halted in front of her door. Julia heard the rasp of the key in the lock, the dull metallic snap as the lock released. Then the door opened and five stern-faced wardresses marched in, followed by the senior medical officer.

The doctor gave her a stern look. "Miss Sydney, if you do not eat voluntarily, I will have to feed you."

Julia glared at him, hatred in her eyes.

He stepped aside and motioned for the wardresses to subdue her.

Five to one was an uneven fight, but Julia successfully resisted their attempts to get her out of the corner for several minutes, kicking out at them with her booted feet. They finally succeeded in grabbing her legs and pulled her from the corner and threw her down onto the bed. A wardress sat on her ankles, immobilizing her legs, while another held her head, and two others grabbed her arms. Julia couldn't move an inch and the first wave of panic flashed over her. They were going to feed her and she was helpless to prevent it.

The doctor knelt on the edge of the plank bed and bent over her. Julia clamped her mouth shut and clenched her teeth tightly, her final act of resistance. He grabbed up the steel gag and pried open her lips with his fingers, then worked the metal between her teeth. When he got it in at last he locked it open, forcing her jaws apart at a painful distance.

Grabbing the long, stiff feeding tube, he shoved it down her throat.

Julia gagged as the tube touched her throat and the instinctive reflex continued as he pushed it down into her stomach. She wanted to cry out, to scream, but she couldn't make a sound. From a glass pitcher, the doctor poured the liquid meal down the tube.

When the food hit her stomach, it clenched painfully. Julia tried to draw up her knees, to ease the pressure, but the wardress held her legs tight.

With the tube still in her stomach, Julia threw up.

Her only satisfaction was that she'd been sick all over the doctor. He pulled the tube out and ran out in haste.

Julia lay weakly on the bed, the mattress and sheet sodden with her own vomit. It was in her hair, down the side of her face, and she felt incapable of wiping any of it away. But it was consolation not to have that hateful tube down her throat.

After making a few ineffectual efforts to clean her up, the wardresses left.

Only dimly aware of her surroundings, Julia thought she heard noises from a nearby cell. Were they feeding another prisoner? She wanted to cry out, but her throat hurt and she could only utter a few scratchy noises.

Drifting in and out of sleep, Julia lost all sense of time. Sometime later, another wardress came in and told her she was being put back in her cell upstairs.

"Please, can I have clean clothes?" Julia pleaded with her.

"We'll see."

She sat in her old cell for a long time before they finally brought her a new dress and cap. Julia sponged herself as well as she could in the icy water in her cell, trying to clean her hair.

Then she took off her boot and mustering all of her meager strength, Julia hurled it against the glass covering the gas jet. It broke with a satisfying crash and Julia heard running footsteps in the hall.

The matron stared at the broken glass littering the floor. "You should be ashamed of yourself!"

Julia smiled in triumph. She wasn't beaten yet.

They took her shoes away and brought her slippers.

The doctor and the wardresses appeared again in the early evening, coming so silently that Julia didn't hear them until they pulled open the door. She jumped for the corner and tried to fight them off again, but realized that her strength was failing. How much longer would she be able to resist?

This time, Julia wasn't sick until they pulled out the tube.

"If you do that again I shall feed you twice next time!" the doctor yelled as he dabbed at the front of his coat.

"Don't feed me at all," Julia managed to croak. He stomped out of the cell.

As night drew on, the gas jet was lit.

Julia barely remembered to scratch off the mark of day four before she drifted into a confusing world of dreams and fog.

She remembered these hallucinatory images from her last hunger strike, the strange visions that confused the mind and ate away at her courage. To combat them, she tried to picture herself back at the cottage in the bright summer sunlight, sitting in the back garden with a book in her lap. Then suddenly she was attacked by a group of MPs, in their striped coats and top hats, who held her down while one of them shoved a giant tube down her throat.

Julia reared up in bed, sweat dripping from her body. She couldn't get away from them, even in her dreams. Tears rolled down her cheeks and she didn't have the energy to brush them away.

This was beyond anything she could have imagined.

Her days became a nightmare of dread, as she lay on her bed listening for the terrifying footsteps that announced the twice-daily arrival of the doctor. Her struggles grew weaker, but Julia forced the wardresses to subdue her each time. She no longer felt any pain when the tube went down, just a numbing despair at the ongoing violation of her body.

She now knew what it meant to be raped, to have no control over a physical assault.

A *male* assault. The doctor, the prison governor, the men in the Home Office who'd approved the procedure, were all guilty of raping her. She hated them with white-hot fury.

Six days passed, then seven.

Julia was so weak she could barely carry the water bucket from the sink in the hall to her cell each morning. Even making a circuit of her tiny cubicle, in the shuffling gait necessitated by the ill-fitting slippers, was almost more than she could endure. Her muscles, her strength, were ebbing away. The feedings did little good, since she threw up most of the broth each time.

One wardress treated her with sympathy; helping Julia with the water, and murmuring encouraging words when she collapsed on her mattress after the feedings, her body too ravaged to move for several hours.

Julia's one daily joy was to stand on the chair under the window, peering out at the world outside. She could only catch a small glimpse of the exercise yard below, but that was enough. Just this simple maneuver took nearly all her strength and she could only stand for a few minutes at a time. Once or twice she thought she recognized one of the women arrested at the Home Office demonstration, but in their prison clothing and caps, she couldn't be sure. Just the thought that it might be one of her comrades lifted her spirits.

Until the next feeding.

Once, she begged to be allowed into the yard, even though she could barely walk. One of the wardresses helped her outside. Julia sagged against the wall of the yard, breathing in the crisp October air in great, noisy gulps.

When the wardress took her back inside, Julia started to cry. Would she ever be outside again?

Night brought the only semblance of peace to her life, the knowledge that she was safe from further assault until morning. But even so, she never really slept, laying on her hard plank bed in a state of semiconsciousness, her mind haunted by increasingly disturbing hallucinations.

Then, as the sky began to lighten toward morning, the gas jet shut off and Julia started to shake, unable to control her fear.

They would be coming soon.

Chapter 23

Sitting on the Liberal bench in the House, David tried to concentrate on the debate around him, but all he could think about was Julia. She'd been in jail for eight days now, and after her deliberate effort to get arrested, he knew she would have refused to eat. Now she was being force-fed.

Nothing more had been said about his having paid her fine, but David knew that he was on thin ice with both the Home Office and the Prime Minister. And with everyone expecting the government to dissolve after the Lords vetoed the budget, his position was even more tenuous. No doubt there would be a Cabinet reshuffling after the elections, and he could easily find himself on the outside again.

It didn't make for restful nights.

He should have had his head examined back in July, when he thought he could gain control over her. She'd taken charge of the relationship from the beginning and led him around by the nose like a tame sheep. She'd been the one who was in control.

Someone tapped him on the shoulder and David snapped to attention. They were calling for a division on this portion of the bill. He stood and followed the other Liberals out of the room. Time to get some work done.

In the morning, *The Times* carried another letter from the WSPU deploring the use of forced feeding on their prisoners. Calling the practice "primitive and barbaric," they cited several medical articles that decried the dangers of the procedure.

Disgusted, David threw the paper down. He was tired of reading propaganda from both sides on this issue. Everyone was more concerned with promoting their political views than with a rational discussion of the medical issues. He determined to find out, once and for all, what was going on.

And once he'd seen the procedure, he could set his mind to rest about Julia's safety.

Contacting the prison governor on the phone, it wasn't difficult to arrange a visit. David could go up to Holloway the next day and observe these forced feedings for himself. Tomorrow, he'd know exactly what was going on, and could go back to worrying about his legislative responsibilities.

He went to that afternoon's session in the House with a lighter step.

At an indecently early hour, the garageman brought the car around and David drove off toward the prison. He didn't often drive in London, but traffic was light at this time of day.

At the gate, the guard checked his name against a list and then waved him through. After parking the car, a prison official met David at the door and took him to the governor's office.

"Ah, Kimbrough, glad you could make it." The governor stepped out from behind his desk and shook David's hand. "Glad to see the Home Office is keeping an eye on things."

A tall man walked into the room. The governor motioned for him to join them.

"Kimbrough, this is Dr. Cleeves, our chief medical officer. He administers most of the feedings and can answer any questions you may have."

"How many prisoners are being fed by force?" David asked.

"Right now, we have ten," Cleeves replied.

"All suffragettes?" David asked.

The doctor nodded. "They came in and refused food as is their usual practice. We monitor their condition carefully, and start the feedings when we think their condition warrants it."

"What do you feed them?" David asked.

"It's a mixture of milk and beef broth. It's highly nourishing and easy to digest."

"How long do you continue the practice?"

The doctor thought for a moment. "I believe we're into the second week on several of the ladies."

"This is the first time this procedure's been used at Holloway, then?"

The governor nodded. "We've consulted with our colleagues in Birmingham, where the procedure was first tried. Their advice has been most helpful."

The doctor looked pointedly at his watch and turned to the governor. "It's time to begin."

The governor pulled open the door and David followed the two men into the hall. They led him down a corridor and through several doors until they were in the wing housing the suffragette prisoners. At the medical room, the doctor halted and gathered up his equipment, and they were joined by five wardresses.

"It takes all these people to feed one prisoner?" David asked with surprise.

"The women actively resist our efforts," the doctor replied bluntly. "They have to be physically restrained."

David swallowed hard. "How exactly does the procedure work?"

"You'll see soon enough," the doctor replied brusquely and strode down the hall. David hastened to catch up.

They stopped in front of one of the grated cell doors. The head wardress put the key in the lock and pulled open the door, then stepped inside.

Suddenly David drew back. He hadn't asked specifically to see—or avoid—Julia, but now that the moment was here, he prayed it wouldn't be her inside.

He sagged with relief when he entered the cell and caught a glimpse of the blond-haired woman lying on the bed.

She was curled up into a ball, her head tucked against

her chest and her arms locked around her legs. David wondered why she appeared to be in such pain.

"Good morning, Miss Perkins," the doctor announced cheerily. "Ready for breakfast, are we?"

While the doctor readied his equipment, the wardresses moved toward the bed. David watched the woman curl up into a tighter ball and suddenly realized that she wasn't in pain or discomfort, but was preparing to resist the wardresses.

Five against one wasn't an even contest, and although the woman struggled, the wardresses pulled her off the bed and shoved her onto the chair.

"We've found that it's easier to feed them in the chair," the governor whispered to David.

He watched with mounting dismay as a wardress took a long leather strap and wrapped it around the woman, pinning her arms and securing her upper body to the chair. Another strap went around her thighs and the chair seat.

"Is all this necessary?" David asked.

"If we don't strap them down securely, they try to pull out the feeding tube," the governor explained. "Tying them down makes the job easier for everybody."

The prisoner glared at them with defiant eyes.

The doctor stood between David and the patient and he could only catch brief glimpses of the process as the doctor forced her mouth open, securing it with a metal gag. Then he inserted the feeding tube.

Lashed to the chair, the woman could barely move, but her body tried to convulse when the tube went into her throat, gagging as it was pushed down. David winced at the sound.

While the wardress held the tube and funnel, the doctor poured the liquid down. Despite his growing horror, David couldn't look away. The mute pleading in the woman's eyes tore at him and he finally had to avert his gaze.

"Enough," said the doctor.

David looked again and the tube was pulled out.

The woman immediately threw up all over her lap as the wardresses and the doctor jumped back.

"They do it on purpose," the governor whispered to David.

David didn't understand how a woman strapped into a chair could voluntarily throw up.

"Now, I told you yesterday if that happened again, I'd feed you twice today," the doctor said grimly to the helpless woman.

David watched with growing horror as the entire process was repeated, down to the vomiting at the end. He doubted more than a few spoonfuls of the mixture had actually remained in the woman's stomach.

"How can they get any nourishment this way?" David asked as the governor led him back into the hall. "It looks as if she lost everything that was put in."

"Oh, some of it manages to stay down," the doctor said cheerily. "And once they learn that we'll keep feeding them until they've taken enough, they'll stop regurgitating it."

David glanced over his shoulder, watching the wardresses unstrap the woman and lead her to the bed.

"Are they going to clean her up?" David asked.

"We can't be changing their clothing three times a day," the governor said. "She'll have to wait until after the next feeding."

They walked past two cells, and stopped at the third.

"Well, here's another," the doctor announced.

David blanched at the thought of watching it again. "I think I've seen enough," he said, turning to the governor. "Perhaps you could answer a few more questions for me."

The governor nodded and they walked back toward his office.

By the time he left the prison, David was shaken.

He could never have imagined that it would be this bad. The suffragettes weren't exaggerating—this was nothing more than brutal torture.

He couldn't rid his mind of the haunted look in that woman's eyes—her defiant gaze at first, her agonized expression during the procedure, the exhausted relief when it was over.

It didn't take any effort to imagine those same looks reflected in a pair of dark brown eyes. Julia was undergoing the same treatment. He knew—he'd seen the list of prisoners.

David drove straight to the Home Office, parked the car, and went straight for his office.

"I don't want to be disturbed," he told the secretary, then shut the door.

David stared out the window, trying to make some sense of what he'd seen this morning.

He still believed in the ethical correctness of forced feedings—prisoners could not be allowed to starve themselves to death. Human kindness demanded that they be saved. But there was no justification for the brutal process he'd observed earlier.

When you were dealing with committed suffragettes, who deliberately sought arrest and fought against each and every prison rule, ordinary procedures no longer applied. Prison was a punishment only if the prisoners didn't want to be there.

All the suffragettes wanted was to be granted the status of political prisoners and be assigned to the First Division. If the government acceded to this request, the hunger strikes would stop, and the need for the forced feedings would stop as well.

The government wouldn't be losing—the women would then have to serve out their full terms and a prison sentence wouldn't be seen as a badge of courage. Everyone could calm down while the government considered how to deal with the issue of women suffrage.

Buoyed with enthusiasm, he dashed out of the office and went in search of Gladstone.

Trudging back from the Secretary's office after a rancorous session, David felt almost physically ill.

The Home Secretary didn't care about the health and well-being of those women. He regarded them purely as a nuisance and thought prison was the best place for them. If they chose not to eat, the doctors would treat them as they saw fit. Granting them First Division status was tantamount to giving them the vote.

David protested loudly, but his arguments went unheeded. The suffragettes had been making a mockery of the police, the courts, and the prison system. Now, they would see that the government was going to hold firm, and not tolerate their brand of terrorist activities.

Then he'd gone on to question David's motives for suggesting any concession to the militants.

That was when David knew his days in the Home Office were numbered.

He didn't bother to go back to his office, but slipped down the stairs, retrieved his car, and drove home. He had no intention of attending today's session at the House. Right now, David didn't think he could sit next to the men who regarded the suffragettes with such callousness.

Sitting at his desk at home, sipping a glass of whiskey, David contemplated his future.

His job was probably secure until the Lords vetoed the budget and the government dissolved for new elections. Then he'd be told, in polite terms of course, that things were not working out and it was time for some changes for the good of the party. All very neat and tidy; no one would know the reason behind it.

Or, he could make this disagreement public, splash the news all over the papers, and force them to oust him now.

David smiled to himself. He knew which course Julia would counsel.

He reached for paper and a pencil, and began composing his letter to *The Times*.

To the Editor:

Having made a firsthand examination of the process, I must add my voice to those who decry the recent government policy of force-feeding the suffragette prisoners who are on hunger strike. The violence that attends this procedure would horrify any person who witnessed it, as I did, and yet it is performed on these unfortunate women at least twice daily.

The government cannot continue to condone the torturing of these women—for torturing is what it is. What else could you call it when a prisoner is strapped to a chair, her mouth pried open and locked in that position with a piece of metal, then a rubber tube shoved down her throat?

There is no place for this kind of treatment in England.

The resolution to this problem is laughably simple. The hunger strikes began in protest against suffragette prisoners being denied the status of First Division or political prisoners. If these women were transferred to the First Division, their protest would end.

I do not advocate the wholesale release of suffragette prisoners. Crimes have been committed and penalties must be imposed, either by fine or imprisonment. But when no other class of prisoner in England, besides the suffragette, is tortured by their jailers, one must question the motives behind this action. Is it concern for law and order, or a brutal policy of revenge?

Until recently, it was determined that the ill effects of four to six days of self-imposed starvation were punishment enough for these women. Now, they are subjected to these barbaric feedings so that they can be kept in prison for what now appears to be an extra week or two before they are again released on medical grounds. What purpose does this serve, other than being deliberate punishment?

I implore the members of this government, the Home Secretary in particular, to rethink this policy and come to the conclusion that the only humane and just course of action is to grant the suffragette prisoners the status of the First Division, and transfer them there forthwith.

I am well aware of the reaction that my letter will raise among my colleagues. But after observing this horrible procedure with my own eyes, I cannot remain silent while the government countenances the deliberate torture of women prisoners.

Your Obedient Servant,

David Kimbrough
Under Secretary for Home Affairs

When he had the wording just as he wished, he copied it out in ink, placed it in an envelope that he sealed and addressed. Heading downstairs, he grabbed his hat and coat. He intended to deliver this personally to *The Times*, to make certain it would appear in tomorrow's paper.

He then went out and treated himself to an excellent dinner at the Savoy, went round to his club and had a few too many drinks, and went home to bed.

It was half-past seven when the first phone call came in. David stared bleary-eyed at the clock, wishing he hadn't stayed out so late.

He was tempted to lay here and let the damn thing ring; at this hour of the morning, it could only mean one thing—his letter was in the paper and the reaction was beginning. But avoiding the phone only postponed the inevitable; he might as well get this over with.

Struggling into his robe, David shoved his feet into slippers and tromped down the hall to his office. He picked up the phone just as the caller rang off.

"Damn!"

Dressing quickly, David left the house, a sure escape from the insistent ringing of the phone. Let his man field calls for a while.

David walked toward Hyde Park, following the path along the southern edge of the Serpentine. At this hour of the morning, the park was deserted and he had the peace he needed to think.

He'd already resolved, when he wrote that letter, that he would not resign. It would add strength to his protest, but David knew that it would have little political effect. No, he'd wait things out and see what happened. The only hope he had of affecting change lay within the Home Office, and as long as he was Under Secretary, they would have to listen to him.

And if he was dismissed for his views, the impact would be all the greater.

He knew he didn't like the idea of going back to being a plain MP, standing on the fringes of power while others made the decisions. But from the moment that he'd decided that he had to speak out against the forced feedings, he knew there was no other course.

His aunt would have been pleased with his stand.

David wondered what Julia would advise if she were here. By the time she was freed, the entire drama would have been played out and long forgotten. In fact, if they held her to the full term of her sentence, she wouldn't be out until after the new year.

Three months. David wondered how long it would take before she broke, before she began eating to avoid the feedings. For her sake, he hoped it would be soon, but knowing Julia, she would hold out longer than most.

There was one small hope—that she'd be released early for health reasons. But that wasn't much of a hope, either. He couldn't imagine that doctor releasing anyone unless they were on death's door.

It was nearing eleven when he finally returned to his house. There was a stack of phone messages on his desk. David thumbed through them. Only one call from the Home Office—and not from the Secretary. Most messages were from other Liberals and a few members of the Cabinet had called. Every newspaper in London wanted to talk with him.

He picked up one slip, intrigued. Christabel Pankhurst wished to speak to him.

Well, he had a few things to say to her as well. David reached for the phone and asked for the WSPU office.

Her question was short and to the point. Was he ready to support the cause of suffrage in the House? David answered her honestly, saying he wasn't. She surprised him by not ringing off after that, instead inviting him to join their protest vigil at Holloway. Members of the WSPU vowed to stand outside the prison walls until forced feeding of prisoners ended.

How could he refuse to join them?

He ate a quick lunch and headed for the train. Getting off near Holloway, he walked the short distance to the prison. He heard protesters singing and chanting from several blocks away and he pitied those who lived or worked near the prison for the disruption to their lives.

David felt more than uncomfortable when he approached the vanguard of protesters, and almost turned around and walked away. But he was here for a reason; to put his newfound conviction on display, and there was no time for second thoughts.

He walked up to the tall woman nearest the front gate.

"I'm David Kimbrough and I'm here to join your protest against the forced feedings."

She stared at him in wide-eyed surprise and David wondered if he'd met the one person in London who hadn't read the papers this morning.

"Miss Pankhurst suggested I come out." He looked around, decidedly uncomfortable. "I've come to believe—that is, I can no longer—"

"Mr. Kimbrough!" a cheery voice called out. "How nice of you to join us."

Turning around, David came face-to-face with a woman who looked vaguely familiar.

She held out her hand. "Katherine Ames. I'm a friend of Julia's—we met briefly at her cottage. I read your letter in *The Times* this morning. Glad you've joined our side."

David started to tell her that he wasn't a supporter of suffrage, then closed his mouth. He didn't want to get into another political debate.

"What can I do?" he asked.

She handed him a placard, bearing the words STOP GOVERNMENT TORTURE.

David eyed it doubtfully. "You want me to carry this?"

She laughed at his discomfort. "That is what you said in your letter, wasn't it?"

"Yes, but—all right. Do I just march around or what?"

Taking his arm, she pulled him along with her. "Come with me. We can walk and talk."

David hefted his sign and followed behind her.

She looked at him curiously. "Why did you decide to do this? Is it because of Julia?"

"I saw them feed a woman here yesterday," he said, trying to suppress a shudder at the memory. "It was appalling."

"I wish more men in the government would follow your example and see it for themselves—we'd have the process stopped within a week if they did."

He shook his head. "Don't be so sure of that. There are many who think these women are getting exactly what they deserve."

They walked to the end of the block and turned back. "Have you heard any word of Julia?" he asked, finally.

She looked at him, surprised. "You didn't try to see her yesterday?"

He shook his head.

"The prisoners aren't allowed to communicate with anyone," she explained. "We don't know anything about Julia's condition—or any of the others."

"But they'd tell someone if she was ill, wouldn't they?"

"Her family, perhaps."

Her family. David had forgotten all about them. Her parents must be worried sick.

"I should let them know," he said quickly. "Do you have their address?"

"Someone at the office will know," she said.

David lifted his sign higher and quickened his pace. As soon as he got back to town, he'd get hold of Julia's parents.

He wanted them to know that someone in the government was concerned about their daughter.

Chapter 24

He stayed at Holloway longer than he planned, and barely made it back in time for the beginning of the House session. David particularly wanted to be there today, to face down his critics and see if there was an undercurrent of support as well.

He'd barely taken his seat when he was handed a note. The Home Secretary wanted to see him.

Sighing, David rose. He hadn't expected he'd be called on the carpet so soon, but here it was.

Surprisingly, his steps were light as he walked down the familiar halls toward the Cabinet office. Now that the meeting was here, he looked forward to getting it over at last.

Several other Cabinet members, or their assistants, were in the office when David entered. They greeted him coolly.

"Sit down, Kimbrough." Gladstone's expression was stern. "I think you know why I wished to speak to you."

The temptation to offer a flippant retort was strong, but David held back. He sat down, feeling like a condemned man facing the firing squad.

"It is important," Gladstone began, "for efficient government, that the Cabinet be composed of like-minded men. We will have our little squabbles"—he looked pointedly at the Naval Secretary—"but on the whole, unity prevails.

"You just threw a wrench into that process."

David remained silent. There was nothing he could say, after all; by speaking out, he *had* broken the unwritten rule of Cabinet unity. But the situation was too serious to ignore.

"Right now, when we are in the last phases of these trying budget debates, it is important that all members of the party support the government. We know we are heading for a crisis with the Lords; we need every Liberal member firmly behind us."

"I have always given the budget provisions my wholehearted support," David said.

"True, but your recent opinions on other matters create the impression of dissension in the Cabinet." He looked around at the other men in the room. "And we are all agreed that at this point in time, the unity of the Cabinet is paramount."

"As is fair treatment for prisoners being held by the government," David countered. He knew there was no hope for him now, but he wasn't going to go down without a fight.

Gladstone peered at him suspiciously. "I don't recall you expressing reservations when this policy of health measures was first proposed."

"That was because I had not seen the process. It may sound humane on paper, but in reality, it is nothing less than torture."

"David, you know our position. These women have made a mockery of the justice system with their hunger strikes."

"Put them in the First Division and the problem will be solved."

"And who's to say that they won't continue their hunger strikes, to protest the fact they are in prison at all?"

"That's an unlikely occurrence," David said. "I've never heard of a single suffragette who has not gone willingly to prison. Putting them in the First Division is not such a great concession—these are respectable women, after all, not hardened criminals."

"Give in on this issue and they'll demand something new," said the Naval Secretary sourly.

David gave him a sharp glance. "I think you and I both know that they won't cease their activities until they have what they want—the vote."

"I suppose you think we should give them that, too?"

"No," David said, carefully choosing his words. "I feel strongly that the budget fight with the Lords should take precedence over all other legislation. But the suffragettes aren't going to go away, however much this government wishes it."

"Things like your letter this morning only encourage them to further outrageous acts," the Naval Secretary sputtered. "We won't have peace and quiet until they're all in jail."

"You can't lock up every woman in the country," David said. "Their ranks swell with every antisuffrage action. The best thing we could do is to ignore them. They thrive on publicity; deny them that and they will wither away."

"Censor the damn papers," one undersecretary growled.

Gladstone turned to David with an apologetic look. "See what I mean? There is a likeness of opinion here—except for yours."

"I'm prepared to stand my ground," David replied.

"That's why I think it might be better for all concerned if you handed in your resignation. We know that new elections are in the offing, given the Lords' antipathy toward the budget. We'll all be out of a job in a few weeks."

"Then why not wait until the government is dissolved?" David asked. "You could have the fiction of Cabinet unity until then."

"That might have been possible, if you hadn't expressed your views in so public a manner. But I fear the PM agrees with me. You can't be an effective member of the government when you speak out so openly against a policy that has the approval of His Majesty."

David stared at him, in surprise. "The King authorized the use of forced feedings?"

Gladstone nodded.

Leaning back in his chair, David tried to digest the shocking news. Did the King really know what was going on?

Even if he did, David knew what he had to do. "I will not resign," he said stubbornly.

Gladstone sighed. "I wish you would be more cooperative, David. I have no other choice but to dismiss you then."

David nodded. "I prefer it that way."

"Of course, there's no need for this to be bandied about in the press. As you say, the government isn't going to last much longer. You may go quietly."

With a defiant air, David rose. "You are throwing me out of the Cabinet for speaking against the forced feedings, and you expect me to keep quiet about it?"

"David, you have a long career ahead of you in the party. This incident will blow over in time, and shouldn't cause you any damage." Gladstone gave him a warning look. "If you cooperate."

"You're not going to buy my silence," he said.

Gladstone shook his head. "You're free to do what you want, of course. But for your own good—"

"My concern isn't for myself, but for those unfortunate women."

"Is it 'women' or one woman in particular who drives your concern?"

"I feel compassion for anyone subjected to that abominable procedure," David retorted. "Be they an acquaintance or a total stranger."

The loud sounds of the division bell penetrated the room.

Gladstone stood. "Time to do our duties, gentlemen."

David lagged behind as they walked back to the House chambers.

He'd done it now; his actions were irreversible. He was out of the Cabinet, in danger of being tossed out of the party, and his political future looked cloudy. Yet he felt almost giddy with relief.

Why didn't he feel more miserable?

Inside the high walls of Holloway prison, Julia huddled in her cell, shivering against the cold. She'd taken to wearing her nightgown under her dress, but that still wasn't enough to keep her warm.

She thought longingly of that summer day at the shore

with David, when the scorching sand almost burned their feet. A day when it was so warm that swimming in the icy Channel was a pleasant relief.

But it hadn't been the sun and the heat that made her so warm there.

It was David.

No matter how hard she tried to stop herself, Julia found herself thinking about David more and more. Her anger with him gradually faded. She knew he'd been trying to help her when he'd paid her fine and obtained her release from prison. He simply hadn't understood why she needed to be here, to carry out her protest against the government in the only way she knew how.

That was the crux of the problem—he didn't understand the importance of her suffrage work, that it was the guiding force in her life.

Or at least it had been, until she met him. Ever since then, she'd felt a constant pull in the opposite direction. The temptation to cut back on her work, to not back up her words with deeds, to stay out of prison.

That had been frightening. The cause had been her work for so long, she couldn't imagine being without it. What else would she do? She couldn't imagine any other work that would give her the same sense of excitement, the same pride in fighting for a just cause. The WSPU gave her the opportunity to lead and to act.

But David had given her a glimpse of another side of life, a side that held its own special appeal. A side where she felt wanted and desired because she was a woman. After fighting the restrictions against women for so many years, it was wonderful to be wanted for what she was, even when she felt guilty for doing so.

How could she reconcile these two sides of her? What did the woman who wanted to be wanted by David Kimbrough have in common with the militant suffragette in prison? Did they have anything in common?

David made her doubt her commitment to the cause. That was bad. David loved her, which made her feel good. David didn't understand her work—bad. David cared enough to try to keep her from harm—good.

No matter how she looked at things, there didn't seem to be any common ground. Her work with the WSPU was incompatible with her feelings for David.

Unless . . .

Footsteps echoed in the hall and with a start Julia realized that while she'd been musing, the gas light had been turned off. They were coming for the morning feeding.

Despair washed over her. She tried to be strong, but it grew harder and harder each day, with each violation of her body and her spirit. She wished they would go away, would leave her here to starve. That slow torture was nothing compared to what they did to her.

You can stop it in an instant, a tiny voice nagged at her. *Tell them you'll eat and it will all be over.*

No! Julia cried back. *I cannot weaken. I demand to be treated as a political prisoner, and will resist the prison system that refuses to do so.*

She heard the rasp of the key in the lock and the door opened. The five wardresses entered, followed by the doctor, carrying his hateful equipment.

"Are we ready to eat today?" he asked cheerily.

Julia buried her head between her legs and locked her arms behind her knees.

David struggled with the letter he wrote to Julia's parents. His position was awkward, to say the least. He couldn't write to them as her lover, yet the very act of writing them seemed presumptuous otherwise.

Perhaps if he explained Julia's connection with his aunt, it would make sense. His position as owner of the estate, and the cottage, gave him a reason to involve himself in her affairs. And as the *former* Under Secretary for the Home Office, he had a right to extend sympathies to the families of the imprisoned suffragettes.

They didn't need to know that they were the only family he wrote to.

But what could he say to them? He couldn't offer to intervene and get Julia out of prison; he no longer had the power to do that. And he couldn't even tell them of her condition, since he didn't know what it was. What else could he offer them except his disgust with the force-feeding process, and reassurances that Julia would be well taken care of when she was finally released? That she had the cottage to go to, where he'd make sure that she was nursed back to health.

Wouldn't they want to do that themselves?

Julia hadn't gone to them the last time—or had she, when she was first released? He didn't even know. There was so much about her that he *didn't* know, and feared he never would.

After tearing up his first four attempts, he finally produced a suitable letter. It was dry, distant, and didn't give a hint of his feelings for Julia, but it seemed the appropriate thing to send to people he'd never met. He stuck it in an envelope, then headed out the door. Someone at the Union office would know where to send it.

He felt decidedly uncomfortable when he entered the WSPU office, both from memories of his last visit here and uncertainty over the reception he would receive. One letter to *The Times* didn't erase every animosity. There were women here who would never forgive him for being a part of the government. And no one yet knew that he'd been dismissed.

He asked for Miss Pankhurst. At least she'd been polite to him on the phone yesterday. He was told to wait and took a seat.

"What do you think you're doing here?" a querulous voice demanded.

David looked up. It was the woman who'd given Julia such a bad time at his aunt's funeral.

"Certainly not the same thing you are," he replied with a smile.

"What do you want?"

"I'm waiting to see Miss Pankhurst."

"Christabel's busy. You can speak to me, instead."

David's dislike for this imperious woman increased, and her open hostility made him suspicious. "I'll wait for Miss Pankhurst, if you don't mind."

"Do you think that one paltry letter to the paper is

going to absolve you for your other crimes?" she demanded in a heated tone. "Every member of the government has to answer for their actions."

"Beryl, this is not the time for speech making."

Jumping to his feet, David had his first close look at the legendary leader of the WSPU. Christabel Pankhurst was an attractive woman, with rounded cheeks and thick, dark hair. But her eyes burned with the righteousness of the cause.

"I want to send this to the Sydneys." He handed her the letter. "Can you see that they get it?"

She nodded. "I understand you were at Holloway yesterday."

David nodded in return. "It was an . . . interesting experience."

She laughed. "We are always pleased to have men working for the cause."

He looked around, unsure if he should be so frank when he was in the lion's den. "As I told you, I'm still not convinced the time is right for changes in suffrage law. But I consider the forced feedings an abomination and I will speak out against them."

"I appreciate your honesty," she said, "if not your opinions." She took the letter from him. "I'll see that the Sydneys get this."

"Thank you."

David hastened back into the street, relieved to have his errand over.

Now, if he could only find out about Julia.

A thought struck him. No one outside the inner government circles knew that he wasn't with the Home Office any longer. He could call Holloway and ask about the condition of all the prisoners, and find out about Julia as well.

The governor at Holloway was reluctant to tell him anything, but when David insisted, he complied, and gave him a terse account of the prisoners' conditions.

When he hung up at last, David's face was grim.

One woman from the first group arrested outside the Home Office had been released due to poor health; two more were in the prison hospital and eating normally. The others had abandoned the hunger strike.

Of Julia and the other woman arrested with her eleven long days ago, there was less information. They were doing "as well as could be expected." Which, knowing what they were going through, wasn't very encouraging.

He discovered Julia had spent time in a punishment cell for some infraction, but was back in her regular cell now and being fed like the rest. That was all the information the governor gave and David didn't ask for any detail. At least he knew she wasn't sick enough to be in the hospital or released.

How much longer would it take until she deteriorated to that point? A few days? A week? He prayed it wouldn't be that long; the sooner she was released, the sooner he could start nursing her back to health.

If she would let him. For all he knew, she was still as furious today as she'd been last week, when he'd paid her fine and set in motion the chain of events that led her to the present situation.

He wasn't going to apologize to her about that. He'd done what he thought was right—and in light of what he now knew about the forced feedings, he'd been right.

David knew he would never understand the strength of Julia's belief in the cause, her willingness to undergo such torture in the name of what she felt was right. But he was forced to admire the strength of her convictions; her utter certainty that what she was doing was right.

He wished he still felt that certainty about his own work. But over these last few weeks, as his doubts grew, he realized that he wasn't certain of anything anymore.

Except that he loved Julia. And had to make sure that she was safe.

Julia clutched at the blanket, pulling it up to her chin. Every muscle in her body ached and she simply could not get warm. Cold seemed to radiate from the floor and walls of her cell.

She should get up and walk around, to get the blood circulating and warm herself. But she didn't have the strength to move. It was a struggle just to keep her mind clear.

Last night, when she'd once again vomited her "dinner" all over the floor, Julia'd been filled with black despair. For once, it looked like she was in a battle that she wasn't going to be able to win.

Was there any point in continuing her resistance? It was obvious they would continue to force-feed her until her sentence expired, she began to eat, or she died.

And as miserable as she felt, the last possibility didn't seem so far off. Her longest hunger strike had been four days; already she'd been in here eleven days and doubted she'd kept more than a few spoonfuls of broth in her stomach after each feeding. She expended all her energy on resisting the doctor and the feeding tube, and to no avail. They simply overpowered her through brute force.

The isolation was the worst. She didn't know anything about the other suffragette prisoners held in Holloway. Were they still continuing the hunger strike, or had they given up? If only she could talk to them, gather strength from their shared experience. But the only people Julia saw were the wardresses, the doctors, and the occasional prisoner who came to clean up her cell, when Julia was too weak to do so.

She rolled over and faced the cold wall beside her bed. In the dim light from the gas lamp, she made out the cross hatches she'd scratched there, marking off the days. Eleven lines, growing more and more wobbly as they went on.

Sudden panic filled her. Had she made a mark yesterday? She tried to remember, tried to visualize herself scratching that last wavering line on the wall, but her mind wouldn't cooperate. She couldn't remember making any of the marks.

Tears welled up in her eyes. If she lost track of the days, she was lost. It would be too easy to surrender to despair, and hopelessness, and the drifting haze that threatened to take over her mind. Everything that made her who she was, that made her willing to undergo this hideous torture, would be swallowed up into that oblivion.

After that, what was the point of existing?

Hot tears ran down her cheeks as she sobbed silently in the isolation of her cell.

She was only dimly aware of the change in the light when the gas was turned off; barely heard the footsteps echoing down the hall as they came toward her cell. And when they entered, Julia couldn't bring herself to move. She lay there passively, unable to muster any resistance, as the wardresses came for her.

They lifted her from the bed and half carried, half dragged her to the chair. Julia slumped forward, unable to sit upright.

"Doctor, I think we should feed her on the bed," the chief wardress said. "She's terribly weak."

He grabbed Julia's wrist, checking her pulse, then nodded.

They carried Julia back to bed. The doctor bent over her, forcing the gag into her mouth, even though Julia couldn't have clenched her teeth together if she'd tried. Then came the tube, and the uncomfortable pressure as it entered her throat and snaked its way down her gullet to the stomach.

Julia drew up her knees, her stomach cramping when the liquid entered it. She wanted to cry out at the pain. Dimly, she thought the doctor poured the liquid down the tube faster than usual, for it seemed like only seconds before he pulled it out.

She barely was able to turn her head to the side before everything came up.

"Damn!" the doctor exclaimed.

Julia lay there, feeling the warm liquid seeping into her dress, her hair, and didn't care. She only wanted to be left alone, to surrender to the fog.

Arms jerked her upright and the doctor poked and prodded her chest with his stethoscope.

"I want her removed to the hospital ward," he said finally. He bent low over Julia. "Can you hear me, Miss Sydney? Your health is very precarious—you must begin eating. I'm having you transferred to the hospital."

Julia managed to crack her eyes and stare hazily at the doctor. "No surrender," she murmured.

He picked her up and carried her limp body out of the cell.

Chapter 25

The insistent ringing of the phone jolted David out of bed.

Groaning, he rolled over and pulled the pillow on top of his head. What new controversy sparked this early morning call? Word must have gotten out about his dismissal from the Home Office and now he was going to be accosted by the newspapers for days.

Whoever it was, they were persistent. Groaning again, he dragged himself out of bed and stumbled down the hall.

He shouldn't have stayed so long at the club—or had quite that many whiskeys.

"What?" he snarled into the phone.

"Mr. Kimbrough?" a woman's voice asked.

"Yes."

"This is Katherine Ames, at the WSPU. Julia's been moved into the hospital ward at Holloway. I thought you'd like to know."

A chill swept through his body.

"Mr. Kimbrough? Are you still there?"

"I'm here," he said, sitting down. "How ill is she?"

"They didn't say. We're hoping this is just a preliminary move and they'll be ordering her release later."

"How soon will you know?" he asked anxiously. "Who will they call if they decide to release her later today?"

"They'll call here."

He glanced at the clock on the mantel. Half past seven. Would the governor be in yet? Thank God he'd established a relationship with the man already—and that he didn't yet know that David had been dismissed from the Home Office.

His career was already in ruins—one more sin couldn't harm him.

"I'm going to try to get a physician in to see her," David said quickly. "Are you going to be there for a while? I'll ring you back when I've made the arrangements."

"I'll be here," she said. "Good luck."

David immediately called the house of his uncle's personal physician. Sir William wasn't too enthused at being woken up at this hour, and was even more unhappy when David told him what he wanted, but after some grumbling, agreed to come with him.

David didn't call Holloway, reasoning they'd be less likely to turn away Sir William once he was there.

Retrieving his car from the garage, David raced through the empty streets of Mayfair. Despite his earlier reluctance, the doctor was waiting for him.

"Don't see why you think I want to be physician to a bunch of law-breaking women," he said as David sped toward Holloway. "What are my regular patients going to think?"

"That you're a humanitarian, bent on saving lives," David retorted. "Think of the headlines: SIR WILLIAM INTERVENES ON PRISONER'S BEHALF; NOTED PHYSICIAN DECRIES FORCED FEEDING."

"If the damn women would eat, they wouldn't have to be fed," he said. "Foolish idea."

"Have you ever seen a forced feeding?" David asked.

Wearily, the doctor sighed. "Yes."

"Then you know how these women are suffering."

Sir William glanced at David. "I doubt your uncle will be enthused about your involvement with this."

"Oh, I'm sure I'll have thoroughly disgraced the family name by the time I'm finished," David agreed with a grim smile. "But if it saves a woman from dying, it's worth it."

They reached the prison in record time. Several precious minutes were wasted at the gate, persuading the guard to let them in, and David was in a fit of impatience by the time he parked the car.

The governor, alerted by the guard, met them inside the entrance.

"What's all this about a physician being called in?" he demanded.

"The Home Office is concerned about the health of the prisoner." The lie rolled easily off David's tongue. "I'm sure you understand that we don't want any awkward questions being asked."

The governor looked from David to Sir William, and back again. "Very well," he said, and motioned for them to follow him.

The strong smell of antiseptic wasn't enough to hide the unpleasant odors of the hospital ward. The supervising matron looked at them curiously when they entered, but then turned away.

Sir William turned to David. "Wait here, Kimbrough."

Another man hastily entered the room; David recognized the doctor who'd performed the forced feedings. He joined Sir William and they went to a bed at the far end of the room. Julia's bed.

David fought with his desire to see her, and the knowledge that he needed to remain circumspect, at least until he knew what her condition was. If she was gravely ill, he didn't give a damn who knew how he felt about her; he would move heaven and earth to get her out of here.

The wardress pulled a screen around the bed and David paced anxiously at the front of the room, waiting for Sir William to finish his examination.

His steps halted suddenly. Where was he going to take Julia if he did get her released?

The perfect answer was his house, but taking an unmarried woman, no matter how ill, into a bachelor's house would be sheer folly. But she obviously couldn't go back to her own rooms at the Union office; she would never get the rest she needed in that hive of activity.

The cottage. Of course! It was the perfect place—away from London, away from friends, where she could recuperate in the fresh country air again.

Sir William and the prison doctor stepped from behind the curtain and stood together, conferring quietly. Sir William's expression was grim and David's heart sank as they came nearer.

"Kimbrough?" Sir William walked over. "Dr. Cleeves here and I concur that the prisoner's condition is serious. I'm going to speak to the governor and make arrangements to have her released."

David nodded, trying to hide his fear. "How bad is she?" he asked Sir William as they hastened to the governor's office.

"She should have been released days ago," Sir William replied bluntly.

David winced at his words.

The governor was less willing to accept the diagnosis. "This is a self-induced illness," he protested. "She has the power to cure herself."

"I was under the impression that you were treating these prisoners," Sir William said. "It doesn't look like she's been getting any nourishment. How much weight has she lost?"

"Some of the prisoners have more trouble with the feeding process than others," the governor said. "Miss Sydney was certainly not a cooperative patient."

"Dr. Cleeves tells me that she managed to keep down only a fraction of what she was fed." Sir William gave the governor a stern look. "She is starving to death, despite your efforts."

"She merely has to eat on her own and all will be well," the governor said.

David's rage exploded. "If you don't release her, she's going to die. Can you imagine the public outcry if that happens? Think who will be blamed."

"I agree the situation is urgent." Sir William placed a calming hand on David's arm. "I understand there are precedents for releasing these prisoners for health reasons. As examining physician, I am prepared to take responsibility for insisting that it be done in her case. Now."

David stared at Sir William, his jaw hanging open in

amazement. He'd never expected to get such support from him.

Then his stomach clenched. If Sir William was being so insistent, Julia must be in very bad shape indeed.

He wanted to race out of the room, dash down the corridor, and run to Julia, to hold her in his arms, to reassure himself that she was going to be all right, once they got her out of here.

He would never forgive himself if she died.

The governor frowned. "I have to consult with the authorities."

David's heart sank. If the governor called the Home Office, he'd discover that David didn't have authorization to be here.

"Any delay in treatment could make the difference between life and death for this woman," David said. "I assure you, the government doesn't want a dead suffragette on its hands."

He saw a flicker of fear in the governor's eyes and dared to hope he could pull this off. All it took was a few strokes of the pen, and Julia would be free.

The governor reached for the phone and David's hopes plummeted. Once he called the Home Office, it would be over. Sir William's diagnosis would be lost in the flap over David's unauthorized actions.

"Mrs. Trent?" The governor spoke into the phone. "Have the doctor come to my office."

Smothering a relieved sigh, David's churning emotions soared again. The doctor would bolster Sir William's opinion.

They waited five long, agonizing minutes before the doctor appeared.

"Cleeves, what do you think here? Should this woman be released?"

The doctor nodded. "She's been a hard case all along, I'm afraid. I don't have any hope that she will cooperate unless she is released."

The governor frowned, then grabbed a form from a drawer in his desk. He wrote quickly, then handed it to Dr. Cleeves and then Sir William for their signatures.

"Normally, we wait for permission from the Home Office to release a prisoner, but because of the medical circumstances in this case, I'm ordering her immediate release." He looked at David. "You can square that with your superiors later."

David nodded, not caring what happened once he had Julia out of here.

"It will take some minutes to complete the preparations," the governor said, and gestured for Cleeves to follow him to the hospital.

David stared at Sir William, hardly daring to believe that they'd succeeded.

"Now what do you intend to do with her?" Sir William asked.

"I want to take her down to Surrey," David replied. "There's a cottage on the estate—she can recuperate there."

Sir William shook his head. "I don't think that's a wise idea—at least for a while. She'll be too weak to travel for some time."

His words brought David to the final realization just how ill Julia was.

"She can't go back to her own rooms—she won't have a moment's peace there. I'll have to take her to my house, then."

Sir William arched a brow. "That might raise a few questions, you know."

"I don't care." David set his jaw stubbornly. "As long as she gets better, it doesn't matter what anyone thinks."

"Why not put her up in a quiet hotel for a time? I can give you the names of several nurses who can tend her. She needs round-the-clock care for the first days, at least."

"Thank you."

David vowed to put her up at the Savoy, where she could recover in the lap of luxury. Julia would find exquisite irony in having the most elegant hotel in London playing host to one of the most infamous suffragettes.

He smiled for the first time that morning. "I'm going to take her to the Savoy."

Sir William laughed and clapped him on the back. "Spoken like a true Kimbrough."

Using the governor's phone, David and Sir William made all the arrangements. When the governor returned, all was ready.

"They're bringing her to the front door in a wheelchair," the governor said. He shook his head. "Why these women have to be so stubborn . . . it's beyond me what they are trying to prove."

David thought he could supply a few answers, but he kept silent.

Julia would be free in a few minutes.

At his first glimpse of her, David recoiled in shock, not believing that this was Julia. But a second look told him that this apparition was really her. Limp brown hair hung beside her gaunt cheeks and she was slumped against the side of the chair. But it was her eyes—those expressive brown eyes that had so enchanted him—that were the worst. Dull, unfocused, barely open.

She looked like hell. He took a deep breath before he approached her, and knelt at the side of the chair, taking her limp hand in his.

"Julia? It's David."

Her eyes flickered open but he wasn't sure if she even recognized him.

"I'm here to take you home."

Picking her up in his arms, he was shocked at how little she weighed. She felt more like a child than the grown woman he knew. David carried her swiftly to the car and gently placed her in the seat beside Sir William.

For a moment her lids lifted and she looked at him through clouded eyes. "David." Her eyes closed again.

His hands shook so hard, David wasn't sure he could control the car, but somehow he managed to steer them through the now busy streets, dodging carriages, omnibuses, and carts on the way to the Savoy.

They stopped once, at Sir William's consulting rooms, where one of the nurses he'd hired over the phone met them. After gathering more medical supplies, they continued to the hotel.

David again carried her inside, to the consternation of everyone in the lobby, and waited impatiently at the elevator while Sir William spoke to the desk clerk. But all went well when the hotel manager himself escorted them to the room, making David doubly glad that he'd called on Sir William. Sometimes, family connections were helpful.

They propped Julia on the sofa, using pillows to keep her upright, and the nurse hastened to prepare some broth.

"She won't be able to eat any solid food for a few days," the doctor explained. David sat beside Julia, his arm around her thin shoulders.

Coaxing her with soft words, he spent the next half hour spooning the liquid into her mouth, dabbing at her lips when it spilled out, urging her to take more. The doctor wouldn't let him stop until she'd consumed the entire batch.

"Now, off to bed with her." Sir William waved David away and he and the nurse put Julia to bed.

"She probably needs to sleep more than anything else," Sir William said when he closed the bedroom door behind him. "We'll make her eat whenever she is awake and she'll be looking better in a few days."

David grabbed his hand. "I cannot thank you enough for this."

"She must be a remarkable woman," Sir William said as he repacked his medical bag.

"She is," David agreed without reservations.

"I'll be back later this afternoon to check on her. I suggest you go home and get some rest. She'll be fine here with the nurse."

David started to protest, then stopped himself.

He couldn't do her any good here, not yet. The nurse was prepared to help her and he'd just be in the way.

There were other ways he could help Julia. Starting with a visit to the WSPU offices. They'd be relieved to know that she'd been released. Then he planned to place some calls to a few well-known newspapermen, and tell then exactly what was going on inside the walls of Holloway.

Julia stretched lazily, breathing in the enticing fragrance of the scented linen sheets. It was such a marvelous dream she didn't want to wake up. But they would be here to feed her soon.

She cracked her eyes, looking for the mark she'd scribbled on the wall of her cell yesterday. Were there twelve of them now?

Instead, she saw flowered wallpaper.

Closing her eyes again, Julia realized she was still dreaming. Very well, she'd remain asleep. This dream was far too pleasant to interrupt.

When she next opened her eyes, she saw an unfamiliar woman in a gray dress sitting beside her bed, knitting.

"Who are you?" Julia mumbled through her parched throat.

"Awake, are we?" the woman responded cheerily. "About time. Thought you were going to sleep the day away." She took Julia's wrist and checked her pulse.

The hospital ward. Of course. Julia vaguely remembered them taking her there. A tangle of images flashed through her mind. The doctor, and the matron. Yet she also pictured David there, and he wouldn't have been at Holloway. Reality and imagination were blurring.

"Do you think you can sit up?" the woman at the bedside asked. "I've some nice beef broth for you."

At the mention of food, Julia instinctively curled up in a ball, clamping her jaws together.

When she didn't feel hands pressing on her, pulling her off the bed, she opened her eyes and looked cautiously around the room.

Julia'd never been in the hospital ward before, but she didn't think it was furnished with thick carpets and maroon velvet draperies.

"Where am I?" she asked the woman.

The woman hastened to her side. "Oh, you poor dear, so much has gone on! This is the Savoy."

Julia stared at her. The Savoy? She must be joking. She was at Holloway—wasn't she?

"That nice man and Sir William brought you here this morning—and not a moment too soon, if you ask me! What they could be thinking of, to do such a thing to you in that prison. I'd like to give them a piece of my mind."

"This is Holloway," Julia croaked.

"No, you're not in that nasty prison any longer. I told you, this is the Savoy." The woman laughed. "One of the fancier nursing assignments I've had, I may tell you."

Julia closed her eyes, trying to get her mind to focus. She wasn't in Holloway, she was at the Savoy. Someone had brought her here. A doctor? Was this mysterious Sir William a doctor? She tried to remember but nothing made sense.

David. She kept picturing him in her mind, but the images were too jumbled to understand.

The woman patted her hand. "Don't you worry, we'll have you back on your feet in no time. I'm going to prop you up with some pillows and we'll have a nice lunch."

"Who are you?" Julia asked.

"I'm Mrs. MacPherson, your nurse."

A nurse. Julia's suspicions rose again. Was this all an elaborate trick to get her to eat? Again, she looked around the room, noting the polished mahogany dresser and brocaded chair.

No one would go to such lengths for a ruse.

Julia felt as helpless as a baby as the nurse lifted her into a sitting position. But as the smell of the broth wafted beneath her nose, she eagerly opened her mouth for the spoon.

She must have slept later, for when she opened her eyes the room was in semidarkness. For a panicked minute, Julia feared she was back in Holloway, under the dim light of the gas jet, but then she felt the soft pillow beneath her head and the soft linen nightdress against her skin and knew that she wasn't.

Trying to sit up, Julia found she was too weak to even raise her head more than a few inches. Finally, she managed to roll herself onto her side and raise up slightly on one elbow, in order to survey her surroundings.

Everything, from the nightstand beside the bed to the heavy draperies covering the windows, reeked of taste and elegance. A lamp stood on a table at the foot of the bed, its light muted.

The Savoy. That was what the nurse had said. Julia lay back against the pillows, a faint smile on her face. She could think of worse places to be.

Like Holloway.

The bedroom door opened and a strange man walked in.

"Ah, Miss Sydney, I see you are awake." He held out his hand. "I'm Sir William Cuthbert, the physician who examined you this morning."

She regarded him with a puzzled expression.

"Don't you remember?" he asked.

Julia shook her head.

"Probably for the best," he muttered. He sat on the edge of the bed and listened to her chest, then checked her pulse. "Good, good. You're doing as well as can be expected. Can you sit up?"

Julia mouthed the word "no."

"I'll have the nurse bring your food in a moment. There's someone here who wants to see you."

He went out the door and to her surprise, David walked in.

"Hello, Julia." He came closer to the bed, regarding her with an apprehensive look. "Sir William said I could pop in for a minute."

"Did you get me out?" Her voice rasped in her ears.

David's expression grew pained as he knelt beside the bed. "I had to, Julia. They'd put you in the hospital ward and I persuaded Sir William to see you. He said you had to be released at once. I know you're probably mad, but—"

With great effort, she reached out and touched his hand. "Thank you."

Relief flooded his face. "You aren't angry?"

Angry? Julia shook her head. She couldn't be angry with David. That all seemed so long ago, now.

Sir William and a new nurse entered the room. "That's enough for now; you can't tire our patient. This is Miss Smyth, who is going to take care of you for the evening. Do everything she says and we'll have you back on your feet in no time."

David squeezed her hand and stood up. Julia gave him a weak smile as he left.

Somehow, David had got her out of Holloway. And this time, instead of resenting him bitterly for it, she was grateful. Grateful that he'd gained her release from Holloway. Grateful that he'd saved her from further humiliation behind those prison walls.

For they'd broken her, and the memory of that shame brought tears to her eyes. That humbling experience would remain with her for the rest of her life.

She'd finally failed at a task she'd set out for herself. Julia, the smart one, always the first one with the answer, the one who dared the others to follow her. Now she'd finally discovered that there was a limit to what she could do, what she could endure.

She'd uncovered that hidden weakness in her, laid it bare at last so that there was no avoiding it.

No one who'd undergone the forced feedings would think any less of her, she knew, but that thought offered no consolation. Julia still had to contend with herself, her bitter disappointment that she hadn't been strong enough to resist them at the end.

That she'd needed David to come to her rescue.

And that she'd been so glad he had.

Chapter 26

For Julia, the next few days passed in a confusing haze. She woke briefly to eat, then immediately slipped back into sleep. It was all she could do to keep her eyes open when the doctor arrived twice a day to examine her.

If she had any strength, she'd be frustrated at this never-ending lassitude, but even that emotion involved too much effort. All she wanted to do was curl up in the warm cocoon of the Savoy's comfortable bed and forget the last two weeks.

For once, she was awake and alert when the doctor visited her on the third morning.

"Well, you're looking better," Sir William said cheerily. "Think you're ready to eat more than broth?"

At the mention of real food, Julia suddenly felt ravenously hungry. She nodded eagerly.

The doctor examined her carefully, nodding as he checked her pulse and her heart.

"You're a lucky young lady," he said at last, putting his stethoscope away in his bag. "I don't think you've done yourself any permanent damage." He gave her a stern look. "But for God's sake, don't ever do anything like this again. I can't promise you the outcome will be as favorable next time."

Julia shuddered at the thought of going through that torture again. After being broken this time, she didn't think she would ever have the courage to try another hunger strike—not if the feedings awaited her.

What did that mean for her future work with the Union? Would anyone respect her, when they learned of her fears? And how could she ask others to do what she was afraid to?

She sank back against the pillow, her thoughts troubled.

"That's a serious face for someone who's been given good news," Sir William observed.

Julia smiled sadly, knowing he wouldn't understand her concern. "I'm fine."

"I'll start you on a thin gruel this morning, and if that goes well, we'll try some bread and pudding this afternoon. As long as you're staying here, you'll want to take advantage of the excellent kitchen downstairs."

"Why am I here?" she asked. "And when can I go home?"

"A hotel seemed the best place to take you. Kimbrough insisted on giving you the best," Sir William replied. "And I don't think you need to worry about going anywhere for a while. You need to get your strength back."

"Where is David? He was here that first day, I'm sure of it."

Sir William smiled. "Strict orders—you're not to have any visitors. Especially good-looking young men. I don't want you overly agitated."

Now that she was alert again, questions flooded Julia's mind. "What happened to the other women in prison? Were they released?"

The doctor shook his head. "You're not to expend one bit of energy worrying about that sort of thing. No visitors and no news until you've gained back some weight and can stay awake for more than half an hour."

The nurse brought the gruel and Julia eagerly devoured it, feeding herself for the first time. That the process exhausted her was a pointed reminder of just how weak she was.

But for once, she didn't fall asleep immediately. Instead, she thought about David, and how he'd come to her rescue again. And how, if the doctor hadn't exaggerated, she probably owed him her life.

Thinking of David was even more frightening than

remembering prison. Julia feared that it was her love for David that had ultimately weakened her in Holloway. He'd distracted her, diverted the energy she'd once devoted to the cause.

She was now torn between two conflicting desires with no solution in sight. Dismissing David from her life hadn't helped; if anything, it had made matters worse. She'd lied to herself about how much she cared for him.

She loved him deeply.

Yet for all she cared, she couldn't forget that he'd been involved in the decision to implement the forced feedings in the first place. Yes, he'd rescued her from Holloway, but he had to bear responsibility for what had happened to her there. In light of that, even thinking of him seemed traitorous. How could she ever go back to him with that issue hanging between them?

Despite Sir William's orders, David resolved daily to visit Julia, once going so far as to enter the lobby of the Savoy before his courage failed him.

He honestly didn't know how he'd be received, and he was afraid to find out. Had she really known what she was saying when she'd thanked him for rescuing her from Holloway? Now that she'd had more time to think, she might not be so eager to see him.

David admitted he had to accept some of the blame for what had happened to her in prison. He'd been at that Home Office meeting, had approved the forced-feeding measure. The argument that he'd approved the plan in order to protect her sounded idiotic now. He hadn't known what a misery the feedings were, or that Julia would resist them so forcefully.

That was one thing he should have known. She was a determined fighter, unwilling to give an inch.

Now he acknowledged that he had been terribly wrong. But that admission might not make much difference to one who'd suffered as she had.

Would his public repudiation of the policy, and the loss of his position in the Home Office, be atonement enough for the hurt he'd caused her? Would the fact that he'd crossed way over the line in his efforts to get her out of Holloway carry any weight?

If it were him, forgiveness would come hard.

He still attended the House, although the news of his dismissal from the Home Office had been announced the day after Julia's release. Response to his "defection," as his detractors called it, was varied, and centered around the issue of the forced feedings.

He found himself in an unlikely alliance with the Labour MP, Keir Hardie, in collecting information about the process. Enough of the suffragettes had been released from prison so that their stories could be told, and David worked with Hardie and even the WSPU to put the details of their torture before the public and in front of Parliament.

They'd even enlisted the support of several doctors, who enumerated the dangers of the forced feedings. David couldn't believe that anyone who read of their concerns would agree to continue the process. But the government did not respond.

David wished there was some way to force every member of the government to go to Holloway and see for themselves what was going on. They should talk to these women, hear in their own words of the agony they suffered.

All over the issue of their status as prisoners.

How could it hurt the government to acknowledge that the women were political prisoners? That tiny concession could even dampen suffragette enthusiasm for more violent acts.

But hard-liners in the Cabinet refused to listen to reason, and now that he was on the outside, his voice was listened to least of all.

He realized that the frustration he felt was probably only one tenth of that felt by the suffragettes, who'd been facing this blank wall of unresponsiveness for years. And he began to sympathize, if he could not condone, the escalating fury of their demonstrations. How could anyone remain peaceful when they were completely ignored?

Not that he'd ever admit that to Julia.

So he stayed away. He didn't even know if she would be angry to discover he'd brought her to the Savoy, instead of Clement's Inn. He hoped she would understand that it was the best place for her now, when she needed total quiet and round-the-clock nursing care.

Later, he'd try to persuade her to go down to the cottage—or even better the big house, where the servants could pamper her. If she didn't want him there, David would accept that, but he wanted her to be able to recover without any concerns.

He couldn't bear the thought that she would still push him away, but he had to face the possibility that she would.

It was shortly after dinner one evening when Julia heard querulous voices coming from the outer room. One was the nurse; the other was—Beryl?

The door flew open and Beryl marched into the room.

"So this is where he's hiding you." Beryl examined the elegant room with a disdainful sneer. "Quite a cozy lovers' nest."

"How nice of you to visit," Julia said dryly, ignoring her taunts.

"Yes, well, I would have been here earlier if someone had bothered to tell us where you were," Beryl said. "As it was, the dragon at the door tried to turn me away."

"She's following the doctor's orders." Julia propped herself into a sitting position. "How are the others? Are they still in Holloway? No one here tells me anything."

"You were the last holdout," Beryl said. "Two women are still in, but they started eating. Everyone else has been released."

Julia's spirits rose. *She'd been the last holdout.* The thought gave her a small rush of comfort. "Have there been any new demonstrations? Arrests?"

"We've an action planned this weekend in Newcastle," Beryl explained. "Will you speak there?"

"I can't," Julia said, even though she wished she could. She had to tell people what the government was doing to the suffragette prisoners. But she knew it was too soon.

"Well, if I had a room like this at the Savoy, I don't think I'd want to leave either." Beryl sniffed her disapproval.

"I can barely walk," Julia said. "It's impossible for me to go to Newcastle."

"When are you planning to come back to Clement's Inn? That is, if you are planning to come back."

Julia stared at her. "Why wouldn't I?"

"Well, if Kimbrough has set you up like this . . ."

"I didn't have much say where they took me," Julia replied icily. "I'll be back when the doctor says I may."

"We'll see," Beryl mumbled under her breath.

Sir William stormed into the room, followed by the red-faced nurse.

"What are you doing here?" Sir William demanded of Beryl. "I left strict orders that there was to be no visitors."

Beryl drew herself up. "I wanted to make sure that Julia hadn't traded one prison for another."

"She nearly traded a prison for a graveyard, that's what she did." The doctor peered at her. "You're one of those suffragette women, aren't you? Damn fools, the lot of you. Now, get out. This woman needs total peace and quiet. I don't want you riling her up."

Julia smothered a smile, wondering who would win this confrontation. Beryl glared at the doctor for a full minute, then turned to Julia.

"I'll tell everyone how *well* you're doing," she said, marching out of the room with her usual haughty arrogance.

The doctor frowned as he checked Julia's pulse. "As I thought, you're far too agitated. No more guests, do you hear?"

"Yes, sir," Julia said meekly. She didn't intend to turn anyone else away, but if his words kept Beryl out, they were welcome.

After the doctor left, Julia thought more about what Beryl had said. Julia had been the last holdout at Holloway. Even if she'd finally broken, she'd outlasted the others. It was a small triumph; she should feel proud.

But it didn't do enough to wash away her failure. Julia knew she would never look forward to prison again; indeed, she wondered if she would ever be willing to take part in an action that she knew would lead to her arrest.

The realization saddened her. She couldn't consider himself a leader of the movement any longer, a lieutenant under Christabel's generalship. Her effectiveness as a tactician was in doubt, for she'd always be tormented by the knowledge of how many women would be sent to jail as a result of her decisions.

Julia didn't think she could ever send anyone to face that horror.

But what was she going to do? She still believed firmly in the rightness of the cause. Working with the less-militant organizations did not appeal to her. She supported the Union's call to battle.

She was a soldier who had lost her nerve.

Maybe, after recuperating in the country, she would regain her courage. Hadn't her last stay revitalized her and brought her new energy? This one would, too.

Julia firmly ignored the truth—that it was her developing love affair with David that had infused her with new enthusiasm. Because that relationship was also responsible for destroying her courage, as well.

She wanted to talk with David, but he stayed away and Julia began to wonder if he wanted to even see her. Beryl had the courage to go against Sir William—why didn't David?

The flowers he sent every few days were nice, but not enough to make up for his absence. She had too many questions to ask him. Why had he brought Sir William in and worked for her release? Was he avoiding her because he thought she was still angry with him—or he with her? Or was it guilt that kept him away?

Every time Sir William came, Julia was tempted to mention David, to ask if she could see him, but she never mustered up the nerve.

If David didn't want to see her, she didn't want to see him.

David knew there was so much he and Julia had to say to each other, but he didn't want to go against the doctor's orders and upset her while she was still weak.

Instead, he sent notes, flowers, books, and anything else he ran across that he thought she would like. It was a shameless attempt to put himself back into her good graces, and he pursued his plan with enthusiasm.

After a short recess for by-elections, Parliament was back in session and David applied himself to harassing his former colleagues about the forced feeding issue, while he continued to work for passage of the Liberals' finance bill. If some saw that a contradiction, he did not. He might not be a part of the government, but he was still a member of the party.

Unless or until they decided to run someone against him in the next general election. David knew if he continued to speak out against the forced-feeding situation, that could become a reality. And with the finance bill heading for the Lords, and defeat likely, a general election was in the offing.

He was in an odd position, working with Labour MPs who were far more radical than himself, ostracized by the Liberal leaders for his defection, and viewed with equal suspicion by the WSPU. He may have lost his job for speaking out against the forced feedings, but unless he was willing to endorse the suffrage cause, they weren't eager to talk with him either. Apparently there was no room for a middle ground on the subject of the women's vote; one was either for it or against it, and even the issue of forced feeding was tangential to the main topic.

He was in a no-man's-land, not belonging anywhere.

If those women really wanted to confront the decision makers, they should take their demonstrations to the country estates of the aristocracy. David chuckled at the idea of picketers outside his uncle's palatial home. The duke would be outraged.

He'd have to suggest it to Julia.

If she ever listened to him again.

He shut his eyes. Would she ever understand and forgive him for his part in supporting the forced feedings?

It was frustrating, not being able to talk to her, to make her understand, to get down on his knees and beg for forgiveness. But he didn't dare confront her now, when she was so weak. Later, when she was stronger, they could talk.

And if the doctor's insistence on not upsetting her delayed the confrontation, all the better. David feared that she would not forgive him, would dismiss him from her life again, once and for all. He was willing to wait to talk to her; at least now, he had hope.

Once she'd told him to go, he wouldn't have any.

So while he waited for her to regain her strength, he made arrangements to prepare the cottage so it would be ready for her. He'd send over a maid from the big house to take care of everything for her, so Julia didn't have to lift a finger. She'd be fed, cosseted, and forced to live a life of leisure. She might not like it very well, but it was what she needed. No cares, no worries—just peaceful rest.

Something he desperately wanted to share with her, and feared she would not let him.

It would be pure hell to know that Julia was at the cottage, and he couldn't see her.

So for that reason, he kept his distance, sending her trinkets, calling the doctor daily for an update on her condition, and forcing himself to stay away from the Savoy.

Finally, he went down to Cranwood, to personally supervise the readying of the cottage for her.

It was the only way he could keep his sanity.

Chapter 27

After a week at the Savoy, Julia was restless, bored, and eager to get away. She was still weak, but could cross the room by herself now, and slept only a little more than usual.

She'd received an anxious telegram from her mother, but Julia sent a quick reply to reassure her. Later, when she was fully rested, Julia vowed to visit with her parents for a few days.

Sir William surprised her with his pronouncement after he examined her in the morning.

"Hmm," he said, listening to her heart. "Think you're ready for a change of scenery?"

"I can go home?" Julia asked eagerly.

"Not if by 'home' you mean going back to that radical hotbed where you keep your rooms. Kimbrough led me to understand you had a place in the country."

"The cottage?"

"Exactly. I think you're strong enough to travel, now. Shall I make arrangements for you to go there?"

"Yes, but—"

Her raised his hand. "No buts. Either you follow my orders or I wash my hands of you. Any strenuous activity now is bound to lead to a setback. Do you want to be flat on your back for another fortnight?"

"No," Julia replied meekly. That prospect sounded unbearable.

"Glad to see you have *some* sense. You'll need nursing care for a while, at least, but I think I can persuade one of the ladies to go down there with you."

"When can I go?"

"Tomorrow, if you like."

"Tomorrow?" Julia's eyes widened. "I can't get ready that soon. I have to pack my things at Clement's Inn, and make arrangements for the cottage to be readied, and—"

"Your only task is to get from the hotel to the train station," the doctor said sternly. "Someone else will take care of all that."

"You mean I can finally communicate with the world?" Julia asked sarcastically. He'd kept her so isolated Julia wasn't even sure what day it was. She couldn't wait to get her hands on a newspaper.

He ignored her jibe. "There must be someone you can trust to pack your things—send them a note. Kimbrough assures me that the cottage is ready and waiting."

"Where is David?" Julia asked. "Surely, you can let me see him, now."

"I believe he is out of town right now," Sir William said.

"Oh." Julia sank back against the pillows, disappointed.

Then she brightened. David would have to come visit her—at the cottage. And maybe there, where they'd fallen in love, they could find a way to resolve their differences again.

Once she was out of Sir William's clutches, he wouldn't be able to keep David away from her. Or anyone else. She'd spend the entire first day of freedom writing letters. Except for the tiny bit of information she'd gleaned from Beryl, Julia didn't have any idea what was going on in the world. She couldn't wait to find out.

Julia gave the doctor a note for Katherine, and later that afternoon a trunk arrived with her clothes, a note from Katherine wishing her well and saying the rest of her things had been sent down to the cottage.

Julia wasn't sure she liked the finality of that remark. It sounded as though they weren't expecting her back at Clement's Inn.

And she intended to be back—if they would let her.

For Julia knew she could never allow herself to be arrested again. She didn't have the courage. In the future, her role would be less visible.

At least one person would be pleased if Julia was out of favor—Beryl. Julia grimaced. She would like to see how well Beryl handled a long prison term—and the forced feedings.

In the morning the nurse helped Julia dress and then held her arm for the long walk down the hall, the jerky descent in the elevator, and across the lobby to the waiting cab. It was the longest distance Julia had walked since she arrived here, and it was a relief to sink back into the padded seat of the hansom and catch her breath.

No matter how much she wanted her life to be back to normal, her body wasn't going to cooperate for a while.

But in the country, she would soon regain her strength and take those long rambling walks she so loved. Her one regret was that Lady Marchmont would no longer be there to talk with. She'd miss that.

Would she be able to look forward to David's visits on the weekend again?

By the time Julia and the nurse arrived at the cottage, Julia was eager to take to her bed again. She barely glanced at the familiar surroundings as she tugged off her clothes and climbed between the sheets. Exhausted from the journey, she fell to sleep instantly.

When she awoke, it took a few minutes for her to remember where she was, and then she half expected David to be there beside her.

But that was foolish. She hadn't seen him since that first day out of prison.

Julia couldn't find her robe, so she struggled into her clothes and shuffled out into the parlor.

"Goodness, you shouldn't be up," the nurse said. "Here, sit down. Are you hungry?"

Julia nodded.

"I've got your dinner keeping warm in the oven," she said, and headed off to the kitchen.

Oven? Julia would have followed her, but the chair felt too comfortable.

"This is such a lovely place," the nurse said, bringing out a tray. "You must love to come here."

"I spent most of the summer here," Julia said. "It was wonderful."

While she ate, she looked around the parlor, reacquainting herself with its familiar furnishings. It looked almost the same as it had this summer, except that her books and papers weren't strewn about the room.

That would happen soon enough.

Julia ate every bit of her dinner—roast beef, tender peas, and suet pudding—then sat back with a feeling of contentment.

It was time to start her life again.

"I want to write some letters," Julia said. "Do you know where my writing desk is?"

"Everything is still in boxes," the nurse replied apologetically. "Sir William thought it would be a good project for you to unpack a little at a time, as your strength allowed. I'll try to find something for you to write on."

The nurse came back with a tablet and pen.

Julia penned a short letter to Katherine, thanking her for packing her things together, and begging for news from the Union, back issues of *Votes*, and a full accounting of everything that had occurred since Julia entered Holloway. With a shock, she realized she'd been isolated from the world for almost a month.

It took her a longer time to write to David. She wanted to tell him how much she appreciated his efforts on her behalf, and thank him for preparing the cottage for her, but she wasn't happy with the tone of the note; it sounded too stilted and formal. She couldn't achieve the tone she wanted while her feelings for David were still so confused.

Finally, she wadded up the note and tossed it in the fire. David's letter would have to wait until she decided what she wanted to say.

In the morning, after a sound sleep, Julia explored the cottage. She laughed when she saw the stove David had installed in the kitchen. Julia realized now she would have to learn how to cook.

Her days slipped into a regular routine of arising for breakfast, reading quietly in the parlor during the morning, taking lunch, a nap, and then reading again in the afternoon before dinner.

She hadn't yet ventured outside, but as the days passed, her steps grew more steady and she was soon moving around the cottage without any difficulty.

A servant came daily from the big house, delivering coal for the fire and food for the kitchen. Julia persuaded the nurse to teach her how to prepare a few simple meals. The woman was a pleasant, undemanding companion, but Julia couldn't wait for her to be gone. She was tired of depending on others and wanted to be by herself again.

But Sir William wouldn't approve until he knew that Julia could care for herself, so she threw herself into her cooking lessons with renewed determination.

As her strength returned, Julia ventured outside at last, bundled up against the cold October winds.

A massive package arrived from Katherine, containing journals and newspaper clippings, and a long, newsy letter. Demonstrations against government officials were continuing, and several women had been arrested around the country and were presumably being forcefed. Julia's heart ached for them and she wished she could send them words of courage, but of course, they couldn't receive any mail. It was another of the hateful restrictions placed on the Second and Third Division prisoners.

Grabbing a recent issue of *Votes*, Julia eagerly read all the news she'd missed. In her haste, she almost missed the article by Christabel, detailing Julia's own release from prison. But a name caught her eye and she read the article.

> We cannot help but compare Kimbrough's recent pronouncements against forced feeding with the determined silence of other members of the government. How can

> they look themselves in the mirror in the morning, knowing the full details of the abuse and torture that is taking place in prison under their direction?

Julia read the words again, slowly. David had spoken out against forced feeding? She quickly looked through the other issues, but didn't find any other mention of it.

Turning to the pile of clippings Katherine had sent, Julia scanned the headlines. There, amid the news accounts of her arrest, and the articles of protest from the Union, was a letter David had sent to *The Times*.

"Having made a firsthand observation of the procedures, I must add my voice to those who decry the recent government policy of force-feeding the suffragette prisoners . . ."

She could hardly believe what she read. David had spoken out publicly against the forced feedings? He'd actually gone to Holloway and seen the process and came away properly horrified.

Her stomach clenched and Julia feared she might be sick. She prayed that he hadn't seen *her*.

But no, he couldn't have. Despite her struggles, she would have known if he was there. He must have seen another prisoner.

Why had he gone to all that trouble?

And what happened after he sent his letter to *The Times*?

Julia hastily riffled through the rest of the clippings, looking for any mention of David. Here it was—bless Katherine for saving this for her!

> The Home Office announces that David Kimbrough, MP for Colton, has stepped down from his position as undersecretary. It was agreed by all concerned that recent disagreements over certain government policies made this move necessary.

Julia stared at the words. Had David been booted out of the Home Office for speaking his mind on the forced-feeding issue?

She found another article, from the Labour paper. KIMBROUGH OUSTED? read the headline. It, too, speculated that he'd been forced out of the Cabinet for his strong public statements opposing the government policy.

Julia sat back in her chair, amazed by the news. Such dramatic events going on, and no one had said a word to her!

David's political career was in ruins—all because of her. She'd attacked Gladstone's house to pay David back for paying her fine, hoping he'd be blamed. With that action, she'd surely sewn the seeds of suspicion. Then he'd dared to go to Holloway, to find out for himself what was going on. Horrified at what he'd seen, he'd gone public with his opposition, and lost his job.

He'd been courageous enough to admit he was wrong, and she knew the effort that must have taken. David was no fool; he knew what his opposition would mean to his political career.

Then why had he done it?

Julia jumped to her feet, papers and newspaper clippings flying to the floor. She hadn't been able to find the right words for him the other day, but she could find them now. She needed to talk with David, soon.

He had sacrificed his career for her, without even knowing if she would care. She had to let him know that she did—and that she was ready to make some sacrifices of her own, if it meant they could be together.

David sat in the library of his aunt's house—his house, now, he reminded himself. It was still too easy to forget that the irascible old lady wasn't upstairs taking a nap.

However, he couldn't forget that Julia was at the cottage, a scant ten minutes walk from the house. He couldn't count the number of times he'd started to walk over there over the last few days, but he always turned back, unsure of the reception he would receive. He felt safer waiting for an invitation from her.

But what if it never came? He hadn't heard a thing from her since she arrived.

On a blustery but dry October morning, he stepped out of the house again, determined to walk off his nervous energy. Tonight, he vowed to visit Julia, whether she wanted to see him or not. He couldn't stand the uncertainty any longer.

He walked down to the village, stopping at the church to lay a few late blooming flowers on Lady Marchmont's grave. The stark granite headstone looked painfully new amid its weathered companions. But it would eventually blend in, just as his own grief would fade over time.

Taking a circuitous route back to the house, his path wandered through the woods, until he rejoined the lane a short way from the pond. The pond where he'd first noticed Julia, on a July day that seemed years in the past.

David picked his way through the scattered underbrush and stepped into the clearing. He halted, suddenly, staring across the water.

There, at the far side of the pond, Julia sat on the grass, tossing pebbles into the water.

His first reaction was alarm that she was so far from the cottage. She wasn't strong enough to be out alone like this. What if she collapsed?

His second thought was that she looked more beautiful than ever and he missed her like crazy. Her absence left a gaping hole in his life that he wanted to fill again.

Slowly David walked toward her.

"I have to admit, you offered a far more fetching sight the first time I saw you here." He kept his tone light, teasing.

She looked up, her eyes widening in surprise, at the sound of his voice.

David stood, hesitantly, waiting for her reaction.

Julia's lips twitched impishly. "Well, if you think I'm going to strip off my clothes in this wind, you're going to be sadly disappointed."

He reached for her, lifting her off the ground and into his arms for a quick hug before setting her back on her feet. Then his face clouded. "What are you doing out here alone? You shouldn't have walked this far. Sir William would have fits if he knew you were out like this."

"Sir William has fits about a lot of things," Julia said dryly. "He said I could do what I wished as long as I was careful."

"I don't think walking out on a day like this is being careful." David stepped back and surveyed her with dismay. "Look at you! Not even a hat and only a thin jacket. What could you have been thinking of?"

"That if I stayed inside for another minute I would go mad," she replied matter-of-factly.

"Does the nurse know you're out here?"

Julia shook her head. "Not unless she's telepathic. She went back to London yesterday."

"Yesterday?" He frowned. "She left you here alone?"

Julia's laugh tinkled in his ears. "David, I'm not an invalid anymore. As long as I don't overtire myself, I'm fine."

"What are you eating?"

She laughed. "You'll find this hard to believe, but I am even doing my own cooking. I can make more than omelettes now."

Smiling at the pride he heard in her voice, David uttered a mock groan. "I knew I shouldn't have put that stove in."

Leaves lifted by the wind swirled around their feet and he saw her shiver. He grabbed her hand. "Come on, you should get back inside before you take a chill."

Her hand felt impossibly light in his, the bones still easily felt beneath his fingers. Even with a jacket on, she looked far too thin, and her face was still pale.

Even so, he thought she looked wonderful.

"What are you doing here?" she asked. "I thought you'd be in London. Isn't Parliament still in session?"

"It's only last-minute adjustments to the finance bill. They'll get by without me."

He hurried across the field, forgetting her weakened condition for a moment, and it wasn't until she pulled on his arm did he slow down.

"Stop a minute," she gasped. "I can't walk that fast."

David swooped her up in his arms and carried her the rest of the way. She felt light as a feather and David vowed to fatten her up with the richest foods he could find. Especially if he could feed them to her, bite by bite, day after day.

Kicking open the cottage door, he set her down on the sofa and stirred the fire until the flames were licking at the coals.

"Tea?" he asked.

Julia started to rise but he gently pushed her down. "I'll fix it," he said gently. "You rest." He grabbed a shawl and wrapped it around her shoulders, then went to the kitchen to fix tea.

Resting her head against the back of the sofa, Julia closed her eyes. David was here; she had so much to say to him and she didn't even know where to begin.

She opened her eyes when he brought in the tea, setting the tray on the table, then he took a place on the sofa beside her.

He glanced around the room. "Either you've developed neater habits since I was here last, or someone is picking up after you."

"And not even a dead flower in sight." She laughed and then touched his arm. "Thank you for all the flowers you sent me in London. Although it would have been nice if you came by yourself."

"Sir William insisted on no visitors. I didn't dare cross him."

Julia took his hand in hers and fixed her gaze on it, nervous to meet his eyes. "David, I found out about what you did, what you said when I was in jail. I'm sorry that you lost your job."

He shrugged. "I knew there'd be elections in a few months, anyway. I might have been put out of the Cabinet then, anyway."

Struggling with what she wanted to say, Julia dared to look at him. "I'm also very proud of you—for saying what you did. That took courage."

The sharp stab of pain in his eyes surprised her.

"Not nearly as much courage as you displayed."

Julia looked away, knowing his admiration was misplaced. "Everyone thinks that, don't they?" she said bitterly. "I doubt they'd be so approving if they knew what a coward I was."

"What do you mean?"

"I failed, David. At the end, I simply couldn't take it any longer." Her hands shook and she struggled to keep her voice from breaking. "I gave up resisting; I let them feed me."

"And you should have given in a damn sight sooner," he yelled angrily. "You were half dead when we got you out of there, do you realize that? Another day or two at the most and you wouldn't have come out."

"That's what I mean," she said softly. "I finally realized I was afraid to die. I gave up on the cause."

Slipping an arm around her shoulder, he pulled her close. "I call that coming to your senses, not abandoning the cause. You're a far more formidable opponent alive than dead."

Julia searched his face. "Is that what we still are—opponents?"

"I'd like to think we are friends."

She lifted a brow. "Friends?"

"Well, maybe more than friends."

Julia twined her fingers with his. "David, I don't know what I'll be doing with the WSPU in the future. I still believe in the fight, and I'll never give it up, but I honestly don't think I could go to jail again. And if I won't do that, I'm not sure they'll want me."

"There are other groups working for suffrage," he said.

"I know, but it wouldn't be the same, either." She sighed. "For the last three years, my whole life has been wrapped up in the Union—until this summer. Ever since I met you, things haven't been the same."

"They haven't been for me either." A warm light suffused his eyes.

She gave a sad laugh. "We both may be out of a job."

"There are worse things to lose," he said. "Like your life. Or your love." He leaned over and kissed her gently. "I love you, Julia."

She lay her head on his shoulder, drawing courage

from his solid strength. "When I first went to Holloway—the second time—I was so angry with you for interfering. I swore I would never speak to you again. But I finally understood why you arranged my release—and that was more frightening than anything."

He squeezed her fingers. "Why?"

"Because it made me realize how much you loved me. And what I felt for you, and how it was changing me. I knew I wouldn't be able to give myself completely to my work anymore, because of you."

"You know I wouldn't ever interfere with your work."

"David . . ." She gave him a skeptical look.

He grinned. "Well, at least as long as I didn't think you were going to hurt yourself."

"David, you have to trust me to take care of myself."

He let out a long sigh. "I know that. And if you hadn't been in prison, I wouldn't have gone to Holloway and observed the forced feedings. I'd still be deluding myself that they were for the best. You forced me to confront reality."

She ran a hand down his cheek, moved by his willingness to change his mind. "David, right now, I can't imagine ever wanting to go back to prison. But if my views change, you have to let me make my own decisions."

"There's a good chance the party may try to take my seat away, and I'll have to fight for it," he said. "I might get my uncle to agree to sponsor me for a seat somewhere. Or I could sit the whole election out." He cupped her chin in his hand. "But the one thing that I know with utter certainty is that I don't want to do any of those things without you."

Tears filled her eyes at his declaration. "You know the real reason I didn't want to die?"

He shook his head.

"Because I wanted to see you again."

"I have no intention of going away." He kissed her with an aching tenderness.

"I don't want you to."

"Even if I manage to stage a political comeback and get reappointed to a government post?"

She shook her head. She wasn't going to let politics come between them again.

"Even if I insist on marrying you and force you to host elegant Liberal Party dinners?"

Her breath caught at his words, while at the same time she laughed at the absurdity of the image. "That may be asking a bit too much."

"Are we talking about marriage—or hosting the dinners?"

He was grinning, but she saw the question in his eyes.

"Why, the dinners, of course. I can't quite picture myself as a model political hostess."

"True, you're liable to poison the food of any nonsuffrage politician who steps across the doorstep."

"Including yourself?" she asked, poking him in the ribs.

"I'm not that foolhardy. I know I won't have any domestic peace unless I capitulate on that issue." He tapped her nose with his forefinger. "But I insist on equal concessions from you."

"Yes."

"No arrests."

She nodded. "For a time, at least."

"No, I mean forever." He regarded her sternly. "You can lead any number of demonstrations, write your inflammatory articles for the papers, and organize any campaign you want, but I will not see you go to prison again."

Julia closed her eyes. He wasn't asking for much—only to give up the whole purpose of the Union. *Deeds, not words*. The motto of the Union. The philosophy that had guided her for the last three years.

But without David's love, she wouldn't have the strength for the fight anymore. If she had to hold herself back, wasn't that better than not being there at all?

Beryl, and some others, would despise her, saying she'd given up. But Julia didn't care about them. The only opinion that mattered was David's.

The choice was hers. And it wasn't that terrible of a sacrifice.

"No arrests," she conceded.

He gave a whoop of triumph and pulled her into his arms, kissing her soundly.

"If I was very good, I would make an honest woman out of you before I made love to you again." The wicked gleam in his eyes belied his words.

"How utterly boring," Julia replied.

"Well . . . perhaps I might relent. If you promise to marry me within the month."

Julia thought her heart would explode from the sheer joy that filled it. She took his hand. They were together, again, where they belonged.

"You're the only man I could imagine spending my life with," she said.

"We'll do just fine," he said, a boyish grin on his face. "As long as we don't discuss politics."

Julia laughed aloud, from sheer happiness.

"I love you, Julia," he whispered, looking down at her with a tender expression in his eyes.

"I love you, too, David."

Author's Note

I came of age in the years of antiwar protests and the blooming of the "new" women's movement. The long-ignored history of women fascinated me. And it was the militancy of the English, and later the American, suffragists that fascinated me most. Here were women of my grandmother's generation staging massive demonstrations, battling police, and going to jail for their political beliefs. What powerful role models!

For simplicity, I kept actual historical figures to a minimum in my story, and I invented Julia's demonstrations. However, the basic details of the suffrage struggle are true.

The WSPU declared a truce during the 1910 elections, buoyed by government promises of a new suffrage bill. But when Asquith refused to pass the bill out of committee, the truce ended. Again, in 1911, government promises were made and broken. The WSPU declared war, and began a serious campaign of violence, including arson. Ultimately, to avoid arrest, Christabel Pankhurst fled to France, but still masterminded the WSPU actions.

Public revulsion toward forced feeding resulted in a new government policy in 1913, known as the Cat and Mouse Act. Suffragette prisoners were permitted to hunger strike until their health was endangered, then would be temporarily released. Once their health improved, they were returned to prison, to serve out their term. Then the process started all over again.

These were not medically supervised fasts. Most of the women refused both food and water, and their health deteriorated rapidly. Many had to be carried out of prison. But the struggle continued.

One suffragette was killed when she threw herself under the hooves of the King's horse during the Derby. Others died in less spectacular ways, their health ruined by hunger strikes and forced feedings.

The outbreak of WWI brought a halt to WSPU action against the government. Agitation for changes in male suffrage brought new demands for including women as well. The House of Commons granted women property owners over thirty the right to vote in 1917. In January, 1918, the House of Lords agreed. Full universal suffrage for English women over twenty-one came in 1928.

The British press coined the term "suffragettes" in 1906, and the radicals eagerly adopted it for themselves, giving the name to the second WSPU paper. Their American cousins preferred the gender-neutral "suffragist," and in this country, "suffragette" was deemed an insult.

(Written in 1995, the Seventy-fifth Anniversary of the ratification of the Nineteenth Amendment to the U.S. Constitution.)

WE NEED YOUR HELP

To continue to bring you quality romance
that meets your personal expectations,
we at TOPAZ books want to hear from you.
Help us by filling out this questionnaire, and in exchange
we will give you a **free gift** as a token of our gratitude.

- Is this the first TOPAZ book you've purchased? (circle one)

  YES NO

  The title and author of this book is: ____________________

- If this was not the first TOPAZ book you've purchased, how many have you bought in the past year?

  a: 0 - 5 b 6 - 10 c: more than 10 d: more than 20

- How many romances in total did you buy in the past year?

  a: 0 - 5 b: 6 - 10 c: more than 10 d: more than 20 ____

- How would you rate your overall satisfaction with this book?

  a: Excellent b: Good c: Fair d: Poor

- What was the main reason you bought this book?

  a: It is a TOPAZ novel, and I know that TOPAZ stands for quality romance fiction
  b: I liked the cover
  c: The story-line intrigued me
  d: I love this author
  e: I really liked the setting
  f: I love the cover models
  g: Other: ____________________

- Where did you buy this TOPAZ novel?

  a: Bookstore b: Airport c: Warehouse Club
  d: Department Store e: Supermarket f: Drugstore
  g: Other: ____________________

- Did you pay the full cover price for this TOPAZ novel? (circle one)

  YES NO

  If you did not, what price did you pay? ____________________

- Who are your favorite TOPAZ authors? (Please list)

- How did you first hear about TOPAZ books?

  a: I saw the books in a bookstore
  b: I saw the TOPAZ Man on TV or at a signing
  c: A friend told me about TOPAZ
  d: I saw an advertisement in____________________magazine
  e: Other: ____________________

- What type of romance do you generally prefer?

  a: Historical b: Contemporary
  c: Romantic Suspense d: Paranormal (time travel, futuristic, vampires, ghosts, warlocks, etc.)
  d: Regency e: Other: ____________________

- What historical settings do you prefer?

  a: England b: Regency England c: Scotland
  e: Ireland f: America g: Western Americana
  h: American Indian i: Other: ____________________

- What type of story do you prefer?

  a: Very sexy b: Sweet, less explicit
  c: Light and humorous d: More emotionally intense
  e: Dealing with darker issues f: Other

- What kind of covers do you prefer?

  a: Illustrating both hero and heroine b: Hero alone
  c: No people (art only) d: Other___________

- What other genres do you like to read (circle all that apply)

  Mystery Medical Thrillers Science Fiction
  Suspense Fantasy Self-help
  Classics General Fiction Legal Thrillers
  Historical Fiction

- Who is your favorite author, and why?_______________________

  ____

- What magazines do you like to read? (circle all that apply)

  a: *People* b: *Time/Newsweek*
  c: *Entertainment Weekly* d: *Romantic Times*
  e: *Star* f: *National Enquirer*
  g: *Cosmopolitan* h: *Woman's Day*
  i: *Ladies' Home Journal* j: *Redbook*
  k: Other:_______________________

- In which region of the United States do you reside?

  a: Northeast b: Midatlantic c: South
  d: Midwest e: Mountain f: Southwest
  g: Pacific Coast

- What is your age group/sex? a: Female b: Male

  a: under 18 b: 19-25 c: 26-30 d: 31-35 e: 36-40
  f: 41-45 g: 46-50 h: 51-55 i: 56-60 j: Over 60

- What is your marital status?

  a: Married b: Single c: No longer married

- What is your current level of education?

  a: High school b: College Degree
  c: Graduate Degree d: Other: _______________

- Do you receive the TOPAZ *Romantic Liaisons* newsletter, a quarterly newsletter with the latest information on Topaz books and authors?

  YES NO

  If not, would you like to? YES NO

  Fill in the address where you would like your free gift to be sent:

  Name:_______________________________

  Address: _____________________________

  City:_______________________Zip Code: __________

  You should receive your free gift in 6 to 8 weeks.
  Please send the completed survey to:

  Penguin USA•Mass Market
  Dept. TS
  375 Hudson St.
  New York, NY 10014